GRAVE DECEPTION

KATHY LOCKHEART

ROSEWOOD
LITERARY PRESS

Editor: Susan Staudinger
Proofreader: Jovana Shirley, Unforeseen Editing, www.unforeseenediting.com

Cover design © By Hang Le

ISBN 978-1-955017-12-1 e-book
ISBN 978-1-955017-13-8 Paperback
ISBN 978-1-955017-14-5 Hardcover
ISBN 978-1-955017-15-2 Large Print

Published by Rosewood Literary Press

For the readers who embraced this series. I hope you love Shane's happily ever after.

GRAVE DECEPTION

AUTHOR'S NOTE

Grave Deception is an emotional, tension-filled romance. This love story contains violence and other content that may be triggering for some readers. I prefer you go into a story without spoilers, but if you would like **a list of detailed triggers**, you can find it posted on my website at KathyLockheart dot com.

S urrendering to death is different than I imagined.

I assumed the final seconds of life would feel quick, but as I plummeted from a bridge toward the glacial water of the Chicago River, my body felt like it was suspended in midair, the winds pushing against me, shoving against the sands of time.

Tonight, a thin layer of fog snaked around steel skyscrapers, their windows glowing against the onyx sky—as if the city's mythical beauty was trying to veil this grisly tragedy. Arctic gusts stung my cheeks and hardened the ashen chunks floating in the coal-colored water beneath me.

I wonder if they'll find my body. Or if I'll sink and Mom will never know what happened to me.

My heart bled for her. The poor woman didn't deserve to suffer yet another loss—this time, her twenty-nine-year-old daughter. Her grief from Dad's death had cloaked her soul with so much darkness that even the sun could not penetrate it. Her heart so fractured, it had hardened her skin into an impenetrable shield, emotionally shutting everyone out for years.

It was only recently, after she'd started therapy, that Mom had made the progress I'd always hoped for, and she was finally on the cusp of turning things around. If I didn't make it, all her progress would drown with me. She'd sail into the empty sea of loneliness, destined to die alone.

I didn't want that for her, and it felt unfair, to lose my life before I'd had the chance to experience some of life's most profound milestones. I would never walk down the aisle or know the joys of motherhood. The closest I'd come to having kids was the stray cat I fed every day. If I died, who would take care of her? I'd been feeding her for months, and now, she had grown to depend on me. Adopting her was my ultimate goal, but my landlord didn't allow pets, so for now, I put out food every morning and night, gave her medication to prevent fleas, and put a cat shelter full of blankets outside to keep her warm. If I never returned, would she survive?

I wished I'd told Shane about the cat; maybe he could have taken over where I left off.

Shane Hernandez. The guy I'd had a crush on ever since he moved in as my next-door neighbor. He was the complete package. Tall, sexy as hell, with eyes that could make you forget about everything going on around you. He was kind, too, always making the effort to stop and ask how I was doing when we bumped into each other in the hallway, and as if that weren't hot enough, he was a detective with the Chicago Police Department, sporting a gun and badge hanging from his belt that hugged his incredible physique. Insert swoon-fest.

I could see flashes of our first encounter.

"LEAVE ME ALONE, EZRA," I SNAP, YANKING MY ARM AWAY.

I walk along the sidewalk toward the double doors of my apartment complex.

"I'm just trying to help you get inside, Willow."

"I don't need your help."

"You've had too much to drink."

Not typical and not intentional. I tried a new mixed drink that was dangerous, how its strength snuck up on you.

But I'm not drunk. I'm buzzed. Big difference. He wants me to be drunk so he can play the part of the noble guy who helps a vulnerable woman get home safely. As if behaving like a gentleman can make up for what he did to me.

"It's over between us," I remind him. "How many times do I have to say it?"

Ezra ignores me and grabs my elbow. Like I need his help to walk.

Asshat.

When I yank my arm away, I lose my center of gravity, and I fall to the ground.

Ezra manhandles me again because it isn't enough that he invaded my girls' night and jumped into my Uber.

"Let me go!" I snap.

But Ezra uses both hands to grab me now.

"She said let her go," a deep voice warns.

Ezra whips his gaze to the figure standing ten feet from us. It's dark outside, the only light coming from two exterior bulbs that cast an orange haze around the mystery man.

"Mind your own damn business." Ezra pulls me.

"Stop!" I say.

Seriously, I'm not a violent person, but so help me, if Ezra doesn't leave me alone, I'm going to slam my heel into his crotch.

"Chicago PD." The shadowy figure flashes a badge that reflects the light from the building. "Step away from her right now, or I'll arrest you for assault."

Ezra pauses. "I'm not hurting her. I'm helping her because she's drunk."

"She told you to stop. Step away from her. Now."

"You can't arrest me for helping her."

"If you don't leave her alone? I sure as hell can."

Ezra glares at the guy, his fingers flexing at his sides.

"But you don't step away right this second?" the guy growls. "Maybe I'll rearrange your face instead."

I have no idea if the cop is being serious or sarcastic, but hallelujah, it works. Ezra moves away from me.

"I was just trying to help," Ezra says before slinking away into the night.

"You okay?" the cop asks.

I stand up slowly. In the dark, I can only make out his muscular body, which is encased in dark pants, a button-down shirt, and a gray wool jacket. He tucks his badge back into his pocket and straightens his tie.

"I'm fine. Thank you," I say, but I can't stop myself from adding, "You didn't need to do that. I had it under control."

I start to walk, losing the upper hand when my high heel hits a crack. Before gravity makes me another victim, a hand catches me by the hip, and I'm pressed against a firm side, a stern face looking down at me.

Holy crap. That chiseled jaw, those steely blue eyes. The guy holding me against his unfairly gorgeous body is my new next-door neighbor. His palm sends a flash of heat through my hip as he holds my gaze for five heartbeats. Five slow, belly-warming heartbeats.

"I've seen you around but haven't introduced myself yet."

He's noticed me. My hormones begin a glee fest, but the blood beneath my cheeks is too busy worrying he might've noticed me drooling over him.

"I'm Shane," he says.

"Willow," I say, adding, "You're a cop?"

"A detective," he says. "I wouldn't be a good one if I didn't say this..." His voice is warm and caring, no hint of animosity. "Gettin' this drunk is dangerous, Willow. You don't know how many girls in this city get assaulted every day."

I step away from him to make it clear I can stand on my own, that my clumsiness is merely from dangerous footwear.

High heels are weapons of mass destruction.

"I'm not that drunk," I say, motioning to where Ezra walked off. "He's just using my slight overindulgence as an excuse to try to weasel his way back into my life. Which will never work."

Shane raises his eyebrows. Seems to consider this with a ghost of a smile, which he quickly drops.

"The guy. Does he normally get that handsy with you?"

"No. He's harmless." Overbearing and a class-A dickwad. But harmless.

"Didn't look harmless," he says.

My neck burns in embarrassment of this scene. Of all the ways I wanted to meet my hot neighbor, this was not one of them.

"I'm sorry I bothered you," I say.

The tone of his voice lowers an octave. "You're never a bother, Willow."

THAT ENCOUNTER SPARKED THE FIRE OF MY GROWING ATTRACTION TO HIM, yet in our subsequent run-ins, I kept getting mixed signals. On the one hand, it seemed like he looked for excuses to stop and make small talk with me, and when he did, he studied me intently, like my every word fascinated him. During those talks, I'd catch him staring at my mouth with this wanton look in his eyes, and other times, his hungry gaze would comb over my body. But sometimes, we'd be in the middle of talking, and he'd suddenly clear his throat and excuse himself, leaving me with the impression he was intentionally cutting the conversation short.

Maybe he was attracted to me but thought dating a neighbor was a bad idea. After all, if we broke up, that would be seriously awkward, running into each other, but still. I wished I could have explored something with him, because as the foreboding water rushed toward me, I realized I'd never have another chance.

No.

I wasn't going to die.

The bridge was only three stories above the river—people survived higher falls than that. The bigger danger was the water, which, in winter, was a hair above freezing. So cold, it would lock up your muscles, making it virtually impossible to swim. Causing death within minutes, if not sooner. And it would endanger anyone else that might try to rescue me.

But so help me, even if the landing broke my bones, I'd fight with everything I had and make it to the shore.

I could do it.

I had to.

I braced myself as the river slammed into me.

And everything went black.

Pain pierced through my body like a thousand daggers stabbing me—each dagger ice, slicing up my skin with their arctic blades. I tried to scream, but I couldn't open my mouth, couldn't open my eyes, either. In a sea of darkness, the only thing that existed was muffled sounds.

Splashes.

Yelling.

Something hard clenched my torso.

"Hold on!"

Something else pressed to the back of my neck, lifting my face above the waterline.

"Willow?" The voice echoed its shock through my ears.

The voice knew my name. How did the voice know my name? Why did the voice seem familiar to me?

My body shifted and jerked, water splashing on my face and going up my nose, dripping a freezing path into my throat. Whoever it was seemed to struggle with my weight—my winter coat and jeans anchoring me down.

I could hear the mystery man breathing heavily, and I could feel his arm loosening its grip around me, undoubtedly weakening from the beginnings of hypothermia.

"Hold on, Willow." There was an urgency to his voice, as if he knew I needed to actively fight against falling asleep. Because it wasn't just falling asleep...

Flirting with the border between life and death, fighting to live was exhausting. My body hurt, my lungs hurt, and trying to stay alive was as tiring as fighting against a violent rip current. How easy it would be to just let go and get carried toward death.

"Grab her beneath her shoulders!" the voice barked. "But be careful. Support her spine!"

Something locked beneath my armpits, and then my back scraped across something as the water receded from my torso, then my legs.

With my body now still, I tried to open my eyes again.

Why can't I open my eyes? Why can't I scream?

I'm so cold. It feels like every cell, every vein, every bone in my body is freezing into pure ice.

I wanted a blanket, to be curled up by a warm fire—anything to get warm.

I tried to take a breath, but I couldn't, and my lungs screamed with death's grip squeezing them.

Help.

"Her pulse is weak," the voice growled, panting. "I don't think she's breathing. Check the ETA on the ambulance. We have less than four minutes before permanent brain damage sets in, another minute or so until she's dead."

Fingers tilted my chin, opened my mouth, and then something warm draped over it. A thrust of heated air burst into my throat. The relief was only temporary though, because the wind whipped against my neck and carved a tunnel into my body, all the way to my bones.

"Coats!" the voice barked. "Give me your fuckin' coats!"

As his mouth returned to mine, blowing another deep rush of oxygen into my lungs, I could hear zippers. And then layers of clothing shielded my body from the assaulting wind.

As the mouth blew another gust of air into me. And another. And another.

In the distance, a siren wailed.

"Come on, Willow. Fight!"

I sensed something just above my mouth.

Then, his lips returned.

Suddenly, I gasped, and my eyes flew open, taking in the scene before me.

I was lying on a snowy embankment with several fuzzy silhouettes of people standing around me. But only one person was drenched, only one had jumped into the ice water to pull me out, risking his own life in the process.

Shane Hernandez.

"Willow." He cupped my cheek and stared down at me, his relief giving way to vengeance. "Who did this to you?"

2

I opened my eyes to a white-tiled ceiling that butted up against stark walls. Colorless and empty, mirroring how I was feeling right now—trapped in a hospital bed with ivory railings that would make it harder to escape this nightmare.

After a few moments, a face hovered over me. And not just any face.

Shane Hernandez.

Making me momentarily forget everything else, except his beauty.

Shane was a gorgeous blend of rugged strength and soft charm. Blue eyes that reminded you of the sky on a warm summer day, black hair that you longed to run your fingers through, a strong jaw that accentuated his full lips—lips you wished you could feel pressed against your own—and tan skin that sheathed his sculpted muscles.

Which bulged against his...teal *scrubs*?

He must have noticed my confusion, because he glanced down at his attire.

"Was soaked when I came in. They took mercy on me and gave me something dry to wear."

Which had the bonus of showing off his arm tattoos.

When he returned his focus to me, the fluorescents illuminated the relief in his eyes that I was awake and the nervous uncertainty that was likely reflected in my own.

"How are you feelin'?" His deep voice drifted across my skin like the welcome heat of a bonfire on a crisp autumn night. His azure eyes held mine so intensely, it felt like they had seized me, shackled me to him while his energy scorched the air between us.

So overwhelming that I had to look away.

"My head is pounding, and I feel exhausted." But not bad, considering what happened. And what could have happened, if it hadn't been for Shane.

"You pulled me from the river." *You saved me.* And risked his life doing it.

I allowed myself to become engulfed in his gaze again, surrendering to the heat this time. Welcoming it, savoring it, even as the walls of the hospital seemed to burn to ash around us. His eyes met my cheek, and he looked as if he wanted to reach out and brush it.

"You scared me." In Shane's eyes, flames of worry became eclipsed by a wildfire of vengeance. "I heard you scream a bloodcurdling scream—the kind you hear when someone's being..." His lips tightened into a line. "I saw you hit the water, but I didn't know it was you until I got to you. What the hell happened, Willow?"

His iron gaze searched my face, trying to pull answers out of my eyes—like if he looked close enough, he'd find them.

I had to break Shane's stare again to have any shot at thinking straight, but when I tried to spur my memories of what happened on that bridge, it felt like an ice pick burrowed into my skull. I couldn't remember what happened before the fall—only fragments of what came after.

"What were you doing there?" I asked.

Shane placed his hand on mine like he needed to feel for himself that I was actually here. Alive. Although his grasp was tender, it torched my skin, crackling embers up my arm and into my ribs.

"Was going for a run," Shane said.

"At night?" I asked.

"I jog whenever I can squeeze it in. Was running on the pathway along the river"—so, he was on the ground level, not above it on the bridge—"when I heard you scream."

What were the odds? Of all the times and all the places for us to be in the same space together in a city that houses three million people. A freak coincidence? Or serendipity?

"How did you fall from that bridge, Willow?"

"Good. You're awake." A nurse in teal scrubs, identical to the ones Shane was wearing, smiled as she entered the room. "Doctor's on his way."

She pumped hand sanitizer into her palms and then checked my IV bag.

"Ms. Johnson." A man with hair as white as Santa's entered the room. Wearing a blue button-down beneath a lab coat, he approached the opposite side of my bed as Shane and pulled a pencil-sized flashlight out of his pocket, shining it in my left eye, then my right.

The assault of light was one of the only things that could break the spell cast by Shane's energy.

"How long have I been here?" I asked.

"Three hours or so," the doctor said. "Can you follow my finger, please?" He held his index finger up and watched my eyes as he shifted it from side to side.

"When can I go home?"

Because that's all I wanted to do—go back to my apartment, crawl under my covers, and sleep until my head didn't hurt anymore. And then maybe spend some time figuring out how I fell from that bridge and why Shane was affecting me *this* much—because the energy I felt from his gaze, his touch, was beyond powerful.

"We're keeping you overnight for observation," the doctor said. "You got lucky. Fractured wrist. Based on the clinical exam, a concussion. Could have been a lot worse."

My wrist is broken? I looked down at my left arm, and that's when I noticed the cast.

"Is she going to be okay?" Shane's brows crinkled into worry again.

"She'll be released tomorrow with a list of things to watch for with a concussion. But she seems to be doing just fine. Once the pain meds wear off fully, you'll probably feel like you were in a car accident, though. Pretty banged up and bruised. I recommend taking it easy for a few days."

"My memory of last night is fuzzy," I said.

"Short-term memory loss is not uncommon with concussions," the doctor said.

"Will she get it back?"

Shane's wary eyes fixed on to the doctor's face as he removed his stethoscope from around his neck and pressed it to my chest.

"Hard to say. Some patients do; some don't."

"What if I take her to the bridge where she fell, have her look around?" Shane asked. "Might that trigger her memory of what happened to return?"

"If there was a prescription to heal post-traumatic amnesia, I'd write one, but unfortunately, many patients never regain their memories. I'm not saying it's not possible, but we need to be patient. Her best chance of recovering them is from rest and time to let her body heal."

"My head is pounding," I said.

"I'll increase your dose of pain medication and have the nurse come in with it. It won't be a full dose this time, since you already had some three hours ago, but it'll help. Meanwhile, a police officer is waiting outside to take your statement," the doctor said. "I'll send him in."

"I'd prefer to do it another time." Not only was I exhausted, but also, my memories were missing. Maybe if I went home and slept for a little while, I could actually give the cops something to work with and not waste their time.

"I'm afraid he's on his way."

Great.

The doctor left the room, but Shane remained on the side of my bed, as he'd evidently done for the past three hours.

"You didn't need to stay here." Though he'd always been friendly in the past, flirty even, staying here was a burden. "I'm sure you have better things to do with your time than to babysit your clumsy neighbor."

Especially since the clock on the wall said it was past one in the morning. A detective needed sleep to be at his sharpest.

Unless...was Shane here on official business? Was the cop waiting outside here with him?

"Is my fall part of an ongoing case of yours or something?" I asked.

That would be just my luck. Fall victim to some serial bridge-thrower.

"No," Shane said.

Then, why?

His ocean-colored gems latched on to my eyes and didn't let go as he placed his hand on top of mine. Again, it torched my skin and crackled heat through my chest.

"I needed to make sure you're okay."

It felt like Shane was looking directly into my soul, wrapping me in the warm embrace of his genuine concern for my well-being. No, more than concern. The haunting shadow in his eyes hinted at an agony he'd suffered when he'd been waiting to find out if I was going to be all right.

But surely, the rest of his appearance—looking like he'd been through hell with dark circles under his eyes and a mop of messy hair that he'd been running his hands through—wasn't from worrying about me. Right? Surely, that level of stress was from physically jumping into the water.

A uniformed police officer dragged me from my thoughts when he entered the room.

"Ms. Johnson."

The guy was in his late twenties, I guessed, and resembled the actor Joe Pesci. Dark brown eyes set in an oval face, thin lips. A slight overbite to his upper teeth. He was short, a broad chest that told me he hit the gym a lot, but his legs were thin, like he often skipped leg day.

As soon as Shane's eyes landed on him, Shane's jaw tensed.

The officer's face tightened when he spotted Shane by my bedside, too.

"Detective," the cop said in a clipped tone.

"Officer De Luca." Shane nodded.

For a second, I seriously wondered if they were about to arm wrestle, but the cop cleared his throat.

"Mind if I ask what you're doing here?" De Luca asked him in a curt tone.

"As I told you in my statement, she's my next-door neighbor," Shane said. "And I pulled her from the river."

De Luca's eyes snapped back to Shane's hand wrapped around mine.

Shane didn't need to say anything for the tension to roll off his body.

Meanwhile, drumsticks performed an evil ritual on my skull.

"I need to ask her some questions, so you know the drill." The cop dismissed Shane with a wave of his hand toward the door.

I pressed my fingers to my temple, willing the ache to subside.

"Would it be okay if I got some sleep first?" I couldn't imagine his interview would be brief—a woman mysteriously landing in the Chicago River. Plus, "My memory is fuzzy. I think it's the pain meds, so I'd prefer to let them wear off first."

"I'm here now," De Luca said in annoyance, as if wasting his drive time here was a bigger offense than collecting more accurate information.

"That's not what she asked," Shane said. "It might be better to wait for her head to clear. Take her statement tomorrow."

De Luca's nostrils flared.

Shane saw his nostril flare and raised him a chest puff.

I wonder if two police officers would get into a fistfight.

In a hospital no less.

"You need to leave, Detective." De Luca glowered at Shane.

"Since I already gave you my statement, I don't. Unless that's what Willow wants."

De Luca licked his teeth and cut his eyes to mine, silently demanding I kick Shane out, but all I wanted was for De Luca to come back another time.

"I'm hoping my head will be clearer tomorrow," I reiterated.

"Do you know how you came to fall from that bridge?"

"No."

"Did you jump?" De Luca asked point-blank.

"What? No."

I couldn't believe he'd asked me so bluntly, with no empathy in his voice.

Tonight, I wound up in a river and almost died, for crying out loud. Equally disturbing, I had no recollection of how it happened. Could he at least try to imagine how awful this felt? This was a lot for me to process, and I was doing my best to not let the anxiety of it all consume me. A little compassion would be appreciated.

"You said you have no memory of it," De Luca said.

Shane stiffened at his tone.

"I don't, but I know I didn't try to kill myself."

"How do you know for sure?"

"I..."

"Been depressed lately?"

Down? A little. But depressed? "No. And I would never kill myself; I wouldn't do that to my family. Plus, I'm terrified of drowning. When I was a kid, I fell into the community pool for a few seconds, and I've had a fear of drowning ever since. If I *were* depressed enough to off myself, it would be something gentle, like

GRAVE DECEPTION | 17

taking a bottle of pills or something. I'd never jump into icy water to drown myself. It must have been an accident."

"I walked the bridge before I came here," De Luca said. "No holes in the railing or any other visible signs of a defect. Bridges are built with a safe pedestrian pathway. But if you were drunk, or being reckless, done it on a dare, climbing around or something, that might be another story."

"No. I'd never do that. I told you, I have a fear of drowning."

"I didn't smell alcohol on her breath when I did mouth-to-mouth," Shane said. "Surely, the hospital did a tox screen."

De Luca glowered at Shane, as if to say, *I don't need you to tell me how to do my job.*

My head's pounding got worse. I pressed a finger to my forehead.

"I didn't see blood or any signs of a struggle," De Luca said to me. "I'll walk the bridge again in the daylight, but there wasn't anything to suggest there was a violent confrontation."

"She has fresh bruises on her upper arms," Shane said. *I do?* He lifted the sleeves of my hospital gown slightly to expose the tops of them. "Looks like someone grabbed her."

"You said you and some pedestrian pulled her from the water," De Luca countered.

"Under her shoulders. We didn't grab her upper arms. Someone else did. Which means there was a confrontation *before* she went over."

"None of the witnesses along the river saw anything until they heard her screaming when she fell, and there were no witnesses on the bridge."

"Someone did this to her," Shane said.

"We don't know that."

"You heard her; she's terrified of drowning, so she didn't do this to herself, and she has bruising."

"She could have bruised her arms, hitting the ice chunks in the water, or it could have been from earlier in the evening or yesterday."

"*Or* someone grabbed her and threw her off the bridge."

I couldn't tell if De Luca was trying to be unbiased or if he was offended at Shane's insistence.

"It's also possible she was intoxicated enough to do something reckless. You know better than anyone the dangers of getting tunnel vision on a case, Detective. Let me do my job."

"Then, do it. Find out who the hell did this to her."

De Luca inhaled an angry breath and pulled up a screen on his phone.

"Let's start from the beginning," he said. "What were you doing before you were on that bridge?"

The nurse walked into the room, carrying a syringe, which she pierced into my IV. "This will make her drowsy," she warned.

I loved her for not asking the cops for permission to administer it first; evidently, leaving a patient in pain for longer than necessary wasn't going to happen on her watch.

I could feel heat radiating down my body, the stabbing pain in my head subsiding as my eyelids went to war, fighting to stay open.

"Get some rest, honey."

Once the nurse left, I tried to answer the officer's question.

"I don't..." I shut my eyes, and it took concerted effort to open them again. "I don't remember what..."

As I yawned long and deep, Shane frowned, his worried eyes pinned on me as he said, "Maybe you should finish her statement tomorrow."

De Luca opened his mouth, as if about to argue his case, but perhaps he saw the exhaustion in my face and he took pity on me. Or maybe my eyes were glassy from the narcotics and he realized he'd be wasting his time, trying now. Because after a deep breath, he cleared his throat.

"Fine. We'll finish tomorrow," he said.

De Luca glared at Shane for several long moments before ambling out of the room.

"Okay, is he your childhood nemesis or something?" I smirked, because, well, *pain meds.*

"I'm goin' to make some calls," he said. "See if I can get someone else assigned to your case."

"So, he *is* your childhood nemesis."

"You almost died tonight." Shane's lips flattened into a tight line. "You need a cop that'll go the extra mile, not someone who'll do the bare minimum."

Bare minimum. Yikes. There was a story there for sure, and if he disliked De Luca so much...

"Why can't you work the case?" I yawned. My eyelids didn't care that a sex god was in the room.

"Conflict of interest, since I know you." With his eyes scouring my face, he looked haunted by something, something he seemingly couldn't leave without asking. "Willow, can you think of anyone who might've done this to you?"

I laughed. Because *narcotics*.

I couldn't remember how I'd come to fall off that bridge, but one thing I knew for certain: "No. No one in my life would ever hurt me."

His face got all disapproval-ish.

"You'd be damn surprised what people are capable of, Willow. You should be careful not to see people through such rose-colored glasses. We need to find out what happened to you as quickly as possible. Because if someone did this to you, they might try again."

3

I woke when light warmed my eyelids, the sun streaming through the blinds of the hospital room. Muffled voices of what I presumed to be a nearby nurses' station rumbled outside of my closed door, shoes squeaking along the hallway—probably hospital staff making their rounds. In here, it smelled like disinfectant that stung my nostrils.

"Morning," Shane said.

My eyes snapped to the chair next to my bed. In it sat Shane, now wearing a blue T-shirt that clung to his biceps for dear life, jeans, and a Cubs baseball hat that framed his sultry eyes.

I once again found myself struck by his beauty and the heat that radiated off him like he was a walking fireplace.

"How's your head?" Shane asked.

I shifted, trying to sit up a little, but immediately groaned. Whatever pain medicine they gave me last night must have worn off because, now, parts of my body felt like they'd been on the receiving end of a baseball bat.

"I didn't expect to see you this morning," I said.

Shane might've felt some sense of obligation to stay last night until I had woken up, given he had been at the scene of the bridge incident. But after that? I'd have thought he would've gone home.

"I got you some things." Shane opened up a plastic bag and set a toothbrush, toothpaste, and some face soap on the nightstand next to my bed.

"You went to the store for me?"

"Pharmacy is close by."

Still, he didn't need to do that. Surely, the hospital supplied necessities.

When he looked at me, my gaze surrendered to his, electricity firing currents beneath my skin.

"I got you your favorite coffee." Shane pointed to a cup with the logo of my favorite coffee shop, Angie's Coffeeteria. "Might be luke-warm by now, but I can see if I can find a microwave to zap it for you."

"How did you know Angie's Coffeeteria is my favorite coffee place?"

Shane scrubbed his jaw as he stared at me. "Anytime I've bumped into you in the mornings, you're always carrying a cup from it."

My cheeks became an inferno, competing with my chest for which body part was hotter right now.

"I'm not sure if I got the right drink," he hedged. "Maybe you get one of those fancy drinks. This is just black coffee. Cream and sugar on the side."

I wondered if I could hide the surprise on my face that he had gone so far out of his way for me. Not only saving my life, but trying to make the aftermath of this dreadful experience as comfortable as possible.

No one had ever done something this nice for me.

Mom had done her best, raising us girls after my dad died, but she was lost in pain with nothing left over to give to a child in their most vulnerable years. I liked to believe that it made me more independent, thickened my skin, even, and that I was stronger because of it. But in moments like this, it reminded me that, growing up, affection was as absent as my father was.

"I also grabbed you some clothes since they cut yours off in the ER." Shane motioned toward a bag on the other side of the room. "They're mine. They'll be way too big for you, but it'll just be for the drive home."

I looked down at my hands, trying to contain the swelling tenderness I was feeling for Shane.

"You have someone you want me to call, Willow?"

I thought about this. All things considered, I was okay. The injuries I'd sustained weren't life-threatening, and they would soon discharge me from the hospital. So, there was no need to bother my friends with a hospital run for a non-life-threatening emergency. Not even Emily. Coming to a hospital in downtown Chicago was a massive ordeal with traffic and parking, and I'd be waiting around awhile for paperwork. Monopolizing most of her day when she was just getting over a cold no less. Something this intrusive was better suited for immediate family.

But I would not burden Mom with this. If I called her to the hospital, I'd have to tell her what happened, and she would discover I could've died. I tried to avoid the cruelties of breaking down the walls she'd built around her grief; it escaped its prison enough on its own.

Which left me with my sister, Hayley. Calling her was a bad idea —the last time we were supposed to meet, she didn't even show up.

I SIT AT THE TABLE, HOPING THIS IS FINALLY THE TURNING POINT IN MY relationship with my sister—a turning point I've longed for, for as long as I can remember. We were close when I was younger, but since Hayley was older when Dad died, it had a bigger impact on her, and as the years passed, Hayley pulled away from everyone—her addiction creating an even bigger divide between us. I never gave up hope that I could get her back, though—a good person doesn't give up on a family member. Even if that family member isn't always treating you perfectly, you keep making the effort with them.

Case in point, tonight, I invited her to have dinner with me on my birthday—just the two of us. I booked us a table at a restaurant with a view of the city. White tablecloths. Candlelight. Dinner plates so shiny, I can see the candlelight reflection dancing across them. And dang it if excitement doesn't ignore my warnings to not get my hopes up too high and buzz inside of me.

I sip my water and stare at the skyscrapers outside the window, imagining all the people getting together right now. How many of them were years in the making?

I check my watch.

Maybe she's stuck in traffic.

I wait another few minutes and then text Hayley.

Me: Are you having trouble finding the place?

I drink another half glass of water.

I call her, but it goes right to voice mail. I leave her a quick message and then text her again.

Me: Are you okay?

No answer, not even after another five minutes.

She's over an hour late. The waiter keeps glaring at me, a line of people near the hostess booth waiting for tables to open up.

Me: Are you still coming?

No reply.

Worry pits in my stomach, and I feel guilty for wondering if she's using again because what does that say about me as a sister? I should have more confidence in her sobriety. That's what a supportive person would do, but the thought isn't coming from a place of anger, but from concern.

Because, now, I'm worried that something's happened to her.

I call her ten more times, I send her more texts, and then finally, after two hours of waiting, my cell buzzes.

Hayley: So sorry. I can't make it. Happy birthday!

How is it possible that a heart can rejoice and sink, all at the same time? Rejoice that she's okay—or at least seems to be—but sink because she blew me off. Again. And somehow, for reasons I don't understand, this time hurts even more than when she didn't show up to either my high school or college graduation.

Tonight would've been just me and her, and it would have gone a long way to healing the wounds created by years of her flaking out on me.

I grit my teeth.

Me: I hope whatever it is, is important.

I feel like a fool for thinking this would turn out any differently, and I flag down the waiter to let him know someone else can have the table— leaving him the money I would have spent on my meal as a tip. As starving as I now am, I'm too humiliated and angry to order food and eat it alone.

I walk home, seesawing between wiping tears from my cheeks and clenching my hands into balls. This is stupid. Yes, it hurts, but I'm fine. This isn't a new development that she didn't show up tonight. In fact, I shouldn't have planned for anything else.

The next day she pops over—an exceedingly rare occurrence. I normally try to bite my tongue, take the high road when she's hurt my feelings. After all, when we were kids, Hayley played a big role in raising me. But enough is enough.

I stand in my doorway, not allowing her inside as she says hello and gets to her point.

"I thought we could go grab lunch."

Seriously? I wasted my entire night getting ready, sitting and waiting at a restaurant just for her to no-show. With no actual explanation, mind you, and she thinks I'll follow her to lunch now, like a puppy begging for scraps?

"What came up last night?" I cross my arms over my chest.

"Oh, uh..." Hayley runs a hand through her hair. "Just, like, a thing with a friend of mine."

"A thing."

"Yeah. I was totally planning on coming, but, you know."

"I don't know, actually," I said. "That's why I'm asking. Why did I sit there for two hours, waiting for you? And why didn't you text me sooner to let me know you couldn't make it?"

"Jeez, Willow. If you're trying to make me feel like crap, I already do."

"You could have fooled me." She hadn't even responded to my text last night.

"You shouldn't feel so upset."

I shake my head in disbelief. *"Thanks for telling me how I should feel,"* I say. *"If you don't mind, I have to go."*

I shut the door and press my back to it, telling my erratic breathing to calm the hell down, that this is progress—me pushing back on her. Staying silent all these years hasn't changed anything, so establishing firmer boundaries with her—telling her that her behavior, at times, is unaccept-able—is an important step to getting our relationship back on track, and our foundation will be stronger for it.

WE'D EXCHANGED A COUPLE OF BRIEF TEXTS AFTER THAT INCIDENT, BUT NOT much more.

Shane's fierce gaze blasted right through me, as if he could oblit-erate the bricks I'd built around myself, uncovering every truth about me.

"Okay, we're goin' to talk about why you have this hesitation to call someone, but for right now? I'll be the one to drive you home."

Butterflies launched in my stomach. "You don't need to do that."

Maybe I should at least try to see if Hayley would show up. As thrilled as I might be to have more unprecedented time with Shane, I didn't want to be a burden. And almost dying last night reignited my desire to get close to my sister, once and for all.

I looked at the nightstand. "Where's my phone?"

"At the bottom of the river, would be my guess."

Damn. I couldn't call anybody even if I wanted to; I had every-body's phone number saved in my phone, not memorized.

"Your keys survived though. They were tightly packed into your jean pocket, I guess."

Well, at least there was that. One less hoop I had to jump through to get home and into my bed.

"Why did you stay here last night?" *Why are you doing so much for me?*

All those years I'd fought for scraps of affection from my family, and Shane was handing it out like it was no big deal.

"I witnessed you fall from a bridge, Willow. You weren't breathing. You think I'm just going to leave and go run errands today?"

Well, yeah.

My answer must've been written all over my face because Shane's lips tightened.

"It's pretty damn obvious that you're not used to people being kind to you."

My face flushed so hot, I had to look down at my hands. Which was silly. I was stronger than this.

"That's not true." My friends were nice. My family was kind even if it wasn't consistent and even if sizable gaps of hurt interrupted the kindness.

"We just don't know each other well enough for an overnight-stay-in-the-hospital kind of thing."

I wasn't sure if Shane believed me.

He stood up, came to my side of the bed, shoved his hands into his pockets, and said, "I want to make sure you're okay. And, until we figure out who did this to you, I don't think it's a good idea for you to be alone."

Now was not the time for my heart to be dissecting all of his words, looking for clues about possible romantic intentions. It was inappropriate. And yet, that's exactly what that traitor was doing right now.

"Which brings me to my next point." He looked down at me for several seconds before speaking. "Until this all gets sorted out, I'd like you to stay at my place."

My hormones elicited a dance squad in perfect formation, cheering, *Yes, yes, yes.* But my pride took over. I was an adult, capable of taking care of myself.

"I appreciate the offer, but no."

"Willow..."

"Look, I'm sure, in your line of work, every incident seems suspicious to you, but there is no killer after me. No one in my life would've done this."

Shane thinned his lips in obvious disagreement.

"Would you have gone to meet a stranger at ten o'clock at night, alone?"

"Maybe I wasn't alone?"

"If you were with someone, they might have been responsible for your fall. And if they weren't, they would've called for help or, at a minimum, run down to the bystanders when I pulled you from the water."

Fair point. But that didn't change the facts: I trusted everyone in my life implicitly, and while it was beyond disturbing that I'd almost died—*I must be in shock, because it still doesn't feel real*—I wasn't going to let Shane get himself all worked up over a non-crime.

"Then, I must've been alone. I must have somehow fallen off the bridge by accident."

Did an accident sound slam-dunk obvious? No. You don't hear about people falling off bridges very often for a reason, but I knew no one in my life would ever try to kill me, and I wasn't suicidal, so it was the only logical conclusion.

I hoped the cops would figure out how the accident could have occurred. Was there a fault in the bridge they'd initially overlooked? Was it one of those bridges that opens like the top of a box when tall boats come along the river, and for some reason, it was slightly open at the top when I happened to walk over it? Because if it happened to me, it could happen to someone else. And they might not make it...

"Willow." A nurse poked her head in. "I'll be in with your discharge papers in a few minutes."

I nodded.

Shane appeared to debate on asking me more questions, but he glanced at the skin beneath my eyes. The makeup concealer industry made a fortune off girls like me, whose skin darkened like crazy on anything less than six hours of sleep.

"We should get you home so you can take a nap before De Luca shows up to take your statement."

"I thought you didn't want him on the case."

Shane's jaw tightened. "I should've known I'd need somethin' tangible to get him reassigned. But he's not a detective, so as soon as he determines a crime has been committed, detectives will open an official investigation."

"The only way to get De Luca off the case is if he's convinced that someone tried to kill me?"

When Shane nodded, I frowned.

He thinks I'm some weak victim, just lying here, waiting for other people to help. But he doesn't know how strong I really am, and maybe he needs to see that.

I threw the covers off my lap, trying to hide my wince. With strain, I reached back to make sure my hospital gown was all sorts of tied up—have an ass-flash would totally hamper my demonstration of strength.

When I dangled my feet off the bed, Shane tensed, looking at me like a baby about to take her first steps.

"What do you have against him?" I asked.

"That's a long story."

My goal was to grab the bag of clothes and change in the adjoining bathroom, but as soon as I tried to stand up, the room started to go black from the drop in blood pressure. I was going down like a sack of potatoes—and not in a cute, romantic dancing-dip way. More like a puppet-that-got-her-strings-cut kind of way, but before I hit the ground, Shane's arm crashed around my back and pulled me upright, slamming my chest to his.

It was just reflex on his part, the way he'd pulled me against him —the guy hadn't had time to plan it out, for crying out loud—but now, we both stilled.

He looked down at me, his worry giving way to something else as his eyes raked over my face, landing on my lips. He smelled like the ocean that shared its color with his eyes, framed by those dark, serious eyebrows that pulled down slightly.

"Easy," he whispered.

He held me for several seconds before setting me down on the bed.

"I stood up too fast," I said to ensure he didn't misread this as me being frail.

"Maybe it's too soon for you to go home."

"No. I hate hospitals."

Now that I was safely sitting on the bed, Shane took a couple steps back and evaluated me.

"Bad experience in one?" he asked.

"My dad," I said, surprised how natural it felt, talking to Shane. "He died when I was little."

Pivotal memories of him flashed through my mind.

I'M FOUR, AND DADDY IS HOLDING MY HAND, WALKING ME TO THE FIELD behind our house to pick wildflowers. My favorites are the purple ones— those are way harder to find than dandelions. I love them so much that he's helped me dig a big rectangle in our backyard for a garden we're going to build, and he's going to let me fill it with them.

"Will you always love me, Daddy?" I ask as we walk.

Daddy looks down at me. His hair glows orange from the sun behind him. "Always."

"Even when you die?"

His eyebrows crinkle.

"Mommy said her grandpa died. Will you still love me when you die?"

"I'll always love you, Willow. Even when I'm gone."

Daddy squeezes my hand.

"But you don't have to worry about that. I won't die for a long, long, long time."

. . .

A COUPLE MONTHS LATER, I PLACE WILDFLOWERS ON TOP OF DADDY'S SHINY black casket. It took me a half hour to find purple ones hidden in the weeds, and I had to walk through thorny bushes that scraped my legs to get them, but Daddy deserves the good wildflowers. Especially since they'll be the last ones I can ever pick for him.

"You lied," I whisper over my tears. I don't think I'll ever stop crying. I think I'll cry every single day for the rest of my life.

I'M EIGHT, HOLDING THE PINK FLYER WITH PURPLE LETTERS THAT THE SCHOOL sent home with us about the father-daughter dance. It has three yellow bubbles with pictures of girls dancing with their daddies with big smiles. My friend Julie said her daddy is taking her shopping for a fluffy purple dress, and he's going to take her out to dinner before the dance, and they'll pick their favorite song and dance to it, and when she gets married someday, they are going to dance to that song again.

A drop splats on the paper from a tear as I stare out the window at the rectangle of overgrowth that was supposed to be my and Daddy's special garden.

I'm a terrible person for wishing somebody else's daddy could've died instead of mine.

I crumple the page and bury it in the trash can, so Mommy doesn't see it and get sad again. Maybe Mommy would be happy if I didn't keep making her sad by leaving these things out.

I NEVER WANTED ANY OTHER FAMILY TO GO THROUGH WHAT WE DID, LOST IN the emotional and financial damage created by grief's aftershocks.

That's why I wanted to open up my own business to help families in distress. Organizing counseling and taking the business skills I'd learned to help them shape their résumés, search for work, and find loans to get a down payment on housing. I'd had this dream for years, and though I had volunteered my time at various organizations, I'd never had the courage to take the leap. Wrapped in the sanctuary of a steady paycheck, 401(k), and good health insurance, I kept postponing. And now, here I was, having almost missed the chance of making my dreams come true.

"I don't remember much," I continued, "but I do remember being in a hospital when they told me the news."

I saw pain flash through his eyes. Pity, empathy would make sense. But not pain.

Why did he look hurt?

Shane cleared his throat, recalibrating back to the task at hand.

"Let me get a nurse to stay in here while you change," he said.

I allowed it, only so I wouldn't break my skull in half and have to stay in here another night.

The nurse was nice, and a few minutes later, I was dressed in Shane's ocean-scented outfit.

As he warned, they were much too big. His T-shirt went down to the middle of my thighs, and his light-gray sweatpants were so baggy, I had to roll the bottom several times and cinch the drawstring tightly.

"I'll go get your boyfriend," the nurse said.

"He's not my boyfriend."

She gave me a smirk, the she-devil, and then vanished into the hall.

Shane returned, pushing a freaking wheelchair into the room.

I glared at him. "I'm not sitting in that."

"Hospital policy. Come on." He patted the seat. "Maybe I can pop a wheelie."

I reluctantly—and I mean, *reluctantly*—let him help me into the wheelchair, only because I was a rule follower. And again, I needed my skull in one piece to escape this jail.

A few minutes later, I got into his car, because, fine, we were heading to the same place, and it made no sense to disturb my friends when I had a ride.

Gray clouds—the thick snowstorm type—lingered in the sky, casting the charcoal skyscrapers in shades of silver and blue. Icy winds beat against the side of the car, and a nearby ambulance wailed, drowning out the vehicle engines that purred near a traffic light.

"Thank you," I said. "For"—saving my life, bringing clean clothes—"everything. And for driving me home."

Shane allowed his eyes to wander from the road for a few seconds, his face softening as he studied me.

"I'm glad you're okay, Willow." He gripped the steering wheel tighter. "When I pulled your head above the water and realized it was *you* who'd fallen from the bridge..."

He didn't finish his thought. Instead, his forearms tightened, and his knuckles whitened.

Having someone care about me this much was, pathetically, a foreign experience. I didn't know where to cram all these strange emotions mixing together, so I settled for avoiding eye contact and glancing around his car, searching for any excuse to change the subject.

"You have a siren." I noticed.

He said nothing.

"Do you ever use it for non-work purposes?"

Shane furrowed his eyebrows, looking at me. "Why would I do that?"

"The usual. Beat traffic, get through red lights, scare people for fun."

He cast his gaze back to the road, his lips twitching up. "Of course not."

"Ever use it to pull over someone you know?"

Again, a sideways glance. "No."

"Would you?"

"Not unless I wanted to be a dick."

I smiled and watched the buildings pass in silence until, finally, we arrived at our apartment complex.

Shane and I lived on the first floor of the ten-story building.

Despite my insistence that I could do it alone, Shane kept a steady hand wrapped around my arm—I swear I could feel its heat through his coat he'd made me wear—as we walked into the building and ambled down the hallway leading to my front door.

When we reached it, I stopped in my tracks, a shiver of unrest drifting through my bones. At first glance, my front door looked as it always did—shut tightly—but when you approach the same door every day, some part of your mind picks up on small discrepancies before you're fully aware of what seems off. Whatever it was, was so small, I stood there, inches away from it, studying the door closely to identify what made me pause. And that's when I realized what it was.

The door was shut, but not fully—a centimeter or so not butting up against the outside frame.

Shane must have sensed my anxiety and seen my eyes wandering over my door, because he stepped closer, scrutinizing it himself.

And then, without a word, he pulled me down the hall, unlocked and opened *his* apartment door, and shoved me inside. *Shoved*, even though it hurt a little.

"What are you—"

He covered my mouth with his hand, a silent warning firing from his eyes.

If I wasn't so startled by it, this might be sexy as sin.

He held his index finger over his lips and flattened his palm, motioning for me to stay. Then, he vanished into his bedroom, brandishing a gun when he returned.

He punched 911 into his phone and handed it to me.

"Stay here," he whispered. "Tell them there's a possible break-in."

Then, he was gone.

4

I stood motionless as a squeak alerted me to my front door opening.

Shane's going inside.

With a gun.

Obviously, Shane thought someone might be in there, so why risk going inside? Why not wait for backup? If he interrupted a burglary or something, Shane might not be the only one wielding a weapon...

I pushed the green button on the phone and alerted the operator to what was going on—a possible break-in—as quietly as possible.

All the while chewing my fingernail.

The level of worry I had for him right now surprised me. Of course I'd be worried about *anyone* in a dangerous situation, but this wasn't anyone. It was Shane, and that's what had me chewing my nail so hard, it hurt.

An eternity later, I could hear sirens growing louder, and Shane's front door opened.

He held the weapon at his side, his muscles relaxed compared to the rigid balls of steel they were when he had left.

"Place is empty," he said.

"So, it was a false alarm?"

"I didn't say that."

"So, someone *had* been inside my place?"

Shane opened a drawer in his kitchen, pulled out a leather holster, and strapped it to his belt. Then shoved the gun inside.

"I don't know," he said. But his tone gave away his lie. He very much thought someone had been inside. "Let's wait for the uniformed officers to do a more thorough search."

And that's precisely what they did. Responding officers swept my apartment from top to bottom and found no evidence that an intruder had been inside. No overturned furniture, no evidence of a scuffle, no evidence that someone had jimmied the door. They concluded I had likely forgotten to lock it on my way out and it just hadn't latched fully.

Which was strange. Living in a big city, I *never* left without locking up. Ever.

But at least that meant there was no break-in.

Not that Shane agreed with that. When the officers left, he ran a hand through his black locks—his biceps trying to distract me by bulging from his shirt—and he repeated to me what he'd said to the officers.

"My gut is tellin' me this is related to what happened to you. You never leave your apartment unlocked," Shane said, "let alone with the door ajar."

He's been more observant of me than I've given him credit for. But I guess that's what makes a good detective—always noticing things.

"And this all happens around the same time you fall from a bridge?" He shook his head. "Until we sort this out, you're staying at my place."

I almost smiled—I did find his protectiveness sexy—but squared my shoulders. I knew he meant well. But I wasn't some victim in perpetual danger, and no matter how good his intentions might be, my independence was something I guarded fiercely.

After growing up without a father, having an emotionally absent mother, and an older sister who'd become more isolating with each year, I'd learned to take care of myself at a very young age. It was my comfort zone, and now, I didn't like to depend on anyone.

The only person in this life you can fully rely on is yourself.

Plus, I'd just been released from the hospital, had a splitting headache, and wanted to lie down and take a nap in the comfort of my bed.

"Sorry. No can do."

"Willow..."

"You heard what the officers said. No forced entry. Nothing missing."

"That they saw."

"No shred of evidence anyone was even inside my apartment."

"No evidence someone *wasn't.*"

And based on the stern look on his face, he expected me to accept his hypothesis as fact.

At work, Shane was probably used to being a boss and telling people what to do. He had a commanding aura about him that likely compelled most into obedience, but I wasn't in his jurisdiction.

I pinched my temples, trying to thwart a growing migraine.

"I'm going to lie down now."

When I stepped forward to leave his apartment, he blocked my path by pressing his palm against the wall to my left, his forearm muscles flexing as he caged me in.

I raised my chin, challenging the air between us, but he matched my determination with a stubborn-ass look of his own.

"Willow, I'm not letting you back in your apartment when we don't know what the hell is going on."

"*Letting* me?" I threw my hand up and immediately regretted it because of the stabbing pain in my shoulder that must've been a torn muscle. Pain Shane must have picked up on, because he glared at my arm with that fiery vengeance again, as if counting down the moments until he could get revenge against whoever had hurt me.

"This isn't your call." I tried to step around him on the other side, but he mirrored my movements and blocked my path. "Isn't holding someone against their will illegal?"

"You were almost killed last night. If you think I'm letting you out of my sight, you have another thing coming."

I glowered at him. "I can't decide if I find your overprotective-ness"—*sexy as hell*—"sweet or mind-blowingly annoying."

His lips curled up on one side. And as if his sort of smile wasn't distractingly scintillating enough, after a few seconds, his gaze traveled down my face and landed on my lips. Standing only inches away, he kept me trapped with his muscular arm, and his mouth parted slightly.

The energy around us shifted. A mixture of anger, and possessiveness, and passion.

I'd never had anyone inspire this reaction inside of me before. I could feel my every nerve stand on end, tempting my lips toward his while he dared me to fight against it.

But if he thought standing here like a panty-melting sex god would make me surrender to his every command, well...my hormones might be completely on board with that, but I wasn't.

I shoved the heat from my chest down to my toes.

"Look, I appreciate everything you've done for me, but I'm a grown woman. I don't feel well. I have a headache. And I'm going into *my* home and crawling into *my* bed and going to sleep."

He said nothing.

Good.

Point made.

I stepped toward his door, surprised he didn't stop me. He didn't stop me when I reached the hallway, and he didn't stop me when I reached my front door, opened it, and shuffled inside. But once I went to shut said door?

He stormed inside, locked the dead bolt, and flopped down on my couch with his feet up.

Like someone who'd been lying on my worn-out cushions so

often that he knew how the sliding glass door stuck, knew some of the drawers in the painted-too-many-times kitchen cabinets didn't fully close, and knew that my coffee table hid a small chocolate stain on my carpet from when I fell asleep, bingeing the Twilight series. And the thing was, he looked like he belonged in my place.

Not that I'd tell him that. He wouldn't hear me anyway, what with all his non-listening to my boundaries.

"What are you doing?" I snapped.

"Mind if I watch a movie?" He picked up my remote.

"Um, yes. I mind. A lot. As I said, I want to sleep."

"I'll keep the volume low."

In my old fantasies, he'd been in my living room, shirtless. In my new fantasies, I was whacking his bossy head with a frying pan.

"Leave," I said.

"Fine." He rolled his eyes. "I'll keep the volume off." He added to himself in an annoyed tone, "I hate captions."

"You'll keep the *TV* off, because you're going back to your place."

"If you think I'd leave you alone after someone tried to kill you, you clearly don't know me very well."

Ugh! I hoped after a long nap, my memory would suddenly come back so I could say this with complete certainty.

"No one tried to kill me. Bridges get caked with ice this time of year, so I must have somehow slipped and fallen. And clearly, I don't know you because I never pegged you for breaking and entering or whatever this is. Please leave."

I crossed my arms over my chest, and we entered a stare-down. In corner one, a female with stick-straight brown hair and chocolate-colored eyes. At five foot five, weighing a mere one hundred and twenty-four pounds, she faced the competitive disadvantage of having arms as thin as twigs. In corner two, we had the most stubborn male specimen to ever walk the earth. A muscular guy well above six feet tall, he could probably throw said girl across the room, using nothing but a deltoid muscle. He could even use his eyeballs as weapons, for God's sake, what with those light-blue specks on the inside—simply winking me into submission.

"I've made my decision," I snapped. "Mind-blowingly annoying."

His lips curled up, and he clicked the button on the remote, the television blaring to life.

"Shane!"

His eyes snapped to me, all humor gone as tension strangled his words.

"Willow, if I go next door, I won't be able to focus on anything because I'll be worried that whoever broke in the apartment is comin' back."

"No one broke in." If they had, there'd have been signs of a robbery. *At least, I think so.*

"I'll keep checking on you if I hear any noise, which'll make it harder for you to rest. Just let me stay here and watch something. I promise you I will be quiet."

It was getting harder to hold on to my irritation when he said sweet things like that and looked all innocently at me, as if unaware that part of me savored the idea of him staying a little longer...

"And if I say no?"

To this, Shane held my gaze intensely. "Let's not cross that bridge, shall we?"

I cocked my head. "Was that pun supposed to be funny?"

"Is that a yes?"

For all the loving things holy.

"Whatever. If you so much as sneeze, I'm kicking you out."

Shane's mouth tugged up again, and he looked at the television. "Do you get HBO?"

I rolled my eyes and wandered into my bedroom, where I shut the door, changed into my pajamas—ignoring the part of my brain that said Shane's clothes smelled sexy—and lay down in my bed, trying to ignore my hot, sexy, stubborn-ass savior who was guarding me with a loaded gun.

5

I thought I would sleep longer—certainly make it past four
o'clock in the afternoon—but the doctor wasn't kidding. With
the painkillers worn off, my body was sore in more places than
it wasn't. I needed a heavy dose of Tylenol.

I ambled out of my bedroom and froze.

*Sweet baby Jessica, Shane Hernandez is sprawled out on my couch.
Asleep.*

In my sleep-deprived haze, I'd forgotten he was here.

The poor guy probably got no sleep last night, running around,
grabbing me clothes and supplies. He was still wearing the same
jeans, T-shirt, and baseball cap that he'd had on at the hospital, his
gun's holster fastened to his right hip. His head was tilted slightly to
the left, angled toward the back of my couch, and his T-shirt had
lifted up a few inches, exposing the tan ridges of his defined stomach. As if that wasn't sexy enough, his arms were crossed over his
chest, his biceps gorging over the pressure from his underlying fists
—swelling the tattoos that wrapped around his arms.

I remembered the first time I'd seen those tattoos.

. . .

LAUNDRY DAYS SHOULD BE OUTLAWED. NO ONE LIKES THEM. AND LAUNDRY days in an apartment complex with one shared room?

The seventh circle of hell.

I gather up the laundry I normally did on Sunday afternoons. I hadn't gotten to it this past weekend, so here I am, doing it during the week.

As I exit my apartment, my eyes wander to my next-door neighbor's door. I've seen him several times since tipsy-mageddon, and not once did he make me feel bad for what had happened. If anything, he's been overly kind, asking if I am okay. Asking if I'd like him to walk me to and from my car each day. I've declined his offers, but I can't stop thinking about him.

My ears become all nosy, listening, curious what he is doing right now. Is he home?

As I make my way down the hallway, I'm not hoping to see him.

I'm not.

I'm just...being a courteous neighbor, making sure I'll say hi if I pass him. That's all.

But his door doesn't open.

My shoulders do not sag with disappointment. This basket is just heavy.

I walk down the long corridor. The laundry room is near the front doors, to the left if you're coming from my place. Guess they put it there for convenience or whatever, but the entire building has only ten washing machines.

So, they're a hot commodity. At least, on the weekends they are. During the week, I have no idea how often they are used, but when I enter the room, I discover the answer is not many.

In fact, only one person is in this room, at the far end, with his back to me.

The splashing grind of a washing machine echoes off the white walls, filling the space with the fresh-linen scent of laundry detergent. If I wasn't wearing socks, you would hear the click of my feet against the yellow-stained tiled flooring, but apparently, the guy doesn't hear me.

He grabs his shirt from between his shoulder blades and tugs it up and over his head, revealing an intricately woven system of tattoos along his back and arms. The guy has some serious muscles, one competing with the next for first place in deliciousness. Muscles that bulge and flex as the guy places the shirt into the washing machine with the rest of his laundry and begins stabbing at the buttons.

God, even his stabbing finger is sexy. I bet his face is smolderingly fine.

My estrogen begs me to throw all my morals out the window and become an instant porn star, party of two. The guy still hasn't noticed that I'm here. Does he always do his laundry in nothing but a pair of workout shorts? If I had known that, I totally would've stalked the laundry room.

My salivary glands activate into overdrive, and I literally have to wipe a piece of spit off my lip.

The guy grabs his laundry basket and turns around.

Ho-ly shit.

The tattoo god is Shane Hernandez, my new next-door neighbor.

Shane has tattoos?

Shane is a laundry room god that will forever invade my sexual fantasies?

Daaaaaaaaamnnnnnn.

"Hey." He walks up to me like he's unaware he's the spitting image of a model for Tattoos Ink Magazine. *Its slogan would read,* Men so sexy, they'll destroy all other men for you. *He means his smile to be friendly, but the way those inviting lips curl up is seductive.*

"Oh, hi."

It's the best my brain can come up with because all the blood has abandoned my head in favor of my lower belly. If this is what the police detective next door looks like, I will need to start robbing banks. Like, now.

"The one in the corner is broken," he warns, pointing to the machine with its lid open.

And when he twists around? His stomach muscles clench slightly, deepening their lines.

I open my mouth to respond, but nothing comes out. He hasn't told me I have the right to remain silent, but evidently, I no longer have the capacity to speak.

I've been attracted to Shane for a while. But this Shane? This Shane elicits   stay-up-all-night-fantasizing-about-what-he-is-doing-on-the-other-side-of-that-wall attraction. This is straight-up imagining-what-he's-like-in-bed attraction.

"I was just doing laundry," I say.

Brilliant.

A trained detective would have never guessed that, Willow. Being that you're holding a pair of rotting clothes, shoved into a laundry basket, standing in a laundry room. What else you got to win him over?

Shane smiles. Like he isn't holding his own laundry basket against the side of his thousand-pack abs. Smart. Sexy. Does laundry. Call 1-800-every-woman-wants-me.

"Most of 'em are free. That's why I prefer doing laundry during the week," he says.

Smart detective. Probably worked recon to find the best day and time of the week to do laundry.

Mental note. My laundry day has officially changed to Tuesdays, 6:34 p.m.

"Cool."

Cool? What the heck, Willow? Cool? You have a college degree. You're independent, and smart, and hardworking, and you have a better vocabulary than cool.

Damn that chest.

His tattoos are a labyrinth of objects woven together, forming an artful blanket across his skin—all of them black, high contrast, giving off a sinister vibe. In my quick glance, I make out a bird with its wings sprawled, a clock with Roman numerals, roses, the sun. They're as fascinating as they are gorgeous.

I'd love to stare at them as he throws that basket down, grabs me by the hips, hoists me up and onto one of these washers, and then...tells me anything I say can and will be used against me. Hard.

"I'll wait for you," he says.

I blink. And I have to remind myself I've come here to do something.

What was it again?

"Do you want me to throw it in for you?" Shane's eyebrows pull together.

"What?"

He grins. "Your laundry. You want me to put it in the washing machine?"

I have laundry?

Oh. Right.

Yep. Holding it.

"I use the machines," I blurt out.

My cheeks suffer third-degree burns.

Shane's lips twitch like he's trying not to laugh at me.

I clear my throat and force my eyes away from the candy they crave.

Oh my gosh, say something intelligent.

"I do laundry on Sundays normally."

Ugh. That's the opposite of intelligent.

Shane raises the smirk even further and says, "Well, maybe I'll have to start doing laundry on Sundays then."

My heart thumps so loudly in my chest, I bet his super-trained detective ears can hear it.

"I'll just get this started," I say.

I don't look at him as I walk to the washing machine; if I do, I'll forget how to use it.

How has Shane been hiding all of that underneath his shirt? I mean, sure, anyone can have tattoos, but Shane seems so straitlaced. His pants are always crisp, his button-down shirt wrinkle-free. He isn't just a rule follower; he's a rule enforcer. And even though he'd made that, "Maybe I'll rearrange your face," threat to Ezra, I'd assumed he wouldn't go through with it, so I had still pegged him as all rules. These tats don't fit the mold that I'd formed of him in my head—a mold that I already thought was beyond sexy.

But this?

This was next-hemisphere sexy.

. . .

SHANE HAD WALKED ME BACK TO MY APARTMENT DOOR THAT DAY.

And now, here he was—again.

6

You're staring at him. Stop being all creepy.

I tiptoed into the kitchen, hoping I could retrieve the Tylenol without waking him, but the cabinet must've wanted a good show because it squeaked, stirring Shane.

He made that stretching sound that people make when they're first waking up. I had never heard anyone make it sound sexy before.

I wonder what noises he makes when he's in bed with a woman.

"Willow?" He pushed himself up into a seated position and rubbed his eyes.

"I didn't mean to wake you."

Shane looked at his watch. "We have to get ready for your statement with De Luca. Starts in an hour."

Right. I still had to finish my statement.

"Thank you for staying," I said. "But I've got the rest of the day covered."

I was attracted to Shane. Completely. But right now, I wanted him to leave. I didn't like people seeing me in pain or weak. It was too intimate—made me feel too vulnerable, I guess—and anything that resembled someone trying to take care of me made me uncomfortable.

Later this week, when things normalized, maybe I'd get the courage to ask him out for a cup of coffee. I had the perfect excuse: thanking him for everything he'd done last night. Most importantly, saving my life.

I reached up on tiptoe, stretching my arm up to reach the Tylenol that I had stupidly put on the third shelf, but my shoulder cried out in pain from a torn muscle.

Shane walked over and pressed a hand to my lower back.

"Sit down."

"I need—"

"Tylenol." His eyes were on the container I'd been trying to reach. "I know. Sit down. I'll bring it to you."

"That's not necessary."

"Do you want to get back to normal as fast as possible?"

I frowned. How did he know which buttons to push?

Buttons. My hormones relived that moment in the laundry room again. This time, in slow motion. The traitors.

"You need to take it easy and let your body heal. Sit down." He nodded his chin toward the couch.

I debated arguing with him, but I didn't want to reinjure myself on the basis of being stubborn.

Instead of walking over to the couch, however, while Shane busied himself opening the bottle and rooting around for a glass, I went to the sliding glass door.

I unlocked it and jerked it up and to the left like I always did each morning. This time, I yiped.

"Willow!" Shane barked.

I grabbed my shoulder, my cheeks flooding with embarrassment.

"I just hit it at the wrong angle."

"Yeah. No shit. Sit. Down."

Shane's hand pressed against my hip, and he guided me over to the couch, waiting until I sat. "Don't move."

I pursed my lips at him.

He saw my pursed lips and raised me a glower.

"Stop trying to be a freakin' hero and rest," he growled.

"I'm just trying to go about my daily life because that's exactly what I'm going to do."

"You're going to do two things today. Give your statement to De Luca and follow the doctor's orders and rest."

I glared at him as he walked into my kitchen and retrieved the glass of water and Tylenol he'd prepared before I almost ripped my arm off my body.

"Here," he said.

I downed the pills and the water he handed me.

"I assure you, I can take care of myself." I had taken care of myself for a long time. When I was a kid, my mom was emotionally and sometimes physically absent for large chunks of my life, so my sister and I had learned to cook, clean, and take care of ourselves sooner than most people do.

I could certainly handle a broken wrist, sore shoulder, and banged-up body.

"How's your head?" Shane asked, ignoring my statement and taking the empty glass back.

Feels like a little maniac is inside of it, shooting a BB gun through my brain.

"Fine."

Shane regarded me with his ocean-colored eyes that were darker around the outside, lighter blue on the inside. I bet he was used to flashing those gems at women and getting them to obey his every command with the sexual spell they cast over them.

"I'd like to rest until De Luca gets here," I said. Polite code for, *Please leave.*

Shane didn't acknowledge my passive request. Instead, he went back into my kitchen, opening up every single cabinet door, one at a time.

"What are you looking for?"

"Ah," he said to himself.

When he pulled out the bag, my mouth fell open.

"What are you doing?"

"You need to rest," was all he said.

He rooted around until he found a bowl, poured the dry pebbles into it, and walked over to the sliding glass door. Evidently expecting it to open like a normal door.

He yanked at the door handle, checking to ensure it was unlocked.

A better person wouldn't have smirked at his frustration. Too bad I wasn't a better person. Because watching him yank it harder and harder while mumbling things like, "What the hell?" and, "What is wrong with this freaking thing?" gave me all sorts of satisfaction.

"You have to pull it up and to the left. Jerk it at an angle," I said.

Shane frowned. "That's a fire hazard."

Duh.

"I'm going to call the landlord today," he announced.

Like I hadn't thought to do it myself. "I already did. Three times, they came out here and fiddled around with it and left, saying the building has shifted and there is nothing they could do about it."

"That's bull. I'll call again."

I rolled my eyes. His sapphires might be capable of putting women under magical spells, but our landlord? Good luck.

Shane jerked the door the way I had told him, and it opened. Icy air drifted into the living room as he stepped outside and set the bowl on the four-foot concrete slab that had been advertised as a "patio" when I'd first rented the place.

Patio, my ass. It was big enough to fit one folding chair. Two, if you didn't mind your thigh fondling the person's sitting next to you.

"How do you know I feed Snowflake?" I asked.

Shane stepped back inside and shut the door with a lot more ease. Locked it.

"You named a stray cat?"

"It's not her fault she's a stray. Maybe someone gave up on her. Didn't give her enough chances to show what a good kitty she is."

Shane gave me a look like he wasn't sure if I was being serious.

"Why *Snowflake?*"

"Because she's one of a kind."

Obviously.

A hint of amusement flickered across his face.

"How do you know I feed her?" I repeated.

"I've seen you do it plenty of times."

He did?

I knew Shane was a detective, trained in the art of observation, but still. My stupid chest warmed at the thought of him being all observant of me.

My chest didn't get the memo that De-*sex*-tive Shane Hernandez was bossy as hell and was sort of in my apartment against my will. So, this was basically a break-in situation. Maybe even a hostage scenario.

"Look, I appreciate everything you've done. But it's time for you to go back to your place."

"We already discussed this. Someone might have broken into your apartment."

This again. If cops *hadn't* swept the place up and down, if they *had* found a single clue that someone had been inside, I'd agree with his concern. But the reality was, while I made it my habit to lock up when I left, I was only human, capable of making mistakes. Like forgetting to lock my door.

"No one broke in; no one stole anything. So, if you don't mind," I said, shooing him with my hand, "I have things to do."

"So, do them. I prefer for you to follow the doctor's orders, but don't let me stop you if there's somethin' more pressing than trying to figure out who tried to kill you last night."

I scoffed, and when he didn't move, I stood up and walked across the room until I was in front of him. I wished I were taller so I didn't have to look up at him like this. I wished my stupid stomach weren't coming to life with flutters with him being this close, and I wished my eyes hadn't betrayed me by appreciating the artful lines of muscles on his forearms as he crossed his arms over his chest.

"Let me rephrase," I said. "Leave my apartment."

He had the nerve to step forward. "I'm not leaving you alone, unprotected."

"You're being ridiculous."

"Agree to disagree."

"This is MY apartment!"

"Which I'll leave once I know you're safe."

"I *am* safe!"

"Agree to disagree."

Images of karate-chopping his windpipe flashed through my mind.

"Are you always this infuriating?" I asked.

"Are you always this stubborn?"

"Why the hell do you care so much if some random neighbor gets killed?"

"Because you're not random! I care if YOU get killed!"

Shane's Adam's apple bobbed, and I swear a look of embarrassment washed over his face, as if he slipped and said something he never intended to.

But that something was everything.

My damn nerves sparked to life, longing to feel his mouth on mine, to taste his tongue, feel his hands in my hair. Because I realized in this moment that even though I didn't *want* to rely on anyone, having someone *want* to protect me felt incredible. Especially when that someone was Shane.

I couldn't remember the last time anyone had done something like that for me. Or if anyone ever had for that matter.

People love you the best way they know how, but in my life, love had always fallen short of feeding my soul the way it was supposed to. Shane's affection and concern for me was the first time I'd felt like the holes in my soul had the potential of filling in.

It exhilarated me, but also terrified me.

I wasn't sure what just happened or if he wanted to kiss me as badly as I wanted to kiss him, but before I could feel what his lips felt like on mine, a meow broke the silence.

Snowflake was on the patio, walking in circles by the glass.

She was a gorgeous cat. Mostly white with black patches and olive-colored eyes.

"I normally pick her up and hold her," I said.

I froze in place, struggling to free myself from the sexual tension. But she was meowing so loudly, she must be worried; I'd never left her alone for an entire night before. She always got some snuggles.

I walked toward the door, but Shane beat me to it, opening it for me so I didn't have to tear a ligament this time.

I stepped outside, barefoot. The half inch of snow on the concrete hadn't melted yet, and it hurt my skin more than it should have—almost as if the insides of my bones were still defrosting from being in the icy waters of the river.

"Hey there," I cooed, petting Snowflake's head. "I bet you were so hungry this morning. I'm sorry."

She rubbed her back on my leg. I hated that she was stuck outside in this cold. Sometimes, I snuck her into my apartment for an hour or two at a time, knowing that I was risking my lease. I petted her for as long as my bare feet would allow in the snow and then came back inside and sat on the couch.

After closing the door and locking it, Shane took a position in the kitchen, his back resting against my countertop.

"I'm sorry for being rude," I said. "I'm overly tired. I'm in pain, and I'm not used to people trying to take care of me."

I had never admitted that to anyone.

"You have nothin' to be sorry for, Willow. I'm trying to help. Even if it doesn't come across the right way."

I sighed and groaned when I shifted my ribs. "I need to get a new phone today."

"I can take you after your meeting with De Luca," Shane said.

I wasn't going to argue with him anymore. Maybe after De Luca determined no one had done this to me, Shane would go back to normal, and we could spend time with each other in a typical way. Because I was even more attracted to him than ever. While I'd normally break out in a rash if anyone helped me like this, for some reason, with him, I didn't hate it. If anything, it felt nice, having Shane look out and care for me. But I preferred we get to know each other better on equal footing.

"You need to push De Luca to open an official investigation. He needs to be shoved. Hard," Shane said.

"Isn't he going to want to talk to you? You were at the scene."

"He already took my statement at the hospital."

Oh, right. Shane mentioned that when De Luca first came in.

"Why can't you work the case?" Not that I wanted him to. He'd be a dog with a bone without the objectivity needed to prove I wasn't pushed.

"Because you're a friend," Shane said. "And I was at the scene. Could jeopardize the prosecution."

Friend. What a callous word to exist in the English dictionary.

"Tell me you're going to push De Luca."

"I'm going to answer his questions and let him do his job."

"Willow, I'm tellin' you, this guy wants to file his report and go home and watch the game. You need to push him because the person responsible for last night might be someone close to you. And they might try again."

"It's winter. The ground is full of ice and snow, and bridges are prone to icy conditions—particularly bridges over water. I've slipped on ice countless times since moving to Chicago."

I was a normal girl, not a woman from one of those *Dateline* episodes. Did I have some relationships in my life that were less than perfect? Yep. But did that mean someone would have tried to hunt me down and kill me? No. Not even close. As I told him before, if I fell off a bridge, it had to be some sort of an accident. Period.

Shane frowned. "Can you think of any disagreements you've had with anyone lately? Friends? Family? Work colleagues? Neighbors?"

I shot him a look.

"I thought you can't get involved in the case."

"This isn't the detective in me asking; this is a friend asking."

I gave him an incredulous stare. "I'm not discussing all of my relationships with you."

Because some of them were complicated and embarrassing. When you have to fight for people's love, you often feel unwanted, and when you feel unwanted, you sometimes wonder if it's *you*. If there's something wrong with *you* that makes you disposable.

"We don't have to get into relationships. Just tell me a little about yourself."

I wasn't stupid enough to think he wasn't fishing around for suspects, but there was no need to be rude to him. He'd saved my life, and maybe he needed to get some questions out of his system to see there wasn't a sinister cesspool of killers in my world.

"I have a mother and a sister. I went to the University of Illinois and moved to Chicago when I graduated with a degree in business."

"Do you have a lot of friends?"

"I have a few close friends. Most of them live in the city. Some of them I haven't talked to in a while, but when we do talk, it's like no time has passed at all."

"Do you have a boyfriend?"

"No."

We stared at each other, a moment passing between us, as if an unspoken line in the sand had just been wiped away.

Shane cleared his throat and, based on his long sigh, appeared to recalibrate with a new line of questioning.

"And your family. What are the dynamics like?"

I bit my lip. "As normal as you'd expect after my dad died."

Shane held my gaze, his voice softening. "You said he died when you were a kid?"

I nodded.

"Do you mind if I ask what happened to him?"

This was one subject I never discussed with people—it was too intimate. But strangely, I didn't run into the shadows of my heart with Shane. Maybe it was because he had been with me in a moment of life or death, so talking about death wasn't as jarring as it normally was. Or maybe it had shoved our bonding into fast-forward. Whatever the reason, I felt comfortable answering him.

"All I know is that someone killed him, but I'm not sure of the details."

I knew how crazy that had to sound to a detective skilled at getting every one of his questions answered, but when I was twelve —after a particularly brutal encounter with my mom—I stopped trying to actively find out what happened to him.

After years of my mother refusing to answer questions about my father, I'd decided to take matters into my own hands and googled my dad's name. Up popped a screen with dozens of people with that same name—Johnson is the second most common last name in this country, and Michael is an extremely common first name, too. Sifting through the pages of results, I managed to come across his obituary, but the only thing it confirmed for me was that he had in fact died. If I wanted to learn any more about *how* he died, I realized I needed to narrow my search by combining his name with the date of his death or city, but before I had the chance, my mom stormed into my room.

Turned out, all the parental software and apps she had on our electronic devices that safeguarded us against internet dangers also alerted her to my sleuthing.

It wasn't her screaming in my face, or grounding me for two months, or even her physical outburst, throwing things around my room, that broke me; it was the look in her eyes, of deep pain and betrayal, that made me feel like an awful person for hurting her by looking into the one thing that had the power to break her. Especially when Mom spiraled out of control for weeks after that. Realizing how badly my curiosity had hurt my mom, I decided to let it lie until she was ready to discuss it with me.

Especially since my devices were so closely monitored.

Over the years, I became conditioned to just accept that my dad was dead, and with all the other drama Mom and Hayley created, sadly, it was only every now and then that I'd get the urge to know how Dad died again.

Each time I did, paranoia swept through me that even without electronic monitoring, Mom would somehow find out if I went sleuthing again, and this time, her anger would be so bad, our relationship would be destroyed. I reminded myself I had one parent left —one—and nothing was worth jeopardizing that.

Plus, I trusted that, someday, she *would* tell me what happened.

"His death has always been very painful for my mom, and I didn't have the heart to keep pressing her for what happened to him."

But after almost dying, how could I go to my grave, not knowing the truth? Not only of what happened, but why Mom had kept it such a big secret. Was it really the right thing to do, to drop it?

Shane scrubbed the side of his face. "Yeah, I can relate to that."

I looked up at him. "You can?"

Shane grabbed the countertop with both hands and crossed one foot in front of the other. "I don't talk about this with anyone." He met my gaze, and something passed between us as the wall he kept up around others collapsed, flooding my heart with affection that he'd trust me with whatever he was about to divulge. "But my dad died when I was little, too. He was a police officer and was shot in the line of duty when I was four."

Holy crap.

I never would've guessed he had endured such a violent loss in his past. That took some major courage to join law enforcement after that. I mean, anyone that joined the force knew the dangers, but when your own father lost his life...I guess I was surprised Shane still took that risk.

"This might be a completely inappropriate question," I said. "But did that ever make you not want to become a police officer?"

I wondered if my question was too intimate, but Shane didn't hesitate.

"The opposite. My dad was a hero, who dedicated his life to protecting others. If I could be half as good as he was, I knew I'd do a lot of good in this world."

My insides came alive with butterflies. Shane Hernandez wasn't just ruggedly handsome or kind. He had a heart of gold. The kind of heart I had searched for, but never found in any other guy.

As we stared at each other in silence for several heartbeats, I wondered if he felt this too, this connection expanding like a fast-growing sunflower. For me, the feeling was unprecedented.

I could have stared at him like this for hours, but a loud knock made me jerk.

Shane clutched the gun strapped to his hip and held his hand up to me, motioning for me to stay put. He pulled his weapon from its holster and approached the door slowly, looking out the peephole, his eyebrows scrunched together.

"Identify yourself," Shane commanded.

It took a second for the person on the other end to answer.

"Uh...Mike? With 1-800-Flowers?"

"Leave them by the door," Shane said. "And walk away."

Oh my God. The poor flower deliverer was probably so confused right now.

Shane stared through that peephole forever before unlocking and opening the door.

Gun drawn.

He stepped into the hallway, weapon first, sweeping from left to right.

I guess he was satisfied that there wasn't some serial killer waiting for me in the hallway because he put his gun back in its holster, picked up a vase of red roses, and came inside, kicking the door closed behind him. Which he locked right after he'd set the bouquet on the counter.

"I wonder if someone knows I was in the hospital last night."

How, though? I pulled the little card from the roses as Shane put both of his hands on the countertop, glaring at the flowers as I read the note.

I miss you. I hope you'll reconsider giving me another chance.

~ Ezra

"Who are they from?" Shane asked.

"My ex-boyfriend."

Shane didn't blink. "Was that the prick who got handsy with you the night we met?"

I nodded, and Shane's face set into stone.

"How long ago did you guys break up?"

"A few months."

"Mind if I ask why things ended?"

Normally, I wouldn't answer this question—it was humiliating —but Shane needed to know that Ezra wasn't abusive or anything.

"I caught him kissing another woman."

And son of a brat if I hadn't let it momentarily lower my self-esteem. I'd been ashamed that I had let *his* behavior impact *my* self-worth, but for a hot minute, it had.

Shane raised an eyebrow.

"I forgave him at first. Tried to work it out."

"You took him back?"

"You don't need to sound so judgy. Sometimes, you have to work at things in life, and I thought it was worth giving our relationship a second chance."

"But it didn't work?"

I bit my lip. "I found text messages with another woman, and that was it; broke it off."

"How'd he take it?"

I shrugged. "How does any breakup go?"

"Did he accept it was over?" Shane asked.

· · ·

"I'M GOING TO DO WHATEVER IT TAKES TO WIN YOU BACK, WILLOW," EZRA declares.

"I'M SURE HE'LL MOVE ON, EVENTUALLY."

Shane said nothing.

"He's tried to get me back before, so these flowers are just par for the course," I assured.

Shane pinched the bridge of his nose.

"What?" I asked.

Shane stared at me for several seconds, keeping his voice gentle. "In my line of work, I've come to see that far too often, our feelings for someone stifle our instincts, and our heart dismisses red flags before our brain has a chance to think."

"Meaning?"

"I know this is hard for you to accept, but I believe someone tried to kill you. And the statistics say it's someone close to you."

I bit my lip, telling my heartbeat to calm down. Just because Shane was a detective didn't mean he was right.

Shane glanced at the flowers, then back at me. "Tell me you see what I'm seeing."

I swallowed.

"That your ex-boyfriend isn't letting you go, isn't accepting no for an answer, and sends you flowers after you were almost killed."

7

"What are *you* doing here?" De Luca asked.

Maybe letting Shane answer my door was a mistake.

"I told you, she's my neighbor," Shane said. "And a friend."

Blech—that word again.

De Luca glared at Shane for a few seconds before spitting out a question. "You think I wouldn't find out?"

"It's not personal," Shane said.

"Trying to have me removed from the case isn't personal?"

"I'm trying to do what's best for Willow."

They exchanged another look before De Luca strolled past Shane into my living room.

My TV was off, its black screen reflecting De Luca's rigid posture as he took a seat on the other end of my couch, which jolted from the weight shift. Outside my sliding glass door, snow flurries drifted to the ground without a care in the world while, in here, my apartment's air thickened with tension.

Tension that was brimming from De Luca's dark brown eyes—eyes so dark, I could barely discern the black pupil from the surrounding color.

"Afternoon."

As De Luca pulled open his phone, presumably to a screen where he took notes, I wondered, *Would De Luca agree with Shane's suspicions?* Because the more I thought about it—even after I tried to open myself up to what Shane had said—I just could not imagine someone having tried to kill me. There had to be another explanation for how I'd fallen from that bridge.

"Do you want me to leave?" Shane asked me.

Ironic. Before, I'd been trying to do just that, but now, when I had the perfect excuse—finishing my statement—something didn't sit right in doing it.

I think it was because De Luca's tone of voice was so rude, his body language screaming he'd rather be anywhere but here. I suppose his simmering animosity could be from whatever was going on between him and Shane, but if that were true, he shouldn't be glowering at *me* right now.

Shane never did. Not even when I disagreed with his theory. He was warmth and compassion, whereas De Luca was cold and hard—and about to probe into my private life. I could handle it alone, but for the first time in my life, I didn't have to.

"I'd rather you stay," I said.

De Luca scowled at me, scratched his cheek so roughly that thin streaks of pink painted his skin, and then started with the basics. Confirming my date of birth, that kind of stuff. And then he got to the questions.

"What were you doing on the bridge?" De Luca asked.

"I don't remember."

"Where were you coming from before you got to the bridge?"

I pinched the bridge of my nose. "I don't remember. I think home maybe?"

"Where were you headed?"

"I don't know."

"Were you with anyone?" he asked.

"I don't remember."

De Luca tugged his earlobe. "Were you drinking or otherwise under the influence?"

"Not that I recall. Didn't the hospital do a test?"

"Initial screens were negative, but I'm asking what you *recall*. You drink a lot?"

"No," I said.

"Use drugs?"

"Never."

"In the hospital, you said you hadn't been depressed lately. But do you have a history of depression?"

I twisted my hands together, my face burning.

"I would remember if I was depressed enough to want to kill myself."

"You said you don't remember."

"That night. But I remember everything before yesterday, and I wasn't depressed."

"She was screaming when she fell," Shane said defensively.

De Luca's stare snapped to the ground and took a few seconds to return to me.

"Anyone threaten you?" he asked.

"Not exactly."

"Not exactly?"

"I'm a human resources manager. My company recently let seven people go. A couple of them got angry. Said some things that they shouldn't have."

Shane's gaze became so severe, I felt like it could snap my spine.

"Like what?" De Luca asked in an ambivalent tone.

"*You're making a mistake, how dare you*—that type of thing."

"But they didn't make a specific threat against you?"

"No."

"Was it your decision to fire them?"

"No. It was management's. I'm the HR manager who has to facilitate the process."

Not soul-crushing at all.

"Were they under the impression it was your decision?"

"No. They knew it was management."

De Luca typed something. "You part of any organizations, sports teams, that sort of thing?"

"I volunteer at a few places that help feed the hungry, give business skills to folks who are out of work."

"Anything unusual occur?"

"No."

"Anything else unusual happen recently? Notice anyone following you or find a tire slashed or anything like that?"

"No. I get some weird DMs sometimes on my social media accounts," I admitted. "But I'm sure that happens to every person online."

"Any of them particularly alarming?" De Luca asked.

"No."

"Anything else out of the ordinary happen?"

"Someone may have broken into my apartment last night," I said.

"May have?"

"The front door wasn't fully shut when I got home."

"Anything missing?"

"No."

"Did you call the police?" he asked.

"Yes."

"What did the responding officer say?"

"There was no evidence of a break-in."

De Luca nodded.

"My, uh..." Ugh, I knew this was going to sound bad, but as much as I believed no one had done this, I couldn't be a stubborn fool, either. "My ex, Ezra, sent me flowers this morning."

"Flowers."

"He wants me back."

"Ezra ever get violent with you?" De Luca asked.

"He got a little handsy with me when I was drunk one time, but I wouldn't classify it as violent."

Another thought crossed my mind—something Shane would pounce on as a motive, but it was too far-fetched to be related to this. And it had nothing to do with Ezra.

"You should subpoena her phone records," Shane said.

De Luca sucked his lower lip between his teeth, biting down harshly.

"Normally takes weeks to get the data back," Shane said. "But it can be a lot quicker if you show exigency."

De Luca's chest inflated.

"What's exigency?" I asked.

Shane was kind enough to answer me, much to the obvious frustration of De Luca.

"A life-threatening emergency, where we need the information to prevent a crime that could result in death or serious bodily injury. For example, if we think your life is in imminent danger from a killer. Phone records don't have pictures or text messages though; you have to physically download that information from the phone. Do you know if you have messages in iCloud enabled?"

"Detective..."

I shrugged.

"If you have it backed up," Shane said, "and it synced that night, we could see if anyone texted you." Shane turned his attention back to De Luca. "You should have her sign a consent to search so you can look into it."

De Luca snapped his head around to Shane, the two men scowling at each other.

That's when I realized that whatever was going on between them was bigger than I first sensed.

After a few moments, De Luca turned back to me. "One last question. Do you think anyone in your life is capable of doing this to you?"

And there it was, point-blank. I felt like this was some sort of loyalty test between De Luca and Shane, which was silly. The question was about what happened last night, not some macho posturing between the two.

Still, after everything Shane had done for me, it felt like a little bit of a betrayal when I answered honestly. "No. I don't think anyone did this to me."

De Luca nodded and stood from the couch.

"This needs to get kicked up to detectives," Shane insisted.

"We have no witnesses that saw someone with her on that bridge. No physical evidence of a struggle. No witness statement suggesting she was attacked. No threats, nothing."

"She can't remember."

"There is no evidence of foul play. Thus, no justification to kick this up to detectives. Probably a reckless mishap or failed suicide attempt." His tone was so ambivalent, you'd think he hadn't just detonated a bomb in my psyche. "I'll see if any video surveillance points to that bridge, but I wouldn't hold my breath."

"So, you're not goin' to open an investigation then?" Shane snapped. "Not even so they can talk to her goddamn ex?"

De Luca glowered at Shane.

"As a witness and a friend of the victim, you know you need to stay away from this case," De Luca said in a calm tone. "It would be a shame for your career to go down the drain over this."

8

"**F**uck." Shane shoved his hands through his hair and paced in my living room. The veins in his arms pulsed like little snakes winding around his skin, and his chest remained permanently inflated. "De Luca is going to close the report. No one will be lookin' into this, Willow."

Shane was trying to protect me, but I needed to protect him by convincing him to stand down.

"De Luca *is* looking into this. Maybe he doesn't do things your way, but he said he's going to look at camera footage."

"Even if we get lucky enough to have a camera pointed at the exact location you went over, do you know how long that might take him? Meanwhile, whoever did this is still out there, and he doesn't appear the least bit concerned by that."

"What is with you two? Because I can tell whatever's going on is not about this case. There's clearly a history there."

"It doesn't matter." Shane pinched the bridge of his nose.

"It does to me," I said, making it clear I'd wait.

Shane stilled for a moment before taking a deep breath. "De Luca and I used to work together, and he frequently cut corners. I reported him for it. And later, it was because of that report that he lost out on a promotion."

Cut corners. No wonder Shane was so worried about De Luca's competence on this. Had De Luca learned his lesson and straightened out, or should I also be worried he might cut corners on my case, too? Even if I was worried, there wasn't anything I could do about it, other than ask De Luca questions and ensure he was following up about it; if Shane couldn't get De Luca reassigned with his weight in the department, I certainly couldn't either.

Not that I'd express my concerns to Shane; I didn't want to fan the flames when he looked on edge enough. His body was so tense, it looked like it was carved out of stone, and his eyes looked darker than I'd ever seen them—a haunted midnight blue.

"Let me see your phone records," Shane said.

"What?"

"You would have access to all your phone records with your carrier."

"Do you *want* to piss De Luca off?"

Shane walked up to me with his hands at his sides, his pupils dilated. "Let me see them."

"Shane..."

"Tell me what's been happening in your life over the last few weeks."

See? I'd made the right call, not telling Shane about that fleeting thought I'd had when De Luca was here. Shane wouldn't see it as a far-fetched motive; he'd probably get spun up about it, and it was going to be hard enough to get him to stand down from this investigation without adding to his concern.

"You cannot get involved in this," I insisted. "I heard what De Luca said."

"To hell with what De Luca said."

"You're a witness and a friend of..." I couldn't mutter the word *victim*. "He made it sound like if you step one foot into this case, your career could be damaged." It must break a substantial policy that law enforcement has in place. "And after you tried to get him taken off the case, he sounded like he'd jump at the chance to get you into trouble. You have to let this go."

"Willow." Shane took a step forward. "I believe you that you wouldn't have jumped on your own. And I believe you when you said you're afraid of the water, so you wouldn't be reckless enough to be balancing on the railing or some stupid shit like that. But where we disagree is your accident theory. There's no evidence that supports someone being able to go off that bridge on accident. And you have those bruises on your upper arms, which leaves one possibility —*someone* did this to you."

Even if De Luca wasn't the most thorough police officer, there would either be camera footage of what happened or there wouldn't be. Shane stepping on De Luca's toes wasn't going to make any of this go faster. It would just get Shane into more trouble, and I couldn't let that happen.

"Even if your career wasn't on the line," I said, "the price tag of your curiosity is my sense of security. It's disturbing enough to know this is being investigated, and for my own sanity, I'd prefer to have De Luca look into this out there"—I pointed toward my sliding glass door—"so it's not in my face every moment of the day."

"I told you, if someone did try to kill you and failed, they could try it again. Especially if they think you might tell the cops who did this to you."

"I have no memory of it."

"But whoever did this doesn't know that. And even if they did, they can't take the chance that your memory might someday come back. Whatever the hell their motivation was for tryin' to kill you before, you can add to that them facing life behind bars if you open your mouth. They have more motivation than ever to finish what they started." His eyes tightened, demanding I acknowledge the danger he thought I was in. "You seriously just want to walk away and not look into it?"

I wasn't walking away or not having it looked into.

"I know you're used to working cases and looking for suspects, but I'm not a case. I'm a human being with a normal life. And trying to convince me over and over and over again that somebody that I love and care about might've tried to end me? It's unfathomable."

"Willow—"

"I'm not being naive," I interrupted. "I'm just being honest. I truly do not believe that anyone I know is capable of physically harming me. Okay?"

I hope I'm not wrong.

Shane's jaw set into frustrated granite as he stared down at me. "What about people you don't know?"

If someone did this to me, it would have to be a stranger, but I'd never meet a stranger alone in the dark, so I couldn't see how that was possible, either. Unless...maybe I was walking and became the victim of a random act of street violence or something. I didn't know, but Shane needed to back off for his own sake.

"If it was a stranger, then they don't know who I am, so they wouldn't be able to come after me again," I said, trying to calm Shane down. "I'm still hoping my memories will come back, but in the meantime, please, let it go."

Shane grabbed the back of his neck and held it for several seconds. "After what I saw outside the apartment that night with your ex...I should've asked more questions."

Was that why he was so upset? He blamed himself for not preventing it?

"We don't know if Ezra was involved in this, and even if he was, this isn't your fault, Shane. So, if that's why you're so obsessed over this—"

"It's not. I just..." His cerulean eyes combed over my face as he dropped his arms back at his sides. "I won't stand back and allow something else to happen to you, Willow. You're too"—he stopped himself, finishing with a whisper—"important to me."

But how could that be?

"You barely know me." I regretted it the second the words

vomited from my mouth because it might come across as ungrateful. I wasn't. I was just surprised. While I'd always sensed a mutual attraction between us, his almost profession was bigger than that.

"I've noticed everything about you from the first time I laid eyes on you," he declared.

I swallowed under the intensity of his gaze as he took a step closer, challenging my space and my assumptions, staring down at me for several breathless moments.

"Your beauty took my breath away." Shane's voice was low, almost a growl, as he studied my eyes, my cheeks, my lips. My heart began to beat so hard, I wondered if he could hear it. "And I loved how you'd always walk with your chin held high with this stoic look on your face, like you were determined to make each day a success."

Shane brought his arm up tentatively, so slowly that it was as if he was unsure I'd allow him to touch me like this. But of course I was okay with it. I *longed* for his hand to complete its agonizing journey to my face, and when his palm pressed to my cheek, my mouth parted in ecstasy. The warmth of his skin washed over me like the shimmering rain of a summer storm.

I'd never felt this immense energy with anyone before, like my body was full of magnets, activated and pulling to his every caress.

"Every once in a while," he continued, "I got to hear you laugh, and its melody would..."

He bit his lip, his chest only two feet from my own, expanding with faster breaths as he swallowed, seemingly struggling to continue talking through this haze that had come over him. It was like watching someone become lost in a memory, only this memory was us. Here. Now.

"I craved that laugh so damn bad," he said. "And I kept finding excuses to run into you."

He brushed his thumb along my cheekbone, leaving a trail of heat over my skin.

"I'd rush over and hold the complex's door open for you." A sad smile tugged his lips up in the corner. "Or I'd collect my mail if I saw you in the mail room—anything to steal a few moments with you."

Something was changing between us right in front of my eyes, something expanding past the boundaries of the romance we'd been dancing around for months.

He studied my mouth with a hunger I'd only seen flashes of before. Now, that flash illuminated into an all-out spotlight as his tone dropped another octave, a need pulsing through his words.

"I kept having to remind myself to keep my distance because..."

Because what?

I hated the way he swallowed harshly—it looked painful—but I savored the way his gaze swept over my face, his eyebrows pulling together, like he couldn't stand keeping his distance from me anymore. He stared at my mouth as if fighting against a desire he'd had since the moment he first saw me—the desire to feel my lips against his own.

My mouth moistened, hoping he'd surrender to whatever internal battle waged in his mind because, my God, I could tell his lips would feel amazing on mine. His tongue would, too. I wanted to feel his hands in my hair, dragging his palms down my back as he kissed me the way I'd only daydreamed of.

Shane trailed his thumb slowly down my cheek and began to trace my lower lip.

Holy mother of erotica, the sensation caused my breath to catch. How could a touch so simple feel more sensual than anything I'd ever felt with a man before? I wanted to lick his thumb, suck it even, and grab the back of his neck and end this agony by pulling his mouth to mine.

Every skin cell on my body heightened, aching to be touched.

I rested my hands on his shoulders, feeling the curves of strength beneath my palms—rock-hard muscles banding together, stretching over his iron torso.

It was surreal, getting to touch him like this, but even more surreal was that I was about to feel his lips on mine. Shane tilted his head, staring at my mouth as he moved his knuckle beneath my chin and tilted it up.

His phone's chime burst through the silence and immediately became my enemy because it ruptured whatever spell had made him abandon his mysterious reservations. He took a step back, and his features rearranged into regret, like he'd gotten lost in urges he shouldn't have allowed himself to act on.

I knew this attraction might feel complicated to him, especially since he was a police detective who became inadvertently caught up in the aftermath of my fall after saving my life. The fact that he also happened to be my next-door neighbor just added another layer of complication on top of everything else.

But why did I get the sense his step back was because of something else? Something bigger and more complex?

"I should order us some food," he said.

Food.

Dinner.

"Crap!"

I almost forgot, and since this was the first time I'd see my sister after the birthday debacle, I was not going to miss this. I needed to hurry, or I'd be late, and that was a major pet peeve of my mom's.

"I'm meeting my family for dinner." Mom, Grandma, and Hayley. "It's my mom's birthday, and we're going to her favorite restaurant."

I hurried toward my bathroom, forcing my mind to put whatever just happened between us behind me for the moment. Later, I could wonder about it all I wanted, but for right now, I needed to focus on getting to dinner on time.

"I don't think—"

"Look, I know you're worried about me, and I appreciate it. But you're treating me like I have a gun to my head. We don't know for sure if anyone did this to me, and even if they did, they're not waiting outside my door with a loaded pistol, ready to take me out."

Shane appeared in my bathroom doorway, watching me frantically start my shower.

"I'm going to the dinner," I said. "I have to get showered and changed."

And brush my teeth because, gross, I hadn't done that since I'd fallen from the bridge.

Maybe it was a good thing we hadn't kissed. I probably tasted like a meerkat.

"Willow..."

"Shane."

He opened his mouth to argue but closed it when I held up my palm, letting him know this wasn't up for debate. As I held my other hand under the shower water, waiting for it to turn warm, Shane's shoulders rose and fell while he appeared to evaluate me.

After another moment, he asked, "Can I please come with you?"

My dang heart did jumping jacks at the thought of spending more time with him. Maybe if we spent more time together, I'd find out the rest of his confession—why he'd been keeping his distance before. More importantly, had that changed?

"Fine. But for right now, I have to get in the shower."

Shane bit his lip but reluctantly exited my apartment, presumably so he could get cleaned up and dressed. He waited to hear the lock of my dead bolt, though, before the door to his apartment opened.

It took me a minute to get undressed with the aches and pains, but I managed to do it alone this time. The hot shower took longer than I wanted it to, thanks to having to wash myself with only one hand, my cast safely outside the shower curtain. The plastic shield thing the hospital gave me, which would protect the cast from water, looked like it'd take a few minutes to put on, and I just wanted to hurry.

When I stepped out, I dried off, wiped the fog off the bathroom mirror, and reached for my toothbrush.

But it wasn't there. Confused, I swept my eyes over my bathroom, and there, on the white porcelain back of the toilet, was my toothbrush.

What in the world?

I always kept my toothbrush on the right side of my sink, next to the toothpaste. Always. And even if I'd absentmindedly put it somewhere else, I would never put it on the back of the toilet. Because *gross.*

Did someone move my toothbrush? Maybe Shane had moved it when he'd swept my apartment to make sure no one was in here? No. That made no sense. But it made no sense that my toothbrush would magically transport itself to the back of my toilet, either.

For a second, I actually considered the possibility that someone *had* broken into my apartment. But if they were looking to rob me, first of all, they would not have been looking on my bathroom counter, and second, even if they were, they'd knock things around so they would fall on the floor, not neatly place them on the toilet ledge.

Maybe they had knocked it on the floor and then set it back there?

No. It was a stupid thought. They'd have set it back on the counter, not the toilet.

Still, I hurried through my apartment to ensure nothing else seemed out of place before returning to the bathroom.

I must've been brushing my teeth while on the phone or something and had to set it down for a second and then forgot about it...

9

"I can't believe I let you talk me into you coming," I said.

Now that I thought about it—without the almost kiss clouding my mind—this was a huge mistake. There was a reason I kept my family life private, and tonight might be a complete shit show.

In fact, I had this nagging gut feeling that something bad was going to happen, and I really didn't want Shane to witness whatever it was.

I had a thick skin when it came to my family—a thick skin that diluted the hurts caused by Mom's emotional swings and Hayley's rejection—but sometimes, I forgot that others weren't used to or prepared to face the unpredictable chaos a family get-together brought.

"I'm surprised you're even goin', to be honest. After what happened last night."

I chewed on my fingernail.

"Your determination to make this dinner, which arguably falls on one of the worst possible days to fulfill social obligations...this have anything to do with your hesitation about calling your family at the hospital?"

I picked at my nail.

"Yeah, I thought so."

An empty pit opened in my stomach. "It might be a cluster."

Shane watched me straighten my coat. "Tell me what role to play."

"What?"

He rested one elbow on the Uber's door, angling his body to see me better. "You're clearly goin' through some crap with your family. It's not my business, so I won't pry. Or I'll do my best not to pry, so long as I don't think whatever's goin' on with your family could escalate to pushing you off a bridge. But I can at least try to make this night easier on you. Tell me what role to play."

Knots of tension unwound in my chest, replaced with appreciation. He didn't know how much his offer meant to me.

"Just a friend is great," I said.

Shane placed his hand on mine—a gesture he probably meant to calm me, but it did so much more.

"I'll make an excellent dinner date."

I was sure he would, but it felt terribly intimate, allowing Shane to see the dysfunction that might be on display tonight.

"I'm warning you, it might be awkward," I said. "My mom's hit or miss with her moods at these things, even though she's the one that insists on them. And my sister is...unpredictable."

"I'm well versed in what grief can do to family dynamics," Shane said.

I met his empathetic gaze, which seemed to wrap around me and pull me into an embrace.

"Sometimes, it's easy to forget that other families go through this," I said.

"Death has so much collateral damage that no one really thinks about. You think about the kids growing up without a dad or the widow struggling to make ends meet. But you don't think about the fractures it can create in relationships."

He truly understood.

Shane continued, "My dad's death destroyed the relationship with an entire side of our family."

That, I was not expecting.

"How?"

"From what I've gathered, my mom was stuck in the anger phase. She blamed the guy who shot my dad, of course. But he was dead, and when your loss is that big, I think your pain branches out to find a home where it can fester. To look for someone to blame—anyone—and when blamin' his killer didn't fill the void, she blamed my dad's father."

"His father?"

"I come from a long line of cops," Shane explained. "My dad's dad was a cop, and so was his dad. When my father was killed in the line of duty, this tension between my mom and his side of the family started to percolate. I think, deep down, my mom blamed them for pressurin' him to go into law enforcement in the first place."

I couldn't imagine losing my child and then having their spouse blame *me* for it.

Shane's poor grandpa. But his poor mom, too, because she was rocking in a sea of agony, probably not intending to create waves of anguish.

Shane's tone deepened. "You would think that people who share the same loss would draw closer together, but sometimes, it's the opposite. Like maybe you see them as walking reminders of everything you lost or something. I don't know. But instead of strengthening the bond between my mom and my father's side of the family, it weakened it."

Weakened a family bond.

As heartbreaking as it was, it felt reassuring to know it wasn't just my family that had gone through this. It made me feel less rejected by my family—a reminder to myself that their rejection had nothing to do with *me*, but rather the aftershocks of grief.

Grief was such an isolating monster. Hurting people so devastatingly that they pulled inward, away from some, while lashing out at others. Eating away at relationships one at a time until we felt lost in the shadows, all alone. Hoping our remaining loved ones would return to us one day.

Maybe if we talked about loss the way Shane and I were now, healing could begin, but it seemed everyone avoided the topic of loss at all costs.

Except for Shane. He was the first person who talked about it so openly, and in doing so, he cast a light into my darkness and held out a hand so I was no longer alone.

"I'm sure my grandfather sensed her misplaced blame," Shane continued, "and probably resented it. The tension between them grew until, eventually, we stopped seeing my dad's side of the family altogether. My grandpa would still send us birthday cards and Christmas presents; he still let us know he cared about us, but we didn't get to see him anymore."

I couldn't even imagine how Shane's dad would feel about that. I bet he'd have wanted everyone to wrap their arms around each other. Not break up.

"How did that make you feel?" I asked.

My question surprised me; it was a thinking-out-loud moment, but even more surprising was when Shane scrubbed his jaw and answered. He tried to keep his tone neutral, but I could hear the pain breaking through his words.

"Let down. I wished they had put their own feelings aside and made the kids the priority, you know?"

Yeah. Grief not only ate relationships; it devoured childhood innocence.

"Because with my dad dying, holidays were tough enough. The last thing we needed was being estranged from loved ones."

My ribs ached; I knew how that felt.

"I've never met anyone that understands these kinds of family complexities like you do," I said.

Shane regarded me, a shared pain etched across his features. "I've never talked about it like...*this* with anyone before."

In all his years, the guy had never opened up like this to anyone, just as I had never opened up to anyone, either—as close as I'd been to Ezra, I'd never gone deep into my family dynamics. I felt sorry for Shane, knowing how isolated he must have felt as he watched other guys clanking beer mugs and playing poker without a care, but I also felt privileged that he'd trusted me with something so intimate.

"Your mom must have hated you becoming a cop," I said.

Shane raised his eyebrows. "More than you can imagine. She threatened to not come to my graduation over it."

Ouch.

"My life felt like a constant tug-of-war," Shane continued. "Because of my dad's death, what I wanted more than anything was to lock up people like my dad's killer. To protect people, so hopefully, their fathers would never get shot. And I wanted to carry on the legacy of our family, to not let it die with him, because letting the line of cops end with him just felt like another death to me. A death I could prevent from happening. Yet, at the same time, I worried me becoming a cop would put a tremendous stress on my mom. She'd already suffered enough, and the last thing I wanted to do was to drag her back into that hell."

Jeez. Whenever I had seen Shane before, he always looked so put together and peaceful. There was a calmness about him, and I never would've suspected that beneath the surface, there had ever been such a storm in his past.

Once again, Shane's words made me feel less alone in my suffering. By unveiling his personal, intimate experiences with loss, Shane unlocked my cage of shame—shame over the hurt I'd felt by my own family's dynamics.

The Uber stopped in front of the restaurant, and Shane held the door open for me so I could escape the bitter cold and walk into the heat of the restaurant.

Where I spotted my mom and grandma, sitting at a four-top.

Shane followed me as we wove around the tables, my wrist still aching despite the Tylenol.

"Do not tell them what happened to me," I said. "My mom misses my dad a lot around her birthday, and I don't want to worry her about your...hypothesis."

"As soon as you take your coat off, they're going to see your cast. What are you going to tell them?"

"I don't know..."

10

To everyone else, the restaurant's ambiance was romantic—charcoal walls with a scattering of pastel-pink flower arrangements; dimmed lighting; white tablecloths with sparkling wineglasses; the smell of rich chocolate desserts, mingling with tomato-rich dishes; and soft violin music, designed to hush the surrounding conversations. But to me, it was like a gorgeously designed cover for an unpredictable book. You had no idea what you were getting into until you turned that first page.

When Mom spotted me, she smiled. A good sign that she was in a decent mood tonight—that it wouldn't be a repeat of last year, when she'd been sullen and had barely talked during dinner.

My shoulders relaxed a little.

Hopefully, Hayley would be in a good mood, too. I wasn't sure what to expect, given we hadn't seen each other since the day after the birthday blowoff, but I intended to talk to her tonight to see if we could put my birthday debacle behind us and take a new step forward.

Mom's gaze shifted to Shane, not hiding her surprise.

"Hey, Mom." I bent down to give her a quick kiss on the cheek.

Then Grandma's. "I hope it's okay that I brought a friend of mine. This is Shane. Shane, this is my mom, Laura."

"Ma'am," Shane said, shaking her hand. "It's good to meet you."

"And this is my grandma, Kathleen," I said.

"Ma'am." Shane shook my grandma's hand too.

Grandma's eyes combed over Shane's handsome appearance—his dark hair, polished with product; his turquoise eyes, reflecting the candle's flames, accentuating his strong jaw. His black pants, light-blue button-down, and navy tie showed off the curves of his rugged body. To say he was the hottest guy in the restaurant wasn't an understatement.

Women were watching him, but he didn't seem to notice.

Shane placed his hands on the neckline of my coat, locking eyes with me—a secret moment passing between us as he silently asked me if I was ready for this.

When I nodded, he slid the coat off my body.

Pain seared through my shoulder with my arm's movement, but I hid it from my facial expression.

"What happened to your arm?" Mom's brows furrowed in alarm.

I kept my face nonchalant. "I fell."

Shane glanced between me and my mother as he draped both our coats on the backs of our chairs.

"When did this happen?"

"Last night. Shane got me to the ER, where they put a cast on it." All true. So far, only lies by omission, and I wanted to keep it that way. Telling an outright lie to my mom would only hurt her when she eventually learned the truth. Even if I was trying to protect her.

A waiter interrupted my mom's incredulous stare, and when he found out we had an extra person, a fifth chair was added. Chairs were adjusted, and after a minute, the four of us were seated with one empty chair remaining.

"Where is Hayley?" I asked.

"Late." My mom's lips flattened into a line.

Not a good sign.

"Is she doing okay?" I asked. Code for, *Has she fallen off the wagon?*

Mom busied herself with straightening the silverware.

"I've been trying to call you," she said. Code for, *Change the subject.* Which she'd do even if Shane wasn't here.

Mom's only coping mechanism in life was her giant broom, shoving anything difficult under the rug. And Hayley's issues were no exception.

The broom gave Hayley a lot of free passes in life. That, and the bond she and Hayley shared, cemented in tragedy, was a connection I was never invited to be a part of. Hayley was fourteen when Dad died, and since I was only four, I guess I wasn't old enough to share in their grief. Making me feel like a bit of an outsider in a family already deficient in affection.

"I lost my phone. I'm going to get a new one tomorrow."

Because by the time I got done with this dinner, it would be cutting it too close to get to the store before they closed today.

I braced myself for follow-up questions about how I lost my phone and where and how I had fallen hard enough to break my arm. Most moms would ask follow-up questions.

But not mine.

She went with, "So, how's work going?"

Small talk, then.

"Honestly? It hasn't gotten better."

When I had chosen human resources as a profession, I thought I would be spending my days hiring new people, developing strategies to retain talent, helping coach the company on ways we could better support our employees. And at first, I was. But for the last two years, it was the opposite. The company I worked for laid people off every quarter. And guess who had to take part in all the *planning* meetings of how many lives to ruin and whose lives those would be? No matter how well they were all performing.

And that was just the tip of the iceberg. The real heartbreak was when I'd have to sit in on the meetings where we let them go. And then there were the follow-up meetings with the people who'd lost the income for their family, seeing them in tears, terrified of how they'd pay their mortgage. They'd show me pictures of their kids and beg me to help, not knowing I lacked the power to do so. My orders were given by management, and, yes, I'd tried to advocate for people. And, yes, I'd laid out plans and other strategies that we could try instead of letting people go, but it always fell on deaf ears.

Increasingly, those situations became harder for me to handle emotionally. It was draining and, candidly, toxic for me. I didn't want to go into work to fire people all the time.

My boss kept assuring me the business was going through a cycle and that it wouldn't always be this way. I'd already researched other companies and discovered that moving would not solve that under-lying issue, so I was just trying to hold on for dear life until this "cycle" was over.

"I'm sure it will get better," Mom said.

Six words that summed up Mom's parenting advice to me over the years. *I'm sure it will get better.* Ironic, since Mom's grief never seemed to get better. She didn't know how to help someone navigate a path toward making things better. To her, life was about accepting the gunshot wound and letting it bleed out for whatever remained of your life.

At least she'd started to turn things around by seeing a therapist this past year, and that was a huge win—offering up more hope than ever that we could finally get close. Hell, when I'd been falling from that bridge, that's all I wanted—more than anything else in my life. So, why was all this hurt and anger and frustration bubbling up now? I guess a year of limited progress hadn't overcome twenty-four years of all these suppressed, unresolved feelings that continued to batter me.

"I've always wanted to start my own business, helping people find jobs and get back on their feet," I said. "I'm going to start researching what that would entail."

Shane's lips curled into an impressed smile.

"What about your current job?" Mom asked.

"It's just some research," I said. "I'd have to learn more before making anything official." Maybe I could start a business on the side and grow it into something full-time. My goal wasn't to get rich; it was just to pay my bills and help people.

A waiter stopped by to top off our waters and to ask if we had any questions about the menu before walking off.

"Have you spoken to Hayley lately?" Mom asked.

Sweep. Under the carpet went my career crisis.

"Just texts."

"You should call her."

"*I* should call *her*?"

"She feels terrible for missing your birthday."

"Does she?"

"You're too hard on her."

I took a drink of my water, refraining from snapping back with what I really wanted to say—*You're too soft on her.*

"If she wanted to spend my birthday with me, she would have been there."

My needs in life probably sounded weak. Needing to be *wanted* by my sister and closer to my mother weren't the goals of super-heroes, but they were human, and I knew if I had those two things, everything in my life would feel more stable—relationships, my anxiety, everything.

But I swear, some days, it felt like the harder I fought for it, the farther it slipped through my grasp.

"How'd you lose your phone?" Grandma asked, trying to change the subject to safe waters. Unaware that it launched an anchor in the choppy ones.

As frustrated as I felt toward my mom right now, I never wanted her to find out about my almost dying.

I locked eyes with Shane. He appeared to measure my nervous-ness and placed his hand over mine.

"Ma'am," he said, "can I just say, I think it's amazing that you guys get together like this? Not all families make the effort with each other these days."

My eyes stung. With a soothing tone, Shane took out his own broom and swept the rising tension away.

"When my husband died, I vowed I'd always make my girls a priority," Mom said with pride.

I was shocked she mentioned Dad's death. Dad was basically the Voldemort of the house—don't ask, don't tell, just exist silently in the shadow of his ghost—and it was selfish to feel the pang of hurt, hearing the word *priority* with the word *girls*. Plural.

I wasn't this needy. I was independent, and I shouldn't fixate on the hope that, one day, Mom would come to love me as much as she loved my sister.

I was just emotional from almost drowning—that's all. When you almost die, it has a funny way of cleaning the lens you see life through. The relationships that aren't as strong as you want them to be feel even more important to fix.

I'd kept my face neutral—I could tell I did—because Mom and Grandma didn't waver in their expression.

But Shane must have sensed the shift in my body language because he gave me a look that would have gone unnoticed by anyone else and placed a hand gently on my knee, where no one would witness his reassuring affection.

Suddenly, his presence here felt like an asset—an asset I was grateful to have.

"I lost my father when I was a child, too," he said.

My mom presumed the comment was meant for her, but I could tell it was meant for me. It was him saying I wasn't alone in this twisted web of pain that comes after the death of the family's patriarch.

"I'm so sorry to hear you lost your father." Mom's brows furrowed into empathy. "They say time heals all wounds, but it never does, does it?"

"No, ma'am."

"Please. Call me Laura."

Translation: Shane just won my mom over.

"What do you do for a living, Shane?" My mom folded her hands.

"I'm a detective with the Chicago Police Department."

My mom's smile no longer reached her eyes. In fact, she dropped her gaze from his completely, fidgeting with her nails the way she always did when extremely nervous. I wasn't sure Shane noticed it, but I did.

And a bolt of hurt shot up my spine because that slight gesture told me more than I'd learned in the last twenty-plus years.

I chugged half of my water, trying to convince myself her wariness over Shane's profession could be due to Hayley. Her addiction with drugs and alcohol had landed her in hot water sometimes, and maybe Mom got nervous, having law enforcement so close. But I knew better. Shane was here as a guest, not here to bust Hayley, if she ever even showed up.

And it's not like Hayley would do something illegal in front of him.

No. My instincts confirmed this had nothing to do with my sister. Mom had just mentioned Dad's death before asking Shane about his profession—Dad's death, which she'd always claimed was too painful to discuss the circumstances of.

And I'd bought that, slinking into shame whenever my curiosity had surfaced.

But clearly, I'd been a fool.

It wasn't until this very moment that I realized she had a much different reason for not sharing the details behind his death.

She's hiding something. Keeping me in the dark as to who killed him. *And has been my whole life.* I could tell by the way she was now avoiding eye contact with me.

Clearly, the reason she'd tensed when she learned Shane's profession was because a trained detective—particularly one emotionally unbiased from the situation—would be able to see past her excuses and omissions if the topic of Dad came up.

It was shocking to realize someone I'd pegged as timid had actively kept this from me my entire life. And beyond hurtful. I was so respectful of *her* wishes and her needs, and evidently, she'd never cared about mine. All those years she'd played the role of *it hurts too much to talk about*. What a crock of shit.

Why would she keep the details surrounding Dad's death from me?

Almost dying had stiffened my resolve; I wouldn't sit back and allow her to lie to me any longer. It might be selfish to do this at her birthday dinner, but after over two decades, I needed to strike now, before I lost my nerve because I knew myself—I'd leave here and talk myself out of this anger, and we'd go back to the spin cycle of dysfunctional secrets, possibly for the rest of our lives.

With my mouth dry, I interrupted Shane's conversation with my grandmother.

"I remember being in the hospital that day," I said to my mom.

Mom couldn't even hide the grimace.

I could feel Shane's stare on the side of my face.

"I remember having blood on me. I remember people talking in hushed whispers. And I remember feeling scared and confused because I was so little, and I remember you refusing to tell me what happened."

"Willow, we're in mixed company," my mom said.

"Mom—"

"Drop it. If you want to have a conversation, we can do it later. In private." Code for, *Yes, there's a ton I haven't told you, but I never will.*

My chest was heaving now at the betrayal, at her lies. Beneath the fancy white tablecloth cloaking my family in normalcy, Shane squeezed my thigh in a gesture of comfort.

It felt like I was at a table of enemies, and Shane was my only ally. I placed my hand on top of his, savoring the solace of his palm flipping over and locking fingers with mine. His embrace was my safe haven in this dinner from hell.

"Who killed Dad?" I pressed. "And why?"

"Drop it," Mom snapped.

The feeble woman had summoned her inner lioness. She glared at me, like I was a horrible person for wanting to know how my father died.

I hadn't thought about the details for a long damn time, but now, I wanted to know, and if last night taught me anything, it was that I didn't have forever to get answers. I pushed aside my inner panic, ignored the fear that I was pushing Mom too far.

"I deserve to know." I even kept my chin up, no matter how fast my heart was hammering.

"You can either drop it or leave."

Look at her, suddenly all strong. Where was this strength when she prioritized her own needs over her small, heartbroken kids all those years ago? I couldn't sit at this table and stare at my mom's lying face for another moment. If I did, I'd start crying—I could already feel it coming—and I prided myself in having a thick enough skin to not break down. Especially not in front of anyone.

I shot up from my chair. "If you'll excuse me, I need to go to the ladies' room."

I wove through the tables and escaped into the women's restroom, where the sobs broke through the dam I'd built to hold them in—cracking open the wound of my father's death.

How could I ever trust my mother again? Was I the only person she was lying to? Did everybody else in my family know the truth and I was the only fool in the dark?

Why would she lie about Dad's death?

Strong people wouldn't let her get away with this, and I was going to be a strong woman. Clearly, she wouldn't answer in mixed company, but so help me, I'd confront her alone another day, and when I did, I would not leave without answers. She would not get away with lying to me for over twenty years.

I stared at myself in the mirror, wiping the stream of vulnerability from my cheeks before emerging from the women's restroom.

Shane stood with his back pressed against the wall, arms crossed over his chest, his shirt now rolled up to his elbows.

"You okay?" he asked.

"I'm fine."

His steely blue eyes grabbed me in their hold as he stepped closer, placing his hands on my upper arms.

"It's okay if you're not."

Those simple words—*it's okay if you're not*—unleashed the tears I normally held back from everyone, flooding my cheeks.

Shane wrapped his arms around me, and in the silent comfort of his embrace, I allowed myself to be weak in front of him. Only, it strangely didn't feel weak, doing this. I felt simply...human, allowing myself to have an understandable reaction to such a life-altering betrayal.

He seemed to know there was nothing he could say to ease my pain. He seemed to know that the only thing I needed right now was the comforting reminder I wasn't alone.

Because I felt so very alone right now.

"Do you want to go?" he whispered.

I did. I wanted to leave, but I also knew if I ruined this dinner, Mom would never forgive me. And with our relationship fractured, I was too scared to allow it to crumble to dust.

After all, she was still my mother. My only parent.

"No," I managed. "Let's just get through the main course and then make up an excuse?"

As I pulled away, Shane reached up and swiped a fallen tear from my cheek with his thumb.

"You okay?"

I would not lie to him. "No."

He nodded, his jaw tightening with concern. "Tell me what I can do to help."

"Being here helps," I admitted. "Being a buffer."

"A buffer." He chewed the inside of his cheek. "I can be a buffer."

He reached down and took my hand in his, as if it were no big deal, but to me, it was everything. His palm was warm, affection seeping up my arm and into my chest, calming the hurts that were stabbing me from the inside.

And then he guided me back to the table.

Mom didn't look up from her menu.

I refused to let that sting.

Shane pulled my chair out for me and gently lured me into it by holding my elbow. Then, he sat down, opened his menu, and put his hand back on my knee.

Again reminding me I wasn't alone in this.

We sat in silence for one full minute. People nearby chatted. The waiter walked by without stopping at our table. The violin music began a new song.

I couldn't take any more of this.

Maybe I'd just leave. She was the one lying, not me, and if she was willing to end our relationship because I couldn't suffer through this? Well...

Shane leaned over and put his mouth next to my ear, whispering, "Breathe."

Then, he pulled back and asked, "So, what do you do for a living, Laura?"

Man, he was good. His tone had no trace of animosity, yet was not overly bubbly, either. The perfect blend of politeness, intrigue, and respect. Even for someone who didn't deserve it.

"I'm an insurance agent." The return of her fake smile told me she was relieved Shane had changed the subject.

"What type of insurance do you work in?" Shane asked.

"I started out my career in homeowners and vehicle insurance, but I now specialize in life insurance. It's never too early to get it, you know." She waggled her finger. "Most people don't think about life insurance until they're much older, but everyone should have a policy."

How did she not realize that talking about life insurance flirted dangerously close to talking about the death of someone you loved? I took a huge gulp of water, trying to swallow my frustration.

"Do you have a policy, Shane?"

"I don't. My grandparents on my mother's side did, though, and they left us quite a nest egg."

"Still, you should get your own policy. I've ensured everyone in my family has life insurance."

Yeah, because that makes up for lying and hiding the truth for years.

"If you ever want to discuss it"—Mom fished a business card out of her purse, then handed it to him—"call me."

Unbelievable. Drumming up business after dismissing my feelings.

I took another angry gulp of water.

A motion that didn't go unnoticed by Shane, who offered me a look of empathy before returning to his role of Friend of the Year.

"Thank you," Shane said, tucking the card into his pants. "If someone younger and unmarried wanted to get a life insurance policy, how would you recommend choosing a beneficiary?"

Shane was beyond kind, keeping my mom talking like this.

"I recommend choosing someone your age. But if you don't have anyone you trust, you can choose a family member, like Willow did."

Shane took a tight sip of water. "Willow has life insurance?"

"As I said, everyone in my family has life insurance."

Yes, but based on Shane straightening the silverware unnecessarily, he probably assumed she'd been referring to everyone her age.

"How big of a policy would you recommend for someone my age?"

I stared at him, but he avoided my eye contact.

"The bigger, the better," Mom said. "The price of life insurance increases as you get older, so while you might not need a big policy right now, it's advantageous to lock in a larger policy today at the lower rates, and that way, you'll have it later in life, when you're married with children."

"That makes sense," Shane said. "Do you think ten thousand is adequate?"

I side-eyed him.

Mom laughed. "Oh dear, no. You want something that can take care of your future family. I recommend estimating the full value of the home that you want to have someday, plus money for your future kids' college funds, as well as living expenses for your entire family for upward of twenty years, just in case."

"Sounds expensive."

"It's very reasonable. Depending on the type of policy you get, you'd be surprised. Willow only pays thirty-five dollars a month for a million-dollar policy."

Shane was the one with the smile not reaching his eyes now as he shifted his gaze to me. "You have a million-dollar life insurance policy?"

Crap. Mom was oblivious to his sudden rigid posture.

"Who's the beneficiary?"

As if tensionville couldn't get any worse, Hayley showed up to the table, looking even more disheveled than usual. Her long hair was stringy with oil at the roots, as if it hadn't been washed for a couple of weeks. Her dress had a purple stain on it that looked like wine, and her eyes looked dilated.

As if she'd just taken a hit of something before she arrived.

My chest ached, realizing she must be off the wagon again. Maybe that's why she didn't show up to my birthday, and then I go and lay into her as if she did it to be intentionally hurtful.

I should have known substance abuse was likely the cause.

I hated Hayley's struggle with addiction; I felt helpless, watching her suffer.

Hayley plopped down at the empty chair and stared at Shane, her eyes tight, looking like she was trying to place him. Hard to do when she'd never met him before, but sadly, she was too high to remember that.

"Who's this?" she asked.

Please do not tell me Shane has ever arrested my sister...

In a city this large, the odds of that had to be low. Right? Maybe she'd hoped to talk to me tonight, just as I'd hoped to talk to her. A talk that would have to wait—I wouldn't have it with her when she was high.

"Hayley, this is my friend, Shane."

"Nice to meet you," Shane said.

After staring at him for a couple more seconds, Hayley moved her gaze to my cast. "What happened to your arm?"

"I fell," I said.

She looked like she was about to ask more questions, but Shane interjected with his own, still fixated on the conversation we'd been having before she'd arrived.

"Who's her beneficiary?" he asked.

"Most people choose their spouse, of course," Mom droned on. "Willow's will change later, but for now, it's me."

11

"Why didn't you tell me?" Shane asked.

He'd been silent on the Uber ride back to my apartment, like he was so upset, he needed time to calm down. He waited until we were inside, alone, before he ambushed me with his frustration.

"Because I knew what you would think."

"You didn't tell De Luca."

"It didn't even cross my mind until I was in the middle of the interview with him, and when it did, I thought he'd become fixated on someone I know for a fact would never hurt me. But you're right; I need to tell him. I'll do it the next time we talk."

Shane rubbed both hands over his face. "I hate to say this," Shane sighed. "But...I picked up on a lot of tension between you and your mom."

"She would never hurt me." Physically. Emotionally? That was another story.

"Tryin' to be diplomatic here, but it sounds like she has a million reasons to hurt you."

"Shane..."

"I'm not sayin' she did," he clarified. "I'm sayin' it's a big policy, Willow."

"My mom's not a killer."

"The two of you have palpable tension."

"I'm sure all families do," I said.

"She always that dismissive of you?" Shane asked with an edge.

My neck flushed, embarrassed by our dysfunctional relationship yet flattered by his fierce protection over me.

"She doesn't like talking about painful subjects."

Shane rubbed his thumb along his eyebrow, his tone cautious. "Like Hayley's drug use?"

Guess it was obvious.

"I sensed some animosity between you two."

I sighed. "She didn't show up to my birthday," I said. "I called her out on it, but she wasn't mad at me. It was the other way around."

"But you're not on good terms with her?" Shane asked.

"I'm not on bad terms with her. Our relationship has always been complicated, but she did a lot for me when we were kids."

I could still remember the times when Mom wasn't there, when Hayley took it upon herself to brush my hair in the mornings and walk me all the way to my elementary school. She was a teenager; she didn't have to do that, especially when she was struggling with her own problems—like being in and out of rehab.

"Does your mom support your sister financially?" Shane asked.

"Not exactly."

Which made Shane inflate his chest again. "Drugs are an expensive habit. Doubt she's contributing to any of the bills, then. Supporting two people instead of one isn't cheap. Is your mom struggling financially because of it?"

"Stop." Being mad at my mom was one thing. Accusing her of the most heinous crime one could commit was another.

"Do you know how many cases I've worked where people have been killed over small amounts of money? A million-dollar policy doesn't strike you as a red flag?"

I glared at him.

"I'm not sayin' this is easy. But, Willow"—he shoved a hand through his hair—"the cops are not looking into this enough. You have to be diligent to protect yourself."

"And how do you suggest I do that? Stay in my apartment forever? I have a job. I have friends. I have a life."

"Maybe you should avoid your mom for the time being."

I laughed. "Wow. And who else is on that list?"

"I would like to make a list," Shane said.

"I was being angrily sarcastic."

"If you'd allow it."

"No. I won't allow it. You'd put everyone in my life on that list."

"Only people that have somethin' to gain. Or have an issue with you. Do you and your mom normally get along?"

"I'm not talking about this."

"I'll take that as a no."

"We don't have some deep hate for each other, Shane. It's complicated."

"You and her have any issues recently?"

"My mom is not a killer. And even if I played a ludicrous twilight-zone game of pretend for a moment, if she was a killer, she'd never kill one of her kids."

"Would your sister benefit from the policy?"

"No. My mom lets her crash at her place—that's it. And Hayley might assume I have a policy, but she knows that Mom would never give her a single penny; Mom refuses to fuel Hayley's drug habit. Only reason she lets her crash there is so she won't be homeless."

Shane appeared to consider this. "Has your mom had any recent financial pressures?"

"I'm not getting into this."

"What about her rent or mortgage? People on the cusp of eviction can get desperate."

"Look." I sighed. "I'm beyond grateful that you were at that dinner. Seriously, it was the only way I could get through it, but I'm not doing this. I am not going through my life and dissecting everyone as a possible suspect. Maybe some families could withstand that kind of suspicion, but mine can't. Mine is fragile. You poke around with questions, they'll take them as *accusations*. You went to dinner with me, so now, they'll think I'm behind it, and I don't want my mom to stop talking to me. I don't want to lose my family, Shane. It's my biggest fear. We might not be one of those close-knit families, but I love them and want them in my life. I already made my mom upset enough by asking her about my dad."

And, yes, I still planned to ask her about it again in private and demand to know why she'd kept it a secret all these years. If she still didn't answer me, I'd resort to doing my own research or hire someone to look into it deeper than I'd be able to.

But asking direct questions about my dad was a family thing. Accusing her or others of murder? I might as well walk away now and never call them again. I'd be shunned forever.

"Please. Drop this. For my sake. I can't stop De Luca from doing what he needs to do, but I can stop you from making it a thousand times worse."

Shane scrubbed his face with both hands. "Willow, all due respect, don't you think you're diggin' your heels in too deep?"

Stubborn. He thought I was being stubborn.

Maybe I was being too stubborn in this situation. But here was the thing: I'd always given people a lot of chances because I believed in forgiveness and redemption and all of that—and no human was perfect. But the thing about taking the high road all the time? Some days, it can make you feel like a doormat, so there was this constant seesaw—of forgiving someone versus standing up to them—that I tried to balance at all times. Did I get it right all the time? No.

But now, everything was different.

Feeling my mom pull away like that at dinner made me realize that there may have been something else obstructing our relationship this whole time—not grief, as I thought, but lies. I needed to get answers from her, the truth and why she kept it from me. Maybe then I could finally feel the connection with her I'd been chasing my whole life.

After almost dying, I wanted that connection more than ever with both her *and* Hayley.

I could tell Shane was about to say something, but he never got the chance because someone knocked on my door.

My heart pathetically swelled, hoping it was my mother, coming here to apologize—I deserved an apology, and I'd insist we go somewhere to talk in private—but my hope died when I looked through the peephole.

Shit.

Shane had despised Ezra since meeting him that night I'd had too much to drink, and now, Shane was convinced Ezra was his prime suspect. As if that wasn't tense enough, Ezra had been trying to get me back for months, and if he saw Shane inside my apartment, he'd jump to all sorts of conclusions.

Allowing the two to see each other felt like a ticking bomb.

I stepped away from the door, deciding I wouldn't open it, but Ezra knocked louder.

"Why aren't you answering it?" Shane whispered.

"I'm not in the mood for company."

Based on Shane's frown, he didn't buy that.

"I'll get rid of them." Shane stepped toward the door.

"No!" I grabbed the handle. "I'll do it."

At least I had a chance of getting Ezra to go away without losing my temper.

In theory...

12

"**B**abe." Ezra's gray eyes rounded slightly when he saw my cast. "What happened?"

His blond hair flowed around his face in staggered lengths that rested on his shoulders, but the most pronounced facial feature was his thin nose, which had a bump in the center from when he'd broken it playing hockey as a kid. Like his cheeks, it was slightly reddened on account of having just been outside in the winter cold.

"It's a long story." One I had no interest in getting into right now. "What are you doing here?"

Ezra's puffy winter coat shifted open when he tucked his hands into his jeans, his eyes soft, just as they were the first time he had bruised my heart.

"Can we talk?"

"Now's not a good time."

"Please?"

"She said now's not a good time." Shane stepped out from behind the door and stood at my side.

A look of hurt washed over Ezra's face as he looked from Shane to me. Then anger when he must've recognized him as the cop who'd threatened to arrest him that night I'd had too much to drink.

Shane took a step even closer to me, his hip practically touching mine.

If I were a fire hydrant, I'd be covered in urine.

"Ezra, this is Shane. Shane, this is my ex-boyfriend, Ezra."

With obvious bitterness in his eyes, Ezra held his hand out—undoubtedly trying to be a bigger person to prove to me that he had changed, but Shane crossed his arms over his chest, leaving Ezra hanging.

Ezra dropped his arm and snapped his eyes to me. "Can I talk to you for a minute?"

"I told you, it's not a good time," I repeated.

"It's important." There was a desperation permeating from him that I had never seen before.

"Please," Ezra said. "It took me a half hour to get here. Just give me five minutes?"

"Ezra..."

"Two minutes," he said.

Option A: I could continue arguing with Ezra, but he was clearly determined to get something off his chest, and every moment Ezra refused to leave, the vein on Shane's forehead looked closer to exploding.

Option B: let Ezra say whatever the hell he'd come here to avoid this escalating.

I sighed, stepped back, and motioned for Ezra to come inside. Much to the disapproval of Shane, who tried to annihilate my ex with the world's most powerful glower.

Ezra walked into my living room and flicked his eyes to Shane.

"Alone?" Ezra said. This time with an edge.

"Hell no," Shane said.

"Shane—"

"I'm not leaving you alone with this guy."

"This guy?" Ezra stepped into Shane's space. "Who the hell are you again?"

Shane matched Ezra's movements, closing the distance between them until they could probably smell each other's breaths. I had to shove my hand against Shane's chest and push *hard* to get him to move.

"Shane, it's fine."

"Willow—"

"I'm fine. Please give us a minute."

Shane's chest rose and fell faster beneath my palm.

"You're right on the other side of that wall," I reminded him.

Shane clenched his jaw and glared at my ex-boyfriend as he put his hand on his *gun holster.*

"Fine. I'll be right outside," Shane said.

I refrained from rolling my eyes.

Ezra looked irritated as F at Shane's posturing and watched him with guarded eyes as Shane slowly left my apartment.

I didn't hear him go inside his own place, though. Must be out in the hallway.

"The hell was that about?" Ezra asked.

"It's a long story."

"Just like your broken wrist is?"

It clearly bothered him, being out of the loop when Ezra probably suspected Shane knew exactly what happened to my wrist. Going from knowing every detail of someone's life to finding her with another man in her apartment, with a mysteriously broken arm, shone a spotlight on the intimacy that had vanished between us.

"Ezra, I really don't have the time for this."

He looked over at my kitchen countertop, his lips curling down. "So, you got my flowers."

"I did."

"You didn't answer my text this morning."

A chill crawled up my spine. For the briefest of moments, Shane got into my head. My potential killer would know my cell phone was missing or ruined from the water, so was this an attempt to divert suspicion away from himself?

I pushed a finger to my forehead, refusing to allow this situation to mind-F me.

"I didn't see it," I said.

"Did you see the note?" Ezra motioned toward the flowers.

"I did."

"And?"

"And what?" I asked.

Ezra regarded me, softening his tone when he spoke next. "I miss you."

He took a step toward me, but I held up my hand, silently warning him to give me my space. A flicker of resentment washed over his face, but he extinguished it and kept his tone gentle.

"I promise if you give me another chance, nothing like that will ever happen again."

"Ezra—"

"Please, Willow. What more do I have to do for you to take me back?"

"I did take you back," I reminded him. "I gave you a second chance, and it still didn't work."

His lips tightened. "You gave up too soon."

"*I* gave up? I'm not the one who was kissing someone else when their girlfriend was in the ladies' room or texting other women behind her back."

He balled his hands into fists. "Willow—"

"Please just go."

"Willow—"

"Go!"

Ezra's eyes darkened, and his jaw ticced.

"How long are you going to make me pay for my mistake? I told you I was drunk. As for those texts you found, I told you, those women texted me, not the other way around. It was just a little harmless flirting. It didn't mean anything. *You* mean everything to me. I want to be with you, Willow, no one else. Does that mean nothing to you?"

"You will not bait me into another argument, Ezra! I don't know how many times I have to say this to you before you will understand. Stop with the flowers. Stop with the phone calls and texts."

He took a frustrated step toward me. "When will you stop punishing me?"

"I'm not punishing you! Relationships end when there's no trust. I don't trust you. I will never trust you, and I want you to leave."

I don't know why he expected this conversation to finally be the one that changed my mind, but I could see a wave of frustration break into outrage with the way he glared at me, his chest heaving. He stomped over to the kitchen, grabbed the flowers, and chucked them against the wall.

The vase exploded like a bomb, shards of glass and water thrown through the air like shrapnel.

I'd thrown my hands up to protect my face out of instinct. My muscles ached from the sudden movement, but I was too shocked to focus on it.

Ezra had never acted like this before. Ever. Not once had I ever seen him lose his temper, let alone throw something that could have hit me. Before I could process it for more than half of a second, my front door burst open. Shane's eyes met mine—relief flaring in them that I was unharmed—before absorbing the broken glass and spilled flowers. He curled his lips and charged Ezra.

Shoving him up against the wall with his forearm pinned to his throat.

13

"I cannot believe Ezra did that." Emily leaned forward, her gorgeous red hair falling like curtains around her ivory cheeks.

Emily, Tracey, Amelia, and I sat at a café by my apartment because ever since Shane left for work this morning—I'd stayed home to nurse my sore body one more day—my anxiety about the last three days, the bridge, Ezra, my family—trapped me in a pressure cooker, and if I didn't escape, I felt like I'd combust.

Seeing my friends would help. Particularly Emily, whom I met after graduating college and moving to Chicago. I'd been drawn to her confidence—envying it, if I were being honest.

Tracey and Amelia, I'd met a little later—Tracey from a different department at my office (she'd since moved companies) and Amelia at my grandma's church function, where her grandma was on the same committee as mine.

The church's bake sale had nothing on this café, though. This place had muffins you would donate a kidney to taste; Costa Rican coffee, freshly ground and roasted on the hour; and ambiance that smoothed away any wrinkles of apprehension going on in your life.

Amber lighting enveloped the tables that were spaced several feet apart—a rare commodity in downtown Chicago—affording you privacy to think or chat with your friends.

"I know," I agreed. "I've never seen him like that before. It was scary."

"I can't believe he sent flowers to begin with," Amelia said with a bite to her tone. "It's been over for you guys for months."

Tracey made no effort to hide the bewilderment on her face. Couldn't blame her; it was an odd thing for Amelia to fixate on, given everything else we'd just talked about—how I'd fallen from a bridge, how cops were looking into it, and how Ezra pulled this stunt with the flowers.

"I don't know how you're being so brave," Tracey said. "I would be beyond freaked out if I almost died and had no memory of how it happened."

I sighed. "I am. I'm trying to hide how much it upsets me, especially when I don't remember what happened because it'll only make Shane more upset. But how the hell did I wind up in that river? I mean, no scenario makes any sense."

I pinched the bridge of my nose.

"They'll figure it out." Tracey placed her hand on my arm.

"Totally," Emily agreed.

Amelia said nothing, and we sat in silence while I tried to stop this unhelpful anxiety that stirred every time I thought about almost dying.

Emily looked like it pained her, not being able to make me feel better. But she must have decided snapping my thoughts back to something else would pull me out of my despair, if only temporarily, because she cleared her throat.

"What happened after Shane pinned him to the wall?" she asked.

"Shane called the cops. Tried to get him arrested for vandalism."

"But he's not in jail?" Emily asked.

"No."

The responding officer disagreed a broken vase met the threshold for vandalism or attempted assault, since it hadn't hit me, and he didn't succumb to Shane's pressure otherwise.

"Did you file a restraining order?" Emily asked.

Amelia pursed her lips, and her chest inflated slowly.

"I didn't." Much to Shane's dismay. "Ezra was out of line, and he deserves to feel like an asshole for what he did, but I don't want to ruin his political career by filing one." That kind of record would follow him everywhere.

Ezra was a lobbyist for a major pharmaceutical company. Honestly, when I met him, I expressed moral concern over it—was he lobbying for bigger profits rather than expanding medicines to save lives? He assured me that wasn't the case and also pointed out this job was a "stepping stone" in his political career—allowing him to frequently travel to Washington and meet key leaders. His endgame was a high-ranking role in politics, and a restraining order could severely hamper his chances at achieving it.

Was I being too soft by not filing one? Hopefully not. I was trying to do what I felt was *necessary* to protect myself without ruining people's lives, careers, or damaging my relationships with family in the process. It was a seriously hard juggling act.

"Is everyone in your life going to be a suspect?" Amelia kept her tone gentle, but I swore offense flashed through her eyes. "I talked to you on Saturday. Does that mean the cops will want to talk to me?"

My palms began to sweat, and the dull ache that persisted in my wrist intensified. This was precisely what I was afraid of—offending the people I cared about. I'd just had a blowout with my family, and the last thing I wanted to do was have a blowout with my friends over this.

"They might."

"I talked to you, too, and I *hope* the cops talk to me," Tracey said. "The sooner they rule out innocent people, the sooner they can focus on who did this to you and lock them up."

"You heard what Willow said. They don't even know someone

did this to her. For all we know, she could've done this to herself—"
Amelia caught herself. Eyes wide. Full of remorse.

Tracey and Emily were too busy throwing daggers at her to make
eye contact with me, but if they had, they'd see my entire neck
swelling in red.

Her words cut deep inside me, filleting my stomach until it bled.

"I'm sorry. I didn't mean it," Amelia said. "Even though you've
been down lately, I don't think you *actually* did it to yourself."
Actually?

Down lately? Yes, that last round of layoffs at work had broken
my heart—one of the people who lost their jobs was a single mother
with three kids, who had no savings, and the hurt from watching
each person suffer through job loss accumulated one on top of the
other. And, yes, my sister missing my birthday had drudged up the
pain of that whole thing too, but was I down in the dumps enough
that even my own friends thought there was a chance I'd done this to
myself?

"You think I tried to kill myself?" I couldn't hide the shock on my
face.

"Of course not," Emily said, glaring at Amelia.

"Then, why did you say it, Amelia?" I demanded.

"I just would hate for cops to accuse an innocent person of something that they didn't do. That's all."

Her words continued to whip my bleeding wound until the pain
was so intense, I had to look away.

Right behind it was anger that surged through my veins, wrapping around my throat until the air tasted like poison. Amelia
seemed more concerned with the potential blowout toward the
people in my life than my almost dying.

Before anyone could say anything else, Emily's eyes settled on
something behind me.

Two hands appeared on the table, a set of male arms caging
me in.

"A word?" his voice grumbled near my ear.

He smelled like the ocean. How could someone so assertive smell so gentle?

Emily and Tracey looked like they didn't know what to make of his anger while Amelia looked at him with guarded eyes.

"Sure," I said. "I'll stop by when I'm done here."

His fingers tightened.

"Now, please." He said it like a command and walked to the side of the room, apparently confident I would obey.

The only reason I walked over to Shane was because I knew he would probably create a scene if I didn't. I needed to get him to leave so I could get back to my friends and smooth things over.

Also, Shane needed to remember that no matter his good intentions, I didn't take orders from him.

He leaned against the wall, committing a crime of looking gorgeous. With his black coat hanging open in the front, he wore a pair of fitted black slacks and a blue button-down that kissed his muscles—making him look like a sinfully hot action star playing the role of a detective in a movie.

I'd venture to say every set of women's eyes was on him right now.

"What the hell are you doin' here?" he asked.

"Conversing with friends. You?" I asked.

Shane pursed his lips. "I told you it would be safer for you to stay home."

"I know."

Shane's chest inflated so much, I wondered if it was going to pop.

"Did you go to the cell phone store without me?"

As a detective, surely, he knew there were other ways to contact friends.

"No. I messaged my friends through social media on my computer."

Shane rubbed his jaw, as if trying to massage away his frustration over my having not followed his advice to become a hermit. "We need to talk."

"I'll stop by after—"

"It's important."

I studied him. He seemed a lot tenser than he had this morning when he'd checked on me before heading to work. Which was saying something.

"About?"

Shane eyed my friends. "Let's talk at home."

"Just say it," I insisted.

He scrubbed his cheek. His poor face would get rug burn if he kept that up.

"Your ex," he said, looking back at me. "Did you know he has a history of violence?"

My lungs stopped pumping air through my body.

"What are you talking about?"

Ezra didn't have a violent history. I'd never once seen him get into a fistfight with a guy, he'd never been arrested, and he'd never been in trouble with the law. The vase was the only time I'd seen him act like that.

"Last night didn't sit well with me, so I dug around a little today."

"You dug around?" I tilted my head. "Are you *trying* to get yourself fired?"

"Ezra has a probable criminal past."

"Probable? What in the hell does that mean?"

"When he was a minor, he was a suspect, questioned in a violent crime, but he was never charged or arrested. Nothin' that would pop up in a basic background check. I had to reach out to the investigating jurisdiction to find out the details of the offense."

"Which was?"

Shane studied me, allowing several seconds to pass, as if he thought my oxygen level needed to rise before I could handle whatever he was about to say.

"Assault and battery."

14

"Assault and battery of who?" I asked.

"Can we talk about this in private?"

I looked over at my friends. Amelia's hurt feelings would have to take a backseat to this development; I needed to hear whatever Shane had uncovered.

"Let me say goodbye."

Shane glanced at them. "Who's the girl in the black shirt?"

I looked at the table. "Amelia. Why?"

His gaze fixed on something specific, and his eyebrows furrowed slightly.

"No reason," he claimed.

But he wouldn't look at me.

"I'll wait for you outside," he said.

And then he walked off, as if he thought I'd let him off the hook that easy. Fat chance. I'd circle back to that one, for sure, but for now, I said goodbye to my friends, explaining there was a development in the case I had to talk about with Shane.

When I left the café, I found Shane standing outside in the crisp winter air.

Gray clouds loomed over the skyscrapers like an ominous warning. The buildings stood so tall, they looked like they were standing up against the imposing threat of snow, as if refusing to accept the reality around them.

"So, who did Ezra hurt? And why wasn't he arrested?"

When we began walking, it took Shane a minute to explain.

"Off the record, the detective on the case knew in his gut it was Ezra based on what information he had. Especially when Ezra showed up with a broken nose."

Ezra said he'd broken his nose playing hockey as a kid. Not in high school.

"But knowin' something and having enough evidence to arrest and charge someone are two different things. Especially when the victim clammed up and wouldn't ID him. Said he'd get beat up even worse if he snitched. On the record, Ezra was just a minor who *allegedly witnessed* a fight that put the kid in the hospital with a concussion."

"Who was the victim?" I asked.

"Ezra's best friend in high school, evidently."

If it was true, I couldn't believe he'd kept this from me. We'd dated for six months, and I thought I knew everything about him.

And while it was possible he was innocent, I found it very hard to believe Ezra wouldn't even mention witnessing his best friend from high school getting beat up, let alone that he'd been called in as a suspect on the assault. Especially since he intentionally lied to me about how he'd broken his nose.

It felt like another betrayal by him. Another thing someone had hidden from me.

"So, you think he's capable of hurting me," I deduced.

"Someone close to you has a hidden, violent past," Shane said.

"We should take it to De Luca."

"I did." Shane's teeth clenched. "Didn't change his mind."

I guess that shouldn't surprise me. Someone in my life being called in for questioning over a teenage fight a decade ago didn't change the fact that there was no evidence a crime had even been committed on the bridge.

"I can't let this go now," Shane said. "Not now. Now that I know about your life insurance and your ex...I need to look into this."

"I'm not going to let you compromise your career over a hunch."

"It's not just a hunch. You have people in your life with real motives, Willow."

I pursed my lips.

"I still can't *imagine* someone I know having tried to hurt me," I said. No matter how logical Shane laid out the evidence, my heart just could not accept this as a possibility. "And I cannot have you tear down relationships with people when I'm working so hard to build them back up."

"Okay, look." Shane stopped walking and scratched his temple. "Let's say, for a moment of pure hypothesis, someone you know did this to you."

I opened my mouth to argue, but he held up his palm before I could talk. Then put his hands into his pockets, as if his relaxed posture could make what he was saying sound less shocking.

"You owe it to yourself to look into this, Willow. Sounds like you're overly considerate of other people, and maybe it's about time they return that favor."

He studied my eyes.

"Besides, if they love you, won't they want you to be safe?"

I opened up my mouth, but, dammit, a good rebuttal to that didn't appear—especially since Tracey had said something similar.

"I will be very delicate," he promised. "I'll never ask any questions in a way that implies I'm accusin' them. But your family loves you. Your friends care about you. If someone did try to kill you, all of them would want you to do whatever it took to keep yourself safe."

Logically, he was right. The people who cared about me would want me to take the steps necessary to stay safe, and Shane understood what was at stake, that he couldn't ask accusing questions without risking the very relationships I was trying to protect. If there was anyone I trusted to handle this delicately, it was Shane.

But still, this was difficult to accept. And no matter how delicate he would be, there was no guarantee that his probing questions regarding their whereabouts at the time of the incident wouldn't offend or hurt the people I cared about. I mean, look at how Amelia had reacted.

"I will be very careful," Shane assured.

I wanted to say no, but even I had to admit that Ezra's behavior yesterday was alarming. And the life insurance policy? That could be a big motive for anyone, I guess—after all, money is a universal motivating factor.

I hoped Shane was wrong. Hopefully, the incident *was* an accident, like I thought, but if someone *had* been with me that night, who was it, and why hadn't they come forward? Was it possible they panicked when I fell, and they ran and then became worried that it would make them look guilty? It would give me peace of mind to at least have Shane explore this with his expertise.

How could I possibly move forward in my life, not knowing for sure?

Damn, if only my memories of the fall would return, it would answer all these questions.

"I'll let you work on this on three conditions," I decided.

"*Three?*"

"First, I'm not living like a hostage. I'm going about my daily life, and this includes meeting up with my friends, going out to dinners, going to work. I'm not going to sit in my apartment every minute of the day with your overprotectiveness suffocating me."

I bet he wanted to dispute this condition, but if he was right and someone in my life wished me harm, the only way to protect me was if I agreed to let him investigate.

Still, his chest swelled, and he held off saying anything for several seconds.

"And the second condition?"

"We work this *together*. I'm not giving you the keys to go investigate my life without being ingrained in what you're doing."

This one looked easier for him to swallow. Probably because he'd need my help anyway.

"Third, you don't do anything that could threaten your job. De Luca warned you to stay away from this case, and he seems to have a stick up his butt about you. So, that means no pulling any official information using police resources."

"Willow—"

"I will not let you jeopardize your career over this."

"I'm not going to stand by and let you get killed."

Someone trying to kill me once was a stretch. Twice? I wasn't on board with that fear.

"No police resources."

His jaw set tight. "You're tyin' both hands behind my back."

"I'm protecting you from yourself."

Shane swiped his thumb along his nose. "I'd like to renegotiate using police resources."

I shook my head. "Best and final offer."

Shane shoved his hands into his pockets. Stared at the ground as if it could help him plead his case.

"Fine," he grumbled.

A wave of panic flooded through me at the turning point this meant in my life.

I hid the tremble in my voice and squared my shoulders. "How do you propose we start?"

Shane eyed my hands, which were flexing nervously in and out of balls, and then offered a gentle smile, like he wanted to ease my anxiety.

"How about I ask you some questions over dinner?"

Shane Hernandez had noticed so many things about me over the past few months, but now, I'd given him permission to dig deep into my life, my relationships. My heart thundered as I wondered...

What question will he ask first?
More importantly, what will he uncover?

15

"Tell me about Ezra." Shane adjusted his shirtsleeves, which were rolled up to his elbows. As if readying himself for some kind of a mental battle.

We had walked to a diner a half block from our apartment that sat about fifty people. Crimson tables rested between a perimeter of olive-colored booths, sitting atop black-and-white checkered flooring. A busy front door chimed every couple of minutes, it seemed, with another person picking up a to-go order from the counter, the activity producing a draft that frosted my skin. Chicago's favorite rock station played on the speakers positioned in the ceiling while the smell of fried potatoes mingled with grilled beef.

A very unassuming backdrop for deep-diving into a possible attempted murder.

I stirred the cubes in my water glass with a straw. "What do you want to know?"

"For starters, give me more specifics about how you ended things."

The memory came back as if it happened only moments ago.

· · ·

I'm at a get-together, and I'm watching Ezra from across the room, talking to a girl I don't know. He's throwing his head back and laughing at something she said.

My body tenses.

I study the girl and wonder if she's his type. Long black hair down to her waist, so straight, it looks like it has been ironed. Her hair is prettier than mine. Shiny, fluid like water. Her body is thinner, too. I bet she can put any outfit on and make it look good. She looks so effortless, talking to Ezra, as if her life has absolutely no complications and she's just drifting from one fun experience to another.

I take a sip of my drink to wash down my jealousy. My mistrust.

To my knowledge, Ezra has not kissed another woman since that night a month ago. When he begged me—begged, begged, begged me—to give him one more chance, he vowed he'd never ever hurt me again like that.

Because it had nearly destroyed me.

His phone buzzes; he left it on the table next to me, and I find my eyes wandering to it. Then widening when I see a text.

Bianca: U have the sexiest eyes I've ever seen.

Bianca? Who the hell is Bianca?

I glare at Ezra, who is full-on flirting with the woman now. Right in front of me. Too bad for him I know the password to his phone.

Yep. Look at me. I'm that girlfriend, dammit.

I pull open the text and feel my stomach drop. They've been texting for days. The words sexy, gorgeous, cute laugh, when can we meet *all pop out at me. I continue reading. Looks like they met in a club two weeks ago and have been texting ever since, talking about getting together soon.*

Anger pierces my heart. It isn't the first time some random woman has texted him, but I can't believe Ezra is doing it again after I confronted him about it before, and I can't believe he has the audacity to make plans to meet up with this Bianca after swearing his faithfulness to me. How naive I'd been.

Cheating is like an iceberg. Cheaters are skilled at hiding their deception below the waterline; if you see anything, it's likely just the tip of how deeply their betrayal actually runs.

His betrayal has turned me into a person I hate—a jealous, mistrustful woman. I've become that girl who watches her boyfriend at parties like he's on some visual leash. Dissecting his every move and word for any clues he might stray.

I'm all for giving people second chances and the benefit of the doubt, but I'm also not a moron, and when my boyfriend is repeatedly behaving inappropriately with other women, it's time to pull the plug.

I walk up to Ezra.

"I need to talk to you," I say.

"Babe"—he looks between me and Ms. Gorgeous—"I'm in the middle of a conversation."

"It's important," I say.

Ezra flashes an annoyed look at me, and his annoyance grows when the gorgeous girl walks away.

He wraps his hand under my elbow and guides me to the other side of the room, where no one can hear him.

"He grabbed your arm?" Shane's jaw ticced.

"The word *grabbed* implies something threatening."

"Did his grasp bother you?" he challenged.

"Of course."

Shane's stare bores a hole through my skull.

"Then, that's all that matters. He's lucky I wasn't there that night."

I wasn't sure what to say to that, so I continued with what happened.

"You embarrassed me," Ezra snaps.

"I can't do this anymore," I say.

Ezra releases my elbow and searches the room for the hot girl. "Do what?"

"This. Us. I can't be with you anymore."

Ezra's eyes snap back to mine, and he flicks his fingernails at his sides, like he does when he's angry.

"The hell are you talking about?"

"I thought I could get past your infidelity, but I can't. Especially when you keep doing it."

"My infidelity? Are you fucking kidding me? I didn't sleep with anyone, Willow. I kissed one girl. Kissed—that's it. And what the hell do you mean, keep doing it?"

"Who's Bianca?"

His eyes narrow. "You went through my phone?"

"She says she's planning to meet up with you."

"I can't control what people send me."

"You can control talking to other women behind my back. Inappropriately."

"So, I can't talk to anyone if they're female?"

He's goading me into a fight, where he'll try to break down my every objection until he gaslights me into thinking I'm overreacting. Just like he did last time.

"I'm not doing the back-and-forth game. I don't trust you anymore, and when there's no trust, there's no relationship."

Ezra glares at me. I assume he's going to try to talk me into staying with him again, but unlike last time, he must see the unwavering decision in my eyes because he looks furious. He licks his bottom lip and eventually shakes his head as he looks me up and down in disgust.

"You're going to regret this."

"He threatened you?"

"I took it more as his ego talking—like I'd let the best catch in the sea slip away. But looking back on it now, maybe I gave him too much benefit of the doubt. Especially after seeing how he behaved with that vase."

Shane massaged his hands and stared at my elbow with a look of vengeance.

"I pride myself on maintaining control. Carrying the badge means I can't give in to the rage I sometimes feel." Shane snapped his eyes to mine, holding them for several heartbeats before continuing, "But last night, when I heard that crash? When I realized he'd thrown that vase that could have hit you?" Shane cracked his knuckles. "You have no idea what I almost did to him."

What if there was another risk to Shane's career that I hadn't considered? What if Ezra did something stupid again, and next time, Shane crossed a line that police are not allowed to cross?

Surely, it was arrogant of me to worry that might happen. Shane had been a cop for years, probably had complete self-control over his emotions.

Right?

"I don't want to cause you any problems," I said.

To this, Shane's eyes once again met mine, only this time, the anger in them melted as he set his hand on the table, a mere inch from my own. I stared at his hand, wondering what it'd feel like on my body, twisting through my hair, touching me in places I'd only fantasized about. As if sensing my desire, Shane allowed his thumb to graze my pinkie, surging an electric current up my arm.

In a low rumble, he said, "Willow, you're the farthest thing from a problem."

My heart responded to his words, to his caress, stretching through my chest toward him, longing for him to slide his fingers up my arm and stroke my cheek instead of my hand.

Based on the parting of his lips as his blue eyes gripped mine, he wanted to do more than just touch my hand, too.

"You give people too many chances." Shane's voice was tender. "Giving that asshole ex another chance after how he treated you. Makin' the effort over and over with your family when even I can see they're not treating you right. As Maya Angelou once said, 'When people show you who they are, believe them.' Think you need to heed her warning."

My stomach stilled under the adoration of his gaze, the thrilling shiver from his fingertips skating across the back of my hand. The touch was so simple yet incredibly intimate.

"You deserve better than that, Willow. You deserve to be somebody's first priority."

He had no clue what his words did to my soul, extinguishing the flames of hurt that I never believed would be snuffed out. I'd assumed the only person capable of healing those wounds was the one who'd inflicted the blisters. But Shane was the salve to my burns, soaking the pain away in his tenderness.

He made me feel like the person I never knew I could be despite not having known him very long.

Some people come into your life like a whisper of a breeze. Others a tornado, their impact immediate and severe.

It felt like my heartbeat was dancing to his movements as he gently rolled my hand over and began tracing little circles on my palm.

"Why do you think that is?" Shane asked. "You givin' too many chances?"

This was a question I had asked myself countless times throughout the years. It took me several seconds to emerge from this sensual fog to offer the hypothesis I had come up with—one I hadn't shared with anyone else.

"Growing up, when my mom was around, she could be so much fun. She'd keep me home from school just so we could make chocolate chip cookies together and watch a movie marathon. She would laugh and put on music so we could dance on the coffee table. I think she was trying to make up for the other times, because in those other times, her grief was like a flu that would affect her every so often, and when it did, she would get sadder and sadder, and it would snowball. When it got really bad, she'd leave and disappear for days."

My vision blurred with the memory.

· · ·

I'm seven, and I'm clutching my teddy bear—the one Daddy got for me before he died. On accident, I had cut Teddy's foot open, but Mommy had stitched it up with purple string. I liked the purple string; it shows you don't have to give up on something you love just because it isn't perfect.

Like Mom. She's not perfect, but I'll never give up on her.

I stare out the window. I have to go to the bathroom so bad, but I only leave my post when I can't hold it anymore. She's been gone six days, and she's never been gone that long, and I feel like the only way her car will come down the road is if I'm watching for it.

I watch the rain wash across the asphalt like it's cleaning a path for Mommy. Headlights appear. I tense and stare at the car coming toward our house.

My heart beats even harder as the lights get brighter and the windshield wipers shove aside the rain. It's as if the car is racing toward me so Mommy can jump out and run into my arms, promising she'll never leave me again.

But the car keeps going.

And my heart sinks even deeper.

I wonder how far it can drop before it stops beating.

"She's not coming back," Hayley snarls.

"Yes, she is!" I say through my tears, even though inside, I'm terrified it's not true. I clutch Teddy tighter. "She's coming back," I whisper. "She's coming back."

"I never gave up hope that she'd return. Giving up hope meant giving up on Mom; it meant giving up on the person I wanted in my life more than anyone. And even if she wasn't treating me the way a child should be treated, I still wanted her. I guess a child still wants her parent, no matter what." I did, at least.

Some people dream of wealth. Some power. I dreamed of love—the unconditional and everlasting love of a mother. Many have it. Some even take it for granted, but for those of us that have never experienced it, its absence becomes a crater in our chest that we'd give anything to fill.

For the first time, the empty ache had started to dull, which shocked me because it was Shane's tenderness trickling into the chasm rather than my mother's—whose everlasting affection still eluded me.

Sometimes, I felt ungrateful for being hurt because I was lucky. I wasn't abused or abandoned forever, and compared to my sister, I'd come out virtually unscathed by it all. But I guess it was only human to long for a mother's love.

"The void in my life without her would've been bigger than the void she created when she'd withdraw. So, I always waited," I said. "And when her car would come rolling back up that driveway, I would rush out the door and jump into her arms. Convinced that if I had given up on her, she would've never come back."

And thus began my pattern of holding out hope that people and circumstances would always get better if you held on long enough. Every time my mother returned, that belief further solidified into cement.

"Plus, after losing my dad, I guess I don't want to risk losing anyone else," I admitted.

"Sounds like your reason for holding on to things for too long is a fear of abandonment," Shane said. "Your dad died. Your mom emotionally abandoned you. Your sister's addiction probably makes you feel abandoned by her, too, choosing substances over you."

I hated that my eyes shimmered. I hated that I'd always wondered if it was me—the reason I wasn't close to my family. That I was lacking somehow. I mean, what kind of person gets rejected by their own family? But then I'd chide myself for having woe-is-me thoughts like that.

"So, you keep making the effort," he continued. "Settling for unhealthy relationships and situations where you deserve better."

I deserve better. I didn't want my eyes to sting even harder because I had a lot of good things in my life, and I refused to let a few less than ideal variables define me. Yet...a soft spot in my heart clung to his declaration and encouraged me to change my ways.

I wish I could say I'd broken up with Ezra because I'd decided to no longer give people too many chances, but the truth was, I'd broken up with him because his lies and betrayals made me fall out of love with him.

"I talked to people over the years about my dad." Shane cleared his throat and shifted in his seat. "Guy that shot him had been a problem for months."

I blinked, taken off guard by the abrupt change in conversation. Confused as to how it connected to what we just talked about.

Shane shifted his fingertips to the back of my hand again, rubbing soft circles over my knuckles as he stared so deeply into my eyes, it felt like he was looking into the hidden crevices of my soul.

"Cops were frequently called on him for a bunch of minor infractions," Shane said. "But from what I've been told, while the rest of the cops became fed up with the guy, my dad saw a desperate guy who was at a fork in the road."

Shane added two more fingers to circle the skin on my hand. I wanted to close my eyes and savor his touch; it affected me so much, it was all I wanted. Like a warm blanket after being pulled from those frigid waters, offering a solace I've never felt from anyone before.

"After years on the force, my dad saw what he believed was a pattern with career criminals, putting them into two buckets—those that had been causin' problems since they were born and those that came to a crossroads in their lives and caused problems after."

His fingers drifted up to my wrist, making it harder to focus on his words.

"I guess a mass school shooting that took place in his hometown heavily influenced my dad. He wasn't a part of it, but hearin' about the twenty-year-old that stormed into that elementary school and started shooting really got to him. And while there's a lot of factors that contributed to it," Shane continued, "my dad fixated on one in particular—how preventable it was. Guess the guy that did it had a bunch of red flags in the days leading up to it that should have been caught. But the guy hadn't shown violent tendencies until those last six months of his life. Evidently, a string of bad stuff happened to him, and when he started becomin' bitter, everyone in his life just walked away. His life continued to spiral, and he got angrier and angrier with the world until he finally..."

Got a gun and killed innocent children.

Shane sighed heavily and pinched the bridge of his nose. "Point being, my dad was convinced that if someone had shown some compassion to that guy when all that shit was goin' down, maybe he wouldn't have turned into a mass murderer. Maybe those kids wouldn't have died."

If I put myself in his dad's shoes, if I swore an oath to protect people, I'm sure I'd be looking for ways to protect people *before* they committed a crime, too.

"So, this guy loses his job and starts gettin' into trouble. Earns himself a few nights in jail on several occasions. Dad sees a guy down on his luck and heading toward a psychological cliff, so to speak, and tries to talk to him. Tries to help redirect his anger, provides him with support groups, things like that."

Shane's jaw tensed.

"My dad picked the wrong guy to try to help. Because the next time he gets called in, this guy was gettin' evicted. My dad went in to try to talk to him, and that's how he ended up getting shot. Tryin' to give someone a second chance that was never going to change."

My stomach rolled. No wonder he was so cynical about what people were capable of. No wonder he believed once someone squandered their second chance, you should walk away.

"I know you want to see the best in people, Willow. But always trying to see the best in people can sometimes cost you everything."

I wanted to believe that he was wrong, that the worst wasn't yet to come...

16

"Mind if we stop in my apartment first?" Shane asked. After the heavy conversation at the diner, we'd gotten my new cell phone and had just walked into our apartment complex. "I'd like to get a notebook for this."

"Sure." I stood behind him as he unlocked his door, opened it, and switched the light on as I stepped in.

Aside from the couple of minutes I had been in his apartment when he thought my place had been broken into, I had never been inside his place.

The inside was absolutely pristine and so free of clutter, it was almost bare. A black leather couch faced a flat screen TV, but there were no decorations hanging on the walls, no plants. Nothing to give the place life, really. The space smelled like Shane's cologne—an ocean scent I wished I could bathe in.

"I'll be right back."

Shane disappeared into his bedroom while I stepped into his kitchen, curious about his morning routine. This whole time, he'd been in here, living in an apartment with an identical layout to mine. The gray countertop contained a blender, a coffeepot, and a compact air fryer. All of them black, all of them so clean, they could pass for being brand-new, straight out of the box.

"Okay." Shane reappeared with a notebook, Post-it Notes, and pens of various colors.

"I would've assumed you would take notes electronically," I said.

"I do. But I like a visual map when I'm lookin' into stuff. Helps me think."

How eerie that, soon, those pages would be filled with details about my life, the people in it, and any issues I'd had with anyone.

My throat ran dry, and I had to tell myself again that this needed to be done. Because each time we stepped closer to this, I wanted to run away.

Shane must have read the look on my face because he set the materials down and stepped closer to me, putting his hands on my shoulders, as if knowing his touch sedated my anxiety.

"This won't be easy, but I'll be here with you every step of the way. Okay?"

I genuinely hoped we'd discover no one had done this to me because I wasn't sure how to move forward in my life if I'd let a killer into my inner circle. How do you ever trust another human being again? How do you ever feel safe again? How long do you have to be with someone before you let down your guard, if you ever do?

"I have one question before we start," I said. "Our goal is to find a good enough clue so De Luca can kick this up to detectives, right?"

Shane released my shoulders. "I'm worried De Luca is going to drop the ball on this one—either to spite me or out of sheer laziness or possibly both. I don't trust him to take the situation seriously."

"But if we find something big enough to show De Luca, won't he realize you've been poking around the case?"

"You let me worry about that."

"No. That guy is just looking for a reason to get you into trouble, and I'm not going to hand it to him on a silver platter."

Shane grabbed the supplies.

"How are we going to hand this over to De Luca without him throwing you under the bus?" I repeated.

But I could see Shane wasn't worried about that; all he cared about was getting to the bottom of whatever happened to me, so he was putting his blinders on, allowing his emotions to get the better of him.

I squared my shoulders. "I'll turn it over to him," I said.

"What?"

"We find something? I'm turning it over to him. And I'm leaving you out of it. Nonnegotiable."

Shane's face tightened. "Fine. Whatever. Now, can we get on with it?"

I took a deep breath and nodded.

"Good. I was going to suggest—"

Shane was interrupted with three knocks that vibrated his front door.

"I know you're home," a female voice said.

Shane dropped his head. Tossed the papers back onto the counter.

"Your car is out front, so whatever case you've been buried in can wait," she shouted.

Shane cocked his head back with a look that said, *You've got to be kidding me.*

Which immediately piqued my interest. I'd never seen a woman at his apartment before.

Shane grumbled his way to the front door and opened it.

"Three voice mails, no answer," she said. "I brought beer. Thought you could use a break from—" Her voice halted, and her eyes widened when her gaze landed on me.

I recognized that face. I had met her once before when I went out with some of my girlfriends for a quick drink. Though I couldn't remember her name.

"Hell hath frozen over." She grinned and slammed a six-pack into Shane's chest so hard, the bottles clanked as she marched past him, looking me up and down with her hands on her hips. "I've met you before," she realized. "You're Emily's friend."

"Willow." I reached my hand out to shake hers.

She shook it right away. Looked so damn gleeful, I wondered if she was mistaking me for someone else.

"Fallon." Shane's voice was clipped. "If you don't mind."

She motioned toward me, her smile somehow growing even wider. "You have a girl in your apartment!"

Shane rolled his eyes.

"When did this happen?" she asked.

"Fallon——"

"Shane has never once had a girl over," she said. "He's like Batman. Keeps his place all locked up and secretive. But you ..." she said, looking me up and down again. "You breached his moat."

"For the love of..." Shane set the six-pack of beer down onto the counter with more force than necessary.

I bit back a smile.

"Okay." Fallon looped her arm through my elbow and guided me to the couch, grabbing two of the beers on her way. "Tell. Me. Everything."

She opened the beers and handed me one.

"Fallon, we're workin' a case."

She scrunched her eyebrows. "I don't remember Emily telling me you're a cop. Are you a cop?"

"No."

She flashed a smirk at Shane. "Nice try. Okay, so when did you two meet?"

I took a sip of the beer, which prickled my throat.

"She's my neighbor," Shane said. "If you don't mind, we have a lot of work——"

"If you think I'm going to leave without asking questions, you're insane." She waved a dismissive hand at him without even looking his way.

I had to bite my lip harder to contain my amusement.

Meanwhile, Shane snapped the top off a beer and took a huge sip.

"Are you his ex-girlfriend?" My cheeks immediately warmed, embarrassed that the question had popped out of my mouth.

Fallon cocked her head back and laughed. "God, no. He's like my brother. I'm married." She wiggled her ring finger at me. "I've been friends with Shane forever, and in all these years I've known him, he's never had a girlfriend."

He hadn't? Never?

A rush of unease swept through me.

He was handsome, sexy as F. Successful. Caring. Kind. How would a guy like that never have a girlfriend?

He didn't strike me as a player with a rotating door of one-night stands, but maybe I'd misjudged him? And had missed all the girls coming and going? He didn't strike me as preferring men with the chemistry I'd felt between us, either.

"I have *never* seen him with a woman. He has never let anyone in his apartment before. Even to 'work a case.' " She used air quotes on that last part.

He didn't? Not even once, not even for a minute?

"He was just grabbing a notebook."

"Girl, this is his Batcave. No one is allowed in. No one. Only reason I get in is because—"

"You basically break and enter," Shane interrupted, annoyance dripping from his words.

"He loves me so much. Now, enough about me. Let's talk all about Willow."

"You're makin' her uncomfortable," Shane chided.

"Am I?" She legit looked worried.

I bit my lip and shook my head. Truthfully? I loved this girl and her easy banter with Shane.

"See? Stop being all alpha protective of her and tell me all about your girlfriend."

"She's not my girlfriend."

"Don't let him get under your skin. He gets all grumpy when he's tired. I can tell he likes you A LOT just by the way he looks at you."

"Fallon."

"I've never seen him look at anyone like he looks at you."

"Fallon!" Shane yanked the beer from her hand and motioned toward the front door. "If you don't mind."

She stood up, and Shane took steps toward her, physically encouraging her to back up to the front door.

"But I haven't even gotten her number yet!" Fallon said.

"Goodbye, Fallon." Shane opened the door.

She stepped out into the hallway. "But I want to invite her out for a drink!"

"Goodbye, Fallon." Shane shut the door.

"You know, she might not appreciate your broody mood, Shane!" Fallon yelled from the other side.

Shane rolled his eyes and walked over to me, rubbing the back of his neck. "I'm sorry about that."

"She's nice."

"She can be"—Shane cocked his head—"a bit headstrong."

"She's cheery."

"Didn't use to be," he said, frowning at the door. "Some days, I miss her old moody personality."

"What changed?"

To this, Shane met my eyes. "She fell in love."

Something swirled around inside my chest.

"How long have you guys been friends?"

"Since we were kids." Shane picked up the notebook, the pens, and the Post-it Notes and set them down on the coffee table.

When he sat on the couch next to me, his leg brushed mine.

Even through fabric, the heat of his skin slowed the oxygen flow to my lungs.

This energy between us was always there, lingering like a flammable gas in the air around us, and when he touched me, it would ignite, the explosion rendering me breathless.

Shane must've felt it, too, because his sapphire eyes met mine and lingered as his mouth parted, his tongue swiping along his lower lip. As the seconds ticked on, Shane looked down to my mouth, his breathing quickening, as if wondering what it would be like to cave in to his desires and pull my mouth to his.

The painful furrow of his eyebrows looked like fighting his desires was hard, doing what he believed was the right thing by not crossing this line with the subject of an open case. And based on how long he lingered like that, it seemed like it took every ounce of his willpower to shift his leg away from mine and recalibrate.

"What I'd like to do," he started, his voice a little shaky, "is make a list of the people closest to you. We'll start with them and go from there."

"The people closest to me?"

"Statistically, most murders are committed by somebody close to that person. What I'd like to do is discuss your relationship with each of these people and understand what the events were leading up to Saturday night. Any arguments, or disagreements, or tension, that sort of thing."

All the saliva evaporated in my mouth, leaving it a desert that stretched down my throat. My heartbeat quickened, and that hamburger that I had eaten no longer agreed with my stomach.

"I don't know if I can do this." Agreeing to it was one thing. Lifting up the hood on all of the relationships closest to me and looking for broken parts was an entirely different situation. This was like giving someone cancer drugs just to be on the safe side when those drugs cause catastrophic side effects.

"I'll be with you through this." Shane's voice was tender, his expression encouraging.

After a few moments, I hesitantly nodded. "Okay. Let's get this over with."

"List the people closest to you."

I took a sip of encouragement from my beer.

"Start with family," Shane suggested.

"I talk to my mom the most, though we're not as close as most families. My sister and I talk off and on, but not nearly as often as I'd like. I see my grandma at family get-togethers."

Shane nodded. He wrote *Mother: Laura* and *Sister: Hayley* on two separate Post-it Notes and placed them on the front page of his notebook.

It was jarring to see it in ink like that, listing them as official suspects in his research. Mom. Hayley.

"Friends. Boyfriends. Coworkers?"

"Ezra was in my inner circle but hasn't been for a while."

Ezra's name was already on a Post-it before I finished my sentence, pinned to the top of his page.

"My best friend is Emily. Second best friends would be Tracey and Amelia."

"Any issues with Emily?"

"No."

"Tracey?"

"No."

"Tell me about Amelia."

Why'd he ask it that way? Different from the way he'd asked about Tracey and Emily?

"Amelia?"

Shane held my gaze firmly.

"Um...we became friends a couple of years ago and our families know each other."

"She looked upset in that café."

"I think she was offended we'd be looking at people in my life as possible suspects."

"You told her we were?"

"No. I told them I fell off the bridge and it was being investigated."

Shane sat back, rolling the pen between his fingers. "Why do you think she would get upset?"

"I suppose because it's offensive to accuse anybody of something that heinous."

Shane didn't look convinced. He scrubbed his jaw, looking down silently.

"You're keeping something from me," I accused. "You asked about Amelia at the café, too."

Shane's eyes snapped to mine, his silence a loud confirmation.

"Condition number two," I reminded him. "We work this together. You tell me what you know."

"I don't know anything for certain," Shane hedged.

"Semantics. Spit it out."

"I'll have a lot of thoughts cross my mind throughout this investigation. Some of them may lead to something, but most of them won't. You sure you want me to share them with you?"

"You already know the answer to that."

Resigned, Shane offered up a slow nod of his head. Like, *Okay. Don't say I didn't warn you.* "Did you notice those scratches on her arms?"

I blinked. "Amelia's?"

Shane nodded again, measuring my reaction.

"What scratches?"

He cleared his throat. "She rolled up her sleeves for a second. Only a second," Shane clarified, as if that were an important clue. "And when she did, she had fresh scratches on her forearms that looked to be consistent with fingernails."

I didn't see them. But then I'd been so distracted, worrying about upsetting everyone, I hadn't been paying attention.

"She mention where she got them?"

I shook my head.

"Okay. That's a question we need to ask."

Amelia had acted shady that day, but, "She'd have no reason to hurt me."

"It's probably nothin'." But Shane's eyes gave away his deceit. He put her name on a Post-it Note and pinned it to the first page of his notebook.

"Okay. Let's talk about your job."

I felt like I was in a tornado, a fresh batch of debris slapping my face with each rotation.

"My company did a fresh round of layoffs last month."

"Anyone seem upset?"

"Everyone is upset when they get laid off."

"Any chance I could get a list of those names?"

"Not without a warrant; it's confidential company information. I'd get fired for giving it to you."

Shane pursed his lips. "Okay, we'll start with people closest to you first. See where that takes us."

No matter how many times we talked about this, I couldn't get past the shock of it. Would it ever go away?

"You really think someone did this to me," I said.

"I do."

"What makes you so sure?"

Shane twisted the pen in his hand. Leaned back against the couch and spoke in a cautious tone. "I visited the bridge today."

Okay, I didn't expect that.

"That bridge is *not* easy to fall off of. I can't imagine a scenario where someone fell over it by accident. Even if someone was being extremely reckless."

Today, I had the whole day off, and I could've gone to the bridge to look around. Maybe the doctor was wrong. Maybe seeing it would spark some kind of memory.

"I'd like to see the bridge."

Shane blinked. "Now?"

"Now."

17

The rust-colored bridge stretched across the Chicago River for the length of thirty cars, connecting a road that snaked between sixty-story buildings whose windows twinkled against the fabric of night. It was hard to imagine something this beautiful playing a role in the grim disaster that unfolded on an evening just like this one.

Tonight, orange construction cones blocked vehicles from entering the bridge, and based on the guy wearing a fluorescent-orange vest, waving his hands at us, pedestrians weren't supposed to be on it either.

"You can't go on there," he said as Shane and I approached it.

Shane flashed his badge. "Police business. We won't be long. Bridge safe to walk on?"

The guy working the bridge looked annoyed as he nodded.

"Were you working here Saturday night?" Shane asked.

The guy shook his head. "No, sir. This job doesn't have activity Friday or Saturday nights."

I guess that would explain the lack of eyewitnesses, but it didn't explain why I would wind up on a bridge that I wasn't supposed to be on.

"We won't be long," Shane said.

As soon as my first step landed on the narrow walking path that flanked the road, my throat went dry. Walking along the same path I must have taken on Saturday, each haunting clink of my footsteps seemed to echo off the surrounding skyscrapers, like a clock ticking down to an ominous end. Adrenaline flooded my limbs, weakening my stomach, as if my body's cells remembered what I could not—how this path had almost cost me my life.

Once we reached the center, Shane positioned himself next to me, but remained silent, as if he knew I needed the solitude of taking this all in.

A scattering of ice sheathed the gray water, which sat stagnant, like it was too cold to move.

I couldn't believe I had fallen into that water. Looking at it now, I was certain that if Shane had not jumped in and saved me, I would not have made it.

I glanced toward the bank of the river, to a void in the snow. *That must be where Shane pulled me out.* The bravery and selflessness it would have required to jump into the dark, deadly waters made my eyes sting.

"You can see what I'm talkin' about." Shane put his hand on the bridge's railing. Which stood up to our chest, and between it and the ground, a crisscross of beams inches apart. Not enough room for a tiny child to fall through, let alone an adult. And the height of the railing made it impossible for someone to get over it without intent. Further, the top of the railing was a cylinder shape, not flat, which made the idea that I'd been recklessly trying to walk on it even more implausible. Also, this was *not* one of those bridges that opened when big boats crossed, so my thought that maybe it'd opened wide enough to fall through was also shot to hell.

"You're right," I said. "There's no way I could've fallen off by accident."

I didn't want this revelation to breach my chest, but it gusted through me like a typhoon, ravaging my fragile insides. My hands became clammy, and my legs wobbled—all while my heart rebelled against it, beating so quickly, it felt like it was spasming.

"I think I'm going to be sick," I said.

"Sit down," Shane commanded.

I did as he asked, the iron's coolness breaching the seat of my jeans, as Shane squatted next to me, putting a calming hand on my shoulder.

"I agreed to work with you on this, but deep down, I didn't truly believe that someone had done this to me."

"I know."

"But someone must have."

"Yes."

"You think they meant for me to die? Not just get hurt?" Even I knew how ridiculous that sounded, but when one faces a reality so shocking and heartbreaking that it will blow up your entire world, one grasps on to straws.

"You don't throw someone off a bridge into deadly, icy water unless you're trying to kill them."

I will not cry. I survived, and I am okay. Just because I don't feel like it, I am. I am okay. I'm okay.

"De Luca visited the bridge," I said. "If he still doesn't think this is foul play, he must think I tried to kill myself."

But I wouldn't have done that, certainly not like this.

Shane sucked the energy from around him to feed his swelling anger while I focused on getting my erratic breathing under control. After a couple of minutes, I stood up, squared my shoulders, and looked decisively into Shane's cobalt eyes as he stood, too.

Strange that I didn't feel embarrassed that Shane had witnessed my moment of weakness with that mild panic attack. With anyone else, I would have because it made me look vulnerable, but with Shane, I felt safe enough to expose the most flawed parts of myself.

"I want to find out who did this." I gritted my teeth. "And I want to put them in prison."

With a gust of wind ravaging his hair, Shane glared at the railing.

"I'm going to find who did this," he said in a low, even tone. "And make them pay."

He stilled in the hollow space of vengeance before placing his hand on my lower back. "Come on. I should get you home before you freeze to death."

The walk back to our apartment complex was poisoned with the drug of truth. I could no longer stay high in the safety of denial, crashing down into the treacherous reality of having been attacked.

When we reached my apartment, Shane looked into each of my rooms, each closet, even the bathtub, before returning to the front door—prepared to give me the time I needed to process this.

He studied me, and even the trained detective in him couldn't hide his worry. "You okay?"

No. It feels like my entire existence has crumbled around me. Who would've done this? Who did I invite into my life that hated me so much, they threw me off that bridge to die? Like an unwanted, disposable piece of trash.

And most terrifyingly, what if Shane was right? What if they might try again?

"I will be," I lied.

Shane's lips pursed. "I'd like to look at your cell phone records. Look at who you spoke to that day."

I nodded, the shock of it all casting me in a daze.

"Can you log in to your account with your cell phone carrier for me? I can start to look over that tonight."

I took his outstretched phone, opened my carrier's web page, logged in, and handed it back to him.

Shane studied me for several seconds, his chest swelling before he finally released a sigh. "You sure you won't let me stay on the couch?"

Part of me wanted him to—the part that felt afraid. But fear was weak, and I needed to stay strong if I had any hope of enduring this.

"I need to process everything."

Shane took a step closer to me.

"You were strong tonight. Going to that bridge could not have been easy."

"I don't feel strong. I feel stupid and naive." And so fragile, it felt like all of my hope, my happiness in life, drowned in that river.

He slowly brought his hand up and cupped my cheek. In his embrace, my fear melted away, surrendering to his calming force. I wished he'd hold my face forever.

"You're not naive. No one can accept that someone tried to kill them without resistance. You're a kindhearted person who sees the best in people, Willow. It's one of your best features that made me start to—" He stopped himself, and I sensed whatever he almost said would've potentially changed things between us. But he kept whatever it was bottled up and settled for stroking my cheek with his thumb as he whispered, "Don't let the asshole that did this take that from you."

I focused on the warmth of his hand, the only part of my body not screaming in hurt. His words washed over me like a sedative, silencing the pain radiating through my bones.

"Thank you," I said. "For forcing me to see the truth."

His gaze turned severe. "How could anyone ever want to hurt you?"

My stomach came alive with butterflies. I didn't think I'd be able to feel anything other than shock and hurt right now, but Shane had a way of making me feel things I never thought possible.

His gaze flickered to my mouth, igniting that energy around us once more.

How could I feel so unlucky, having let someone in my life that wanted to kill me, and yet so lucky, having found Shane? A person who made me feel important, wanted, desired, and like I mattered more to him than anything else.

Shane's chest rose and fell quicker, a fresh look of torment ripping across his features as he parted his lips.

I wanted him to kiss me. I wanted to feel his words and compassion rush down my throat and into my chest. I wanted every part of him, his body and mind, to escape into passion, to feel him on top of me.

He lowered his face closer to mine. One agonizing inch at a time, exploding my greedy need with every beat of my heart. I stared at his mouth drawing painfully closer to my own, and then, so gently that it was almost a whisper, Shane pressed his lips to mine.

Oh my God.

I had imagined this moment many times after Shane had moved in next door, but this was better than any of those daydreams. His lips were warm and gentle as they opened slightly and took my upper lip between them. He stepped closer to me and allowed his mouth to open wider, just enough for his tongue to breach our lips and connect with my own.

He pulled my head to get more of me, and I grabbed his shoulders, pressing my chest against his. I groaned as his tongue connected with mine again. And again.

I wanted him to touch my body, to get carried away with this current of passion.

But suddenly, Shane pulled back like my kiss had burned him.

His eyes were shut tightly, his jaw set in tension. If I didn't know better, I would think he looked angry. Especially since his hands were now at his sides, balled into fists.

My heart spasmed at the look on his face.

"I should let you rest," Shane said.

I didn't know what just happened, but it left me frozen in the ice of confusion and hurt. I knew he probably didn't want to get involved with the subject of an active investigation, but his reaction seemed to go deeper than that...

"Good night, Willow." He didn't look at me as he walked out the door and shut it behind him.

"Lock the door," he insisted from the other side.

It took me a minute to move my feet. I dragged them through the anchor of fresh pain until I reached the dead bolt and latched it shut.

Only once it latched did Shane's apartment door open and close.

The wall separating us felt like it just got thicker.

My whole life, I had felt rejected by my family—be it emotionally or in favor of substances. With Shane, I had only felt acceptance and compassion and even desire. Until now.

Now, I felt rejected by him, too. And with him, I never saw it coming.

I lay on my bed and stared at my ceiling, trying to convince myself he wasn't rejecting me; he was just trying to maintain a professional relationship until the case was closed. When that didn't work, I tried to convince myself that my growing feelings for him weren't strong enough to warrant this mental purgatory. And when that didn't work, I decided to try and force my mind into escaping turmoil.

Researching what it would take to open up my own company seemed like the perfect distraction. First, I searched online for what legal steps were required to set up a small business and what the legal and tax implications were to do so. I took notes on the different corporations you could form, how to handle the funding and money, and what paperwork needed to be filled out.

And then I opened up an online form and filed to open an LLC.

I smiled at having taken the first official step forward in my dream.

But when my escapism ended, my mind went right back to spinning with thoughts of Shane, so I decided to still it with a book.

I retrieved the current novel I was reading from my nightstand, but within the first two paragraphs, I was confused. Some character named Quincy was ranting to the main character. Only...Quincy hadn't been introduced yet.

I flipped back a couple of pages, thinking maybe the author did this surprise on purpose, but no. His name peppered the pages of the last chapter and the one before it.

Come to think of it, I distinctly remembered leaving off on chapter fifteen, when the main character had just adopted that cat—who reminded me of Snowflake—yet my bookmark was now on chapter twenty.

Maybe I'd read the next five chapters and forgot? Maybe this was part of my short-term memory loss. But so far, my short-term memory loss was confined to the bridge incident. Not other random details, like completely forgetting portions of a book I had read.

Or moving my toothbrush...

But then I didn't remember leaving my apartment that night either, so there were at least a few minutes before the bridge I didn't remember. If not more. Maybe I'd been reading this book before I left?

Yeah, I tried to tell myself.

That's what it had to be.

Right?

18

"And he just pulled away? Just like that?" Emily asked.

I nodded.

Emily made her *yikes* face.

I knew it. I knew I wasn't overreacting.

I nursed my glass of wine while confiding in my best friend as we sat at a secluded table in a pub three blocks from my apartment, where I'd met Emily after work. The place was dark—leather seats and black walls—with somber music playing in the background that matched my current mood. After what happened last night with Shane, I needed somebody to help sift through this confusion because I didn't trust myself to read into this situation with Shane correctly. After all, my mind was mostly churning through the bridge incident. My heart, on the other hand, wouldn't stop obsessing over what happened between us.

"You think he regrets it," I deduced.

Emily took a sip of her drink, which was not a good sign. She only did that when she was trying to be very careful with her words, and she was only very careful with her words when she was trying not to hurt somebody's feelings.

My heart put a seat belt on and said, *Buckle up; this is going to suck.*

"He's a protective alpha, right? Typical cop that's out there, trying to protect everybody? Maybe he sees you as a damsel in distress and got carried away."

Ouch. My heart just crashed into the windshield.

I didn't want anyone to see me as a damsel in distress, and I didn't want Shane to have some kind of hero complex where he felt the need to rescue me. *Again.*

Emily must've read the pain in my face because she quickly tried to backpedal.

"Maybe you're wrong," she said. "Maybe it's all in your head. I mean, boys can be totally moody sometimes. Maybe he just doesn't want to get involved with you while he's investigating the case?"

"A friend of his—you've met Fallon before, right?"

Emily nodded. To the best of my recollection, she'd only met her once or twice as part of a broader friend group.

"She showed up unexpectedly and admitted that he's never had a girlfriend. He's never even had a girl over to his apartment before."

To this, Emily raised her sculpted eyebrows. "Never?"

"Never."

Another sip of wine. Another look, like she was choosing her words carefully. "Any idea why?"

"Nope."

"Did you see him this morning?"

"He stopped by briefly before he left for work to let me know he was leaving."

"What did he say?"

"Nothing. He was running late, so he had to hurry."

"So, he was rushed. Possibly too rushed to talk about what happened," she mused.

Emily took two slow sips of her drink and then set it down.

"Okay, here's what you do," Emily said. "The next time you see him, he'll either pick up the romance where it left off or he won't. If he acts like it didn't happen or if he acts weird at all with no explanation, then you know that, in his eyes, the kiss was a mistake, and he doesn't want to take it any further."

My heart lodged in my chest. Why did I care this much? It shouldn't hurt this bad, the prospect of him not wanting me.

If he didn't, where would we go from here? As much as I appreciated him investigating my fall, how uncomfortable would it be to work with a guy that I was completely into if he rejected me like that?

"Okay." I nodded. "I'll feel him out the next time I see him."

I could do this. I had to do this.

A waiter interrupted us, offering a refill we didn't need yet. When he was gone, I geared up for the second question I'd come here to ask Emily.

"What was up with you the other day?"

Emily shifted in her seat. "What do you mean?"

"You were staring at Amelia like something was bothering you."

Did she notice the scratches, too? I wouldn't bring them up myself—doing so would imply I was suspicious of Amelia, and it didn't feel concrete enough to make those kinds of implied accusations.

Emily looked like she considered denying it, probably not wanting to add to my worry.

"I'm sure it's nothing."

"What's nothing?"

A pause.

"Amelia. She's been acting off lately. I thought it was weird how perturbed she'd been that Ezra had sent you flowers and how defensive she was being. And then, ever since we met you that day, she's been up in arms that Ezra might get blamed for your fall."

"She's worried about *Ezra*? Why?"

Emily shrugged. "I don't know. When I asked her about it, she bit my head off."

I frowned.

"I'm sure it's nothing," Emily said, though I wasn't sure of her sincerity. "I mean, Tracey just left town all of a sudden, and I know *she'd* never hurt you."

Okay, this was beyond disturbing that Emily was having to *convince* herself that Amelia would never be capable of something like that.

"I'm sorry. I shouldn't have said anything," Emily said, seemingly reading into how much it bothered me.

"Don't be."

"I just hate that any of this happened to you. I've had bad dreams ever since you told me."

"Em..."

She bit her lip. "You deserve to get your happily ever after, Willow. You've been through so much in your life, and you don't deserve to be going through any of this."

Her eyes shimmered.

"I bet that cop is totally into you. I mean, look how protective he's been," she said.

"You're just saying that to cheer me up."

"Speak of the devil." She nodded her chin toward the door.

You have got to be kidding me.

I purposefully didn't go home after work, and I purposefully didn't tell Shane where I was going so I wouldn't have to talk to him before Emily and I had a chance to fully dissect every word from last night and properly catalog it in our own case file.

The mysterious case of Shane rejects Willow.

"Willow, can I have a word?" he asked.

Emily flashed a look at me that said, *Good luck.*

I stepped with Shane to the side of the room and wrapped my arms around my stomach, like it could hide the bruises on my heart.

"How did you find me?"

"You mean, when you didn't answer my calls?"

My face heated. He couldn't be this dense—to reject a girl and expect her not to need a second to process it.

"Process of elimination," Shane answered. "Walked a direct route from our place to your work. Got lucky on stop number six. What are you doing here?"

"We talked about this," I said. "I'm going to live my life like normal."

Shane shoved his hands in his pockets. "I know. Doesn't mean I won't worry, though."

But he wasn't worried enough last night to stay in my apartment for more than thirty seconds after he kissed me.

"I want to talk to you about what I discovered today with the phone records," he said.

So, this was just about the case, then. He wasn't here to say he thought about it all day and wanted to clarify why he had acted so weird last night. Or wanted to kiss me again.

"What did you find?" I begrudgingly asked.

He looked over at Emily, then back at me. "I'd like to talk alone."

But I didn't want to be alone with him. Not until I knew where we stood. Once I knew where we stood, I would know how to act around him, but right now, I might misinterpret everything and humiliate myself again.

Speaking of interpreting things, I studied Shane's face, which was hardened. That had to be a bad sign. Right? Yet he had come all the way here, just to check on me. A good sign?

Ugh. This was impossible. I wished Emily could come over here and give me her opinion, but if I wanted to understand where I stood with Shane, I would have to do something different.

Don't wait for him to clarify things. Clarify them yourself.

With my heart pounding, I kept my gaze fixed on his as I tested the energy between us, taking a step forward, bringing our faces closer. Shane appeared to assess my movement, frustration cascading through his features.

He broke eye contact.

And took a step back.

Point. Clarified.

How stupid of me to think he'd felt the same way for me as I did him. And he wasn't just pushing me away because of his career; if that were true, he would've said as much in order to spare my feelings and humiliation. This wasn't about his career; it was about me. He wasn't interested. As for yesterday's kiss, Shane must've gotten caught up in the heat of the moment. I had misread everything going on between us.

His affection for me was cruel. It had given my heart false hope—that, for once, someone's care for me would be unending. My mom's affection came and went. My sister's was a faucet that cranked down to zero, and then someone, evidently, despised me so much, they wanted me dead.

Shane's rejection ripped my chest open, flooding it with hurt and humiliation. And anger, because I was stronger than this—than craving affection in the first place.

The worst part was, I didn't understand why he'd changed his tune—from cupping my cheek yesterday to avoiding eye contact today.

Maybe the bridge incident made him look at me with nothing but pity. Maybe he would never get involved with someone that needed so much help. Maybe he saw me as a victim and would never see me as the strong, independent woman that I actually was. Or maybe, after saving my life, he felt a sense of responsibility for me.

Whatever his reasons, I didn't know how I'd ever look Shane in the eyes again, let alone work with him to find the answers we needed so we could both move on with our lives.

"I'll text you later," I said.

After I had time to process this new, uncomfortable reality.

It was my turn to not meet Shane's eyes.

"Willow, wait," he said. "We need to discuss this. Now."

I was grateful for the plans I'd made; they afforded me a perfect excuse to delay spending time with him.

"I can't. My mom gets off work in a few minutes, and I'm heading there after this."

Maybe Mom wasn't willing to talk to me in front of Grandma and Shane. But if I confronted her and didn't let her off the hook, she would have to answer my questions.

"Postpone," Shane said.

"I can't."

When I'd reached out to her, I told her it was important. If I rescheduled or showed up late, she would use it as ammunition to wiggle out of my answers. Because how important could it be if I didn't even show up on time?

"What I found is alarming," Shane said.

Alarming? "Then, tell me what it is."

Shane glanced at Emily, then back to me. "It's not somethin' I'm going to talk about in a hallway conversation like this, pressured for time."

"So, give me the CliffsNotes."

"When can you meet?"

I evaluated him. The hurt side of me wanted to keep putting him off, but the sooner we found something that we could hand over to De Luca, the sooner Shane could get off this case, and I wouldn't have to interact with a guy who'd rejected me.

"Give me an hour," I said. "I'll swing by when I'm done."

"Let me come with you."

"No."

Mom would never talk if Shane was there, and I needed space from him.

"I'll swing by as soon as I'm done," I repeated. "I have to get back to Emily."

"Willow..." Shane said.

But I didn't listen to him. I walked back to the table and sat down. It was irresponsible of my heart to fixate on his rejection more than whatever he had found with my cell phone records. But there it was. I couldn't even glance in Shane's direction because if I looked at him, I might start to cry, and I was not about to cry over some guy who didn't want me. Let alone let him see just how much his rejection had affected me.

Based on Emily's eye movements, Shane must have lingered by the wall for a minute before walking out of the bar.

"Okay, he's gone. I take it, it didn't go well?"

"Is it that obvious?"

Emily pursed her lips. "Screw him. You're a total catch, and if he doesn't want you? That's his loss."

His loss. That's what people said to me when Ezra messed around on me. When my sister blew me off. Her loss. Funny how everyone around me was losing out on so much.

"We're next-door neighbors that share a wall. Do you know how uncomfortable this is going to be now? He probably thinks I'm a pathetic puppy that fell for him."

I pinched the bridge of my nose. This was the last complication I needed in my life.

"Give me your phone," Emily said.

"What?"

She didn't wait for me to comply; she grabbed my phone and flipped it over so my face unlocked the screen and then began typing.

"Don't you dare text him!" I tried to grab my phone, but she held it away.

"I'm not texting Shane."

"Then, who are you texting?"

But she didn't answer me. A slow smile curled up on her lips as she continued texting. After a minute, she said, "There."

She set the phone back on the table.

"Remember the doctor that you met in the bar last week? And you guys totally hit it off and exchanged numbers?"

"Yeah?"

"You guys finally have that date you planned to go on."

I glared at her. "Seriously, Emily? Now is not the time for—"

"You want to coexist with Shane and not have it awkward, right?"

I pursed my lips.

"If you go on a date with this doctor, it'll make it very clear to Shane you've moved on."

I frowned. "Shane wouldn't even know about the date." Because I wouldn't tell him.

"Oh, I'm betting he will." She smirked. "He seems to find you every other time you're away from him."

"Why do you have such a mischievous gleam in your eyes?"

"Because based on the way he looks at you? I think he *is* into you. And I can't wait to find out what his reaction is going to be when he finds you out with another man."

19

"How did Dad die?" I asked, my tone a bit curt.

It wasn't fair to her that Shane's rejection compounded my frustration toward my mom and her deceptions. It was weak to wonder why no one wanted me, and it was pathetic to feel like no one ever would.

Evidently, I couldn't make people love me, but I sure as hell could —and would—get answers I deserved.

My mom blanched. "It's nice to see you too, Willow."

I kept my shoulders square, pretending I wasn't terrified inside.

I had never confronted my mother like this, but after thinking about it more, I knew this was my last shot to get *her* to be the one to tell me. Once Shane started asking his questions, she might be so offended, she would refuse to share with me again. I could never forgive her if I had to learn about this by researching it on my own or from a stranger, like a private investigator, and since playing softly over the past two decades had not worked, I decided on a stronger approach.

Especially since the fate of our relationship hung in the balance of her honesty. There was no way to get closer to her until we obliterated the lie standing between us.

"How did he die?" I repeated.

We sat in the living room of my mother's twelve-hundred-square-foot bungalow outside the city. This was the bungalow that we had moved into after Dad's death. Her living room was full of muted blues and grays, like she wanted to be surrounded by colors that made her sad. The pictures on the walls were from decades ago —all snapshots of happier times with Dad in them. It was like Mom's life had frozen in place the day Dad died, and she never moved forward.

Her body had, though. She looked like she'd aged four decades, not two. Deep lines ground into the skin around her sunken eyes, her cheeks hollow from being too thin. Her skin was unnaturally pale, even by Chicago winter standards, and her shoulder-length dark hair had spouted grays and had started to thin.

She sat in Dad's old recliner, stirring the cup of tea she'd made herself when I'd first arrived. Staring at me as I tried not to show any trace of anxiety.

"I know this isn't easy to talk about," I said. "But he was my father. And I want to know what happened."

Mom's voice was a whisper. "What difference does it make?"

"Closure, Mom. So I can move forward with my life."

She regarded me, her face softening slightly. "And you can't move forward with your life without dredging up the past?"

"I remember having blood on me," I said. "Were we in a car accident?" Was he drinking and driving?

She took a long sip of her tea.

I clenched my fingers, trying to find my patience. "I haven't pressed you enough over the years because I've been tiptoeing around *your* feelings. But you've never considered mine."

"That's not true."

"You talk about Dad like he's a superhero. I would always listen to your stories, and I would believe every word of it."

"Your father was a loving husband and father. Nothing I told you was a lie."

"If he was so perfect, then why won't you tell me what happened to him?!" I pressed my hands together to keep them from shaking, chiding myself for letting the tone in my voice escalate.

She set her tea on the side table. "Your father was an extraordinary dad to you girls."

Keep pressing, Willow. Now or never. Don't recede back into submissive habits. You've spent your whole life letting people walk all over you. Stand up for your needs.

"Maybe he was. Or maybe he was..." I started.

"He was what?"

"Why are you hiding the details of how he died?"

"Because I don't want to taint your memories of him, okay?"

"Taint my memories. How would knowing the details taint my memories?"

"Willow, please...drop it." With every word, my mother receded into her pain.

"Did he hurt me?"

"I'm not ruining your father's memory over one bad day."

One bad day...

"I was in the hospital when he died. Was I hurt?"

"No human is perfect."

"Was Hayley hurt?"

"I'm not erasing all his wonderful memories, so if that's what you want, please...just go."

"Did I kill him?" I knew I was small, but did I pick up a gun or something?

"No, of course not!" she replied incredulously.

"I'm not leaving until you answer me."

Now, Mom's chin went up. "I'm not talking about this."

My heart pounded harder.

"If you won't give me answers, I'll look into it on my own. I'll even hire someone to get them for me if I have to."

Her eyes welled with tears, and she shot out of her chair. I bit back the apologies and desperate words trying to escape, to smooth over the wrinkles of pain.

Now or never, Willow.

If she refused to be honest with me, I wasn't sure how I could ever talk to her again. Ironic that all I wanted was to feel close with my mom, but all the lies she'd swept under her rug stood between us now.

Mom started pacing, a nervous energy radiating from her steps. "How did he die?"

She added finger flexing to her pacing.

"Did he hurt you?" I asked.

No answer.

"What happened?"

"Stop."

"Why?"

"I don't want the circumstances of your father's death to define you."

"What does that mean?"

The muscles in her face softened, and her lower lip quivered. "Why can't you just let this go?"

"I'll find out what happened with or without your help. I can either hear your side of the story or not."

Her lip quivered harder, beating my anger down. I hated seeing Mom so sad. I hated that it was affecting me right now because she deserved to feel sad after keeping all of this from me for so long. I hated that I thought she deserved it.

This was all such a mess.

Mom swiped a tear from her cheek. I allowed the silence to tick on as she chewed her lip until, finally, she cleared her throat.

"He was a good person," she said, "who made a mistake."

Mom collapsed into the chair and wouldn't look me in the eye when she finally answered the question I had been waiting for my whole life.

"Your father was stressed out over finances and had too much to drink. He got into a verbal altercation that escalated to the point of getting himself killed. He was shot once in the head. And I couldn't stop it."

Mom shoved her face into her hands, and her shoulders shook.

She had to know that wasn't even close enough to being a full explanation, but I tried to bite my tongue to allow her words to come at her own pace.

"I kept it from you to protect you," Mom said. "I couldn't save your father. And in the aftermath of his death, I have been so self-centered with my grief that I failed both of you girls. I failed Hayley and allowed her to become addicted to drugs and alcohol. You were the only one in the family who wasn't living under this dark cloud, and I was not going to rob you of that. You still had the chance to go after your dreams, so why would I take all of that away from you?"

"It's not your fault that Hayley is an addict."

Tears ran down her cheeks. "Of course it is. I emotionally checked out, and I left Hayley holding the bag. She would have to step in and take care of you whenever I had a breakdown and left for days at a time. Days! Even though she was also in the throes of extreme grief. What kind of horrible mother does that to her own children?"

Mom wiped away tears of shame.

"It's not a question of *why* she started doing drugs," she said. "But why wouldn't she have? I was the one person who could've and should've protected her, and I never did."

That's why Mom had always been Hayley's enabler. She didn't favor Hayley, as it often felt to me throughout the years, but in reality, her actions toward Hayley stemmed from guilt.

And that's why they seemed so close and why I always felt as though I were on the outside, looking in. Mom had built this impenetrable wall meant to protect me, both from the truth and from the toxicity that she and Hayley lived. Undoubtedly, she thought I deserved more than a mother and sister who were broken by the events of the past.

"Who killed him, Mom? And how did I end up with blood all over me?"

20

"Okay, after you logged in to your cell phone carrier's account for me, I obtained the last three months of cell phone records," Shane said.

He sat on my living room couch while I tried hard to listen to him, but my mind kept wandering to what had just happened with my mom.

Over the years, I had always assumed my dad had simply been in the wrong place at the wrong time. After all, this was a man who had picked wildflowers with his little girls and doted on his wife. Who could've hated him enough to kill him intentionally? In the absence of information from my mom, I had even spun multiple tales of what may have happened. The most probable, I had decided, was when I had seen news stories about a series of armed robberies at gas stations nearby. I had imagined that maybe similar robberies had happened years before, and maybe my father had been paying for gas and had become a victim to an armed robbery gone wrong.

But with the few details she'd provided, my mom just repainted the entire picture of the circumstances surrounding his death.

Dad had been stressed about finances. Dad had been drinking.

Just that one day? Or in general, had he been using alcohol excessively?

He'd gotten into a verbal altercation and, in her words, "gotten himself killed."

Gotten himself killed.

And Mom "couldn't stop it."

"I started with the day of..." Shane continued.

That was not a picture of a wrong place, wrong time. It was a picture of a man becoming unraveled.

Did Mom sell insurance back then? Was there insurance on her life? If so, might he have attacked her in a desperate attempt to get that money?

And how did I get blood on me? Was that why she shut down in the middle of our conversation, refusing to divulge anything else?

"...and compare the list of all incoming and outgoing phone calls to the contact list you provided me."

Did my sister know what really happened? In my shell-shocked state, I hadn't even thought to ask Mom that question.

"I paid particular attention to the hours leadin' up to your fall."

Grandma had to know, too, didn't she? She was, after all, helping to keep the details of his death a secret.

"Three calls in particular were of interest."

In fact, everyone in our family would have had to have been in on it.

"The first was from your friend Tracey. You called her an hour before your fall. That call lasted for six minutes."

How could they all do that? What were they hiding that was so bad? Because that's what they were doing—hiding it.

"The second was an incoming call from Amelia. Shortly after Tracey's. That call only lasted three minutes."

Who had killed him? When I pushed Mom for an answer, she had shut down.

"But the third call," Shane said, pointing to a piece of paper, "was an incoming call from Ezra."

Which meant she knew the killer.

"Which means the last person you spoke with that night was Ezra."

You don't keep that kind of information a secret unless the killer is someone in the family. Right?

"Willow, are you listening to me?"

I blinked and snapped myself out of my trance. "Yes. Ezra. Last person I talked to."

Shane studied me. "Are you okay? You haven't been yourself since you got back from your mom's."

I didn't answer.

"What happened?"

With the pain of Shane's rejection anchored into my stomach, the need to talk through this shocking twist in my life swam to the surface. And broke through.

"I confronted her about how my dad died."

Shane pierced me with his indigo eyes. "Did you finally get some answers?"

It would be easier to stay angry at Shane if he wasn't so sincerely compassionate.

"Sort of."

"What happened?" Shane set the papers down on my coffee table.

My pride wanted to tell him nothing—if he cared so much about me, he shouldn't have pushed me away. But my heart chided me; Shane not wanting me did not take away from how kindhearted he was.

"My dad was murdered. Evidently, he'd been drinking and stressed about money, and he got into an altercation."

Shane's eyes raked over my face, and the familiar pang of hurt jolted. If he made me feel this cared about, some girl would be so lucky to become the object of his everything.

I wish I could've been her.

"Did she say who killed him?" Shane asked.

"No. I tried to ask her more questions, but she shut down again. Like she always does."

"I'm sorry."

I rubbed my eyes. "I thought finding out how my dad died would give me some kind of closure. But it just ripped the wound open and left me with more questions than answers."

I hated how my eyes welled with tears, and I hated that, out of all the people I could talk to about this, I was most comfortable doing it with Shane. It would be easier to keep my feelings at bay if that weren't the case, but he was the only person in my life who could understand what this felt like. And the way he was looking at me— his eyes soft, a line creasing between his brows—I could tell that he not only understood, but he also cared deeply about how hard this was for me to process.

"I don't understand why she kept it from me all this time."

Shane paused. "It wasn't right, lying to you. You deserve the truth. I'm sure, in her own way, your mom was probably tryin' to protect you."

I slouched my shoulders and tried to hold on to the anger I felt toward my mom.

"Aren't you supposed to be the cynical one here?" I asked.

Shane was changing a little, wasn't he? From the cynic who didn't believe in second chances to someone encouraging me to cut my mom some slack.

"You're making it hard to stay mad at her," I said.

Shane's lips tugged up on one side. He stared at me, grabbing hold of me with those azure eyes.

"I'm sorry she's kept this from you for your whole life. That must be overwhelming."

What a great way to put it. Overwhelming.

He put his hand on my knee the same way he had the night we'd had dinner with my family, when he didn't want me to feel alone in that mess. I wish my pulse didn't react to his touch, or his gaze, which slowly trailed to my lips. I wish my lower belly didn't heat up when his thumb brushed light strokes against my thigh. If he wanted a platonic friendship, he shouldn't touch me like this or stare at me with that wanton desire, his tongue wetting his lower lip as he studied my mouth.

This was real, wasn't it? He was attracted to me. And if he cared about me and wanted me, maybe I'd misunderstood. Maybe he did have feelings for me. My heart stretched through the barbed wire surrounding it, reaching for Shane—never needing him more than I did right then.

But suddenly, Shane dropped his hand. He cleared his throat and moved over another two feet from me. Two feet that might as well have been a mile.

It felt like I had been shot in the chest. Not only losing out on the physical feeling of his mouth on mine, caving in to my desires, making me forget all about my hurts, but also, pushing me away after we'd shared such an intimate profession.

What was wrong with me? Was this romance all in my head?

Shane's rejection was the last thing I should care about. There were much bigger priorities in my life right now, like getting to the bottom of what happened on that bridge and processing everything I had learned about my dad. It was juvenile to feel hurt right now, to have my eyes once again burning, but I couldn't stomach him looking at me with pity, a needy girl with unfulfilled feelings for him.

As if the universe wanted to side with Emily, my phone buzzed with a text from the doctor she'd set me up with.

"Tell me that's not Ezra," Shane said, trying to eye my screen.

"No. It's a guy I have a date with."

Shane's eyes snapped to mine. I swore I saw a flash of jealousy, but you can't be jealous of something you don't want.

"I don't think it's the best time for you to be dating."

Well, I was certainly not going to sit around here and feel sorry for myself that Detective Rejection wanted nothing to do with me. And I did not know how long it was going to take to solve this case, so even if I wasn't into this date, at least it would make it clear to Shane that I was moving on.

Because you know what? I didn't *want* Shane anymore. I refused to chase after someone again. Screw him.

"So, the phone records," I said, "we should turn these over to De Luca."

Shane stared at my phone, his chest inflating and deflating before he shook his head. "They aren't evidence of anything."

"Ezra was the last person to talk to me, and he had a conniption fit in my apartment, where the cops were called."

"It's not enough evidence to prove foul play. We need somethin' more than an angry ex."

Dammit. What else did we have to do to get detectives to take over? Because I couldn't keep working with Shane; it stung too much.

"Okay, so Ezra," I said. "He's the first person we talk to, then?"

Shane scrubbed his jaw. "Yes."

I nodded.

Normally, I wouldn't rush Shane out of my apartment so quickly, but our business for the evening had concluded, and I needed to be alone to strengthen my walls for when I was around him next. Plus, I wanted to stop my mind from spinning.

But even after he left, I couldn't relax. I tried reading, again perturbed about what in the world happened with my bookmark. I tried watching a show, but when none of that worked, I resorted to cleaning my kitchen.

With everything going on, I hadn't used my kitchen much. A handful of dishes sat in the sink, so I began rinsing them off.

Only...

The water wasn't draining. It was filling up so quickly; there was obviously some sort of clog. I began scooping water out of one side of the sink with a cup, and only when I reached the bottom did I discover what the culprit was.

It wasn't leftover bites of food; it was hair.

A wad of my hair the size of a golf ball.

I had never had a clog like this before. Not in my entire life. How did this much hair get into my drain?

It's probably just from...natural shedding of hair, I guess?

But that made no sense. First of all, I hadn't noticed any hair loss. Second, why would it be in a clump like this? And third, why would it be in the kitchen sink? Why not the shower drain, where most hair naturally falls out?

I set it on the counter and looked at it. It looked like a drowned hamster, and it smelled like curdled milk.

Something about it didn't sit well with me, made my blood pump faster through my body. I didn't brush my hair near the sink, and even if I did, I wouldn't allow my hair to pile into the drain. I would wipe it up. It would take *a lot* of hair to create a clog this big, so why hadn't I noticed any issues with my drain before? It should've drained slower before stopping completely.

It was almost as if this clog had appeared suddenly.

Come to think of it, I hadn't washed dishes since I'd gotten home from the hospital. Since I'd found my apartment unlocked...since I'd found my toothbrush on the back of the toilet, my bookmark in the wrong location.

I seriously thought about calling Shane over, but my bruised ego was tired of turning to *him* for everything. Plus, it sounded so crazy. Even if I called the responding officers from the possible break-in, I could just imagine my conversation with them.

"Yes, sir, I'm worried someone may have broken into my apartment and moved my toothbrush, moved my bookmark, and shoved a wad of my hair into my sink. Can you come dust for prints?"

"Any sign of a break-in, Ms. Johnson?"

"An unlocked door."

"So, the only things are this toothbrush in a different spot from where you thought you left it, a bookmark, and a clogged drain?"

"Yes."

A cutting stab of a glower. "Yes, Ms. Johnson, we'll escalate this to the top of the crime lab immediately."

I rolled my eyes.

Maybe the sink had been draining slower lately, and I hadn't noticed it. Maybe I'd knocked one of my brushes into it, and hair had accumulated or something.

After all, if a burglar had broken in here, they'd have taken something. Not taking the risk or time to shove my hair into a drain. What possible reason would they have to do that?

It made no sense.

Yet...it was getting harder to assure myself someone wasn't responsible for this. If I told Shane, he'd go ballistic and probably insist on staying at my place from now on.

The next time I talked to De Luca, I should at least mention it...

21

"Do you know how upset you made Mom?" Hayley stormed into my living room. "She's been in bed all day, Willow. What the hell?"

It had shocked me when I answered the door to find my sister here. But I guess I should've seen this coming.

"I never meant to upset her," I said. "I was just trying to get some answers."

"You know when she gets like this, she can spiral. What the hell were you thinking?"

"I'm trying to get closure."

"By making my life a living hell? In case you forgot, I'm stuck living with Mom at the moment. So, when she yells at me? I just have to sit there and take it, and as usual, you never have to deal with any of it."

"What does that mean?"

"Mom will never yell at *you*; she never has. She has always sheltered you from everything, just like she did with Dad's death. You got to go on and have a happy life while *I'm* the one that paid the price by dealing with Mom's heartbreak."

"I was four," I reminded her.

"You've grown up. Happy, unlike me."

Happy? Did she think family secrets made me happy?

"Do you know who killed Dad?" I asked.

Hayley narrowed her eyes, a flash of resentment breaking through her gaze. She looked like she was struggling between the orders our mother had always given her and her apparent jealousy toward me.

"I should say so. Seeing as how I was there when it happened."

I rocked back on my heels.

"You *saw* him get killed?"

She stood there for what felt like an eternity and said nothing, just like Mom had said nothing for all of these years.

"Mom should have told me the truth a long time ago," I said.

"Stop blaming Mom. She's not the one who killed Dad and ruined our lives. You want someone to blame for our screwed-up family? Blame the son of a bitch that killed him! He's the one you should hate! He did this; he took everything from us, so stop blaming Mom!"

"So, it was a man?"

Hayley looked like she debated answering my question, if only to throw it in my face, but Mom had worked hard to keep me from finding out the truth. And Hayley was at the mercy of Mom, who was allowing my sister to stay in her house. She couldn't stray too far from Mom's wishes or else she'd be homeless.

That's it. I'm hiring a private investigator to find all the answers to this mystery, including how much my family members knew all these years.

As if she could read the intent in my eyes, Hayley said, "Stop digging up the past. You won't like what you find."

"The hell is that supposed to mean?"

"I had to pick up the pieces the last time Mom broke down, but I'm done being left holding the bag. Go back to your fucking fairy-tale life and stop ruining what's left of ours."

Hayley stormed out.

No wonder she'd struggled her entire life. Everything made sense now, and a flood of compassion and empathy opened up in my heart for her. Hayley had been suffering with these demons for so long. No wonder she turned to drugs and alcohol.

In addition to the pain of witnessing Dad's death, she'd been left alone at times to care for her younger sister in the wake of tragedy. Mom was an adult and didn't even pull that off. Instead, she left it on the shoulders of a teenager.

It should come as no surprise that Hayley had seeds of resentment toward her. And as if that wasn't bad enough, she'd watched Mom shelter and protect me from the truth for years when she was never there to protect Hayley from the horrible reality.

Maybe that was another reason Mom didn't want to talk about that fateful day, not only because of her grief over Dad, but also, because it would bring back horrible memories for Hayley.

Maybe it was Mom's way of trying to protect Hayley from at least part of it all.

If I had known any of this, I would have been more compassionate toward Hayley all these years.

Maybe this secret stood between me and Hayley, too.

22

This was a mistake. I seriously wanted to cancel this date, but here I was. Wearing a light-blue dress with a neckline so low, I couldn't wear a bra with it. The dress came to my thighs, showing off that muscular line in my legs that I'd worked hard to get. I kept my hair stick straight versus styling it up and put minimal makeup on my face—a little color on my lips and thicker eyeliner on my eyes, but otherwise going for the more natural look. I finished it off with a pair of stud earrings and black stiletto heels.

A totally inappropriate outfit to wear in Chicago's rigid winter temperatures, but I had bigger problems in life.

When the knock came, I grabbed my dressy coat, my purse, and opened my front door.

Clay was holding a bouquet of pink roses.

His eyebrows shot up, and a smile etched across his face. "You look...wow."

"You do, too."

And he did, wearing fitted dress pants, a gray shirt that showed off his muscles beneath his black coat, and his blond hair styled with gel.

"These are for you." He handed me the bouquet.

Luckily, it was already in a vase, so I didn't have to scrounge around, looking for one.

"Thank you." I smiled and set the flowers on my table.

"What happened to your arm?" he asked.

"I fell."

"What type of fracture?" His tone was curious. "Hairline? Transverse? Oblique?"

"Hairline."

He smiled. "Glad it wasn't compound. Those are incredibly painful."

This wasn't exactly a cake walk either, but the ache had faded a little more each day.

"Shall we go?" He motioned with his arm.

I was surprised he merely asked for a medical clarification rather than how I'd broken it, but hopefully, his lack of curiosity would continue through dinner—I didn't want to get into it.

I stepped out into the hallway and locked my door.

At the precise moment Shane's door opened. Wearing his running gear—a fitted black shirt and pants that hugged his hips—he froze when he saw us.

His gaze gradually descended my dress and back up.

Then, he glared at us.

Glared.

Leaning in his doorframe with his arms crossed like some kind of possessive alpha.

Clay shot me a WTF look, but I just smiled as if Shane's behavior were totally normal. Did I want this date? No, not with this timing, but if I had any hope of enduring my lease, I needed to do this.

I reached down and took Clay's hand.

Which snapped Clay out of his WTF trance and put a smile on his face.

"Clay, this is my neighbor, Shane. Shane, Clay. We were just leaving." I tugged Clay down the hall. "Where do we have reservations?"

"You're going to love this place," Clay said. "Best Italian food in the city."

"She hates Italian food," Shane said in an annoyed tone as he locked his door and followed us down the hallway.

"No one hates Italian food," Clay said.

"She does."

"How do you know?" I challenged.

"Couple months back, you and one of your friends were walking down the hall, heading out to dinner, tryin' to decide where to go. You told her no Italian. You hate Italian."

My cheeks flushed. Did detectives catalog every word you ever said?

"We can go somewhere else," Clay said.

"No. I can find a salad or something."

I shot Shane a shut-up look.

"You sure?" Clay asked.

"Yeah."

"Okay, great, because this place is supposed to have killer chicken Parm."

"You're really goin' to take her somewhere you know she doesn't like just so you can get the dinner *you* want?"

"Shane—"

"What's your problem, man?" Clay asked.

"If you invite her out to dinner, you should take her somewhere she can actually eat."

"Shane!" I snapped.

Shane's eyes landed on me, his jaw set in frustration. And when Clay helped me slip my coat on, his fingers brushing my neck, Shane looked at Clay's hands as if they were the enemy.

I pretended not to notice as I stepped outside, eager to put Clay at ease.

"Is that the car you were telling me about?" I asked.

A red Corvette sat a few spaces down, so shiny that it looked like it had just been driven off a car lot. Its angles looked like something from the future; the slope of the roof slanted down toward the rounded trunk with a spoiler on it.

"You like it?"

"It's gorgeous."

Shane glared at Clay, then at his car, and I could tell by the look on Shane's face that he was about to say something to get under Clay's skin. Why? Why was he acting like this? Before Shane had the chance to mutter whatever rude grenade he'd prepared, I pulled him off to the side.

"What is your problem?" I whisper-demanded.

"I don't like him."

"You don't know him."

"He cares more about himself than you."

"And you know this after meeting him for what, ten seconds?"

"All I needed to see. You deserve better."

"You know nothing about Clay."

"Do you?" Shane challenged.

"Why are you out here, anyway?"

"I was about to go for a run."

"Well, be on your way, Hernandez. I have a date to get to."

Spoiler alert: the date was boring as hell. Dr. Arrogant would not stop talking about himself. I don't think he asked me a single question about me or my life. I couldn't wait to get home.

Not that I would ever admit any of this to Shane. I hated that he had been right, but he was a seasoned detective and had spotted Clay's selfishness quicker than me. But in fairness, Shane's magnetism had distracted me in the hallway.

Thankfully, the dinner was finally over. We sat in his ostentatious Corvette, ambling along a road in downtown Chicago, while Clay droned on again about all the cadavers he'd dissected in medical school.

Just what every girl longs to hear.

Suddenly, red and blue lights cut through the evening's darkness through the rear window.

I looked at the speedometer, but Clay wasn't speeding.

"What the hell?" Clay pulled off to the shoulder.

I looked behind us, and when I realized the lights came from an unmarked squad car, my hands clenched.

He'd. Better. Not.

The unmarked squad car's door opened, and a silhouette emerged.

It can't be him. So help me, if it is...

The blue and reds shone behind the man as he walked toward our car. Painfully slow. And when he reached the car? He came to *my* side rather than Clay's and tapped on my window.

It took me a second to figure out how to roll it down on account of my immense irritation.

"A word?" Shane said.

"What the hell, Hernandez?" I asked.

He opened the door, as if he were being chivalrous instead of a level-ten dick.

"Step out of the car."

"No." I tried to shut the door, but Detective Dick kept it pried open with his ridiculous forearm strength.

"I'll repeat myself one more time. Step out of the car."

"Or what? You going to drag me out?"

Shane's eyes flared with anger. "Don't tempt me."

"Go ahead. I double dog dare you."

While Shane and I entered a glaring competition, Clay stirred to life.

"What's your deal, dude?"

"Shut up," Shane snapped.

That's all Clay needed. Dr. Arrogant apparently would not tolerate being spoken to like that. He shoved his door open and launched himself out of the driver's seat.

Shane put his hand on his weapon, because, yeah, he was wearing the damn holster on his belt.

"Back in the car." Shane held up his palm.

"Screw you." Clay walked around the hood of his car and approached Shane.

"Clay, stop!" I demanded.

Clay took another step toward Shane. "Get away from my car and away from her."

I lunged out of my seat. *The last thing we need is a shoot-out over egos.*

"Take one step closer to me," Shane said in a tone that added, *I dare you.*

Clay did.

But before Shane could manhandle him, I jumped between them, shoving my hands against Shane's chest until he backed up to the rear of the Corvette.

Clay stood at the side, then ambled toward the front of the vehicle. Thank goodness.

"What the hell are you doing?" I demanded.

"You know who that guy is?"

"You're acting like a lunatic! How did you even find us?"

"When he picked you up, I got his plates. And I ran them while you were at dinner."

"Is that even legal?" I asked.

Traffic slowed as vehicles drove past us, looking at the lights and the scene we were making on the side of the road.

"He's got unpaid child support in three states."

Wow. Clay told me he didn't have kids. But this was a moot point; I'd already decided I wasn't going on a second date with him.

"Well, thanks for the warning. If you don't mind, I'll get back to it then."

But when I took a step forward, Shane moved in front of me, blocking my path. "Get in my car. I'm takin' you home."

"News flash: I don't need you to protect me from him."

"Get in the car, Willow." Shane nodded toward his sedan.

"Is that what this is? You see me as some sort of perpetual, helpless victim that needs your protection?" I stepped closer to him and got in his space. "I'm a big girl. Pulling us over tonight was completely out of line."

"You deserve better."

Even though I didn't think Clay could hear what we were saying, he must have lost patience with this whole thing because he walked up to me and gripped my elbow.

"Come on." He tugged me toward my open door, but in a flash, Shane grabbed him and pinned him to his shiny Corvette trunk—his hands behind his back.

"Touch her again, I'll fuckin' pummel you."

"Shane!" I said. "Stop!"

What had gotten into him?

"What the hell, man?!" Clay snapped.

"Let him go!"

Shane and I locked eyes. His chest heaved with fury, and when he looked back at Clay, his lips curled in disgust. But he pushed off him.

Clay spun around. Stood nose to nose with Shane, both men huffing white puffs out of their nostrils as the blue and reds flashed across their skin. Car tires crunched against snow salt as vehicles chugged between skyscrapers, watching a standoff between two men.

"Get back in the car," Clay snapped to me.

"Talk to her like that again..." Shane warned.

Clay looked at Shane's hand, positioned on his gun's holster, then at the unmarked sedan's police lights, then at me. His lips curled as he stood there, glowering.

"You're not worth this hassle."

I had to launch myself in front of Shane, both palms on his chest to stop him from whatever vengeance he was about to carry out. "Stop."

I could feel his heart beating, even beneath his coat, as he watched Clay slam the passenger door, walk around the hood, climb inside, and drive off.

"What has gotten into you?" I demanded.

Around us, snowflakes drifted lazily from the black sky, street-lights illuminating them as they shimmered to the ground, creating a magical scene that was straight out of some fairy-tale romance. Unfortunately, it wasn't.

"You can't keep acting like this," I said. "It makes me think you actually want me when you don't."

I tried to push past him, prepared to walk home in my ridiculous heels, but he blocked my path and looked down at me with angry eyes.

"You think I don't want you?" he snarled.

"I know you don't."

Shane's jaw set with frustration. "I've never wanted another woman more in my life." He took a step forward, and I took a step back, moving toward the hood of his car, mirroring his movements. "You're all I think about." Another step from him. Another from me. "All I want to do right now"—another step—"is pin you to the car and show you what I've been imaginin' doing since I first laid eyes on you."

I swallowed, the puffs of white fog coming from my mouth, quickening.

He stood there. Glaring at my parted lips as if they were the enemy. Glaring at me like I'd committed a felony for even thinking that his feelings for me weren't mutual. Based on the look on his face, I'd say his feelings were stronger than I'd ever imagined.

"I don't understand. You pushed me away..." I said.

"To protect you, Willow! I've never felt this way about *anyone*." He pinned me with his fierce stare. "With other girls, it'd be easy to avoid feelin' anything for them, but the connection I have with you isn't just physical. As soon as I started kissing you, I knew if I let it go any further, it would mean so much more than I could handle. My heart would want to go all in with you, so I've been struggling to hold back. To protect you."

I had seen Shane come unglued—pinning Ezra against the wall

of my apartment and just now, in the way he'd handled Clay—but suddenly, I was witnessing the fabric of his heart unthreading.

Mine opened from its wilted hurt to blossom.

He cared about me. Deep enough to do what was best for me, even if it hurt him.

Seeing the look in his eyes, I felt like a fool for having ever questioned it in the first place. I guess when you experience as much rejection as I have, when something feels too good to be true, it doesn't surprise you when that person walks away.

"Protect me from what?"

I was trembling now, not from fear of his aggressive pursuit, but from the winter winds whipping around my bare legs.

A movement Shane noticed with furrowed eyes.

"Get in the car," Shane said. "We can talk in the heat."

23

Shane Hernandez has never wanted another woman more than me.

As I sat in his passenger seat, Shane's words danced around in my head like joyful music while my heart replayed the encounters we'd had over the past several months. Every stolen glance in the hallway, every time he'd held a door open for me, my attraction toward him had grown. And now, to hear confirmation that it *had* been mutual...

It felt like my heart was jumping out of my chest.

When your heart leans toward someone, all you want is for their heart to lean back.

"What did you mean, you pushed me away to protect me?" I asked.

Shane pulled his sedan out into traffic and tightened his lips. "I'd rather talk about this when we get back home."

I blinked. "Why?"

His gaze met mine. "Because I want to be able to look you in the eyes."

Holy romantic mother of moments. His stare was so hot and sexy, it could melt an iceberg.

This *must* have to do with getting involved with me during an active case. Right? Or what if...

What if Shane sensed something about our situation that I never considered before? While he might be good for *me*, what if I wasn't good for *him*? My life was so chaotic right now, and I seemed to draw him into situations that brought out the worst in him.

"I feel like I'm a bad influence on you," I said.

Shane cocked an eyebrow and looked at me before returning his steely eyes to the road. "How so?"

"I feel like whenever I'm around you, chaos ensues. With Ezra. Clay. I feel like I'm drawing you over to the dark side or something."

Shane's lips twitched in amusement, as if the very idea of *me* turning him bad was ludicrous. "There's a lot you don't know about me."

I blinked. "Meaning?"

"I've always had a darker side to me, Willow. It's something I have to actively keep in check. This isn't the first time it's been tested."

Did he seriously think I was going to let *that* go without an explanation? Nope. Not even waiting until we get back to the apartment on that one. I stared at him, making it clear I'd wait.

He sighed and shifted in his seat.

"When I was a kid, after my dad died, we lived in a trailer park for part of my life. A shitty one," he said. "There was this family that lived next door with a girl my age. Wasn't long before I suspected somethin' ugly was happening in that house."

Shane sucked his bottom lip into his teeth, as if fighting against the undertow of a terrible memory.

"The girl went to school with me. She never had enough to eat. I could tell she was being neglected, but the first time I heard her scream..."

Shane chewed the inside of his cheek.

"There were these drug dealers going to that house all the time. I got in the habit of watching when they would come, keepin' my ears open. Sometimes, there would be no noise. Other times, I could hear her scream like someone was hurting her. I called the cops, of course, but by the time they got there, the drug dealers were gone, and no one was ever hauled away in handcuffs. I kept tryin', but the guys were too slippery to get caught. Meanwhile, those awful screams kept coming."

As if Shane hadn't suffered enough, losing his dad, he was an earwitness to some horrific abuse happening to that girl...

"Did your mom ever hear?" I asked.

Shane shook his head. "My mom was always workin' two, three jobs at a time, trying to keep us afloat. I told her about it more than once, but she told me to mind my own business and stay out of it. That interfering might put me in danger."

My chest sank.

"Lookin' back on it, I know she was just protecting me, but I wish she had done something more."

I thought it was bad enough when I felt helpless to make my mom feel better, to help Hayley get out of her spiral. I couldn't even imagine hearing abuse and feeling powerless to stop it.

"Anyway, this goes on for a while, and I felt so damn helpless since I was just a kid. Still, I tried. I had gone to my mother, and I had gone to the police on multiple occasions. They took me seriously, especially being the son of a fallen officer, but the dealers seemed to know every trick in the book to evade them. Seemed like they were always one step ahead. If I'd been more patient, maybe they would have eventually caught them, but at the time, it felt like that wasn't going to happen until someone died or something. I even stormed over there one time."

"What happened?"

"The front door swung open, and this dude tried to run me off with a semiautomatic. I almost fought him. But I got scared because he was twice as big as me, and if I lost, I worried he would shoot her and her family."

My heart ached for Shane. He was such a kind soul, always wanting to help people, even when he was grieving himself. He was stronger than I would have been. It was hard enough for me to get through the days when Mom was struggling with her grief. I couldn't imagine coping with her incapacitating sadness, enduring my own, and taking on the trauma of a next-door neighbor.

"She and I are still great friends, but she doesn't know that, to this day, I still have nightmares about her screams. And when I'm in those nightmares, that helpless feeling creeps back in."

My eyes burned. Admitting something that vulnerable couldn't have been easy.

"I should've snuck her in to stay at our place instead of leaving her in that trailer to fend for herself. In hindsight, there was more I could have done. And I have to live with the guilt of having failed her."

My eyes blurred with tears.

"You didn't fail her, Shane. By the sounds of it, you were the only person trying to throw her a life raft."

He cleared his throat and took a few moments to gather his thoughts.

"When I joined the police force, I took an oath to serve and protect. And I promised myself one thing: if anything like that ever happened again, now that I was in a position of power, I'd do whatever I could to help that person."

And his next-door neighbor had survived what he believed to be an attempted murder. Now, it all made sense. Even if he had not been attracted to me, Shane would've stepped in and done everything that he had done, anyway.

Shane had to be the most selfless, kindest person I had ever met. It took strength to reach out and help someone, especially when that someone battles your efforts every step of the way, as I had. Despite my pushing back, Shane never faltered, and that took a level of heroics, if you ask me.

In fact, that's what Shane was. A real-life hero.

When his dad died on the police force, Shane would've had every reason not to risk the same fate by putting his own life on the line in order to protect other people. And yet, he did the opposite. He dedicated his life to helping others, just as his dad did. He sacrificed relationships, time, and probably a tremendous amount of emotions, just so he could wake up every day and help protect those in need.

My heart bled for him.

It swelled for him.

It longed for him.

Shane Hernandez had just captured every last fragment of my heart.

"You don't have to answer this," I clarified. "But was that girl Fallon?"

His friend—the only friend I'd ever seen, come to think of it—that had found me in his apartment.

Shane's chest inflated slowly. And then he nodded.

"I never told her this." His voice dropped lower, pulsing with an ominous tone. "In fact, I've never told anyone this. But one day, she confided in me that the guy beat both her and her mom." His jaw locked. "That was it. The next time I saw the guy, I did something..."

Shane made a right turn and waited until the car straightened out before continuing.

I leaned forward, eager to hear his next words.

"Our trailer park was surrounded by open fields, and there was this one field that you had to walk past in order to leave. The field must've been abandoned because no one ever did anything with it. No farming, no mowing. The grass and weeds were as tall as my shoulders."

We came to a red light and stopped, the windshield wipers trying to combat the growing snow.

"It was the perfect hiding place for anyone who wanted to ambush someone."

Ho-ly crap.

"The guy was alone. Like always. I stayed hidden in the weeds so he couldn't see me, and then I jumped him. I took him by surprise, so his weapons were useless to him, and I landed a couple of good blows before he even realized what was goin' on. Which helped. It stunned him long enough to let me finish what I'd set out to do."

My mouth was dry. My throat a desert. "Did you kill him?"

Shane's jaw tensed. "I wanted to. But I left him alive."

Good God. I never imagined law-enforcing Shane would've attacked someone like that. That must be the darkness he said he had to work to keep at bay. Being a police detective, witnessing what heinous criminals were capable of, had to have challenged his calm resolve throughout the years.

"Have you ever been tempted to do something like that again?" I asked.

His eyes pierced mine. "Yes," he said. "With you."

My breath caught in my throat.

"When I find out who tried to kill you..." Shane's knuckles whitened as he looked back out the windshield.

The cold violence cutting through his eyes sent a shiver of fear through me, warmed only with desire.

I didn't know what to say to that, didn't know exactly what he meant. Did he mean he was fighting the temptation to get vengeance? Or was it a threat?

"Is that why you wouldn't date me? You're trying to keep your rage under control?"

It made sense. The closer he'd let himself get to me, the harder it might be to control his fury.

"No."

"Then, why? How does not dating me protect me?"

"It's because of what happened after my dad died."

24

W e parked, then went into my apartment, where I took off my coat and shoes and leaned against the living room wall.

Shane put his hands in his pockets and finally settled into what he wanted to say. "My mom struggled. A lot. Obviously, she struggled financially to support two small kids on her own when she had been a stay-at-home mom before that. But the bigger part..."

Shane walked over to the sliding glass door and watched the snow fall to the ground from the beginning of a winter storm.

"They didn't have a lot of money, but they loved the hell out of each other. You could see it in all the family photo albums and feel it through all the stories that were told. You know, you see these relationships where the love fades; people even wind up in divorce. But every once in a blue moon, there's a love like no other. My mom used to describe it as the kind of love that could make the moon shine brighter." Shane looked up at the sky.

His tone was somber as he continued, "When my dad died, it gutted her. She thought she was hiding it from us. She would wait until she thought we were asleep. Or wait until she was in the shower. But my sister and I could hear her cryin'. It was the kind of crying that I had never heard before. This deep, visceral wail, like her heart was literally bleeding."

My throat swelled. I knew that kind of crying; I'd heard my mom cry like that, and years later, I would come to understand that I had been going through two different types of grief—the grief of losing my father and the grief of watching my family suffer from his loss.

"With each of my milestones in life, there was this black cloud cover. Like my high school graduation. All the other parties I'd gone to had these brightly colored balloons and music playin'. Dancing. And we did celebrate," Shane caveated. "It wasn't like my mom wasn't capable of being happy. It just..."

His breathing shallowed, and for a minute, I didn't think he was going to continue.

"The elephant in the room was that he was missing it. When my mom thought I wasn't looking, I could see how sad she was. I'd catch her crying in the corner. It wasn't just the grief of losin' him; it was losing out on him being part of every experience we'd had. Seein' her kids growing up without a father."

Shane walked over to my refrigerator, opened it, and pulled a beer out. He held it up. "May I?"

I nodded.

"Do you want one?"

"No." I rubbed my arms, this conversation chilling my bones.

Shane took a long pull from his beer, then set it down and grabbed the countertop.

"My dad's death devastated my family. Financially. Emotionally. I was only four when he passed, so I never had a father in the Little League stands, cheerin' me on. My mom couldn't be there because she was busy workin' her ass off. Yet she was still struggling to keep the heat on. Christmas mornings...Thanksgivings...birthdays...were all other kids' dreams; for me, holidays and special occasions of any kind were so painful, they became my nightmares."

My chest tightened as Shane looked at the floor, his voice low.

"I wanted to be happy because I thought if I could just find a way to be happy, then maybe Mom might be happy again too."

My stomach ached, remembering how I'd had those same thoughts when my dad died. When I hid the invitations to father-daughter dances and Father's Day crafts. Thinking I was the one making Mom unhappy by reminding her of what she'd lost.

"But those first years, every Christmas mornin'...I'd check under the tree to see if Santa brought me the only thing I wanted in the entire world."

My eyes welled with tears, picturing a desperate little boy in pajamas, running to the Christmas tree. His heart destroyed when, once again, his naive hope to ever see his father again was shattered.

He sighed and scrubbed his face with both hands. "It was even harder on my sister and my mom. And to watch them suffer like that?"

He took a sip of beer. "I will never allow myself to be in a position where I could leave behind a wife and kids the way my dad did. Never. It's my biggest fear in life."

A tear escaped my eye.

"I'm in law enforcement, and that will never change. I work every day to try to chip away at making this world a little safer for everyone else. But, when I decided to become a police officer, it was with the condition that I'd never get seriously involved with *anyone*, Willow."

I silently gasped.

"I will never leave behind a woman I love, and I'll never leave behind children to suffer the hell of not having a father." His tone was as firm as concrete, making it clear he would never change his mind on this.

My chest literally hurt, like it was burning from the inside.

"That's why I never allowed myself to act on my feelings for you, Willow." Holding my stare, he added, "And I never will."

Every remaining fragment of my heart fell for Shane at that moment. Yet it shattered at the sacrifice he was making. Shane would spend his entire life alone. He'd never be showered in daily love, would never wake up on Christmas morning to his own kids jumping on him in bed. He'd never watch them unwrap birthday gifts, or watch their first Little League game, or attend their school play. He would never hold his own child in his arms or kiss his bride on their wedding day.

He'd dedicate his life to making the world a safer place and retreat to his empty apartment, alone, every night.

Watching as the rest of the world fell in love and got their happily ever after.

I didn't want that for him. Selfishly, I wanted to be with him or else my heart would never be whole. But even if he didn't choose me, I wanted him to be happy.

"Shane..."

"I'm sorry I gave you mixed messages." He chewed his lip. "Candidly, I've never had to fight this hard before to keep my distance from someone."

But then I fell from the bridge. And his long-standing promise to help someone going through anything like his neighbor had us spending a lot of time together.

"I don't think you should shut yourself off like this, Shane. I think you deserve your happily ever after. And you wanting to dedicate your life to protect people..." My lower lip quivered. "The right woman won't look at that as a liability. She will look at it for what it is—heroic."

"This isn't about convincin' her to take this risk," Shane said. "I won't allow it."

"But I don't think you should make that decision for her. That's a decision that you make as a couple together."

"This is about protecting her," Shane said. "Before it ever gets to that stage. There's no point in having a relationship if I'm unwilling to let it become serious."

That's why he never allowed women over to his apartment; he didn't date, because why bother? He wouldn't allow a relationship to get serious, let alone lead to marriage, and he was too much of a gentleman to lead a woman on.

"Shane—"

"I know you want to talk me out of this, but I'm not changing my mind, Willow. And for the record? It's not because my feelings for you aren't strong enough. It's the opposite. If there is one person I want to ensure I never hurt, it's you."

My chest warmed at his loving comment, then froze from the consequence it left behind.

"But pushing me away hurts." Spending the rest of my life searching for a man half as remarkable as Shane hurt.

"I'm sorry, but I'll never put you in that position." Shane held my gaze. "Friendship is all I can ever offer you, Willow, if that's something you'd be willing to accept." His voice was low, like he feared my answer.

It took me a second to respond—not that I'd ever say no; it was just a lot to process. Something I would have to continue to process for who knows how long. But in the meantime, I didn't want him thinking I didn't care about him enough to keep him in my life in whatever capacity he could handle.

I offered a sad smile. "Of course."

He looked like he wanted to pull me against his chest and hug me. But instead, he let a few seconds pass and then cleared his throat.

"I guess we should talk about the next step in our investigation." His tone was tense, like he had to force himself to change the subject.

I nodded. Pretending my heart wasn't on fire. Maybe it would've been easier to go through life, assuming he didn't want me. Because if we both wanted each other...knowing nothing could ever come of it was as painful as being dipped in acid.

"Why don't you call Ezra and see if he'd be willin' to talk in person?"

"I already did," I said.

Shane stilled.

"I'm meeting him for coffee in the morning."

Shane set his beer down. "The hell you are."

"He's not going to talk to you, Shane. The last time he saw you, you had your forearm on his throat."

"If you think I'm going to let you meet with a guy that may have already tried to kill you once, you obviously know nothin' about me."

"I have an idea how I can meet him and still keep myself safe..."

25

Goose bumps erupted all over my skin and exploded up my neck to my scalp. My heart joined the party, thumping against my ribs.

I feel like someone's watching me.

But that was stupid. I was inside my apartment, alone, the door locked. Safe. And if need be, Shane was on the other side of my apartment wall, having left less than an hour ago. There was absolutely no reason for this alarm circulating through my bloodstream.

To prove my point, I hoisted myself up off the couch and went into the kitchen, grabbing a small bag of popcorn out of the cabinet.

I tried to eat a kernel, but my stomach was too busy pleading with me to *run*.

I slammed the popcorn down.

This was moronic. Maybe this case reminded me that out there, other people did get hurt. Other people were in danger.

That's probably all this was. My body in some sort of heightened sense of alarm, even though it was unwarranted.

I moved back to the couch and flipped through the channels until I got to the comedy station.

But something drew my eye to my sliding glass door, which looked out over the space between two buildings. In the summer, it contained a small garden area intended to be a gathering place between the surrounding apartment buildings—one of the features I loved, because it reminded me of the garden my dad and I had started to build. In the winter, the space was a barren chamber of concrete—dark, the only light coming from the surrounding windows.

It was out there, forty feet away—a figure.

A human figure.

They're staring right at me.

All the saliva in my mouth evaporated, and my heart started pounding.

They weren't staring at me. This was in my head. I couldn't even see their face—heck, I couldn't even see if it was a man or a woman. Just because they were facing this way didn't mean they were staring at me. There were tons of first-floor apartments, and they could be staring at any one of them. They were probably just out there, smoking or something, since you couldn't do that inside.

But my sixth sense wouldn't stop screaming at me.

They aren't staring at anyone else, Willow.

They're staring at you.

Run.

Despite my trembling limbs, I got up and stood in front of the glass. Staring right back. And when I did, the figure walked into the night, swallowed by its darkness.

* * *

"I emailed you a Word document a few minutes ago," I said.

Shane eyed me. "Come right in."

My cheeks heated. I'd stormed into his apartment without knocking. *What is wrong with me? I never do this kind of stuff.*

And Shane was in his boxer briefs, his hair messy—how did

messy hair look even sexier, by the way?—sitting on his couch, sipping a cup of coffee. His tattoos wove around his skin, trying to distract me from my mission. Trying to make my eyes wander to all the curves of his muscles and his airbrushed-looking stomach.

Being only friends with him was going to be seriously hard.

Rule number one: I needed to avoid ever seeing this much of his skin again.

"I'm sorry for barging in." And now that I was thinking of it, "Don't you lock your door?"

"Not since you were almost killed, no." He set his mug down on the coffee table and looked at me with those ridiculously sexy sapphires of his.

"Why?" Chicago was a major city with the crime rate to prove it. Not a safe small town.

Shane's steely gaze remained on me. "Because if you're ever in trouble, I'm not wasting precious seconds getting to you."

My neck blazed now, and my stomach warmed.

Rule number two: He couldn't say things like that.

"You think someone might come after me again?" I asked.

"You know the answer to that."

Last night's figure flashed through my mind. There one minute, gone the next. So swiftly, I'd questioned if I'd seen anything at all. Plus, seeing a figure outside a huge apartment complex didn't mean someone was stalking me. But with the toothbrush, bookmark, and clogged drain, I'd feel safer if Shane looked into this.

"I know we're looking at my inner circle or whatever, but that's a list of every guy that's DM'd me on social media in the past six months," I said, referring to the email I'd sent. "Thought we should look into them, just in case."

I wished I could get my hands on company records without a warrant—and without risking my job—so we could look into the people who'd been recently fired. But one step at a time...

Shane stared at his phone, then glared at me. "This is a huge freakin' list."

"Noted. Where do we begin?"

Shane scrolled along the document on his phone, then sat back on the couch and evaluated me. "What brought this on?"

"Just...being cautious," I said.

Shane eyed me skeptically. "You're gettin' scared."

"No."

Even more skepticism oozed from that perfect face.

"You sort it in any specific order?" Shane asked.

I nodded. "Yes. From creepiest and most persistent to the least."

Shane frowned. "You get *any* sleep?"

Not really. "How long will it take?"

Shane stood up, and my inappropriate eyes wandered down his ripped stomach. When I met his gaze again, he smirked.

Rule number three: I had to stop fantasizing about what he looked like with no boxers on, and he had to stop liking my obvious enjoyment of his eye candy.

Damn saliva in my mouth.

He stepped toward the kitchen, but stopped and put his hand on my hip. Kissing the top of my head.

Damn heart. How long would it take to get the memo I wasn't allowed to feel sparks from his affection?

"I'll get started on it later this morning, but first, you need to convince me again to go through with your suicidal plan."

26

My potential killer walked through the front door of the café, his eyes scanning the place for me.

I waved, trying to get his attention before he spotted Shane, who was sitting six tables to my right. It took forever to convince Shane to sit that far away from me after losing the battle to have him stay outside, but at least he wasn't parked right next to me. Still, it was too damn close if you wanted my opinion. Because if Ezra saw him, he wouldn't be answering any of our questions.

And I had a lot of questions. I wanted to ask about his past with the assault and battery accusation. And most urgently, about being the last person who talked to me before I plunged into the icy Chicago River.

I felt safe, meeting Ezra here, since it was a public coffee shop and I was sitting at a table along a wall of windows facing a public sidewalk. The place was fairly busy, morning rush hour in full swing with a line of ten people at the counter, ordering coffee to go, while a few others had the luxury of camping out at the tables. Some talking to another person, most staring at their cell phone screens as they downed a cup of caffeine. The smell of freshly ground coffee mixed with the sweet scent of chocolate pastries while the hum of cappuccino makers blended with people's voices. All very mundane. Safe.

But what I didn't feel great about was Shane, who glared at Ezra like he was reconsidering this entire setup. And the tight look on his face? Made me wonder...

Will Shane control his emotions long enough for me to get the answers we need?

Ezra spotted me, smiled, and walked over, carrying a fresh bouquet. Wildflowers this time.

My heart ached at the memory of putting wildflowers on my dad's casket. I had to shove it aside to focus on the task in front of me.

"Morning." Ezra had styled his blond hair with fresh product and wore black slacks and a gray shirt beneath his wool coat.

He handed me the flowers and, right before he sat down, kissed my cheek.

A loud clank drew my eyes toward Shane, who was glaring at Ezra.

"I got you your usual," I said, nodding to the coffee on the table.

He didn't take a sip right away, instead clearing his throat.

"Listen, I'm sorry for how I behaved the last time we talked. I don't know what came over me when I threw that vase."

His tone seemed sincere, and he looked at my hand like he wanted to take it in his, but he forced himself to give me space.

"I've never seen you act like that before."

Ezra wiped his lips. "Yeah. I'm not sure what happened. I guess I just..." He squeezed his lower lip. "When we first broke up, I convinced myself you just needed some time and that you would eventually come back to me. But now, we're coming up on the sixth-month mark, and that feels like a milestone. If I don't get you back soon, too much time will have passed for you to give me another chance. And..."

Ezra stared at me as his lips fell into a somber grimace.

"Willow, I keep trying, but I just cannot imagine my life without you in it."

I kept the tone of my voice calm, careful with my word choice.

"If you wanted me in your life, why haven't you been completely honest with me?"

Ezra blinked. "What do you mean?"

"I know about you being a suspect in an assault when you were a teen."

Ezra's brows started with shock but then settled on anger.

"Let me guess. That neighbor cop looked into me."

That's not a denial.

"Why did you keep it from me?" I asked.

"Why is this guy poking around in my damn business?"

"The whole time we were together, you never once mentioned it."

"Because I threw a vase at your wall? He's what, trying to convince you I'm some violent felon?"

Out of the corner of my eye, I saw Shane tense at the tone of Ezra's voice. I doubted Shane could make out all our words, but Ezra's body language spoke volumes about how pissed he was.

"Why did you hurt that guy?" I asked.

"Why is he looking into me? Does he want to get into your pants or something?"

"Why did you hide it from me?"

"That's it, isn't it? He wants you, and he knows I might win you back, so he's trying to discredit me."

"He doesn't want to get into my pants, Ezra. You keep asking me to trust you, but to do that, I need you to be honest with me. Tell me what happened."

Ezra was clearly struggling to let go of his anger over my neighbor poking around in his business, but eventually, he must've realized that if his plan was to convince me to give him another chance, he couldn't do that with a big secret standing between us.

"I was at a party and walked in on my buddy taking advantage of a girl. So, I beat the crap out of him."

I blinked. "Why would they name you a *suspect* if you were just protecting someone?"

"Because cops don't take too kindly to vigilante justice."

I wasn't sure I believed him. What a noble version of events to explain a criminal past. The old Willow would have accepted his explanation at face value, but the new Willow had come here to see the look on his face, his demeanor, to try to sort out fact from fiction.

"Why didn't you tell me?" I challenged.

"It isn't something I'm proud of, Willow. And you know I'm working toward a career in politics. If I want to get elected to a senior role, like governor or senator, being a suspect in a violent attack isn't something I can have out in the open. So, I keep it to myself."

Ezra's boss was well connected in this city—and Washington—so with one phone call, he could drastically cut down, if not eliminate, Ezra's career.

"Is that why you asked me here?" Ezra's brows furrowed in offense. "Because your neighbor dug up dirt on me?"

"No," I said. At least, not fully. "There's something I want to ask you."

Ezra waited.

"Saturday night, you called me. But I don't remember what we talked about."

Ezra chuckled lightly. "I barely remember it myself. Drunk dial. I was at a club with my boys, talking about how much I wanted you back."

My cheeks heated.

"And I do want you back. I've changed, Willow, I swear."

"Is that what you said when you called me on Saturday night?"

He smiled. "I think so? Honestly, I don't remember a lot about that call. Ended up passing out at three a.m., so the bouncer tossed me into an Uber."

He was at a club all night? Until he passed out? That would be something we could prove.

"Who paid for the Uber?" I asked.

Ezra looked confused. "Me. Why?"

"Can I see your app?"

"Why?"

I didn't answer him.

"Is this a trust test?" Ezra asked. "To see if you can trust me again? Because I swear I was not with a girl. Look." He pulled out his phone, opened up the app, and showed me the ride data from Saturday night.

Uber arrived at the club at 2:58 a.m. and dropped Ezra off at his apartment twelve minutes later.

His story was checking out, but...

"Did we see each other Saturday night?"

A line appeared between Ezra's eyebrows. "No. Why?"

Was it possible that sometime between the phone call and his three a.m. ride home, he had seen me?

"What happened Saturday night?" Ezra asked.

I took a sip of my coffee, unsure how to answer this.

Ezra's eyes landed on my broken wrist. "Did that happen to you on Saturday night?"

"I should go."

His voice hitched in alarm. "Willow, did someone do that to you?"

"It doesn't matter."

"To hell it doesn't. If someone did that to you, so help me, I'll..." Ezra composed himself before finishing his threat.

That look in his eyes seemed completely genuine. Was it real? Or was that old, gullible me resurfacing?

"What happened?" he pressed.

I sucked my bottom lip between my teeth, debating how to answer this.

"I fell off a bridge."

Ezra sat back in his seat. "You *what*?"

"Shane pulled me out of the water."

It took several seconds for Ezra to digest that, like my proclamation had punched him in the chest.

"Your neighbor?"

I nodded.

"How did you fall?"

"Police are trying to figure that out."

"You don't remember it?"

I shook my head.

Ezra looked down and to the side, putting the pieces together.

"Wait, are you asking me if *I* had something to do with it?"

I said nothing.

His jaw settled into offense.

"In a city of three million people, your neighbor happened to be at the exact time and place you went off a bridge, and you ask *me*? You should ask him these questions."

"What did you mean, I'd regret it?" I pressed.

"This is un-freaking-believable," Ezra snarled. "I didn't push you off some goddamn bridge. Maybe no one pushed you. Maybe you did this to yourself."

"What is that supposed to mean?"

"I heard you've been depressed lately."

"From who?" I asked.

"The anniversary of your dad's death. All that crap going on at work. Plus, all the stuff going on with your family."

I raised my chin and pretended his words hadn't penetrated my confidence. He was the third person to suggest I may have done this to myself—De Luca, Amelia, now him. If three independent people thought it might be true, could it be?

Was it possible I was so down, I was suicidal?

"When we broke up, you said I would regret it. What did you mean by that?"

"*That's* why you're asking me this?"

I waited.

Ezra sighed and rubbed his eyes, but thankfully, the anger from his voice dissipated as he answered, "I was angry, and I thought you'd eventually see what I did—that we're meant to be together."

I pressed my fingers against my temples, feeling so damn confused. Everything Ezra was saying made complete sense. He'd shown me his receipts. He answered all of my intrusive questions. If another failed attempt to win me back had resulted in some explosive fight where he had tried to kill me, why would he send me flowers and show up at my apartment soon after? For all he knew, I would remember who had done it. So, why risk it? It made no sense.

"Thank you for coming." I stood up next to the booth. I needed time to digest all of this and figure out my next steps. If it wasn't Ezra, who else could it be?

Ezra mirrored my movements, looking desperate to get his point across before I walked away.

"Willow, please. I swear to you, I did not hurt you." He brought his palm to my shoulder. "I would never hurt you. I want you back."

"Take your fuckin' hands off her." Shane yanked Ezra's hand away from me, twisting his arm.

"Dude, what the fuck?" Ezra cried out rather than fighting back. Smart move for a future politician to *not* fight with a law enforcement officer in public.

"Let him go," I said.

Ezra could fight back, this could escalate, and since Ezra's touch hadn't been violent, Shane would be the one in trouble.

Shane shoved off of Ezra, who rubbed his forearm, glaring at him.

"What the hell is he doing here?" Ezra looked from me to Shane, betrayal locking his jaw. "He was here the whole time?"

"I..."

"What was this, some kind of attempt to set me up?" His question was dark and laced with warning.

"No." Not exactly.

Ezra glanced between me and Shane one final time.

"You'd better be careful trusting him, Willow. He's getting into your head, making you suspect everyone in your life, but from what you told me? There's only one person in your life that was anywhere near your fall on Saturday."

27

"So, he offered no proof as to his whereabouts at ten o'clock Saturday night," Shane argued.

I could feel my blood pressure spiking, and I jogged faster through the crosswalk. We'd left the café only minutes ago, after Ezra had stormed out.

The city was like a breathing organism. The "L" train roared overhead as vehicles crowded together in morning rush-hour traffic, their tires careening past us with no regard for human life. Wind cut through the buildings like a turbine, burning our noses and cheeks, not caring that it hurt. Seventy-story buildings cut any hope of the sun warming our skin.

"He showed me the Uber receipt." I clenched my fists. "He got picked up from a club and went directly home."

"*I was too drunk to remember what happened Saturday night* is not an alibi, Willow. It's a red flag."

A red flag.

I gritted my teeth, my head pounding as hard as my heart. How many goddamn red flags had we uncovered lately? Yet we never ruled out any of them! None of them. Ezra looked like a suspect, then he didn't—no, wait, he still did. I thought meeting him would get some answers, but no. Just more questions. Just like everything else in my life—the closer I got to the truth, the further it seemed to slip from my grasp.

I couldn't take it anymore. I pinched the bridge of my nose, fighting back tears. Fragments of conversations and implications bouncing through my thoughts.

Your ex-boyfriend isn't letting you go, Willow.

Your mom has a million reasons to hurt you.

Will your sister benefit from your life insurance policy?

Can I get a list of the people who were fired from your work?

That list of guys who've sent DMs is freaking long.

Amelia has scratches on her arms. She tell you how they got there?

And then the ones others had pointed out.

You've sounded really down lately.

The anniversary of your dad's death. All that crap going on at work. Plus, all the stuff going on with your family.

I had been feeling sad. Ezra had broken my heart a few months ago. Grief always surrounded the anniversary of my dad's death. I felt more alone than ever, my family and I on the outs again. How much can one person be pushed before they snap? Was it possible...

Was it possible I had done this to myself?

If I was depressed enough to end my life, would I have blocked that out too? Just like I blocked out the fall itself and blocked out whatever happened to my dad that left me covered in blood?

Ezra's words echoed through my head.

In a city of three million people, your neighbor happened to be at the exact time and place you went off a bridge?

There's only one person in your life that was anywhere near your accident on Saturday—Shane.

"We need to look closer at the timeline," Shane urged.

"Enough!" I ceased walking.

He rocked back on his heels and must've noticed my hands trembling because he softened his expression.

"I'm not tryin' to make your life difficult."

"But you are!" I said. "I know you don't mean to, but you are!"

Anger coursed through my veins at how much my life had been upended. And I knew it wasn't fair for me to feel this way, but instantly, all my anger was directed at Shane. He was the one that had been in my ear since this all started. He was the one making me look at everyone in my life like a murder suspect. Tearing my life to shreds along with any semblance of peace and normalcy.

I didn't know who I could trust anymore, and I couldn't continue living in this never-ending nightmare. I felt like I was going crazy. Looking at every person in my life through the lens of a police detective—it was just too much to take.

"You keep planting these seeds of doubt in my head with everyone!"

"Willow..."

"No, listen to me! Do you know what this feels like?" I said, taking a step toward him. "Imagine someone putting the most painful moments of *your* relationships under a microscope."

Shane put his palms up in surrender. "Look, I—"

"You know what that does? It makes you feel crazy! I don't trust anyone anymore! I don't trust Ezra, I don't trust my mom, or Amelia, or people at my work, or strangers who've DM'd me. I don't even trust *you*!"

Shane stilled, and his eyes hardened. "What are you talkin' about?"

"You were with me that day by the bridge! In a city of three million people, that's pretty coincidental."

His understanding evaporated, his eyes tightening in offense. "You think I would hurt you?"

"According to you, someone did. If we're throwing everyone else I care about into the mix, why not you?"

Shane's face darkened, and he took a hostile step closer to me. "You actually think, after everything I've done, that I would harm a hair on your head?"

I don't know why I took a step back, but I did. Repeatedly. Until my back pressed against the skyscraper behind me. If pedestrians were gawking at us, I'd be none the wiser. Right now, it was like Shane and I were alone, angry energy swirling together in a toxic bubble.

But if he thought putting one palm against the wall next to my head was going to intimidate me into shutting up, he had another thing coming.

"I don't know what to think anymore! That's the whole point. I don't even trust myself! Because you know what? I've been sad lately. Ezra's been trying to get me back, which has made all the pain of him breaking my heart resurface, reminding me of just how damn lonely I feel! I also hate my job, but I've been stuck without a plan for so long, it feels near impossible to move forward. And then...there's my family...who have been lying to me about my dad for years! I might've only recently confirmed this, but in my heart, I think I knew it all along. So, yeah, I've been down. And I never thought I was the type of person who would plunge to my death willingly, but maybe I was wrong. They say every human has a breaking point. Maybe I reached mine."

"You were screamin' bloody murder when you went off that bridge."

"Out of terror, I'm sure."

"If you wanted to kill yourself, you wouldn't have screamed like that."

"Says who? I watched a documentary one time about suicide off the Golden Gate Bridge. Do you know what they found when they interviewed the handful of people that survived?"

Shane's jaw tensed.

"Over ninety percent of people regretted it the instant they jumped. Even if I was screaming because I didn't want to die, it doesn't mean I didn't jump."

"You're terrified of drowning."

"But maybe I hadn't woken up that morning, intending to kill myself. Maybe something made me snap, and the bridge was right there when it happened."

"You don't remember the fall itself, but you remember the days and weeks leading up to it. If you were depressed enough to want to end your life, you would have remembered that, Willow. I really don't think you did this to yourself."

"Well, maybe you don't want to hear this because it would make you think less of me."

Anger punched through his eyes. "That's insulting."

"Maybe you don't want to admit to yourself that, deep down, you do wonder. Maybe you have some distorted image of me that doesn't quite jive with this hot mess of a girl who was so desperate to escape it all that she jumped from a bridge? Maybe you'd want to have nothing to do with that girl. And you want to prove to yourself that I'm not the type of girl who'd do something like that."

"How can you think so little of me?"

"Maybe the real reason you don't want to be with me is because you think it's true; you think I did this to myself."

Shane's jaw clenched. "Which is it, Willow? You think I'm a homicidal lunatic?" He paused. "Or a guy who is such a piece of shit that he would reject someone if they were hurting inside?"

My throat burned. "I..."

"Listen to my words carefully." His angry eyes captured mine as he rested his other palm next to my head, caging me. "I would never harm a hair on your head. And if you were hurting so badly that you would consider ending your life, I would spend every waking second proving to you that life is worth living."

"Shane..."

"I've always been honest with you, so hear me when I say this: There is *nothing* you could ever do or say that would make me think less of you. And there's nothin' you could do to make me want you less."

My lip quivered. He needed to keep those things to himself if we had any hope of keeping our emotions in check.

"What if you're wrong? What if you're seeing danger where there isn't any because of what you went through with Fallon? What if you're projecting those fears onto me?"

I hated myself the instant the words left my mouth. The instant I saw the look on his face. I felt ashamed, sickened by it. What was I turning into?

And how selfish was I being, allowing this—whatever this relationship was—to continue? Because it wasn't just my sense of stability that was on the line.

Shane was coming unglued. Even if he didn't jeopardize his career by getting involved in the case, he pinned Ezra up against the wall by his throat. And then nearly broke his wrist in the coffee shop. Not to mention, he pulled Clay over without due cause. I was not an expert in law enforcement, but none of this could be good. Shane was unraveling, and it was all my fault.

"Listen to me very carefully." Shane's voice was low and even. "My instincts are crisp as hell, and they are not contaminated by what happened with Fallon. Everything in my gut tells me someone did this to you, and I will not stop until we find out who it is. And make them pay."

"But if it's not because of what happened in your past, why are you this obsessed with it?"

"Because I'm falling in love with you, dammit!"

My breath snagged at the base of my throat as I studied his eyes —indigo yet burning red. I was pinned between him and the wall, his massive forearm muscles caging me in next to my ears. And all the vehicle engines faded until all I could hear was the beating of my heart.

As it thumped for Shane.

Shane looked at my mouth one final time, then claimed my lips with his. Silencing my fears and worries. Channeling his frustration into passion.

My chest pressed against his, expanding with each stolen breath. I wished we'd had this argument somewhere else, somewhere we could rip each other's clothes off and take our frustrations out.

His tongue assaulted mine in the best possible way while I greedily surrendered to it. Pulling his body tighter against mine. Grasping for the strength to not rip his clothes off and take him in public.

My cell phone's ring invaded our slice of heaven.

I ignored it. And welcomed Shane's fingers breaching the hem of my shirt.

My cell phone rang again.

I wanted to smash my back pocket against the wall, if only to make it shut up. But it didn't stop our hands from wandering, our mouths from dancing, pedestrians hooting and hollering at us as they passed.

When my cell phone rang for the third time in a row, Shane stepped back.

"You should get it," he growled breathlessly. "It must be important."

No. Nothing was important. Nothing but Shane, and his profession, and his mouth on mine. But evidently, he would not continue kissing me until I stopped whoever the hell was calling me from interrupting us again.

"Hello?" I couldn't hide my annoyance.

"Willow. Officer De Luca here. Got a minute?"

"I..."

"I'll make it brief. Remember I told you I'd pull the cameras near the bridge?"

Shane was looking at me, obviously concerned about whatever my face was telling him.

"Yeah?"

"Reviewed them. Only one camera had the angle of where you went over, and the quality is shit. It's dark, and you can't make out much, but you can see what happened right before you went into the water."

My heart raced in my chest.

"And?" I pressed.

"I'm sorry for not believing you, Willow. Shows *two* people on the bridge that night. Can't tell if the other person was male or female, but we can see a confrontation."

Shane's eyes grazed down to my free hand, and his brows furrowed when he noticed it trembling.

"We can see that in the scuffle, you're pushed over the railing."

28

"Do you recognize anything?" Detective Rosse, who was now in charge of my case, asked.

De Luca, Rosse, and I sat in a conference room at the Chicago Police station while Shane stood against the wall with his arms crossed so tightly, I worried his body would suffer vascular damage. Like the place wasn't already tense enough with its metal chairs, dramatically long rectangular table, and a mirror that was undoubtedly two-way glass.

A minute ago, they'd lowered the lights so I could see the flat screen hanging on the wall better. Not that it helped. I squinted at the footage.

"Can you play it again?"

The video rewound and started from the beginning.

"Why is the quality so bad?"

It was so grainy, I could see pixels. While I could make out two dark figures, if the footage wasn't time-stamped and the location confirmed by the police, I wouldn't even know one of them was me.

"Camera is a half block from the bridge. Only caught the incident in the upper right corner of the footage." And they'd zoomed in as best they could. "Do you recognize anything about the other person?"

I watched it again. Two figures appeared to face each other. Arm gestures suggested we were arguing—an argument that led to a wrestling match. And in that wrestling match, I went up over the railing. The other person stood on the bridge, watching as I fell into the deadly waters of the river below.

They crouched down, watching the water—presumably watching me get rescued by Shane—before they took off running.

"I can't make out anything," I said. "I can't even tell if it's a man or a woman."

"I don't see a lot of hair," Shane said. "Might indicate male. Although it could be a female with a short haircut or her hair pulled back."

I squinted at the footage again; Shane was right.

No long hair.

Rosse asked, "Know any women who have short hair?"

"No."

Rosse noted that in the digital notebook on his iPad. "We'll prioritize questioning men first, but we won't rule out a female."

We had already gone over everything else with him, filling him in on the life insurance policy, Ezra wanting me back and him calling me that night, the scratches on Amelia's arms, everything.

"I want to circle back to something you said," Rosse added. "You mentioned your company recently let several people go, and two of them were particularly disgruntled?"

"They'd put in over ten years with excellent performance evaluations and were panicked about losing their income," I said.

"Would you have met them outside of work?"

"No. I don't think so," I amended. "I mean, if they were crying and asked me to meet them somewhere public, there's a slight chance I might have, but I don't think anybody from work would've done this."

"Why's that?"

"I'm not the one who makes head-count targets. Executive management makes those. My job in HR is to help facilitate the head-count reductions, as directed by management. So, they would know this wasn't my fault."

Rosse evaluated me. He had bushy eyebrows and a square jaw that looked as if working Chicago's darkest cases had turned his face to stone.

"Sometimes, people misplace blame," he said.

I guess that was possible, but, "I didn't know them well, and I wouldn't meet a stranger late at night. Alone."

"Now that we have proof of foul play, I'll be contacting your company to get a list of those names."

He went silent for a moment, typing into his iPad.

"Anything else that you can think of that you haven't already mentioned?"

I was about to say no, but shut my mouth. A gesture Rosse surely noticed because he set his iPad down and stared at me.

"It's probably nothing." I hoped.

A line appeared between Shane's eyebrows.

"But right after that night, I noticed that my toothbrush had been moved."

Shane pushed off the wall.

"And later, I discovered that my bookmark was in the wrong spot. And then..."

Shane's body was a statue, his unblinking eyes fixed on me.

"I found this...lump of hair in my kitchen sink. Each of these things seemed strange at the time and made me feel uneasy. I even wondered if someone was playing mind games with me, but since nothing was missing, I thought I must be projecting my fear onto the situation."

"And you didn't mention this to the police?"

"Because I probably put the toothbrush in the wrong location and forgot which chapter I was on in my book. As for the hair, I don't know. Maybe I knocked my hairbrush in the sink one day and didn't realize it or something."

"You notice anything else in your apartment that's off?"

"No."

"*When* did you notice these items were out of place?"

"The first time I used them after getting released from the hospital. First time I brushed my teeth, the first time I read that book, and the first time I washed dishes."

Rosse poked at his iPad screen. "Let me ask you this: when you got home from the hospital, you found the door unsecure, correct?"

I nodded.

"Let's say someone *is* responsible for the items. Could all three have happened when your apartment was open?"

I nodded. "But why would anybody move those things around?"

Rosse captured me in his hardened gaze. "Just collecting facts at the moment, Ms. Johnson."

He set his iPad down again, as if that were all he needed.

"There's one other thing," I said.

Shane's going to have an aneurysm over this.

"There's a chance I saw someone watching me the other night."

Yep, Shane's forehead vein is about to explode.

"Outside my sliding glass door, I saw a figure, but I couldn't see well, so it might have been nothing."

Kaboom. The vein in Shane's neck exploded, too.

I twisted my fingers together as Rosse gathered the details—the date, the time. The whole while, Shane clenched his hands into fists and paced.

"I think I have what I need to get started."

I looked from Rosse, to De Luca, to Shane.

"Where does this leave us?"

"I'll be in touch when I know more. Meantime, take precautions to keep yourself safe, Ms. Johnson. Lock your doors. Don't walk at night alone. Don't meet anyone alone. Whoever did this to you is likely about to get formally questioned by law enforcement. Psychologically, they can feel backed into a corner. Turning up the heat on them, so to speak."

Yeah, but, "If the police are looking at them, they'd be risking their neck, trying something again. More likely to get caught." Right?

"When people who've committed a crime are backed into a corner, they don't always think rationally. And, in their mind, there's only one person who can identify them as your attempted killer."

Ice shot through my limbs.

"So, things are about to get a lot worse," I said. "More dangerous."

Rosse offered me an empathetic look. "I'd vary your routine if I were you. Just to be safe."

29

"Pack a bag," Shane said.

"Just slow down for a minute," I said. "This changes nothing."

"It changes everything." His eyes snapped to mine, his stare so intense, it almost cracked me in half.

He was right. It did change everything.

Rationally, I had been going along with Shane's investigation because it was the responsible thing to do. But deep down, I guess I never fully believed it. Until now.

Now, any fragment of hope that there was some alternative explanation we hadn't thought of yet had been obliterated. Blown up, the ashes of the life I thought I had falling around me until my once-colorful existence became entombed in gray.

I couldn't even cling to the hope that this person was a stranger anymore. Not only because of the statistics that it was likely someone I knew, but also because I would never meet a stranger alone, let alone in the dark of night like that. And I would never go for a walk late at night by myself—to bump into a stranger who happened to be a killer.

Which meant it had to be somebody I knew.

My lungs began to spasm, causing my fingers to tremble. Shane's gaze locked on my hands, and he stopped pacing.

"You okay?" His tone was deep with concern.

I shook my head.

I don't think I'll ever feel okay again.

"Someone in my life hates me enough to want me dead."

I wasn't one of those people that had dozens of friends. I had a small group of close friends; I had my family. And once, Ezra. Even though we had our ups and downs, these were all people that I trusted with my whole heart to never wish me harm. I never imagined that someone I invited into my inner circle could hate me so much, they would want me dead.

I felt completely and utterly shocked. Scared of what was going to come next. But I also felt angry.

What had I ever done to someone to warrant them throwing me off a bridge into the icy river? No matter what disagreements or arguments we might've ever had, nothing escalated to the point of murder. How dare they try to rob me of my life and all the things that I wanted to do.

I clenched my hands into balls. "My whole life, I've taken the high road when people have hurt my feelings or made mistakes," I said. "I'd forgive them and move forward. I forgave Ezra the first few times I saw problems with him. Long before I saw him kissing that other girl, I'd seen his eyes wander and caught him flirting. And every time my sister rejected me, I reminded myself she was going through a hard time, and I needed to be there to support her. I kept inviting Mom back into my life each time she abandoned me. I kept my friendship with Amelia, even though she'd gotten snarky with me for no reason frequently. And Tracey, who became selfish at times, breaking plans whenever a hot date asked her out."

Shane stepped closer to me.

"I always hold on to hope that things will get better, the same way I held on to hope when I was a kid, believing my mom would return whenever she left us. But how long do you hold on to things that are not good for you?"

Because reflecting on it, allowing people to mistreat you repeatedly isn't taking the high road or being a kindhearted person; it's just giving them a free pass to treat you like a doormat. And sends the message that you're okay with it. I held on to toxic relationships for far too long.

This tendency bled into other areas of my life as well. My job, for instance, which I'd continued to hold on to long after I'd grown to hate it.

I was angry at myself for having allowed this pattern of holding on to unhealthy things for so long that it almost cost me my life.

Whoever did this to me was probably someone who'd thrown up red flags along the way, someone I should have cut out of my life long ago. It was time to sift through these people, not only to find out who my killer was, but to also weed out the toxic relationships from those that lift me up rather than bring me down.

"I need to stand up to people, stand up for myself. All the time. Not just once in a while. And I need to decide what boundaries I'm comfortable with."

"Starting with me," Shane said.

I eyed him, confused by what he meant. Confused why that look of desire washed across his features as he unleashed that stare at me —the one he'd had before he kissed me against that skyscraper.

"When I saw that footage tonight, something changed for me, too. Seeing someone try to kill you, seeing you almost taken from me..." Shane paused. "I know this contradicts everything I told you before," he started. "And if you're not comfortable with it, you need to tell me."

His eyes pierced mine, and he took a step closer, studying my face, my eyes, my lips, my jaw. And he shook his head slowly, speaking in a soft tone this time. "I've been falling for you for a while," he admitted. "From the first moment I laid eyes on you and your beauty, I felt something. And when I met you, I was mesmerized by you. Most people would have been sheepish after a stranger witnessed their ex getting handsy with them, but you squared your shoulders to me and said Ezra was using your *slight overindulgence as an excuse to try to weasel his way back into your life.* Right then and there, I knew you were special, and I found myself wanting to learn everything I could about you. You might think I notice things like what coffee shop is your favorite or that you feed a stray cat because I'm a detective, but that's not it. I notice you, only you, Willow, because everything about you intrigues me. And all this time, I've been falling for you. Fought it with everything I had, but it was like fighting a rip current. A losing battle. And the more time I've spent with you, the faster that rip current shot me out to sea. And now, my heart is completely invested in you. And there's no goin' back."

"But you said—"

"I don't know what the future holds for us. I can't even think about that right now. All I can think about is you and how damn angry I am that someone did this to you. You don't deserve it. You're sweet and kind and would never hurt anyone, and whoever this Goddamn monster is that threw you over that bridge?" Shane's jaw ticced. "They deserve to suffer. When we find them, I want five minutes alone with them."

His affection, laced with vengeance, took a minute to digest.

"I don't want you to feel this angry." I wanted him to be happy. Always, because the truth was, I'd been falling for him, too.

"You know what's buried beneath the anger?" Shane asked. "Fear. I can't remember the last time that I've felt afraid. Because being in a dangerous job is a different fear—survival. But there's a fear far worse than dying."

He stepped even closer, so close that I could feel the heat coming off his chest, and looked down at my lips.

"Having someone you care deeply for die and not being able to stop it."

I sucked in a breath.

"I'm not going to die," I assured.

Shane stretched his fingers at his sides, the blue in his eyes darkening as he stared at me. "I lost my mom. When my dad died, part of her died too, and she was never the same again. I lost my sister when he died, because she changed. She went from being this hopeful, cheery person to the sullen version of herself who doesn't seem to be as happy as she once was. Over time, I lost my dad's entire side of the family because of the dynamics created in the aftermath of his death."

Shane tentatively traced my lower lip with his thumb, staring at my mouth, as if unable to imagine living without it pressed to his. His touch felt so incredible, I had to actively focus on his next words.

"I've lost enough in my life, Willow, and I will not lose you."

He began breathing heavily, his eyes glued to my lips, his hand sliding up my face, cupping my cheek.

"Are you still in pain?" He took another angry step toward me.

"What?"

"From the fall," he growled impatiently. "Are you still in pain?"

What? "No?" *Not really. Why?*

"Good." He pushed me against the wall.

Not gently.

And crashed his mouth to mine.

Oh. My. Word.

He stroked the side of my face with his knuckles as I opened my mouth, surrendering to Shane's tongue as it slid inside me. A flash of heat radiated down my throat, rippling over my chest, and engulfed the sensitive flesh between my legs. Flesh that came alive like electricity that had been turned on, now begging to be touched. Especially when he grabbed my hip and raised my arm above my head.

It was all like magic pixie dust that activated a hibernated part of my passion that entirely surrendered to the heat of his mouth on mine. Erasing any space between us, he pressed me harder against the wall, taking out all his anger and frustration out on my body.

We'd kissed before, but this... this was different. He'd professed his feelings for me, and though I didn't know where we'd go from here—feeling didn't mean he'd changed his stance on marriage—fighting to resist this wasn't working.

I pressed my tongue harder against his, making him groan into my mouth.

I wanted to swallow that groan; I wanted to eat it and feel it reverberate throughout my entire body as I pulled him on top of me. I wanted to see all of him and feel all of him. Inside me. Tasting me. Looking me in the eye as he made me his own.

He grazed his teeth along my jaw and kissed down my neck, thrusting his hips against me, pressing his excitement between my thighs.

"You feel what you do to me?" he asked.

"Yes," I whispered, breathlessly, my chest heaving.

When his mouth reclaimed mine, his hand breached the fabric of my shirt and slid up my belly, sending a spark of electricity to my chest as he moved his hands slowly over my skin, one agonizing inch at a time until finally, he palmed my breast.

And possessively squeezed it so hard, I cried out. A good cry. A please-do-it-again cry.

If this was angry Shane, I wanted to make him angry every day. I'd find reasons to pick fights with him, just so he'd throw me up against the wall and have his way with me. I would secretly pray that someone would cut him off in traffic or piss him off so he could come home and release his frustrations like this.

My nipple hardened even more as Shane pinched it between his thumb and finger, sending a shockwave of heat between my thighs. I pressed my breast harder against his hand.

"Don't stop," I whispered.

He grumbled a grouchy laugh and slipped his tongue deeper into my mouth, silently assuring me he had no plans to stop anytime soon.

He robbed my mouth of his, an icy need abandoning my lips as he looked me in the eye.

"You like this?" he asked, moving his hand to my other breast. And squeezing it.

"Yes," I managed.

"Tell me what you want, Willow."

He squeezed my other nipple, making my head fall against the wall, my back arching.

"I want you," I said.

He pulled my flesh against his, all my soft parts pressing up against all his hard ones, as I glided my hands over the contours of his shoulder muscles, feeling them tense beneath my palms.

Shane shot two hands around my thighs and lifted me up, wrapping my legs around his waist. Not breaking the kiss, he walked us a few steps to my kitchen.

And set me down on my table.

This time gently.

Standing between my knees, he guided me backward until I was lying down, him hovering over me, kissing me. Then inching my shirt up so he could move his kisses to my stomach. And continued to travel upward.

He moved my bra up, groaning at the sight of my exposed breasts, and when his mouth reached my nipple, I sucked in a breath. He swirled his tongue around and around my sensitive bud, sucking on me, tasting my skin, engulfing the fire between my legs into an inferno.

I locked eyes with him, his tongue firm and tight, then soft and tender as it spread its love to my nipple, around and around until my head fell back against the table. I could feel his groan of approval against my skin, and every inch of my body begged for his attention.

His mouth moved from one breast to the other, his tongue dancing over my skin, my nipples, while he'd palm the other side as he worked his ecstasy.

All the while, the heat between my legs was becoming unbearable.

He continued kissing, sucking me, nipping at me, though, as if he enjoyed making this wanton need grow until I couldn't take it anymore. I shoved my fingers into his hair, tugging it, until finally, his lips moved away from my breasts, leaving my skin lined with frosted goose bumps from the wetness.

He kissed up my neck, my jaw, and then my mouth again.

But his hands... his hands began to move. He was strong enough to hover over me, pressing his lips against mine while he unbuttoned my pants and slipped his hand beneath my panties.

Shane held my gaze as he slowly slipped one finger between my folds, a groan escaping my lips as he growled.

"You're so wet for me."

My body heated even more at the praise in his tone, and I didn't dare take my eyes off his as he slid his middle finger down, breaching my entrance.

"Shane," I whispered.

"I'm just getting started, Willow."

I grabbed his shoulders, and when he thrust two fingers inside of me, I arched my back. He moved his thumb to the sensitive bundle of tissue at the top of my center, knowing explicitly how to move his hand. The right pressure, the rhythm and cadence of his touch.

"You like that?" he asked.

I nodded, licking my lower lip.

He curled his fingers inside of me, hitting a delicate patch of nerves that made my eyes roll back as he pulled his fingers back slightly, then in. Over and over.

It felt so good the rest of the universe collapsed into nothing. The only thing that existed were his fingers stretching me, filling me as he worked the bundle of nerves on the inside, and circled the sensitive bud on the outside with his thumb. His eyes, watching me, his mouth falling open in lust as I began to move my hips against his palm. The sounds of my moans, his breathing, the smell of arousal electrifying the space around our bodies.

Shane moved his fingers softer at first, then harder, knowing my body better than my own, his jaw locking as he watched my facial expressions.

I liked that he watched me. I cherished how he'd notice when he'd hit me at the right pressure, and then do it again and again until he could see the wave inside of me building.

Desperate for its release, I pressed one of my hands on top of his and pushed down harder. He swirled his thumb over the apex of my center, making me start to come unglued.

He brought his mouth back to mine and whispered against my lips, "You feel so good, Willow."

That was all I needed to hear. I collapsed under the pleasure of his words, biting his lip and squeezing my legs so hard, I wondered if it hurt him.

"Willow," Shane groaned as I shuddered.

He continued to work my body until the last of my trembles subsided, and then he kissed my jaw, my neck.

I pushed his chest so I could sit up, and then I rubbed my hand on his engorged jeans, watching as his eyes shut, and his head fell back with a groan.

I wanted to taste him. Lick him. Feel him inside my mouth, and return the pleasure he'd just given me. And then I wanted him to pin me down and claim me.

Because if my orgasm was that strong with just his hand, I couldn't imagine how hard I'd come undone with him inside of me.

I unbuttoned his pants.

But suddenly, a harsh pounding on my door thwarted our passion session.

Three knocks.

With a fist, by the sound of it.

Shane looked at me with despair.

"I won't answer it," I whispered.

I unzipped his pants and began to pull his jeans down.

Bam. Bam. Bam.

"Ignore it," I whispered.

Shane looked less sure this time, glancing at my front door before letting me pull his pants down another couple of inches.

Bam. Bam. Bam.

"Willow, it's me. We need to talk right away."

30

"Why are you harassing Ezra?" Amelia snapped.

She didn't wait for me to invite her inside, just stormed past me into my apartment. Like it wasn't irritating enough that she'd interrupted Shane and me. Also, what was with the word *harassing*?

"He told me about your little coffee shop ambush." She glared at Shane. Who remained a statue against the far wall with his wrists crossed over his engorged pants. If she wasn't so self-centered, maybe she would see she'd interrupted something *intimate* with her incessant pounding.

"Since when do you and Ezra talk?" I crossed my arms over my chest.

Shane's eyes hardened as he looked at her hair. Which was in a bun. Amelia normally wore her hair down, but if someone had styled their hair in an updo that night, it might match the silhouette on that video.

"You're pretty upset that I questioned him," I said.

"Because he's a good guy and he doesn't deserve this. His boss has connections and might even fire him."

I eyed her. "How do *you* know that?" I'd never mentioned it.

Amelia's eyes twitched, and understanding etched into my bones.

How could I have been so blind?

A memory fired the clue I'd dismissed a while back. It was one of those things where, at the time, your instincts weren't *screaming* at you. But it was more of a gentle *huh-that's-odd* type of whisper.

I walk into the club where I'm meeting Ezra and several of my friends.

I arrive fifteen minutes early, so I assume I'm going to be the first one here, but I'm not. Sitting at the bar with their stools facing each other, Ezra and Amelia are talking. They're leaning forward, likely so they can hear each other over the noise of the music, but their faces are only a foot apart. And the way they're smiling at each other, it makes me uncomfortable.

How are they already halfway through a drink?

"Hey." Ezra smiles when he sees me. He stands up and gives me a kiss.

Amelia smiles too. But it doesn't meet her eyes.

"Why are you here so early?" I ask.

"Finished work a half hour ago," Ezra said. "Either had to go all the way home and then run late or just come directly here."

I look at Amelia.

"Got lucky with the 'L' train," she says. "Normally have to wait several minutes, but when I showed up to the platform, one showed up right away."

I guess that tracks.

Of course it does. Amelia is my friend. Why would I feel suspicious?

But what if I had been wrong back then? Ezra kiss-cheated on me one time and text-cheated another. Did it not stand a reason he might've been capable of full-blown cheating? Maybe even with one of my friends?

"You need to tell the detectives that Ezra wasn't involved with that bridge incident."

"I don't know that," I said.

"Ezra would never hurt anyone."

"He hurt me when he cheated on me."

"He didn't full-blown cheat."

Interesting. If she hadn't had sex with him, would she consider that not cheating, then?

"So, there are degrees to cheating now?"

"Ezra's boss has connections with politicians in Chicago."

"You said that already," I reminded her. "How exactly do you know that?"

"If those cops show up and ask him questions, one phone call, and Ezra won't be able to pursue a political career in this city. He could even lose his job."

"If someone had feelings for him, losing his job would be unfortunate. Since he might have to move."

I was testing her, and sure enough, her lips hardened.

"He doesn't have enough savings to weather that. How can you not care?"

I did care. But that wasn't the point of our conversation.

"How do you know all that about him?" I challenged.

"Tell the detectives to back off."

"How long have you two been close?" I asked.

Amelia huffed. "You're ridiculous."

"So, it doesn't bother you then? That he's been trying to get me back ever since I broke up with him?"

There. Right there. That flash of anger in her eyes confirmed it. She did have feelings for Ezra, and, yep, it bothered her that he wanted me back. A lot. That was why she was so fixated on him sending me flowers; it hurt her feelings.

I remembered something Ezra said about that night, how he'd called me to beg me for another chance.

I knew I shouldn't ask her questions about the case, but now that I could see the look in her eyes, I couldn't stop myself.

"Were you with Ezra the night I fell?"

She looked disgusted. "We're done here."

Amelia tried to walk past me, but I blocked her path.

Shane pushed off the wall and came closer.

"Did you know he called me that night?"

"You know, if you go around, treating everyone in your life like some psychopathic killer, whenever they figure out what happened, none of us will be here for you when you come crawling back to apologize."

"How did you get the scratches on your arms?"

"Go to hell, Willow."

Amelia walked around me and stormed out of my apartment.

31

"**Y**ou okay?" Shane asked.

I didn't know what level Amelia and Ezra may have betrayed me, but something else she said formed a pit in my stomach because it reminded me of the fear I'd had since day one.

"She's right," I said. "Once Rosse starts questioning everyone, people are going to be so offended, they may shut me out of their lives."

"That's not true."

"Maybe not for everyone, but my family? Our relationship isn't strong enough to have someone poking around like that."

Look how upset I'd made my mother when I confronted her about lying to me my whole life. My questions had already driven a wedge in our relationship, and now, Rosse was going to probe her about my life insurance policy, her whereabouts, and probably ask her point-blank if she'd tried to hurt me. Mom would feel attacked by me. Again. This time pegged as an awful human whose own daughter sent cops to her house, accusing her of attempted murder.

She might never talk to me again. And when Hayley found out

about it, she would probably never talk to me again, either.

I scrubbed my hands over my face.

"Willow." Shane walked up to me, has dark hair accenting his blue eyes as he brought his palm to my cheek—brushing my skin with this thumb, as if he knew his touch was what I needed. And when he spoke, he kept his tone cautious. "Have you ever seen Amelia get violent?"

"No."

Relief did not flood Shane's face. I could see the wheels turning in his head, undoubtedly thinking about her hairstyle, the scratches on her arms, and whatever mysterious relationship she and Ezra obviously had.

"I need to talk to my mom and sister," I said. "I need to talk to them before it's too late."

Shane's lips tightened. "I don't think that's such a good idea."

"The last time I talked to them, I upset them. I can't risk ending things like that. I need a chance to mend things—or at the very least, get better closure."

"I still don't think it's a good idea."

"Rosse agrees the hair points toward a guy."

Shane frowned. Looked at the front door Amelia and her bun had walked through. "It's not concrete enough to risk your life."

"I'm sorry, but I'm doing this with or without your approval."

Shane bit his lip and then placed both of his hands on my upper arms. "I'm going to say somethin', and you're not going to freak out."

"Prefacing anything with that sentence will make anyone freak out."

"I made some calls. Put a...contingency plan in place, just in case things went south."

"A contingency plan."

"With Amelia showin' up here and Rosse about to question people, I think it's time. I arranged for us to stay in a cabin. Couple hours northwest. Wooded area, near a lake. It'll be beautiful this time of year."

"I have to work. So do you."

"The place has internet. You won't have to take full vacation weeks if you work remotely."

"Weeks?" My mouth gaped. "Are you crazy?"

"Hopefully, it won't be that long, but even if it is, I have plenty of vacation time built up."

"No. And in case you forgot, I've already missed work, and I don't want to ask the company for exceptions to be made for me to work remotely."

His jaw tightened. "I'd like you to pack a bag."

"No."

Shane glared at me.

I guess we weren't going to get back to making love right now.

"You're not safe here."

"Most everyone in my life knows that I live next door to a law enforcement officer. Even if they did want to hurt me again, they wouldn't be stupid enough to come to my place."

This was so surreal, plotting out possible attack points.

No, I wasn't planning them out. Shane and Rosse had to be wrong. Whoever did this was counting their lucky stars that they had gotten away with it, and they would never come back and try again.

The real question was, would I ever figure out who did it?

If I didn't, I could see two scenarios playing out. Either I would cut almost everybody out of my life out of fear or I wouldn't, and my attempted killer would remain in my life forever. I could sit across the dinner table with them someday and have no idea that they tried to end my life.

The thought made me sick. Neither scenario was acceptable. The only acceptable solution was to find out who did this.

And in the meantime, for me to talk to my mom and sister before it was too late.

"I'm heading to my mother's house. You're welcome to come, but you'll have to stay in the car."

32

"I'm sorry I upset you," I said.

I held the photo frame, staring into the eyes of a man I would never know. He had his arms around me and Hayley, Mom standing next to him with a smile on her face wider than I'd ever seen it. Mom's smiles never reached her eyes like that anymore, and her eyes didn't sparkle with optimism.

She sat in her rocking chair, clutching a glass of amber liquid. She had taken up smoking again, evidently, blowing out a long puff of poison as she stared at me with impassive eyes. Mascara clumped in the corners, her eyeliner smudged, like her cherry lipstick.

Shane sat parked out front, unwilling to leave me alone until they identified that person on the bridge. He even made me come up with a signal "just in case" something happened and I couldn't get to my phone—to flicker the lights. Even then, it was nearly impossible to get my bodyguard to stand down.

But he understood what was at stake with my coming here.

My goal was simple. I needed to put my family's past behind me once and for all. Because if I didn't let go of it, resentment would spread its weeds and strangle my soul. I'd become a bitter version of myself, filled with the heavy anger from my past anchoring my heart, preventing me from sailing into the clear skies of my future.

And after experiencing the joy I felt anytime I was with Shane, I was choosing a different destiny. I was choosing happiness over hurt.

To do that, I would no longer fight against the current of trying to morph my relationships with my mother and sister into something that they weren't. I would try one last time to learn whatever Mom was willing to share with me, and then I would accept these relationships for what they were.

Only then would I be free.

I sat on Mom's couch, her living room reeking of stale smoke.

She tapped her cigarette above an ashtray, its ashes flaking off and joining a little mountain of old ones.

"I still don't understand why you lied to me." I kept my voice low and even. Sad, not accusatory.

"I told you, I was trying to protect you."

"But how?" I pressed. "How does keeping me in the dark protect me?"

My mom pursed her lips. "Remember what you told me when you and Ezra broke up?"

I stilled; I'd been vulnerable at that time in my life and shared what Ezra had done. Not typical with the lack of depth in our relationship.

"Remember how it affected your self-esteem? Even though *his* offensive actions had no bearing on your beauty or talent?"

My hit to my self-worth only lasted a week, and, yes, I was aware of how pathetic it sounded to let him affect me.

"Imagine if that was something dark that would haunt you and you'd question your self-worth for the rest of your life, not just after a breakup. I didn't want that for you, Willow. I wanted you to feel the sun on your face."

My stomach ached with an open pit expanding.

"Does everyone else know what happened to Dad, except me?"

She took a long drag of her smoke, not making eye contact. With each second that passed, my body grew colder, lacking the warmth I craved.

"Why did you single me out?" I asked.

"I didn't single you out," Mom said. "I tried to protect your sister, too, but she—" Mom tightened her lips, which were surrounded by premature wrinkles, caked with makeup.

"She what?"

"When someone dies, you don't talk about the bad parts of them, Willow. You talk about the good parts. Especially with their children. I was honestly trying to protect you," she repeated. And this time, pain seeped through every syllable.

"I thought if you knew everything, it would hold you back. You'd see yourself as less than worthy, preventing you from getting into healthy relationships or pursuing your dreams."

My *dreams*. Mental note: I needed to check the status of my LLC filing and set up bank accounts for it once I got my ID number from the state of Illinois.

"Why would Dad getting killed make me feel less than worthy?"

Mom took another long drag. The cloud of smoke billowed from her mouth as she looked up at the ceiling—or maybe up to the heavens—as if willing them to give her the right answers.

"Dad did something to get himself killed." I deduced. "He hurt someone, didn't he?"

"I didn't want the weight of this on you. I wanted you to be free of it. And," she added, "I suppose we all want our loved ones to be remembered by their best qualities, not their worst."

"Was it a child?" That would explain the hushed whispers echoing through my nightmares.

Her eyes snapped to mine.

"Did Dad do something to a kid?"

"No." Mom's eyes shimmered with tears.

I had to remind myself this wasn't just about me. Mom lost the love of her life, the father to her children, and in her own way, she was trying to honor his memory—at least through the eyes of his daughters.

"Then, why are you *still* keeping it from me?" I whispered.

She'd warned me loud and clear, but I kept asking.

I wiped my tear.

Mom took another long drag of her cigarette and flipped it into the ashtray.

"Because of *who* killed him," she said.

Who?

Who had killed him? Keeping this a secret from me my whole life was because of *who* had killed him? Who was it? That meant it wasn't a stranger, then. It had to be someone close to us. Someone she was protecting, then.

But who? Were they in jail? And who, in her eyes, would be worthy of a lifelong cover-up for the sake of her daughter?

Hayley said it was a *he*. But Gramps was dead before Dad died, Mom and Dad had no brothers, and there were no other men in our lives—at least none I was aware of. And once I called Hayley on it, she gave me that strange look that I had interpreted as guilt for having let a detail slip. But what if it wasn't guilt? What if she'd said it to steer me away from the actual killer?

Suddenly, a hypothesis crashed into my head, as if it had been there all along. My mom's suffocating grief...had it been heightened with guilt? Not wanting to sully his name—was it because he was doing something terrible behind closed doors? Domestic violence turns deadly every day. Had my mom and dad had a relationship that, at times, turned violent, and in one of my dad's outbursts, Mom had killed him? And hadn't been charged because it was self-defense?

It would explain her extreme emotional swings that I'd chalked up to grief—leaving the house and kids that she felt she'd destroyed. If she took a life—the life of the father of her children—she'd only be able to reassure herself so many times that it was necessary.

But it would only be human to replay that horrifying event

repeatedly, thinking, *If I had done this or that, perhaps I could've gotten away, and he'd still be alive. And my daughters would still have their father.*

Was that the dark family secret?

Mom flicked her cigarette over the ashtray four more times, even though it didn't need it.

"Who killed him?" I whispered.

Mom took a long drag, as if summoning the courage for something. Her eyebrows pulled together, deepening the wrinkle between them as she shook her head.

"Willow, sometimes, the past is best left in the past. I can assure you, he loved you girls more than anything."

My chest ached, and seeing the torment in her eyes made me feel terrible for having asked her so many times for answers. Because now that I wondered if my mother might have taken Dad's life in self-defense, I realized my every word was a shovel, digging up pain.

No matter how curious I might be about what happened, I would never confront my mom about this again. I would allow her the space to heal. These were her boundaries—talking about Dad's death was off-limits—and I needed to accept it once and for all. Did that mean I'd give up on getting answers? No. I'd hire a private investigator and leave her out of it so she and I could move forward in whatever space this left us. Would I feel as close to her as I could if she had been honest with me? No. But again, I needed to accept this version of the relationship we *did* have rather than trying to hope it would change.

And accepting that made me feel the first wave of peace I'd had in a long time.

My cell phone buzzed.

Shane: Rosse just texted me. He has an update and is going to call you about it.

Me: What is it?

Shane. He didn't say. When your phone rings, answer it.

I didn't know how long I had before Rosse called, but I felt a small measure of closure with my mother to put this portion of our relationship—where I inundated her about our past—behind me. And now, I had one more person to clear the runway with.

Hayley, who just walked into the house.

It was time to find out if she had any desire to have a relationship with me or if I was about to close this door forever...

33

"What are you doing here?" Hayley spat when she spotted me.

"Hello to you too," I said.

"You know, your *boyfriend* is sitting outside in a car, not looking conspicuous at all."

"He drove me here."

Mom extinguished her cigarette, flipped the footrest down on her recliner with force, and marched over to my sister. Holding her head between her hands as she stared into her eyes.

"I'm not high, Mom. Thanks for the vote of confidence, by the way." Hayley kicked her shoes off and dumped her coat on the floor.

"I want to talk to you," I said to Hayley.

"Now's not a good time."

"It's never a good time."

Hayley went to the refrigerator, pulled out a bottle of water, and walked toward the hallway that led to the back bedrooms.

I blocked her path.

"Well, I don't want to talk to you right now, so move."

I kept my face neutral, as if her words hadn't blasted another hole in my heart. Why did this still affect me? Her constant rejection was the only common thread in the fabric of our relationship.

But something had changed.

Me.

Did she even want a relationship with me? I would no longer pursue one if she didn't, and before I closed the door forever, I'd get some things off my chest.

"It's important," I said, keeping my tone strong when I added, "Please."

Hayley glared at me.

"Hayley, you could spend a few minutes talking to your sister," Mom said.

As if we were kids and not grown adults. Hayley was ten years older than me. You'd think out of the two of us, she wouldn't need Mom to step in and referee.

"Five minutes," Hayley said. "I have plans."

Hayley plopped into the chair Mom had been sitting in.

"I'll give you girls some privacy," Mom said. "But when you're done, there's something important I want to tell you girls."

Interesting. Mom hadn't sat us both down and talked to us for years. I could tell by the nervousness dancing across her face that it was something she wasn't expecting we'd react positively to.

Mom disappeared into the back hallway.

I took a breath, focusing on what I wanted to ask her, nerves sweeping through me. Deep down, I'd felt fairly confident I would always have a relationship with my mother. My sister, on the other hand...our relationship felt like a rock dangling precariously over a cliff—one that, for years, had taken all my energy to keep it from falling into the cavern, where I'd never see it again.

"What do you want?" Hayley looked at her watch.

"I want to know what I ever did to make you so angry."

She glared at me. My sister hated talking about anything emotional—collateral damage from our dad dying.

"Do you have to be so freaking dramatic all the time?"

"You rarely answer my calls or texts, and if you do agree to hang out with me, you don't show up half the time."

"I'm busy."

"That was an excuse I swallowed for years, but it doesn't work anymore."

"Willow, for God's sake, not everything is about you."

"If you don't want things to change between us, that's fine. I'll stop trying and leave you alone." I wasn't going to beg to be in someone's life that didn't want me there; I deserved better than that. "But I deserve to know the reason why. What did I do to make you hate me so much?"

My sister's eyes rounded slightly. Our whole life, I'd chased after her, and I had never thought about it before, but maybe a part of her found some comfort in that chase—having someone work that hard to want to spend time with her. And now, I was ending it.

I wouldn't feel guilty about it, either. She could look hurt all she wanted, but it was nothing compared to the hurt that she had caused me throughout our lives. I was simply accepting this for what it was and hoping to understand what got us here.

Hayley looked down and began cracking her knuckles—something that she did whenever she felt anxious. I wondered if she was processing this—the official end of our relationship as we knew it.

"I don't hate you," she whispered. It was the gentlest tone I think she had ever taken with me. "I envy you."

She wouldn't—or couldn't—make eye contact with me, as if embarrassed by her confession.

"Envy what?"

"You got to live a normal life," she said. "I never did. You were only four when Dad died, so you didn't know what you lost. But I did."

I wanted to tell her she was wrong, that I had more memories and heartbreak than she gave me credit for. But I said, "I've envied you all of these years because you had more time with Dad than I did."

My sister's lip quivered, as if pain wrapped around her and squeezed until she could no longer breathe.

"He didn't deserve to die," she whispered.

If I asked her if Mom killed him, would she tell me? Would that be a betrayal to Mom, who'd made it clear she wanted to close that door forever? Was it my secret to uncover?

When Hayley's eyes met mine, they were shimmering.

"He died in front of us."

My stomach dropped like the anchor of a big ship.

That's why I had blood on me that day in the hospital. They must have checked me over to make sure I hadn't been hurt, too.

"But you don't remember it because you were young enough to block it out. You got to move on with your life without knowing what happened to Dad."

Hayley's eyes filled with tears, and it stunned me. I'd seen a lot of sides to Hayley in our years, but I'd never seen her vulnerable.

"I didn't get that." She cleared her throat and swiped angrily at her cheek. "Any time I felt Dad's loss, whether it was a holiday or just a random day where I really missed him...I didn't have the luxury of not knowing why he wasn't there."

Hayley curled her lips, her tone venomous. "Someone killed my father and took him from me."

Was that why Mom and Hayley had such an up-and-down relationship? Up, because Mom supported Hayley through everything. But down, because if Mom was the one who killed him, maybe Hayley knew that and held on to that blame.

Hayley picked at her fingernails harshly.

"Every time Dad wasn't there, every event that he didn't get to come to, that's all I could think about—that someone murdered him."

I kept my voice soft, not wanting to sound accusing. Just wanting to understand her better.

"That's why you started doing drugs," I realized.

She wrapped her arms around her chest. Hayley had always

244 | KATHY LOCKHEART

seemed so powerful to me, but right now, she looked frail, her shoulder bones poking out of her too-thin frame.

"It was the only way to escape this...anger inside of me."

Good Lord, poor Hayley.

"Who killed him, Hayley?"

To this, her features fell into vengeance, and she cracked her knuckles so loudly, they sounded like bones snapping. Her tight eyes were lost in a sea of rage, her jaw clenched. Any mention of the person who murdered our father flipped a switch, transforming her from a broken soul to an enraged human who'd give anything to annihilate the person who stole our father from us.

Looking at her now, I could see how much anger had been festering inside of her this whole time, destroying all of her relationships in its path, and maybe, as the only act of love I'd now get from her, she wanted to protect me from planting its seed inside of me. Because she shook her head, making it clear she would not answer.

Instead of feeling frustrated, though, I felt protected by her because maybe she thought the answer would make me just as bitter as she was. And she cared enough about me to not sentence me to that fate.

"Do you resent me for not knowing?" I asked.

Hayley took a few seconds to answer. "Sometimes."

I pretended my stomach didn't clench. At least this was a major healing moment between us, though—one we might finally move forward from.

But if Shane were here, I know the exact question he'd ask. I was confident I knew the answer, and the old me would bite my tongue, for fear of rocking the boat. Especially at such a perilous moment in our relationship.

But I needed to square my shoulders and protect myself. Uncover the truth, no matter how uncomfortable this was going to be.

"How badly do you resent me?" I asked.

Hayley swiped her cheek. "What, you want a number from one to a hundred?"

"Have you ever wanted to hurt me?"

Her eyebrows slammed together in confusion. "Why would I want to hurt you? You're not the one that killed him."

I studied her, scrutinized even, until I was confident I believed her. Hayley was a mess and always blowing me off, but she'd never been violent with anyone. The only person she ever hurt was herself.

"Why did you ask me that?" Hayley wiped both cheeks.

"It doesn't matter."

"Bullshit. Why'd you ask me that?"

I said nothing.

"I might be envious that you got to live without this fucking burden, but I would never hurt you, so why the hell would you ask it?"

Shit. *She's furious at me.* I'd gotten my answer. There was no need to do more damage by telling her why I'd asked it.

"I should go."

"Answer the question."

I stood up.

"Answer the question!"

My heart began pumping harder, like my blood was so thick, it had to work in overdrive. Hayley and I had just had the most intimate moment of our entire relationship, exposing hidden truths behind emotions that had confused me for years. It was the first time I felt true hope that we could grow closer together after this.

Answering her question would make the waters of our relationship even more turbulent, yet she'd never let it go.

She couldn't blame me for asking it, either. If I had to stomach people like Mom being a suspect, Hayley had to be in that mix, too.

The old Willow would have run out the door without replying, but I resolved to be open and honest, even though others hadn't always extended that same courtesy to me.

"I didn't just break my arm," I said. "I was pushed from a bridge."

Hayley's eyes rounded into full-on alarm. "Someone attacked you?"

I hated the shock on her face, worried it would drudge up feelings about Dad's death, worried it might make her go out and drink.

"Are you okay?" she asked.

I gave a gentle shrug.

"Who did it?" she asked.

"I don't know."

She seemed to digest this all.

"Wait." Her eyebrows furrowed, obviously piecing together my earlier question. "You think *I* had something to do with it?"

"I'm asking everyone if they had reason to hurt me."

Hayley stood up. "You see me as such a lowlife, you think I'm some cold-blooded killer?"

"Hayley—"

"What, because I'm an addict, I'm a killer too?"

"No, I—"

"How dare you accuse me of something like that?"

I'd had to ask, but there was no way I would've been meeting up with Hayley that night and not remembered. Getting to meet up with Hayley would've been a tremendous deal to me, and she was so hard to get ahold of, it would've been something we planned for days, if not weeks, in advance.

"I didn't mean to offend y—" I started.

"You don't matter enough to consume me with hate, let alone be worthy of murder."

She stormed off down the hallway, away from my interrogation. Away from my re-shattered heart and any hope I had to glue our relationship back together.

All these years, I had longed for the emotional breakthrough my sister and I had just had. And then I ruined it.

Long ago, I'd come to terms with the probability Hayley and I may never have a relationship. But that was when the crumbling of our relationship was due to her drug use and lack of effort. If our relationship ended as a result of the question I had asked—one she perceived as a heinous accusation—how could I ever live with that? Because this time, it wouldn't be Hayley's fault; it would be mine.

My cell phone rang, dragging me from the depths of my mental hell.

"Hello?" I choked out.

"Willow. Detective Rosse. I have a development and need you to come down to the station."

34

Once again, we were in the conference room at the Chicago Police station.

"Whatever it is, it must be substantial for them to bring us in," Shane said.

He squeezed my hand, probably assuming my anxiety was from this case. And not from ruining any hope of fixing things with my sister.

"You okay?" he asked for the fifth time since we'd left my mom's house.

"I'm fine," I lied. "Let's just hear what the detective has to say."

The conference room was cold, royal-blue walls with fake wood flooring. A flat screen hanging on one side, a whiteboard on the other. I wondered how many other lives were ruined in this room and how many victories from solving crimes. At least this room seemed to experience the lows and highs; my mom's home seemed to only encase the lows.

"Ms. Johnson." Rosse stepped in, holding his tie from swaying as he sat down, holding a gray folder. "Appreciate you coming in on such short notice."

"Of course."

Rosse's eyes settled on Shane. "I need to speak to her in private," Rosse said. "I'm sure you understand."

This piqued my interest. He had let Shane in the room when we first reviewed the surveillance footage, so why not now?

"I'll wait for you in the lobby." Shane squeezed my knee.

"It might be a little while." Rosse took out a pair of bifocals from his pocket and opened the folder. "I'll be happy to drop her off when we're done here."

Hope swelled in my chest that they'd cracked the case.

Shane looked reluctant, maybe even downright stubborn, about leaving me at the station.

"I'll call you when I leave here," I said.

Shane pursed his lips. "Yeah, okay. I'll grab some case files and meet you at home."

Case files. Code for the ability to work from home—or actually, the cabin—if whatever Rosse was going to say was about to heat up this case.

Shane gave me one last look of worry before leaving the room.

Rosse cleared his throat. "I'd like you to review the footage again."

"Why?"

He fired up the flat screen and fast-forwarded to a section of the footage that gave us the best view of the suspect. Still grainy, still a dark silhouette of a figure.

"Are you sure you don't recognize this person?"

Seriously? He called me all the way down to the station to ask me a question we had already covered?

A little annoyed, I stared at the image all the same, willing something to come to me.

"No."

Rosse nodded, as if unsurprised.

"Have you had any contact with Ezra lately?"

"Not since the coffee shop." Which I'd already filled Rosse in on when I'd met with him the first time.

"Anyone else?"

I told him about Amelia and how she was pissed that Ezra might be considered a suspect and answered his follow-up questions. Then, I told him about my conversation with Hayley.

When we finished the entire exchange, he glowered at me.

"You shouldn't be talking about this investigation with anyone," Rosse chided. "It could undermine the case."

I twisted my hands in my lap. "I'm sorry. It won't happen again."

Rosse pursed his lips and looked at his file. "I wanted to give you an update on the investigation. We formally interviewed Ezra, and he has no alibi."

"I saw the Uber app," I reminded him. "It showed he got a ride home at three in the morning from that club."

"Yes. However, I talked to the owners of that club and got a list of names of people that were there. The people that were hanging out with Ezra couldn't account for his whereabouts for over an hour that night."

"Ezra said he got drunk and passed out."

"Then, I asked the owner if I could see the security footage. They have one security camera at the front of the club and one in the back. One of them shows Ezra leaving the club at 9:23 p.m. You were pushed off the bridge at 10:01 p.m. He returned to the club at 10:28 p.m."

My stomach swirled with bile. "Did anyone see where he went?"

"No."

"Did he tell them where he was going?"

"He didn't notify anyone he was leaving. You remember what time his call came into you that night?"

I shook my head. I had willingly handed over my phone records to expedite this.

Rosse looked at the paper in front of him. "He called you at 9:14 p.m. That call lasted five minutes and thirty-three seconds. Four minutes after that call ended, he left the bar."

My heart started beating faster.

"I went to the club and made the walk myself," he said.

He made me wait for it—confirmation of Ezra's likely guilt or innocence arriving with whatever words Rosse spoke next.

"I could walk to the bridge and get back in time."

"But how would he have gotten me to meet him there? I would never go meet Ezra at some random bridge."

Rosse folded his hands on the table. "What if he told you he was suicidal? And he was going to jump? Would you have gone to try to stop him?"

Yes. Yes, I would. But...

"That's a huge hypothetical," I said.

"Maybe," Rosse agreed. "But my point remains. Ezra would know what to say to you to lure you to that bridge."

I felt like I was going to be sick.

"So, Ezra's the primary person of interest," I deduced.

A mixture of relief and heartbreak washed through my veins—relief that we were close to the end of this, but heartbreak because I had blown up my relationship with my sister for nothing. I should've kept my mouth shut. I should've let the investigation unfold naturally and not been so impatient to get answers.

Rosse asked me a million questions related to my relationship with Ezra in much more depth than our first meeting. It took over an hour to wrap it up.

When we finished, Rosse stood up. "Come on. I'll drive you home."

Twenty minutes later, I stepped out of Rosse's car.

"Thank you," I said.

"I'll be in touch, Willow."

He waited until I was inside the double doors of my apartment complex before I heard his engine rumble away.

I stepped into the hallway with my head in such a fog; I didn't notice the figure until it was too late.

35

He stepped out of the laundry room.

"Do you know what you did?"

I startled and glanced past his shoulder, down the long corridor of doors that led to mine. In my fog, I hadn't looked to see if Shane's car was in the parking lot yet. When I texted Shane after leaving the station, he said he was on his way home. Did that mean he'd beaten me here? Or was he still on his way, imminently about to walk through the complex's front doors behind me and stumble onto this scene?

If he saw Ezra here, Shane would lose his shit. And not only would Shane get in trouble for that, but the entire case could be jeopardized because of it.

And if Ezra was guilty, I wanted to do everything in my power to make sure he could never hurt anyone again.

"A detective showed up at my work today." Ezra took a step toward me. "A *detective*. People saw that, Willow. They heard they were asking questions about an attempted homicide!"

"They're interviewing everyone in my life." I kept my voice calm and neutral, and I clenched my hands so he wouldn't see them trembling. Because the look Ezra was casting was one I had never seen before.

His eyes were wide, his lips curled.

"I've been questioned before for assault and battery. Those charges were never filed, but if you add that to getting questioned on an attempted murder? If they name me as a person of interest? The combination of those two will end *any* chance of a political career."

"They're just trying to figure out what happened."

He stepped forward. "And I'm trying to protect my goddamn career!"

I glanced around quickly. If things got heated, I'd run out the front door or grab the fire extinguisher hanging on the wall and smash him with it.

"Don't you get it? This could ruin everything for me! Everything!"

"If you didn't get arrested or charged for anything, I'm sure it'll be fine."

"Oh, well, as long as you're sure, that's all that matters. Are you fucking naive?"

Even though he took another step into my space, I stood my ground and raised my chin.

"Do not take that tone with me."

"My boss has been looking at me sideways ever since that detective left. He'll probably fire me over this regardless!"

"Guidelines issued by the Equal Employment Opportunity Commission say you can only lose your job if—"

"Stop spouting HR crap at me. We both know how the real world works, Willow. If he wants to fire me, he will find a way."

"Well, you can't blame me for that. It's the Chicago Police Department investigating a potential crime. So, if you have a problem, take it up with them."

I tried to walk past him, but his arm shot out and stopped me, blocking my path.

"They'd better back off."

"Let me get past."

"If you cost me my political career, so help me..."

I glared at him. "Is that a threat?"

He licked his teeth. "That detective is making a big freaking deal out of me going for a walk."

I said nothing. Heeding Rosse's warning to not discuss this case.

"After I talked to you, I was too upset to sit there, so I went for a walk to clear my head."

That's why he was here. He thought if he could convince me, I could what, assure Rosse that Ezra would never do this and get him to back down? Ezra wasn't just reckless or a liar; he was desperate.

"Thanks for clearing that up," I snarled. "Now, move out of my way."

His jaw tightened. This wasn't going how he planned.

"I was upset because I love you and want you back."

I laughed out loud at how ludicrous this was. Him blocking me so I couldn't move yet declaring his love for me.

My laugh probably wasn't smart. It seemed to enrage him, based on the tightening of his face.

"See? This is the same goddamn attitude you were giving me that night when I called you. But would you meet me? No. Would you even listen to a damn word I said? That's why I called you a bitch."

I flinched. He'd never called me a name once in the entire time we'd been together, but I could see it playing out. Him, after one too many drinks, calling to try to get me back and getting angry when my answer hadn't changed.

"And then I went for a walk because I was afraid I'd screwed everything up. But I never saw you, Willow. And I meant it when I said I'd never hurt you."

But he just admitted to sabotaging everything with me. He knew I would never tolerate anyone talking to me like that, abusing me by calling me a name. By his account, he was drunk, angry—plenty of motive to fall off the deep end. He had the opportunity and an immense hole in his alibi. And he had lied about it all.

Not that I was going to tell him any of this. I'd call Rosse and tell him everything that Ezra was doing right now.

"That's why I sent you flowers the next day. I felt bad for calling you a name, Willow. But think about it. If I thought you were dead, I wouldn't send you flowers."

I reached into my bag, digging around for my cell.

When I said nothing, Ezra's voice hardened. "I would never hurt you, Willow."

I looked at him, deadpan. "I don't believe you anymore."

Wrong. Thing. To. Say.

His eyes flashed with fury.

He stepped even closer to me.

"You're being a bitch, you know that?" he growled.

"Move, or I'll kick you in the balls so hard, your voice will permanently sound like Mickey Mouse."

"Back off, Willow, and get it through your thick head—I didn't hurt you."

"Yeah, you seem like a harmless bunny rabbit." I glared at his arm, caging me into the hallway.

I tried to push past it, but he stepped forward until his face was inches from my own.

I shot my knee up to kick in between his legs, but he twisted his hips to block it, and when he did, it threw my center of gravity off.

I landed on my back with a yelp, and Ezra towered over me, his fists clenched at both sides.

Evidently, my yelp had been rather loud because a door swung open, footsteps ran toward us, and Ezra was slammed against the wall, his cheek smooshed against it as his arms were twisted behind his back.

"You ever lay a hand on her, I'll rip your heart out with my bare hands!" Shane barked.

36

"You okay?" Shane cupped my jaw, looking into my eyes, as if decoding my every movement.

"I'm fine."

But Shane could see past my lie.

How could I be fine? I knew Shane was right; it was the right thing to do to file the restraining order, but that didn't make it any easier. If Ezra didn't turn out to be the person who'd pushed me from the bridge, that order of protection would have a detrimental impact on his political career.

I wasn't even sure the judge would grant the emergency order of protection, but after learning that Ezra was the primary person of interest in my attempted murder case, he granted it. In twenty-one days, there would be a full hearing, but for now, an interim order was in effect.

Shane stroked my skin and lowered his voice, as if it could soften the blow of what he said next. "Don't get mad."

"Worst way to start a sentence."

"But I grabbed some things from the store for you. Toiletries, so you don't have to pack so much."

I pulled his hand away from my face and kissed his palm. "I'm not going to the cabin."

"Willow..."

"They took Ezra away in cuffs, so he's locked up."

"For a few hours. Maybe the night. But since he didn't technically lay hands on you, it's unlikely it'll be much longer than that. If we could file charges for being an asshole, he'd be locked up forever."

"Rosse's getting close," I assured.

"Charging someone with attempted homicide requires a thorough investigation. It could be days, weeks, or even longer before charges officially come."

"Exactly. Going away right now helps nothing."

Shane moved closer, our noses only inches apart. "It keeps you safe."

"I ruined my relationship with my sister, and I had that huge blowout with Amelia. This has done enough damage to my life. We both know this won't be over until whoever did this to me is in jail anyway, and God only knows how long that could take. I have a life, Shane. I can't just run away with you and stay locked up in that cabin forever."

Something flashed through Shane's eyes. Something with heat and fire.

He brought his hand to my hip, his voice dragging low through his words.

"What if you don't think of it as running? What if you think of it as somethin' else?"

I tried to hide the fire rippling beneath my skin at his touch. With one look, he had the power to bring me to my knees. Literally. And he was unleashing it right now, beneath those dark eyebrows and matching black hair that I was now fantasizing running my fingers through.

"Meaning?"

"No part of you wants to get away with me for a few days?"

I swallowed. Of course I did.

"Don't you think that's a little manipulative, Detective Hernandez?"

His mouth curled up on one side. "I'll do whatever it takes to protect you."

And then he did. As he moved his lips to the base of my throat, leaving a trail of kisses up my neck, my greedy need to feel him performed a hostile takeover of my thoughts.

He kissed me until I couldn't take it anymore, and then, as final evidence he was trying to use every tactic to get me to change my mind, he stopped.

The tease.

"Sleep on it," he said. Obviously relieved we had a few safe hours with Ezra locked up. "We can leave in the morning."

37

Outside, a crashing sound preceded Snowflake's scream. I launched from my couch, yanked at the sliding glass door—damn, my shoulder still hurt a little when I did that—and jumped out onto my patio.

"Snowflake!"

The little house I had put outside for her had crashed against the door in the whipping winds and momentarily pinned her. Scaring the crap out of her. But thankfully, it did not appear to injure her.

She rubbed her back against my bare calf. My freezing calf.

"It's okay. It's just another winter storm." I picked her up and cradled her against my chest. "Come on. You can watch TV with me."

But my sliding glass door was closed.

I'd shut it out of habit, protecting my apartment from the subzero temperatures outside. The subzero temperatures that assaulted my skin, lining my entire body with goose bumps. Without my big, fluffy blanket on the couch, my T-shirt and thong might as well have been a death suit.

I yanked the handle, but the door didn't move.

Crap.

I hated this door. I hated how it stuck and how the landlord could never figure it out, because Shane was right. This was a hazard. I had mastered the art of opening it from the inside, but not from the outside. I tried to repeat my movements on the outside, but the door acted like it was nailed shut.

My body trembled harder.

In this weather, frostbite would set in crazy fast.

When I put Snowflake down, she scurried into her little house as I battled with the door. I pulled horizontally, I jerked vertically, I jerked at angles. But it wasn't budging, all while a winter wind whipped against my skin, freezing me all the way to my bones.

My teeth chattered as I looked around, trying to decide my next step. It was the middle of the night. I could walk around the entire building to the lobby, but that path would take me through snow with bare feet. Not to mention, I'd risk someone seeing me nearly naked.

Humiliation would kill me before hypothermia.

I walked to the patio next to mine and banged on the glass.

No lights were on inside. No movement.

Now that I thought about it, I didn't even know if Shane was home. I hadn't heard him in a long time. Was he asleep?

"Shane!" I knocked.

Maybe he would let me bring Snowflake inside. I reached down to pick up the cat, but she ran off and out of sight.

Dammit.

I was convulsing from the cold.

"Shane!" I knocked again, louder this time.

His light came on.

Hallelujah.

The blinds covering the door opened a crack, revealing Shane standing there in nothing but a pair of boxer briefs. His hair disheveled.

He opened the door quickly and pulled me inside, shutting the door and blinds behind me. If I wasn't damn near hypothermic, this might have been sexy with me standing here in nothing but a T-shirt. But sexy goes out the window when you can't talk straight because your jaw is frozen half shut.

"What are you doin' out there?"

"Th...the...c...cat...g...got...s...scared."

"Jesus, you're shaking."

Shane grabbed a blanket from the back of his couch and wrapped it around me, then pulled me to his chest. His skin felt like an inferno, so I could only imagine I felt like an icicle.

"How long were you out there?"

He rubbed his hands up and down my back.

"N...not...l...long..."

"Why did you go outside in nothin' but a T-shirt?"

"Th...the...c...cattttt."

He smirked down at me. "Stop talking." He pulled me tighter, my cheek pressing against his wonderfully warm chest.

"You're like an ice cube," he groaned. "I would offer you hot chocolate, but all I have is coffee or beer."

"I...I'm f...fine."

"You're not fine."

He pulled the blanket tighter around me.

"I'm...s...sorry I w...woke you."

"You're far more important than sleep, Willow."

He held me close, the warmth of his body eclipsed by the warmth of his heart, which shimmered a glistening path to mine.

Shane stared at me with an intensity that promised to melt the ice away, his throat rolling with a swallow. His eyes combed over my face. Gravitating to my lips. Threatening to burn them with one scorching kiss.

Every cell in my body came alive, and a shiver ran down my spine, only this one wasn't from the cold. The skin on my back sizzled with his every stroke, my chest swelling as it pressed against his muscles.

My lower belly warmed at the sight of him—layers of muscles entrenched in ink, all of them flexing with desire.

Sucked into his gaze like I'd surrendered to hypnosis, I licked my bottom lip and savored the way Shane's eyes dilated at the sight of it, his chest rising and falling faster as he stared at my mouth.

I wanted his lips on mine.

I wanted his hands to touch more than just my back.

I wanted Shane. All of him. His heart, his body, his soul. But even though he'd professed feelings for me, he'd been uncertain about what it all meant for us—hadn't committed to being with me. Feelings didn't change his biggest fear, his decision to never get serious with anyone. And for that reason, I should walk back to my place now before I let this go any further because, unlike the frenzied rush of hormones with the kitchen table incident, this was something I could feel all the way to my core. If I went through with this, Shane walking away later would be a sledgehammer to my heart.

But if all I could have was his body, then tonight, I'd take whatever he was willing to give.

Shane moved his hand to my face, cupping my cheek and stroking my cheekbone with his thumb.

"Let me run you a warm bath," he whispered.

But I wasn't shaking anymore. And I couldn't stand being away from him for another minute.

I shrugged the blanket from my shoulders, took a step back, and pulled my T-shirt up over my head, standing in nothing but a thong.

Shane's eyes glided down my shoulders, chest, abs, legs, and back up again.

Meeting my eyes with a hungry need pulsing through his gaze.

"You're gorgeous."

When I stepped out of my panties and kicked them to the side, Shane stood frozen.

Here I was, giving myself to him. Waiting for him to claim me.

His eyes fixated on the space between my legs, and then he walked up to me and crashed his mouth to mine.

Oh. My. Word.

His lips were an ember, igniting everything throughout my body, his hand on my jaw scorching my skin. Heating the space between my thighs.

It wasn't enough. No amount of kissing this man would ever be enough. And when he opened his mouth and allowed his tongue to lightly press against mine, I groaned. I reached my hands up to his shoulders, our kiss gaining in momentum as I nibbled his lower lip and pressed my mouth harder to his.

I loved every thrash of his tongue, every growl from his throat as his hands wandered down my body, until he pinched a nipple between the pad of his thumb and finger.

Making me yipe.

"Tell me what you want," he demanded.

I swallowed. "I want to feel you inside me."

He groaned, and trailed his fingertips down my breasts, down my stomach, and then slipped a finger past my folds and into my entrance. Making my back arch with pleasure.

He looked like a hungry man as he began to curl and move his finger, watching me, kissing my jaw, my neck. Sucking on my nipple.

And then, he dropped to his knees and threw my right thigh over his shoulder.

Looking up at me, he licked my folds.

I groaned, shoving my hands into his hair as he worked his tongue slowly up to the apex of my sex, and began to suck.

I jerked from the overwhelming sensation and pulled his hair in approval when he began circling the bundle of nerves with his tongue. Groaning, hungry to feast on me.

Shane Hernandez was a powerful man, one who could command most people to do what he said, but right now, he was on his knees. Pleasuring me. Listening to the tempo of my moans as he dipped his tongue inside me, and then trailed it upward again. Sucking on me. Circling. Over and over.

I could feel the wave building. Especially when he teased my entrance with his finger and plunged it inside.

"You're so wet for me," he growled, his voice vibrating against the sensitive skin.

His praise was making my wave rise higher and higher and I pulled his head harder against me, inviting a nip of his teeth—a brief glint of pain followed by an avalanche of ecstasy.

And then I crashed. Hard, as he savored every drop of my orgasm, leaving me spent.

I gasped when he stood up and spun me around, pressing my chest against the wall.

Roughly.

He positioned himself behind me.

Holy crap. This was so hot. So damn hot, the kind of passion that's too big for gentle lovemaking.

"Are you on the pill?" he asked in a hungry, impatient tone.

He ran his hand along the base of my back, lower and lower, until he reached around and met my center.

I cried out, "Yes."

I was surprised he started touching me again, but I liked that there was an anger to it, as if making him wait for it since we'd first met had made him suffer. I liked his anger. I liked feeling the pressure of his fingers as he dipped two of them inside of me from behind. I liked that with his free hand, he grabbed my breast as he stared into my eyes, watching my mouth fall open, my body squirm beneath his movements.

His hand was magic, like a key to the lock of my ecstasy. I tried to hold still, especially when he held my back in place, but he was bringing me to the cusp again.

"Shane..."

"Not yet."

He stopped, pulling his hand back, making me whimper. He stepped out of his boxers, my eyes glued to the pleasure waiting for me as he coated his shaft with my arousal. Before he grabbed my hips roughly and tugged them back a bit.

"Grab the wall," Shane growled.

I gladly obeyed and gasped when he filled me in one angry movement.

Then, he started to move.

With one hand on my hip, Shane's other hand grabbed my neck and twisted my head until his lips claimed mine. His tongue in my mouth. His movements were frenzied, an explosion of pent-up sexual tension that demanded release between us.

"You make me crazy," he groaned into my mouth. Licked my tongue.

He pulled my hips back and pressed my torso down lower, keeping a hand on the nape of my neck.

"You don't know how long I've wanted you," he growled.

Angrier and angrier, he thrust his hips, as if the months of waiting for this were unfair—an injustice that deserved an extraordinary vindication.

I could feel a wave building with him hitting just the right spot, moving at just the right tempo, just the right beat. He cupped my breast, moving so perfectly against me.

"Shane..." I groaned.

"Not yet," he demanded.

I clawed at his wall as the wave rose even higher. I couldn't hold on much longer. I couldn't.

I turned my head and looked up at him, locking my eyes with his. He looked wild with pleasure, his jaw tight, his fingers claiming my hips with such force, they might leave marks tomorrow. Marks I would savor.

Keeping his gaze fixed on me, he moved faster and faster until...

"Shane..." My fingernails dug into the paint.

"Now," he growled.

His sapphire eyes looked darkened with sensuality as we both hit our release, riding each other's waves until every last tremble and moan subsided. Leaving me quivering, spent from the most sensual experience I'd ever had in my life. Locked in each other's gaze the entire time.

I pressed my temple to the wall, panting.

Shane stepped back, spun me around, and crashed his lips to mine. He grabbed the backs of my legs and hoisted my legs around his waist as he kissed me, walking me to his bedroom.

Clutching me with a possessive, desperate hold.

"That wasn't enough." He threw me onto his bed. "Give me five minutes, and I want to go again."

I smiled. Especially when I realized how he planned to spend the five minutes while we waited for him to be ready again.

Shane fell to his knees and sank his mouth to my center.

38

I woke up to morning sunlight streaming through Shane's blinds, stretching across his tattoo-covered torso. His eyes were still closed, and his chest rose and fell lazily with each of his hypnotic breaths. He looked so peaceful with his black hair tousled, his tan skin stretched over bands of muscles.

But as soon as he woke up, he wouldn't feel peaceful anymore. Reality would come crashing back, and we'd have a very hard conversation in front of us.

One that was going to hurt like hell.

Last night, after making love three times and falling asleep in each other's arms, it felt like the gaps in my soul had been filled with his affection. And now, lying naked in his bed, I never felt like I belonged anywhere else but right here, with Shane.

It was strange to think how many years I spent fighting for a sense of belonging within my own family. Maybe I'd been searching for this feeling in the wrong place all along.

And now that I had it, the thought of ever letting it go incinerated my heart.

It was like spending your entire life alone, in the center of a ballroom dance floor, watching other couples dance while you stand there, feeling like an outcast. And then suddenly, the dance floor clears, and a prince's eyes land on you. In a sea of people, he wants you, only you, and he motions for you to join him.

You glide your way into his outstretched arms, your heart pounding, and as soon as you start to dance, you've never felt happier or more wanted in your entire life. In that moment, you never want the music to end. Because once the music stops playing, reality will bring you right back to your lonely little spot, surrounded by other happy couples dancing. Only this time, you will be painfully aware of what you are missing out on.

And you know that no matter how many more princes come into the room, none of them will hold a candle to how that one special prince made you feel.

But Shane made it very clear early on that he would not allow himself to be in a serious relationship with anyone. Yes, he'd developed feelings for me, but that wouldn't change his position. It would just prolong this heaven and plunge me deeper into hell when it ended.

How could I ever be with another guy after Shane? Shane, who jumped into a freezing river, risking death to save me. Shane, whose protection for me extended to how I allowed myself to be treated by others.

I knew what the answer was. I would search for a man who would make me feel a fraction of what Shane had made me feel, and I would spend the next twenty years searching for that feeling, just like I had spent the last twenty years searching for that emotional connection that I was craving from my family.

I was stronger now, after everything I had overcome and learned, but I would continue to go through life like a leaf blowing through the air, unanchored and never belonging to anyone. Just as I'd always been.

My throat swelled painfully. I swallowed and forced down the emotions as I looked past him to a photograph sitting on his dresser of a man holding what appeared to be Shane when he was a toddler. The guy had Shane's eyes, the same hair.

"It's my dad," he said.

Damn, Shane looked sexy when he opened his eyes. The gradients of light and blue speckles mixed together in a harmony of color, pulling me closer with a simple look.

"Do you remember him?"

"Not as well as I want to," he admitted, running his fingers through my hair.

It felt like a clock was ticking down toward the end of our time together and closing my window of opportunity of getting to know him better. Soon, the fragments of his soul he'd be willing to share with me would go back into their lockbox. And I'd no longer have its key.

"What do you remember?" I asked.

Shane trailed his fingertips along my bare back, looking up at the ceiling as he considered this.

"One of the best memories I have was when I was four, shortly before he died. Whenever he would leave for work, I would sit on the front porch, and he would get in a squad car and turn the lights on for me as he drove away. It was this ritual, I guess you could call it, that he had started to say goodbye to me. He'd do the same thing when he got home."

"Sounds sweet." I kissed his chest.

Shane stroked my arm as his voice faded with the memory. "It was. Until the day I was waiting on the porch for him to come home and his squad car pulled up with no lights on. And it wasn't my dad that got out. It was two uniforms." He cleared his throat. "I never saw my dad again."

My stomach walls ached at the image of a little boy waiting for his daddy, who would never return.

"It was one of the worst moments of my life." Shane's voice was a whisper. "Seein' my mom collapse like that. Because when you're a little kid, your parents are like superheroes. They're indestructible.

So, when my mom collapsed, I remember it made me feel unsafe. Like she was vulnerable, and if she was vulnerable, how was she supposed to protect us? And then, when I learned the reason she collapsed was because my dad had been killed, I think it just took away my entire sense of security."

What a great way to put it...your sense of security. How very true. Seeing parents weak or vulnerable has the power to make you feel unsafe when you're a kid.

Shane continued to stroke my hair, his voice sounding lost in the past. "Remember feeling like...when you have a nightmare and you wake up, you're so relieved that it wasn't real? Because the nightmare was dark and all you felt was terror and sadness and despair and hopelessness. Your heart is pounding, and you're sobbing, and you're runnin' away from this monster that's chasing you, but he's gaining on you." He paused. "It kind of felt like, one day, I was playin' with my soccer ball in the backyard, and the next day, I was in that nightmare that I never woke up from. It became my life, and I had to learn to live in the darkness with that monster."

My eyes stung. Because it was the perfect analogy to describe what it felt like.

"That's awful," I whispered.

Shane swept my hair over my shoulder.

"It came in waves," he said. "The first was shock, of course. It didn't feel real. Every time I would see a police car, I would look inside and think maybe my dad was in that one and that's why they couldn't find him—he'd gotten into the wrong car. Or maybe he was out fighting crime and had lost track of time and hadn't come home yet."

How heartbreaking. I could imagine an innocent little boy grasping at all sorts of explanations as to why his dad was suddenly gone.

"When it finally did sink in, I never knew sadness could be so debilitating. I couldn't think straight. I wasn't eating very much. I couldn't sleep. That lasted for a long time. A long damn time."

When little boys were supposed to be playing T-ball and making lists for Santa, Shane had been drowning in grief. I wished I could go back in time and hug that little boy, to tell him it was okay to be sad, to miss his dad. To cry.

"After a while, sadness turned into rage. I was so angry that he had been killed. When I was ten, I used to draw these superhero costumes, where I planned to find anyone who'd ever killed a police officer and beat them up." Shane's lips curled. "I even talked my mom into makin' me the costume for Halloween, though she had no clue what it was actually for. It was blue and red, because those were my dad's favorite colors, and it had a letter *J* stitched on with black felt. *J* for justice."

My stomach rolled, imagining a ten-year-old child enduring all of that.

"I eventually realized it would never work. I was too small to beat up adults, and I had no way of tracking all those bad guys down. So, after a while, I just felt...lost, I guess. Kind of existing without feelin' much. I didn't have a lot of friends because I wasn't very fun to be around."

I kissed his chest and looked at him intensely in his eyes.

"I admire you even more because of what you've overcome." Because he'd overcome his adversity far better than I ever had.

Shane brushed my collarbone, looking at me with a ghost of a smile, as if I were the remarkable one. But he was. Strong and brave and honorable. His life could've gone a million different ways with all of that trauma and pain, and I was impressed he hadn't allowed it to ruin his life.

"After the first few years passed, I remember feelin' like I had this responsibility to be the man of the house. I tried to never show my emotions."

In some ways, I could relate to that. I tried to keep my emotions locked down so that I wouldn't upset my mother. I wondered if Shane ever failed the way I had.

"Were you able to *always* hide your feelings?" I asked.

Strangely, I wanted to hear that someone else had cracked like I had. Because when I was younger and I let the grief upset me in front of my mother, the only way I got past the guilt was to convince myself it was only human. That any human under the same circumstances would sometimes crack under the pain.

"There was this one day I couldn't hold it in because it was the hardest day I'd had after he died," he said.

I wondered if Shane understood how intimate I felt with him sharing this with me. Even more intimate than what we'd shared last night.

"The day we left our house to move into that trailer park gutted me because leaving that house was like leaving my dad behind. That home housed the only memories I had with him. The kitchen counter he had set me on when he'd put a Band-Aid on my knee. The backyard, where he used to play catch with me. The front porch, where we used to sit and watch him go to and from work each day. Leavin' it all behind was like leaving him behind all over again. And I was terrified his memory would fade without being surrounded by the only place I'd ever shared with him."

My lip quivered.

"I couldn't hold it together that day. And the worst part was, me breaking down made it even harder on my mom. It's not like she wanted to leave that house. She had no choice. We couldn't afford it. We could barely afford the trailer we moved into."

He continued to stroke my back, lost in thought.

"Thank you for sharing that with me," I said. He'd been an integral part of my life at one of my lowest points. It was touching to be let so deeply into his.

But my bliss was pierced with barbed wire that wrapped around my chest because we might feel happy right now—and maybe that would go on for a while—but eventually, he would remember the heartbreaking reason he'd pushed me away in the first place.

When Shane professed his feelings for me, he said he didn't

know what the future held for us—that he couldn't even think about that right now. Then, he kissed me and got lost in passion.

But now, I did need to think about that because passion with Shane only made my feelings for him grow deeper. And I knew deep down, no matter how much he may care for me, his biggest fear in life—leaving behind someone he loved—would rear its ugly head and steal him from me. Maybe it would happen on the anniversary of his dad's death, or maybe he'd have a close call with a suspect at work, but inevitably, something would pull him from this bliss. And when that happened, when he did the noble thing and walked away...

I would be destroyed.

Each day I spent with him would be like giving him another fragment of my heart, and the longer we were together, the less of my heart would remain when he left me.

"You okay?" he asked.

I tried to wash away the sadness inside of me, unsure how to approach this conversation. I mustered a fake smile, pretending my chest wasn't burning.

When everything you've ever wanted is right in front of you but still just outside your reach...was it truly better to have loved and lost than to have never loved at all? Because I was pretty sure I was falling in love with Shane. Maybe already had. And I wasn't so sure the aftershock of losing this with him was worth the earthquake of bliss we'd gotten to share.

Maybe it was. Maybe, someday, I'd wake up and decide it was all worth it. But not right now. Not when I was about to tell him I couldn't do this.

"I think it's best if I go," I said.

At the tone of my voice, Shane lay on his side and propped himself up on his elbow, brushing the backs of his fingers along my jawline.

"What's wrong?" His eyebrows furrowed.

I brushed his hair with my fingertips, trying to sound strong. "Last night was fun, but we both know this is a mistake."

Shane's head jerked back. "Since when?"

"We both know how this is going to end."

"And how is that?" Shane asked.

"With you leaving me."

Based on the tightening of his eyes, he was offended. "I told you, I can't stay away from you."

For now. Later though...

"We're caught up in infatuation," I started.

"Infatuation?" he choked out.

"But once that fades..."

"Is that all this is to you?"

"I'll be left out in the storm to pick up the pieces."

I was a coward. A braver person would take whatever time she could get with him—a day, a month, a year. But as much as I wished I'd convinced Shane to not live his life alone, one night of lovemaking didn't erase the last twenty years. If anything, the closer he got to me, the more he'd probably be afraid of leaving loved ones behind, and the more likely he'd be to end it.

This wasn't fear talking. It was me trying to protect my heart.

Shane's face tightened into shocked anger. He swallowed, as if I had just told him his puppy died.

"I didn't realize you were afraid of..." He paused, pinched the bridge of his nose, and clenched his eyes shut. "You lost your dad. Of course that would...what was I thinking?"

Shane shoved the covers off, shot out of bed, and slammed boxer briefs on.

Moments ago, I'd been entwined in his arms, closer to him than... well, than I'd ever been with anyone in my life, really. And now, he wouldn't even look at me; he was so disgusted. His every movement, every lack of eye contact, pulled him further away—like he'd been swept into a current, stealing him from me.

I felt panicked. I wanted to pull him back and accept him for as long as he'd let me. Yet my heart would never survive that in the long run.

"I just don't want to be left," I managed over the lump in my throat. "My mom left every time I felt safe, and—"

He held up his palm. "You don't have to explain. And for the record, I'm not mad at you. I'm furious with myself." He licked his bottom lip. "What the hell was I thinking?"

Shane left his room. Left me. Alone, naked, and heartbroken.

39

I wasn't sure what to do. I sat on Shane's bed, covering my nude body with a sheet while I held my hand to my mouth, trying to contain my sob.

In the kitchen, I heard cabinets opening and closing harder than necessary. The refrigerator door opened and closed. And then eerie silence haunted the space.

I was stronger than this. I didn't need to cower in his bedroom. I could lick my wounds later, when I was alone, and I could scream into a pillow and sob in my bathtub, but right now, I needed to face this.

I stood up and realized my panties and T-shirt were still in the living room. Talk about a walk of shame, humbling to have to walk out there in the nude.

Metaphorical for how naked I felt with my feelings.

Before I had the chance to walk out there, though, Shane appeared, leaning against the doorframe. He had his arms crossed over his bare chest, the tattoos strangling his torso, and clutched in his right hand were my clothes.

"I'm sorry for getting angry," he said.

"I'm sorry for making you angry."

"I've been selfish."

I chuckled and shook my head. "If you think putting your entire life on hold to protect me is selfish, we have different definitions of that word."

"If you'd allow it, I'd lock you in my bedroom forever to protect you from this world."

My heart thumped in my ears.

"But that's not what I'm talking about. I was so caught up in *my* fear," Shane said. "I failed to stop and think about yours. Because you're right. If I'm killed in the line of duty, you would be left to pick up the pieces by yourself."

I blanched. "That's not what I was talking about."

Shane's blue eyes looked so deeply into mine; it was like they were fishing for answers. An explanation.

No wonder he got so upset. Of course I'd always be worried about something happening to Shane, especially in his line of work. But I wasn't talking about him dying.

"I was talking about you leaving me. Breaking up with me," I said.

Shane's head jerked back an inch. "Why would I break up with you?"

"Because your biggest fear is to leave someone behind, and you're a cop, and..."

Understanding softened Shane's face. His lips even tugged up into a half smile as he pinched the bridge of his nose again and shook his head. "I thought you were breaking up with me."

"I am breaking up with you. As a preemptive strike."

"No"—he locked eyes with me—"you're not."

"I know we're not officially together, but put whatever term you want on this. I'm breaking up with you before you choose to break up with me later."

He sat down next to my hip and ran his fingertips up my arm, smiling wider. "No."

"I am."

"I don't accept."

"Shane..."

"Willow." He brought his face inches from my own. "I've made my decision. If you want to leave me because I'm a jackass or something, I'll accept it. But not because of this."

"You said you never wanted to be in a relationship if you were a cop."

He grabbed hold of my gaze so tightly, I didn't think I could ever wiggle out of it.

"That was before I met you," he said. "Before, that was an acceptable sacrifice to make. But once I met you? It was an impossible sacrifice to make. Meeting you changed everything."

My heart had the audacity to feel hopeful. But I couldn't let it all the way in. Just like I couldn't let every car that passed by my childhood window completely flood me with hope.

"I know this might sound sudden." His thumb moved to my collarbone. "But I won't fight it anymore, Willow. Because after gettin' to know you, I can't imagine not being with you."

"But your biggest fear—"

"None of us is guaranteed a tomorrow. Is my job more dangerous than most? Yes. But no one knows what the future holds. You could have died when you were pushed off that bridge, and the very idea of losin' you completely guts me. So, I've realized that I need to grab ahold of happiness when I can and not let fear hold me back. Because I refuse to live a life without you in it, to live a life filled with nothing but emptiness and regret. You, Willow, are worth the risk. The real question is whether I'm worth that risk for you."

Which was everything I'd ever wanted to hear. But was I okay with him making that sacrifice?

Was allowing himself to be in a loving relationship really a sacrifice, though? Wasn't a bigger sacrifice spending his life alone?

"What if you change your mind?" I asked. "If you go to work one day and there's a shooting or something and there's a close call, you might start to think differently."

I adored Shane. And nothing would make me happier than surrendering to my feelings for him. But I was not one of those women willing to surrender my control. If any circumstance existed that might change his mind, I would not choose to dive into this.

"I won't lie and say the fear isn't there anymore," he said. "It is. But I refuse to let that fear dictate my life to the point I can't be happy, and I won't be happy without you, Willow. Because of you, I'm finally ready and willing to take a risk. The only question is...will you give me the chance to make you fall in love with me?"

I didn't realize how fast I was breathing until now. But there it was, my chest rising and falling so quickly that I wondered if I might faint.

"I'm already falling," I admitted. Like him, I think I had been for a while. Slowly, like the leaves of a tree beginning to turn color. A handful at first. And then it spreads until the entire tree is blazing red.

Shane's lips curled up on both sides. Illuminating the entire room with his joy. Then, he crashed his mouth to mine.

And pinned me to the bed.

* * *

THREE HOURS LATER, I FINISHED THE DELICIOUS BREAKFAST SHANE MADE, and I decided it was time to go home and shower.

Shane gave me clothes and shoes to temporarily wear and then walked me to my door and made sure I got in safe. Especially since I had to go back in through the patio door, not having my key on me. It took him only two yanks before the damn thing opened.

Mental note: I need to work on upper body strength.

I stumbled inside with frozen feet, laughing with Shane behind me.

"Did you do this?" I looked over my shoulder at him as I walked to the giant bouquet of flowers sitting on my kitchen counter. Blue and red roses.

Shane's smile fell. "No."

He glanced at the front door. Right. Delivery guys leave flowers at your doorstep; they don't enter and leave them inside. And my dead bolt was still locked.

From the inside.

Whoever brought these must've come in through the sliding glass door because there'd be no way to lock the dead bolt behind them without the key.

Which was beyond creepy. And odd. Wouldn't they have struggled with the door, like we had?

Shane motioned for me to hold still as he advanced into my bedroom, then my bathroom, checking each closet, the bathtub, even under the sink cabinets.

All the while, I inched toward the flowers—a moth to the mysterious flame that was a little card with my name on it, dread filling me as I reached for it.

"Willow, don't—" Shane started.

But it was too late. I'd plucked it from the tightly packed flowers —their scent wafting through my apartment like some kind of ominous warning.

Inside was a handwritten poem.

Willow,

Roses are red.

Violets are blue.

Drop the investigation,

or I'll fucking end you.

40

"Where the hell is he?" Shane demanded.

"You need to calm down," Rosse insisted.

"You kidding me?" Shane shoved a hand through his hair. "The front door was dead-bolted."

"I'm aware."

"He broke into the apartment."

"We don't know the perp is male," Rosse reminded him.

"Bullshit we don't."

"We're dusting for prints."

"You know what it'll tell you. So, answer the question. Where the hell is he?" Shane snarled.

Rosse joined the two uniformed police officers processing this probable break-in with its suspicious, creepy threat—since it obviously had something to do with his case.

"Maybe someone has been breaking in all along, and I didn't know," I said. "Remember the toothbrush, the bookmark, the hair in the sink?"

"When you came home from the hospital, was the sliding glass door locked?"

"I think so." It had to be. Even though I hadn't checked it myself, surely, between Shane and all the officers, somebody confirmed it had been locked when we first walked in. "But even if I didn't, it gets stuck, so it's super hard to open; I couldn't even open it myself last night, so I'm not sure how they'd get inside."

Was it possible the jammed door made the lock unreliable?

"Tony, step outside." Rosse gestured with his arm.

One of the uniformed officers opened the sliding door after three yanks and stepped outside. Rosse closed it behind him and flipped the lock.

"Try to open it." He motioned to the handle.

The uniform grabbed the handle. Tugged it. Hard. Multiple times, but the door wouldn't open. Rosse unlocked the latch, and the officer tried again. The door stuck, just like it had for me last night, but with enough force, the officer got it open on his fourth attempt.

"Thing's a bitch." The cop frowned at the track.

"Carpet's wet from melted snow," the cop noted. "Could all of it be from you?"

I looked at the spots, remembering my path to the kitchen, Shane's to the other rooms.

"No," I said, pointing to a path neither of us had taken. "That wasn't from us."

"Whoever was in here came through this door," the cop said. "But their footsteps outside are long gone."

Four inches of snow had fallen in the last hour with whipping winds covering up any shoe imprints.

"Was Ezra still being held last night or not?" Shane asked.

Rosse stared at Shane.

"I can find out on my own," Shane reminded him.

Rosse scratched the side of his face. "He was released late last night."

"Son of a bitch," Shane said. "Plenty of time for him to pull this stunt."

"There's a restraining order," Rosse said. "So, if it's him, we'll be able to bring him in and charge him with breaking it. We'll process the scene for prints. Look into the source of the flowers," Rosse said. "But for your own safety, I'd be careful to assume it's him. Assumptions can be dangerous; you could let your guard down with someone else."

Had he changed his mind from the last time we spoke? Was Ezra no longer suspect number one?

"Who *do* you think did this?" I asked.

The detective regarded me. We both knew we were not just talking about the flowers. We were talking about the bridge case because, obviously, the flowers were from whoever had tried to hurt me.

"Unfortunately, it's too soon to say."

"Just run down what you know," I said, putting my hands on my hips.

Shane stood to my left, his eyes watching me, as if worrying I'd fall over from fear.

Fat. Chance. I was angry. Beyond angry. Whoever the hell did this, I wanted them locked up, put in jail, end of discussion.

"The ex-boyfriend obviously has a motive. One man we spoke to, who sent you direct messages on social media, has a record, but so far, his wife is maintaining his alibi."

First, gross that the guy was married and messaging some stranger online. Second, after everything we had uncovered, I was still skeptical that a stranger had pushed me.

"We'll pull surveillance cameras and knock on some doors. See if any neighbors saw anything."

"Perfect. I'll wait here and hope the killer doesn't return," I said sarcastically.

"We're working as fast as we can."

"I know. I'm sorry." My nerves were converting me into a class-A witch. "I just want to move on with my life, and every time I turn around..." I gestured toward the flowers.

Rosse gave a pity nod.

"Can I ask you something off the record?" I inquired.

I wanted Rosse to tell me if this was Ezra or not. As Shane told me, knowing something and gathering enough evidence to prosecute were two different things.

"Do you think it's Ezra or not?" I asked.

The detective shoved his phone back into his pocket and kept his eyes on the floor for several seconds before looking up at me. He glanced at Shane, then back at me, and I wondered if he would normally not answer this question but for Shane standing there.

"Just tell her," Shane said. "She won't hold you to it if it doesn't pan out."

Rosse let a deep breath out of his nose. "Your ex made some innuendos to his jail mate last night."

"Innuendos?"

"Not enough to be a threat and hold him. But enough that if it were my daughter?" Rosse's ominous eyes stabbed at mine. "I'd tell her to pack a bag and get out of town until we catch the son of a bitch."

41

I t was after sunset when the winding road turned into the half-mile-long driveway. Night canopied the dense forest that surrounded the quaint cabin. With its outdoor lanterns creating an amber glow along its wooden exterior, the wraparound porch, and the chimney already blowing smoke above the snow-covered pine trees, the place was picturesque. Like something out of a postcard.

Not the safe haven for a dangerous hideaway.

"Guy on the force is lettin' me use this place. Had his uncle, who lives in town, set everything up for us already." Shane put the car into park.

I followed him inside, where a log fire already crackled in the living room.

"Had him stock up on a few days of food, if you're hungry," Shane said, locking the dead bolt behind me.

I shook my head, and then, while Shane checked each window, ensuring everything was locked up and secure, I took in my surroundings.

The living room contained a two-seater royal-blue sofa facing an oversize window, the fireplace in the corner, and a worn oval-shaped coffee table with a crescent-shaped dent on it. They had painted the kitchen cabinets white with fake marble countertops. All of it glowing orange from the gorgeous fire warming the space.

I walked up to it and held my palms out.

"Not bad, right?" Shane appeared behind me, slipping my coat from my shoulders.

"Still feels like overkill."

I couldn't believe it had come to this, and I couldn't stop questioning if these precautions were too extreme. I mean, if the person wanted to kill me, why leave me a threatening note? Why not hide in the corner of my apartment and off me right there? But the fact that I was debating the likelihood of my death was what sealed my decision to go to this cabin with Shane. And it was only temporary.

I tried to look at the positive. The good thing about the flowers was that it presumably left a trail of evidence pointing to the person who bought them, and the person who bought them was most likely the person who had pushed me off that bridge. Which meant we were far closer to catching them than ever before.

"Thank you," I said. "For arranging all of this."

Even though I hoped it wasn't necessary, it was kind all the same. Another example of Shane's fierce protection over me.

Shane stood behind me, holding my hips as he brushed his lips against my neck. It was just a whisper of a kiss, yet it shouted throughout my entire body, echoing throughout my chest and awakening every inch of my skin, which now begged to be touched by his rough hands. He pressed his chest harder into my back, and as he dragged his lips upward to my jaw, I shut my eyes, feeling the worry and disappointment over being driven from my home wash away with the waves of pleasure now dancing across my body.

"And I promise I'll make this stay memorable," Shane whispered, allowing his tongue to briefly caress my neck.

"You're trying to get my mind off of it," I managed, struggling to think coherently with my lower belly warming to a boil.

"Is it working?"

Part of me wanted to hold on to my anger over this situation, but I'd already allowed this person to dominate my life and rob me of any sense of security. I didn't want to give them the power to control every aspect of my life—namely, the good fortune of being alone in a cabin with Shane. I would not squander this and pout.

Even if I wanted to be upset right now, I couldn't be—not with Shane's fingers breaching the hem of my shirt, kindling flames along my belly, my chest, which he grabbed as I turned my head and surrendered my mouth to his.

I ran my fingers through his silky black hair, feeling his excitement grow as he pressed his hips against my lower back. His tongue was gentle and sweet as it danced with my own, my desire to feel him swelling in my thighs.

Shane turned me around so we faced each other. Damn, the amber glow made him so much sexier, the way it bronzed his skin and the flames reflected in his blue eyes. I could stare at those eyes forever, memorize every pixel as he tilted his head and pressed his mouth to mine again.

With the pops of firewood crackling, the smell of its burning wood billowing into the room, I opened my lips and welcomed Shane's tongue against mine, groaning as I ran my hands up through his hair. Each time I'd kissed him, it had felt like the first—that urgent, desperate need for his mouth to never leave mine overwhelming my thoughts. Especially when he trailed his fingertips down my back, pulling at the hem of my shirt.

He broke our kiss and pulled it over my head, allowing himself a hungry gaze of my body, before I helped him get his shirt off—marveling at his tattoos, which appeared to be engraved even deeper into the ridges of his muscles. I placed my palms against his firm chest, feeling the beat of his heart. He let me study his celestial body for only a moment before he grabbed the back of my head and pulled my mouth to his.

Though gentle, his kiss was needy and urgent. He walked me

backward, and when the backs of my legs hit the couch, he relinquished his hold on me long enough to strip me out of my shoes and remaining clothes. Followed by his own.

Last time, he'd claimed me. It was my turn to claim him.

When I pushed *him* down onto the couch in a seated position and climbed on top of him, I could tell by the slight rounding of his eyes and smile that I'd surprised him. I buried my fingers in his hair as I kissed him harder, relishing his groan as I rocked my hips along his lower stomach. He grabbed my breasts as I lifted my hips up slightly and then sank down on top of him, connecting our bodies.

Shane growled and grabbed my hips as I began to move. Slow at first, trailing kisses along his sharp jaw, holding his shoulders, but then I picked up my pace and leaned back, staring right into his sapphire eyes. Watching his every reaction as I tilted and moved on top of him, finding the spot that made his eyes roll into the back of his head.

I could feel a wave of my own building, too, grinding that delicate spot against him.

Shane kissed my nipples, crashing that wave closer to the shore.

"Don't stop," I whispered, pulling at the back of his head.

He gladly obeyed, tasting and sucking as he stared up at me with hungry eyes, our bodies working together in an artful dance.

And then...then the wave began to crash, so powerfully that my body started to lock up. Shane kept his eyes on mine, listening to my every moan as he grabbed my hips and pulled at them to keep our dance going.

And just as the last trembles of my wave began to subside, Shane pulled my lips to his and growled into my mouth.

Before stilling beneath me.

We made love again and again the next night.

And the night after. As the days strung together, I existed on the seesaw of elation—for getting so much exclusive time with Shane—and hopelessness that they would ever close this case.

42

"What is taking so long?" I asked.

"I know it's difficult to maintain patience," Detective Rosse said on the other end of the phone.

"I thought between the flowers and the fingerprints, there would've been an arrest by now."

"Attempted murder is a significant charge, one that the district attorney requires sound evidence for."

"I can't wait here forever," I said. "I have to get back to my job in person. The Wi-Fi here is terrible."

He said nothing.

"How much more time do you need?" I pressed. "Ballpark."

If it was longer than a few more days, we needed to go back.

He sighed and spoke in a low tone, like he was answering me reluctantly. "Give me another twenty-four hours."

I sat up. In the week and a half we'd been here, I'd talked to Rosse every day for updates. Every day was more of the same. *We're working on it, crime scene results, questioning, yada yada.* Never once had he given me a timeline. Let alone one so short.

"There's been a development," I surmised.

Shane was spread out on the couch with his feet up, glancing at me with questions in his eyes. The poor guy was so damn worried they'd never get enough evidence to put my attempted killer behind bars. Ironically, being a detective gave him a front-row seat to how many people got away with crimes. Shane had been trying to hide his worry, but he frequently cracked his knuckles as he glared at my un-ringing phone.

Sensing they might be close was thrilling. But what if it wasn't the ending we hoped for? What if the DA reviewed all the evidence and declined to press charges? I didn't want to burst into tears in front of Shane while I was on the phone, upsetting him by finding out that way. If this was bad news, I'd find a gentle way to break it to him.

First step: privacy, so I could find out what was going on.

I opened the door of the cabin and stepped out onto the snow-lined porch.

Nestled deep into the woods of northern Illinois, the cabin was surrounded by emerald pine trees, dusted with snow. Occasional deer walked by, often in the early morning hours or at sunset, when the orange light softened the forest into an amber glow. Right now, that glow was fading to black—just like the probable conclusion of Rosse's investigation.

I brushed the snow off the antique rocking chair with my palm, cursing when a sharp pain sliced into my skin.

Even the chair wants me to leave this place and get back to my life.

I sat down, squeezing my now-bleeding palm.

"We confirmed the flowers were from Ezra. He was released with enough time to buy them and go to your apartment. The flower shop employee remembers him."

Holy shit.

I waited for him to say more.

"So, that's the development? He's been the one who threatened me?"

That's it? After days, all we had was confirmation my ex-moron sent me threatening flowers? Surely, they'd figured that out days ago and just hadn't been willing to share it with me until now.

"No." The detective took a deep breath. "You sitting down?"

A blood drop splattered onto the snow from the wood that had pierced my palm. I quickly studied the wound, relieved it didn't look deep enough to warrant an emergency room trip.

"I've got the warrant in my hands, Willow. We're going to arrest Ezra for your attempted murder."

A tornado of emotions blew through me. Relief that they had found the person responsible and were going to arrest him. That this was finally over and I could put it behind me. But also shock.

How could I have been in a serious relationship with someone and never suspected they were capable of violence like this? It hurt to realize Ezra willingly and purposely tried to end my life. And for what? Because I wouldn't take him back? Because he had called me a bitch that night and panicked and thought it was all over? I had no idea what he must have done or said to lure me to that bridge— likely threatened suicide or something. But even more bizarre than shock, staying well past its expiration date, was pity.

I couldn't believe I felt a little sorry for Ezra. I shouldn't. A normal person would feel nothing but disgusting hatred for him, and I did feel those things. But Ezra was likely going to spend years in prison. And a small fragment of my heart wilted at the end of this tragic love story.

"So, it's over," I said.

The detective was silent.

"It's over, right?" I repeated.

"Ezra's not at his apartment. He's been fired from his job, so coworkers haven't seen him for days."

"So, you can't find him?"

"With how many cops we have looking for him, I can't imagine he'll last more than a day. We'll pick him up."

Relief pumped through the blood that oozed from my cut, but sometimes, relief makes you let your guard down.

43

The shape outside looked like nothing at first. It sat among a sea of forty-foot-tall pine trees, whose limbs appeared black in the early evening sky.

I gazed out the kitchen window as I washed fresh blood from the stupid cut on my palm. It wasn't that bad; Shane didn't need to curse himself for not bringing a first aid kit, and he certainly didn't need to rush into town to get bandages.

I glanced out the window again, only this time, the shape moved.

My heart launched a cannon of needles through my body.

Because now that it had moved, I could see it wasn't just any shape.

It's human.

I had never seen another person out here. This cabin was ten acres away from the next one and three miles from the main road that led into a town with one convenience store–slash–gas station–slash–grocery store.

I darted to the living room and looked out the front window, thinking maybe Shane was back already. But his car wasn't there.

I ran to the kitchen window.

I'm overreacting.

I'm just being paranoid.

I squinted to get a better look at the person, but it was dark outside, and all I could make out was a shape. A man, I think?

He walked into the woods and vanished.

Probably just a neighbor. Probably out for a walk at sunset and had walked too far.

I yanked the kitchen drawer open and grabbed a butcher knife just to be safe.

The figure came back out of the woods. He stood next to an ancient pine tree and stopped.

He's staring right at me.

I ducked down beneath the window so he couldn't see me. Which was stupid. He already saw me. And he likely noticed there was no car outside—that I was in here all alone.

There was no way Ezra would have been able to track us up here, right?

I needed to call Shane.

I crawled out of the kitchen toward the bedroom, where my cell phone was charging on the nightstand, but I didn't make it that far.

Because the figure walked right by the bedroom window. All I could see was his shadowed profile, so I couldn't see his face to confirm it was Ezra.

If it were an innocent neighbor, he wouldn't walk past a bedroom window in the back of the cabin like this, and if he needed something, he could've knocked on the front door.

I needed to grab my cell phone, hide in the closet, and call the police. And Shane. But this cabin was so tiny, it wouldn't take that unknown figure long to find me. A minute, maybe two, if I was lucky. And we were out deep in the forest. Lord knew how far away we were from the closest police station. I might have a knife, but he could knock it out of my hand or overpower me or have a gun or some other weapon.

But if this guy did wish me harm, my only hope was to get as much distance between me and him as possible.

Hide.

Or run.

I looked at the nightstand, ten feet to my right. At the front door...and then I shot up like a missile, unlocked the dead bolt, and ran into the sanctuary of trees, not looking back.

I didn't need to run all the way to town. I just needed to be deep enough in the forest to get away from whoever that was and wait until I heard Shane's car pull up so we could call the police.

I wove through a blanket of trees so fast, my lungs burned. It felt like icicles were piercing them from the inside with each breath I took, and now, my feet were screaming in agony. Even through the adrenaline, the snow attacked my skin.

The butcher's knife trembled in my hand as my body shivered. A blanket of goose bumps erupted, failing to keep me warm as I risked a look back at the cabin. Behind a curtain of trees, I couldn't see it anymore, which was good. If I couldn't see it, whoever that was probably couldn't see me.

But what if he followed my footprints?

My bare feet screamed in agony from the cold snow. It felt like being stabbed by a thousand needles, yet I couldn't go back to the cabin. Not until I saw Shane's headlights approach.

I could only hope it wouldn't be long because I was wearing nothing but a thin layer of cotton pajamas.

I glanced up at the surrounding trees, spotting an empty oak in the middle of pines. Its branches offered an escape from the snow and a better view to watch for headlights.

I ran ten feet to it and grabbed the first branch, my injured palm yipping in protest. The bark was as thick as a baseball bat, and it scraped my arms as I tried to pull myself up.

Two hands grabbed my hips.

I screamed and spun around, pressing my knife's tip against the chest of a dark figure, who threw his hands into surrender.

"Easy!" he said.

Chest heaving, standing in the snow, I kept the blade of the knife against his chest until my eyes adjusted to the blackness. Only then did I lower my weapon.

"Hey." Shane pulled me to his chest. "It's okay. You're safe."

"S...someone's w...w...walking around tt...th...the cab...bin."

"It was me." Shane shrugged off his coat, wrapped it around my shoulders. "I was getting logs for the fire so you can lie down after I bandage your hand."

"No. Y...your c...car wasn't out f...front. You w...weren't back y...yet."

"I parked on the side this time, sheltered behind two pines."

I melted into Shane's chest and savored the way his arms tightened around my body.

"Jesus, you're not wearing shoes?"

He picked me up, one arm under my legs, the other beneath my back.

"I can walk," my ego assured. But my icicle feet told my ego to shut the hell up.

His steps punched through the snow.

"Next time, call me instead of confronting a stalker in the dark, okay?"

I pressed my cheek against his shoulder as he carried me through the icy forest and back into the warmth of the cabin. Once inside, Shane wrapped me in two blankets and added three more logs to the fireplace before bandaging my palm.

"Thaw," he said, kissing my forehead.

But I only warmed up for a few minutes before my cell phone rang. Shane brought it to me from the bedroom and looked at me with anxious eyes.

It was Detective Rosse's number.

44

"I have news," the detective said. No *hello*. No *how are you*. Just straight and to the point.

"Good news or bad news?"

"You sitting down?"

Shane sat by my feet and pulled them onto his lap, pretending not to be apprehensive over whatever the detective was about to say.

But failing.

"I am," I said.

"We got him," Rosse said. "Ezra's in lockup."

I closed my eyes and let out a breath that felt like I had been holding since I hit the water.

"He is?"

"Caught him at O'Hare with a one-way ticket to Mexico."

I set my hot chocolate down on the coffee table. "He was going to flee the country?"

"Appears so. But we got him."

All the anxiety that had been swirling around inside of me released its grip on my ribs, and I could finally relax for the first time in a long time.

I smiled, and at the sight of my smile, Shane's muscles loosened. He put his elbow on the armrest of the couch and pressed his thumb and middle finger to his closed eyes. I wondered if he was fighting back tears.

"How long ago did this happen?" I asked.

" 'Bout an hour ago. He's in Cook County Jail right now."

"So, it's over?"

"No judge will grant him bail after trying to flee."

It was over. Ezra was behind bars.

It felt like I had been trapped under the weight of a boulder that had just been lifted off my body, and I was finally free to stand up, brush myself off, and walk away.

My hypothesis over *why* Ezra had tried to kill me bugged me, though, because it was incomplete. He'd been trying to get me back for six months, so what happened that night that culminated in murder? And if he had tried to kill me, why was he so stupid to leave a threatening note in my apartment that would put a target on his back? He hadn't even covered his financial tracks of having bought the flowers.

Would I ever find out the answers to these questions?

"I'll be in touch, Willow."

"Okay."

"Have a good night."

"Detective Rosse?" I took a deep breath. "Thank you."

"I'm glad we caught him, Willow. I'll be in touch soon with next steps."

I hung up.

"They got him."

Shane's smile stretched so wide, I could see his teeth. He jumped on top of me and kissed me like we'd been separated by war—his lips firm and urgent, his fingers twisting through my hair.

I couldn't believe that it was finally over. This nightmare had consumed less than a month of my life, and yet it felt like it had transformed everything.

"I adore you," Shane whispered against my lips.

We only kissed for a minute before my cell phone chimed with a text.

"It's from my mom." I squinted, confused. "She said she has something important to tell me."

45

"I'm moving to Texas," Mom said.

I literally froze in place, as if her words harnessed the power of immobilization.

When I had arrived at my mother's place, the first thing that struck me was how gorgeous she looked. She had a fresh haircut, her hair styled with loose waves around her face, her makeup was pristine with a rosy glow to her cheeks, and she wore a silk black shirt with fitted jeans. In all our years together, I couldn't remember her taking such good care of herself. She looked amazing. Ten years younger, at least.

Last time, she'd been smoking—something she only did when she was anxious. Like, say...telling us big news.

"What?" I asked.

"This is what I'd wanted to share with you and Hayley a couple weeks ago, but you left before I had the chance," Mom explained. "There's a large insurance firm looking to open up a branch in Texas. I would be the leader of it with expansion possibilities across the southwest. I interviewed for it and got the job."

"I thought you liked your job?"

And I didn't want her to move. Texas was what, a three-hour flight away? Our relationship might not have been *Brady Bunch* perfect, but if she moved away, we would never get a chance to have the type of relationship I had been trying to build for the last twenty years.

But she was a grown woman, entitled to live her life however she wanted.

"I do," she said. "But..."

Mom motioned for me to take a seat on her couch.

"The truth is, I've been thinking about leaving Chicago for a long time," Mom admitted, looking down at her hands. "Everywhere I look, there are reminders of your father."

Looking back on it, this should not have surprised me. Mom had said things throughout the years about how nice it would be to move to another state and get a fresh start. At the time, I had chalked it up to her daydreaming, but I shouldn't have.

Of course Mom would want a fresh start. Chicago was where her love story ended in tragedy. Chicago was where she stayed to raise her two little children, but having Grandma nearby to help might have been the main reason. But now, we were both grown.

"I've been wanting to do this for years, but I felt I couldn't go because your sister was so reliant on me."

Reliant. That was a kind word. And given that Hayley's problems were rooted in the trauma of Dad's death, I could see why Mom had never put her foot down as much as I thought she should've.

"I..." The selfish part of me wanted to say, *Don't leave. Especially because I'd learned this morning that my life is about to change forever...*

But I had never seen her look so peaceful. While her moving away from me might hurt, it was surely something that was going to make her very happy.

And you know what?

It was time for me to make a different decision. For over twenty years, I had tried to change the relationships with my mom and sister into something that it never became. How long do you hold on to a relationship that only exists in your hopeful wishes? How long does it take to accept things for what they are rather than what you want them to be?

Asking her to stay would not only be selfish; it would repeat the same cycle.

It was time to let go and accept things the way they were.

"I'll miss you," I said.

Relief flooded my mom's face, and her eyes welled with tears.

"I'm sorry for not being the mother you deserved," she said.

My throat swelled. Funny how a simple acknowledgment and apology were especially healing to a complex wound.

"Your sister told me what happened to you. That you'd almost died."

I wasn't sure what to say.

"I wish you had told me."

"I didn't want to worry you," I said.

Ironic, how she'd spent years keeping things from me to protect my heart, and I'd done the same to her.

"I hope you know how much I love you," she said.

My turn to cry. I knew this moment of adoration was born in a goodbye rather than a genuine change in our relationship, but I appreciated it all the same.

"I'm glad you're finding your happiness, Mom. You deserve to be happy."

Every human deserves happiness, no matter how hard we have to fight to claim it.

"I started seeing a therapist who helped me process some of my feelings. I should have handled the birthday dinner with you better and when you came to me afterward to talk about your dad."

Wow. The apologies continued unraveling resentments tied around my bones.

"She helped me realize I wasn't just processing grief. Or guilt over Hayley's issues. The biggest obstacle I've had in my life is shame. Shame that Hayley is struggling with addiction. Shame that I wasn't a better mother to you when I should've been. Shame that your dad died and I wasn't there to stop it, and shame in how it all went down, what he—"

Mom shook her head, unable to finish.

"I think a fresh start will do me good."

Footsteps came up the front walkway.

"Where will Hayley go?" I whispered.

My mom pursed her lips. "We're figuring that out."

Translation: no idea. But it was time for Hayley to leave the nest. Once and for all.

The front door burst open, and Hayley looked at me and Mom. At our hands, at the closeness between us. Which may have been upsetting to my sister to see Mom being so kind to me after I'd hurt Hayley with my questions over the bridge incident.

"You told her?" Hayley asked.

Mom nodded.

"When do you leave?" I asked Mom.

"They want me to start right away. I fly out tomorrow."

"Tomorrow?" I choked out.

"I'll still have to come back to pack up my stuff."

Yeah, but if she was starting a new job tomorrow, packing would be a weekend trip at best. I wish I'd had more notice to talk to Mom.

I hoped Hayley had more notice than I did—or at least was given some kind of grace period to find alternate housing. Because she looked damn stressed. She fidgeted by the front door, scratching the side of her face with her fingernails.

Hayley rarely answered my calls as it was, and after I offended her? Once my mom left, there would be nothing forcing us to talk again. Hopefully Hayley would get her life together, but if not, she might jump from house to house, couch hopping, and if she wasn't able to pay her cell bill, there'd be no easy way to stay in touch with her.

No matter how justified my questions might have been, I wanted to apologize to Hayley for offending her. And now might be my last chance to do it.

"Can I talk to you?" I asked her.

She bit her lip, looking unsure.

"I won't take long," I said.

Hayley's defeated shoulders showed a subdued version of the angry girl who had stormed off the other day. My heart flickered with hope that she didn't want to leave things on bad terms with me before Mom moved away, either.

"Sure. There's something I want to show you, anyway," Hayley said. "Can I borrow your car, Mom?"

Show me? What in the world would she want to show me? And why was she acting so off? Not looking me in the eyes?

I followed her to Mom's car and tried to put her odd behavior aside; Hayley's world was getting turned upside down. Perhaps she was going to ask me for help and felt embarrassed to do it in front of Mom.

"I want to apologize for our fight," I said.

"It's fine."

Clearly, she was still upset by it, though. Hayley scraped the skin of her palm with her nails and wouldn't look at me.

"I should have known better than to ask you if you'd want to hurt me."

Hayley looked out over the steering wheel as she turned onto a side street. We hadn't been driving long, but we'd entered a neighborhood I didn't recognize.

"I guess if I were in your shoes, I would have asked the same thing," she said absently, as if only half listening.

She pulled in front of an abandoned house. With the sun tilting in the horizon, its disheveled appearance had nowhere to hide. It was a tiny box house with a flat roof and plywood nailed over the windows, the front lawn littered with beer cans, broken glass, and Styrofoam containers.

"Is this where you're moving to?"

Maybe Mom had given her some money to help find a place to fix up.

"No," Hayley said. "Come inside with me?"

A man with a matted beard and puffy red coat stood on the corner, staring at me.

"I want to show you something," she said when I hadn't moved.

"This place is clearly abandoned; we have no business walking in."

Hayley's eyes tightened. "You don't recognize it?"

"Why would I?"

"Because it's where Dad died."

46

The house smelled like urine had soaked into its baseboards for years. The walls had been spray-painted with black, orange, and bright green paints. Numbers, symbols. Gang signs perhaps. But thankfully, the place was empty.

I took timid steps across the kitchen floor, the linoleum peeling up in the corners and stained yellow. The air was cold and stuffy, no circulation or heat, but Hayley didn't seem to mind.

"Maybe we should go." I didn't like the idea of getting in trouble for trespassing.

"This is where he died." Hayley pointed to the kitchen floor. "You were right there." She pointed to the hallway. "And I was right there." She pointed to the adjoining living room. "Mom was at the store."

We lived here?

A haunting chill seized my muscles.

My dad had felt like a ghost my whole life. And now, here I was, standing in the very spot where he took his last breath.

I wished I could remember more. The kitchen felt vaguely familiar to me. So did the living room. It was as if some brain cells

306 | KATHY LOCKHEART

still remembered the layout of the house, but none of the horror that happened inside.

"Why did you bring me here?" I asked.

Hayley opened a drawer in the kitchen and pulled out newspapers, spread them across the countertop, as if she knew I'd be unable to resist finding answers about his death.

"You can read it for yourself."

Some part of me screamed that I should run. Hayley was staring at me, her eyes slightly widened, frame tilted toward mine. After twenty-four years, the answers to the questions that had haunted me my whole life were only a few steps away.

My version of a drug I could not resist.

I inched toward the countertop, toward the words that could forever alter my life.

My past. My present. And my future.

The first thing that I noticed was Dad's picture. The second thing I noticed was the headline.

TWO KILLED WHEN FATHER PULLS GUN ON COP.

Police say Michael Johnson turned violent after police served him an eviction notice. The suspect pulled a gun on a police officer, turning a routine visit into a deadly shoot-out. Residents could hear shouting as tension escalated, culminating in both men firing one round. Both fatal.

I staggered away from the kitchen counter.

Away from the new reality before me.

An eviction notice.

A standoff.

Why did this sound so familiar?

Was it ingrained in my brain? Buried somewhere deep in my psyche?

It all made sense now, why mom was so ashamed—because Dad had murdered a police officer.

This was the deep family secret they had tried to keep from me. This explained why Mom didn't tell me everything, why she thought I would live under the shame of what had happened that awful day.

Because being the daughter of a man who killed a police officer? That was quite the dark cloud to live under, and I wasn't so sure I would've been able to crawl out from underneath its horror.

This was why Mom had taken on the burden of carrying this immense secret—to give me the best life possible.

All the while, Hayley had lived with this darkness. All her anger, all these years—I now understood her better than I ever had and why her suffering had transformed her into a toxic person.

I remembered the conversation Shane and I had about grief. Grief wasn't just a monster, eating relationships in its path. It was a cancer, spreading into every infected orifice it could find.

"That cop killed him," she said. "Came into our home with a loaded gun and shot our father dead."

I've had a challenging time accepting our dysfunctional family dynamics. But this whole time, Hayley and Mom must've struggled to accept the reality surrounding Dad's death. Their hearts having twisted the facts. Yes, technically, Dad had been shot by someone, but he'd been the one to pull the gun on an armed police officer. Even if the police officer had fired first, it would've been in self-defense, not murder.

Grief had warped their perception of those events.

I turned around and looked at my fallen sister. At her hollowed-out cheeks, her stringy blonde hair that looked light brown with all its oil at the roots, and her clothes that were too baggy for her body.

I knew nothing I could say now could unravel the twenty-plus years of brainwashing she had done to herself.

"Is any of this ringing a bell?" She rocked from her left foot to her right.

"I was only four," I reminded her. "I don't remember what happened."

"Yeah. Don't remind me," she said.

And then she pulled a gun from her coat pocket.

And pointed it at my face.

47

"What the hell are you doing?" I put my hands up.

"Give me your phone."

"Hayley..."

"Phone! Now!"

When I pulled it from my back pocket, she yanked it from my hand and held it up to my face to unlock the screen.

"Hayley, I don't know what you think—"

"Shane..." she spat.

My blood thinned.

"I figured you were the pick-up-on-the-first-ring kind of guy. Do you know who this is?"

Silence.

"A man who remembers voices. Impressive. Listen, I've got your girlfriend here with a gun pointed at her head. If you like her better with her brains inside of her body, you should come to the address I'm about to text you. Oh, and don't bring or notify a single cop."

Nausea lurched bile up my esophagus.

"Now, that's no way to talk to a lady, Detective. You'd better hurry. I'm running out of patience, and if anyone comes by to check on us, boom."

Hayley hung up the phone and threw it on the floor.

"What are you doing?" I asked.

"How does it feel?"

"How does what feel?"

She rocked from side to side and swiped her nose with the back of her free hand. "Knowing the truth about Dad?"

"Why did you call Shane?"

"Answer the question. How does it feel?"

I needed to tread lightly. I didn't know what might set her off and make her pull that trigger.

I had no right to be this shocked, witnessing Hayley going off the deep end. For years, she'd constantly leaned over the cliff of disaster.

"It's awful. I wish I had known all of these years. Why didn't you tell me sooner? This isn't a burden you had to bear alone."

Hayley's eyes filled with tears, and her lip quivered.

"Oh, because *Willow was so little* and *she's so lucky she doesn't remember*. Let's all tap-dance around Willow and make sure she has a perfect life while the rest of us live in hell."

Even with a gun pointed at my head, I hated hearing her suffer like this.

"Please put the gun down, Hayley."

"Screw you."

"If you wanted me to know so badly, why didn't you just tell me before? You know I kept asking Mom about it when we were kids until she shut the topic down."

"If you cared half as much as you said you did"—she sobbed, shaking with violent tears—"you could've figured this out a long time ago. There's Dad's name in black and white in a newspaper article. You could've put the pieces together if you actually gave two shits."

"I do care. I didn't dig into it because Mom begged me a long time ago to let it go, and if I went against her wishes—even if I did it on my own and tried to be discreet—there was a chance she'd find out and would be so upset that I might've lost her, too! I chose to let it go so I could keep the one parent I had left, Hayley, but of course I care about what happened to Dad!"

"You do *not*!" She stepped closer, the gun now only three feet from my forehead. "You claim you wanted the truth, but deep down, you knew you didn't want to hear it! You just wanted to look like the concerned sister that wanted to find out what happened to her family. You were playing a role, but you were never one of us."

"Hayley, please. Put the gun down."

"And now, Mom's moving away, and everything's just going to keep getting worse."

"Killing me will not solve anything. You don't want to spend the rest of your life in prison, Hayley."

She laughed this ominous, heartbroken cry and rubbed her runny nose with the back of her wrist. "I won't be here anymore."

At first, I thought she meant she'd flee, but I could see something else in her eyes...something disastrous.

Is she going to kill me and then herself? Why call Shane then?

"Hayley, you don't want to do this."

"Shut up!" she screamed so loud, spit sprayed across the room.

"Mom will be destroyed if you do this."

"Serves her right for abandoning us to go start her happy life. I mean, what the hell? What kind of mom makes one daughter live in hell and lets the other one live in a fairy tale? And just when the one daughter can't take it anymore, she up and moves to Texas, leaving her behind. Nobody cares about me. Nobody ever cared about me, except Dad!"

"That's not true. Mom has always taken you in when you needed help."

"While threatening to kick me out on the streets! Just like the day you had your fucking fall."

I stepped back, my hips hitting the counter.

"What are you talking about?"

"You want to hear what *caring* sounds like? Mom told me if I got arrested one more time for possession, she was throwing me out for good. And when I asked her for money for groceries, she said she'd buy them for us herself from now on. But I needed cash. I owed money to my dealer, and she wouldn't give me any. And then what do *you* do, Willow? When I go to you, asking for a little money to help, do you give it to me? No. You lecture me about spending money on drugs."

"You came over that night?"

"And when I turned and walked away from you, you kept lecturing me. You followed me on your high horse, yelling at me for giving Mom a hard time when *she* was the one giving *me* a hard time! *She* was the one holding me back in life, making me live with this secret. And the daughter that got everything handed to her wouldn't even give me fifty bucks."

"The night I went over the bridge, I was with you?"

"I told you to back off. But did you listen? No. You grabbed my arm and started searching my pockets. And when you found a *tiny* pack of powder, you said you were calling the cops. You gave me some damn speech about how time in jail would sober me up."

"You tried to kill me."

"I was just trying to get my drugs back! *You're* the one that wouldn't let it go and turned it into a wrestling match! You're the one that threatened me! You told me you lived next door to a cop. If you turned me in, I'd be homeless!"

Betrayal ate through my veins like acid.

Hayley had *long* hair, but we knew it was possible the person in that grainy video might've had longer hair pulled back into a bun or something.

"You swore you hadn't hurt me," I said. "You made me feel bad for even asking it."

"What did you expect? That I'd confess and get arrested for that?"

I had expected I could see through her if she'd been lying, but I was wrong.

My stomach churned. I could picture it all. Her showing up at my apartment unexpectedly, begging for money, looking high—like she'd fallen off the wagon. Me following her to talk some sense into her. That's why my apartment door wasn't locked. I must've run out in a hurry after her and chased her down before we had a confrontation that climaxed on that bridge.

"After you threw me over the bridge, did you stay to make sure I made it out alive? Or did you just walk away without even looking back?"

"I saw you get pulled from the river and saw you moving when they loaded you into the ambulance, so I knew you were alive. Figured you'd tell people what I'd done, so I needed to run, and to do that, I needed cash. Mom would never give me any, so I went back to your place to look for some. But when I couldn't find any, I panicked. I paced in your apartment for a while, trying to think of how to leave town with no money."

My heart clenched at her treason. I had to grab the counter to keep my weak knees from failing.

"I couldn't tell Mom what I'd done—she'd kick me out for good. So, I called a few hospitals until I found the one you were at and asked if they'd allow you visitors. I was going to beg you not to press charges. When the nurse found out I was family, she gave me the update that you were fine but had no memory of what had happened."

Giving her the chance to get away.

"When I saw you at Mom's birthday dinner," she said, "I was petrified you'd remember it all once you saw me."

That's why she'd looked so off.

But if she'd been in my apartment, looking for cash, she must have been careful to leave everything in place or I would have noticed. Except for...

"Why did you move my stuff?" My toothbrush. My bookmark.

"And clog my drain with my hair?" Hair she must have gathered from all my combs and brushes.

Her face darkened.

"Because once again, everything was going to work out just fine for you. Just like it always has! It was all going to go back to the way it was before—with you living in your happy little bubble and with me trapped in a dark nightmare, reliving Dad's murder over and over again. It wasn't fair, especially after how mean you were to me that night, so I wanted you to crawl out of your skin, like I always have."

Emotions can be the strangest thing. The realization that my sister threw me off that bridge was the only thing I should be fixated on. And, yes, of course, that hurt immensely. But, while I'd never forgive it, an unplanned confrontation that turned violent was bad enough.

Going into my apartment and trying to *purposefully* mess with me psychologically? Somehow, that was an even harder pill to swallow. Imagining her moving my stuff and gathering my hair from my brushes and shoving it into my drain while I was being treated at the hospital. The betrayal stung so deep, it was like my heart shattered and fell to pieces at my feet.

I will not cry. Not for her. Not anymore.

My sister never loved me the way I loved her.

"Were you spying on me?" Was that figure I'd seen outside my apartment Hayley?

She glared at me. "Spying? Get over yourself. I checked on you outside your apartment a couple of times."

"Why?" I asked.

"I wanted to see if you were with the traitor."

"What does *that* mean?"

"You didn't read far enough." She pointed at the newspaper article.

I was scared to move, scared it was a ploy to shoot me in the back. Still, I turned my eyes to look at the newspaper article again.

I read beneath the fold, where the article went deeper into what led up to the eviction notice. Evidently, my dad had fallen on hard times financially, and after being laid off, he fell behind on his rent. My heart spasmed at that, thinking of all the people in my job I had to help lay off. It went on to say that as Dad's stress level rose, he'd started to get into verbal altercations with people, the police being called on a few occasions for it. Until, finally, the eviction notice pushed him past his breaking point.

In a confrontation with an officer, Dad insisted everyone leave him and his family alone. That he wasn't going to raise his kids homeless. The tension escalated until he drew a gun, the officer responding in like. Escalating voices and crying kids in the background, and then shots fired.

To the right of the article was a picture of the fallen officer.

My stomach sank to the earth's center.

I recognize him. Those same eyes, that same jaw and smile.

It matched the photo Shane had in his bedroom of his fallen father—the police officer shot in the line of duty.

Oh my God.

My father killed Shane's dad.

48

I threw up in the sink. It burned my esophagus even worse than my eyes burned from tears.

I remembered the blood on me in that hospital room after Dad had died. Only...it might not have even been his blood. It might have been the blood of Shane's father. Who was I closest to when the shots rang out? Whose blood had splattered onto me?

While I was a four-year-old girl, standing in this bloodstained kitchen, Shane was a small boy, sitting on the front porch. Waiting for his dad to come home from work. Having no idea his father was a corpse, lying on this floor.

The hurt was so overwhelming, I thought I might pass out.

So was the realization of how deep my sister's resentment ran. Grief had planted seeds of anger inside of her, weeds infesting her feelings until they'd grown into vengeance.

"You ran to the officer," Hayley snarled. "Dad told you to stand still, but you didn't listen. You ran to the officer and got in between them, and that's when the officer must have thought Dad was about to shoot you, so he fired his gun, killing Dad. If you'd just stayed put, Dad would still be alive."

I'd run into the middle of the standoff? Causing gunfire to ensue?

I felt faint. Like the room was spinning.

Logically, I knew I'd only been a four-year-old. But my heart didn't seem to care, flooding my veins with the poison of guilt. If I hadn't done that, maybe Dad would still be here.

Maybe Shane's dad would be, too.

I took deep breaths, trying to force those thoughts into the back of my mind because, right now, I needed to focus completely on convincing my sister to put the gun down.

"When did you find out it was *Shane's* father who shot Dad?"

She glared at me. "When I saw Shane at dinner, he looked familiar. It took me a couple of days to place him."

If I hadn't let Shane tag along to that birthday dinner, could this all have been avoided?

"Don't do this," I said.

"Put your hands behind your back."

"Hayley, I know we had a fight on my birthday, but I love you more than you know."

"Oh, you do? You love me so much, you wouldn't even give me money when I needed it. You love me so much that when I tried to leave your house, you followed me and threatened to turn me into the police."

"I'm sure I was doing what I thought was best for you."

"Bullshit. You've always done what is best for yourself. Hands behind your back. Now."

"If you kill me, I'm not the only one who will die," I said. "I'm pregnant."

49

H ayley's eyes widened in shock for several seconds before tightening into disgust.

"How could you have a baby with that man?" she spat.

"Hayley."

"How could you?! His dad killed our father!"

"Shane's a good person."

And it's not like I had any idea that his family was connected to ours; this was another price tag I was paying for the secrets that were kept from me. Not that I'd provoke her right now by pointing that out. Or pointing out that our dad was the one at fault for this, not Shane's.

Hayley paced with the gun still pointed at me, a wild look in her eyes as she struggled to process this.

"This could be good," she eventually mumbled to herself. "He'll be more cooperative then."

Good? She viewed my unborn child as a pawn in her twisted game? And what did she mean, more cooperative?

How am I supposed to talk her down if she's lost it that bad?

The scary thing was, Shane would do whatever it took to save me, but not because of the pregnancy. I'd just found out a few hours ago. Hadn't even told Shane yet.

I couldn't believe I was pregnant. It was reckless of me to assume missing *one* pill wouldn't be a big deal. I always took my pill with my morning coffee, but I had spent that Sunday morning in the hospital. I didn't realize I had missed a pill until Monday and then thought nothing of it.

"You're going to kill me." This shock wouldn't relent.

"Only if I have to," Hayley said.

What did that mean? What would constitute her having to kill me? What was her endgame here?

My mind raced, feeling like the answer was right in front of me. *Think, Willow.*

She lured Shane here and insisted he come alone. Why? And why *here*? In the kitchen where our dad and Shane's dad had died all those years ago. Two guns drawn, two bullets, two heartbeats that stopped.

She had to know that Shane would come here armed and would be prepared to fire at the person threatening my life. Was this some sort of test to see if he loved me? It made no sense. And even if he didn't love me, he'd absolutely fire his gun if Hayley turned her gun on him, giving him no other choice. Any threatened person would.

, And that's when it clicked. The significance of the location. Shane, the son of the officer who'd killed Dad. Her comment about her not being here anymore. My sister's resentment that I'd had a life of happiness while she'd lived "in hell" all these years, and her bitter hatred toward Shane's father that now extended to Shane.

What she had planned was far worse than my death.

Hayley would pull a gun on Shane, knowing he'd pull one too. Maybe her goal was to kill him before he could pull his weapon— revenge against the son of our dad's killer. But the more probable outcome was that Shane would fire, too.

She was going to force me to watch her and Shane kill each other.

And make me live in the hellish aftermath, just like she had after Dad died.

I felt dizzy, a hostage to a haunting tragedy mirroring the one from over twenty years ago.

I should never have come here with Hayley. I should never have gotten in that car with her or given her the benefit of the doubt. I should have cut her out of my life long ago. I'd given Hayley too many chances.

Just like Shane's dad had given my father too many chances.

My breaths started coming so quickly, I couldn't get enough oxygen, but I needed to snap out of it and focus. Any minute, Shane would show up, walk through that door, and she was going to kill him. As some sick, twisted revenge against his father.

And if it didn't go according to her perfect plan? She'd kill me and my unborn child.

I was not about to let that happen.

I waited until Hayley turned her head to see what sounded like an engine approaching.

And then I lunged.

I grabbed her wrist and bit her hand that held the weapon.

Hayley shrieked as I slammed my body into hers, and we both crashed to the floor—me on my left side, her on her right.

She gripped the pistol even tighter, straining to control its aim.

I tried to twist the gun away from me, but Hayley now held it with two hands, and with her adrenaline pumping, she was strong. So damn strong.

I couldn't twist the weapon, so I released it and grabbed the barrel, pushing it away from me as my sister growled over tightened lips—her discolored teeth covered in spit and hatred.

Hayley slammed her elbow into my temple.

For a second, the pain was so intense, I thought I had been shot, but Hayley pushed herself up off the floor.

I rolled onto my knees and sprinted out the front door.

I made it across the front lawn.

I made it to the sidewalk.

I locked eyes with the man I had seen standing on the corner with a big, fluffy red coat.

"Help!" I screamed.

Pop, pop, pop.

My right leg gave out, and I collapsed onto the concrete sidewalk.

"Holy shit!" the man yelled and dropped to the ground on his belly.

At first, all I felt was a tight pressure in my thigh, followed by the warmth of my blood streaming inside my jeans. But then...a burning pain seared through my leg.

I tried to get back up.

Run, Willow.

Run, or you're dead.

And your baby is, too.

I took one step and fell down again.

I got up and glanced over my shoulder.

Four houses away, Hayley was walking toward me slowly, her right hand casually gripping the weapon that had tried to end my life. It was pointed to the ground, as if she knew she had already killed me and was just waiting for the blood loss to do its work.

Because my leg was bleeding crazy fast. It already pooled beneath my knee and spread down my calf, and I could feel its warmth dripping down my ankle as I hobbled away from her.

I limped across the snow-covered lawn, blood leaving a bright red streak behind me, giving away any hiding spot I might find.

I had to keep going. I hobbled between the houses, around the air-conditioning units, and moved to the back of the house to my left, my footsteps straddling the line between the tiny backyard and a field behind it.

That's when a brief recognition hit me of where I was—a memory buried in my mind, just as this field was buried beneath the snow.

This is the field where Dad and I used to pick wildflowers.

Each step felt like someone was taking an axe to my thigh, and the blood now soaked my lower leg. I looked over my shoulder and saw my sister following.

"Hayley, stop," I said.

But my voice was weak. Not that it would've mattered. If there was anything I could've said to her to get her to stop, I would've said it by now.

I made it one more house down before my leg gave out.

Even then, I kept going.

For the sake of my baby, I crawled on my hands and knees through the snow, praying someone lived in one of these houses. Praying they'd be courageous enough to come outside and help me. Praying something would slow Hayley down so I could find a hiding spot to stop the bleeding.

Time was the biggest weapon. If I didn't stop to slow the bleeding down, I'd die. But if I stopped, Hayley would shoot me again, and I would die, anyway.

Despite using every ounce of adrenaline my body gifted me with, I was moving so slowly, I could hear the crunch of Hayley's steps behind me, growing closer and closer.

Crunch.

My elbows wobbled from fatigue.

Crunch.

I kept crawling.

Crunch.

My vision blackened along the edges, and I fell to my side.

My body landed across the line that separated the backyard and the snow-covered field. Some part of my heart recognized this exact spot in the field, where my father used to hold my hand.

Crunch. Crunch.

I reached down to my belt buckle and loosened the leather strap, pulled out the metal tooth, and then slid the belt from around my waist.

Crunch. Crunch. Crunch.

It wasn't easy. I barely had enough strength to get it out, and each of my tugs was echoed with a louder crunch of snow as my sister stepped toward me.

I wondered why she hadn't finished me already. She had hit my leg from much farther away than she was right now. But I couldn't think about that.

I slid the belt under my thigh and fastened it through its loop. Then, I yanked as hard as I could, screaming in pain as the tourniquet cut off the blood supply to the bullet wound.

Crunch. Crunch.

I was panting and fairly confident I was about to vomit.

Hayley stood over me and looked down at the mess beneath her. My hands were sticky, the white snow stained in crimson.

"Hayley, please," I whispered.

"It wasn't supposed to go this way," she said. As if that made being murdered by my sister less heartbreaking.

I loved her. Even as she stood above me, even after all her years of pushing me away, I loved her. I hated that she'd become so broken inside that she'd turned into this.

Hate had infected her soul, spreading until it extinguished the light of the Hayley she once was.

My life didn't flash before my eyes, but a happier memory of her did.

I'm holding Hayley's hand as we run through this field behind our house, jumping over yellow wildflowers and giggling as Daddy chases us.

I love Hayley. I hope we stay best friends forever.

HAYLEY RAISED THE GUN AND AIMED IT AT MY CHEST.

I placed my hand over my unborn child. "I'm sorry," I whispered to him or her. "For not protecting you."

I shut my eyes, wishing my last moments on earth weren't as a failing mother.

"Put your fucking hands up!"

My eyes snapped open to see Hayley's eyes widen as he approached her.

Shane emerged to my right, walking between two houses with his gun drawn, pointed directly at my sister—his arms straight as tree branches, his eyes fixed on the woman about to kill me.

Hayley stared blankly ahead of her as Shane took another step, closing the distance between them.

She allowed Shane to take two more steps.

"This one's for you, Dad," she whispered.

"Hayley, no!"

Like on the bridge, time surrendered to an almost standstill. I lay on the alabaster snow, crimson pooling around me as the orange glow of the setting sun wrapped around my sister who stood over me, arm raised, her finger on the trigger.

Shane wasn't wearing a coat. He was in black slacks, his button-down rolled to his elbows, as if he'd left a meeting when he'd gotten Hayley's call and hadn't bothered to do anything but grab his keys. His forearm muscles clenched as he gripped the weapon, looking over its barrel as a revolver swung toward him.

Shane's eyes widened slightly as she turned. I could see a moment of hesitation on his face, but when her aim landed on his chest, two pops echoed off the nearby houses.

Hayley and Shane both stilled.

They dropped their arms.

And collapsed to the ground.

50

"Shane!" I tried to shout.

Another surge of adrenaline must have coursed through my body because I gained enough energy to crawl over to him.

He was lying on his back, his eyes open. And I could hear a wetness in his lungs as he fought for air. His chest heaved up and down with each desperate gasp.

In the distance, I could see that guy in the red coat on his phone, advancing slowly toward us, probably uncertain if the gunfire was for sure over.

"Call 911!" I shouted. I wasn't sure he would hear me, though. My voice was so weak, and I was so tired, but maybe he was calling for help already.

"Shane," I cried.

I collapsed onto my right side next to him, and with my last ounce of strength, I pressed my left hand against the wound on his chest. Trying to slow the bleeding.

Shane's cerulean eyes locked with mine, only the color seemed to drain from his. They weren't bright anymore, more like a bluish gray.

"I"—he gasped for air—"didn't get to you"—gasp—"in time."

My eyes welled. "Shh. Save your strength."

"I'm"—gasp—"sorry."

The tears broke over my cheeks.

I wasn't a doctor, but even I could see his life fading away. I could hear it in the wet rasps that were supposed to be his breaths. I could see it in the way his lips were losing their color, along with his skin. And I could see it in the way his eyelids began to sink.

"Don't close your eyes," I cried.

Shane's breaths sounded like snoring, his chest caving in and out. His blood oozed outward beneath my hand.

No, he can't go like this. Not like this.

He lay helpless, watching me die, too, after all he'd done to protect me. Shane kept his eyes on me, but they were only half open now.

"No! You will not leave us, you hear me? You need to fight...fight for me. Fight for us. Fight for the family we're going to have. I'm pregnant, Shane."

I regretted the words the minute they left my mouth because I shouldn't have told him that his deepest, darkest fear was coming true. His words echoed through the broken chambers of my heart.

My worst fear is dying and leaving behind a woman I love. Children raised without a father.

Shane's fading eyes filled with tears. He dragged his arm over to me and placed his hand on my lower belly.

"Tell our child"—gasp—"about me." His voice had lost all its strength, a mere whisper. "Tell him or her"—gasp—"I love them."

A single tear breached the rim of his eye and slid down his cheek.

"You can tell our child yourself," I cried. "Don't leave me. Don't leave us."

"I'm"—gasp—"sorry."

Then, his eyes closed.

51

A sharp poke on the top of my hand woke me.

I struggled to open my eyes, my body feeling as though it were weighed down with lead. A faint beeping mixed with the sound of someone clearing their throat.

A sharp pain seared again.

And again.

I tried to open my mouth, but it was sandpaper, and I had an unpleasant taste on my tongue, like I hadn't brushed my teeth for a couple of days. The air smelled faintly of commercial bleach, but at least I was warm.

After a fourth poke, I dragged my eyelids open.

"Sorry, honey," a female voice said.

My blurry vision sharpened into focus to see a nurse standing over me. Wearing royal-blue scrubs with her graying hair pulled into a messy bun, she had a mole on her cheek the size of a pencil eraser.

"You must have shifted in your sleep," she said. "Had to restart your IV."

She stabbed the needle in the top of my hand again.

And that's when everything came flooding back to me. The shooting. My blood loss. Shane. The baby...

"My baby," I said. "Did the baby survive?" My throat was so dry, I had laryngitis.

The nurse taped the needle with white bandaging and looked down at me with pity. "You're still pregnant, as far as we can tell. But it might be a couple of weeks before we know for sure."

My eyes burned. How could I feel heartbroken at the thought of losing a child I didn't even know existed until this morning? Was it still this morning?

"And Sh..." Shane. Did Shane survive? I swallowed the lump in my throat. "Did..." My eyes welled with tears.

"Get some rest." The nurse used one of those voices that people use when they don't want to give you bad news.

"Please, just tell me," I begged.

The nurse looked at me and must have seen the desperation on my face because she sighed and took pity on me.

"I'm sorry for your loss," she said.

This couldn't be real.

Shane's worst nightmare had come true.

Shane is dead.

Shane, my protector, my lover.

The most honorable man I'd ever met, the best human I'd ever met.

Shane, who had sacrificed his own happiness just to protect the possible heartbreak a woman might go through if she lost him. Shane, who reluctantly surrendered to his feelings, lost his happily ever after before it even started.

Shane couldn't be dead. He couldn't be.

There was no way he was dead.

The nurse was wrong.

Shane had to have opened his eyes again. He was alive, somewhere. We were going to go home in a few days and feed Snowflake, hold on to each other even tighter, thankful to have survived. We'd have ultrasounds, and we'd feel the baby kick and grow. We'd buy a crib and laugh when we'd struggle with the assembly. We'd hear the first cry of our newborn as both our eyes filled with tears, and we'd have sleepless nights and bottles and little hands to hold. And there'd be zoo trips, and date nights, and lots of smaller moments too, like washing dishes and kissing under the mistletoe, and a million more experiences to be shared.

And his little boy or girl would wait on our front porch for Shane's car to pull up to our driveway each night. And run into his arms.

Shane wasn't gone. He would not miss out on all of that. He would not miss out on life.

"I'll let the doctor know you're awake," the nurse said.

And then she left me in this room, all alone in my nightmare.

He was alive.

He had to be.

There couldn't be a scenario where he was dead.

Maybe if I said it to myself enough, it would be true.

It felt like my insides were on fire, and I clenched my stomach, hoping that our unborn baby would survive so I could hold on to a piece of Shane forever.

I rolled onto my right side, not even caring that my thigh was in pain from the bullet wound they must have repaired, and I stared at the large, empty space.

Behind me, the door to the room opened, followed by voices guiding in something on wheels.

I couldn't imagine having to share this room with anyone; they should have put me in a private room, where I could grieve alone, without a stranger witnessing my despair.

I closed my eyes and whimpered in my hands, trying to stop my sobbing.

The wheels rolled louder along the floor.

"Closer," a hoarse voice whispered.

What if the pain from my heartbreak was enough to kill the

baby? How could I possibly put one foot in front of the other? How could I get discharged from this hospital and go back to that apartment with all its memories? Yet how could I ever leave it?

I appreciated that story Shane told me so much more now. About how one of the hardest moments of his life was having to leave his house behind, the only place that held all his memories with his dad.

That's all I would have with Shane now. Memories. Memories of those days in the rustic cabin in the woods that I'd been so impatient to leave behind. Memories of us falling in love. My heart ached at the thought of never seeing him again. I would never get to touch him again or feel his heartbeat beneath my palm.

I felt like my insides were on fire as I sobbed harder, my head throbbing from crying so hard.

A warm hand lay on top of mine and squeezed.

I didn't want the comfort of a stranger. I just wanted to be left alone.

I tugged at my hand, but the person kept their grip around mine.

I opened my eyes and followed the guy's hand up his arm—an arm covered in tattoos. My heart lurched in my chest as my gaze cascaded over his hospital gown. And I met two sapphire gems staring back at me.

52

"**S**hane!"

I lunged off my bed and onto the little space between his body and the hospital bed's railing. Not the smartest move I ever made, considering my right arm jerked back and my IV almost came out. The one the nurse had poked me six thousand times to get situated.

"Easy!" one nurse yelled. "He has a chest injury, honey. You need to be careful."

"You're alive!" My eyes were so blurred with tears, I could barely make out his smile. But I could feel his palm when he brought it up to my face and stroked my skin.

"I was so damn worried about you," he whispered.

"I thought you were dead," I cried. "The nurse. She said, 'I'm sorry for your loss,' and I thought—"

I couldn't even finish the sentence. Even knowing he was okay, it hurt too badly to say something so devastating out loud.

I wiped the tears from my cheeks and noted his heartbroken expression.

"It was your sister." Shane grimaced. "She didn't make it. I'm so sorry."

Hayley was dead. My sister, my only sibling. I knew she might be —I'd heard the gunshots—but it was still a shock to hear the finality of it.

A normal person would fixate on her being nothing but a villain, especially since she'd almost killed me, Shane, and our unborn baby. But she was still my sister—the one who stayed with me when Mom had gone off for days at a time—and it would take a while to mend the laceration in my heart from knowing I'd never see her again.

But Shane had nothing to be sorry for. She'd tried to murder him, tried to murder me, and consequently, she died in the process. Of course I did not wish this terrible fate upon my sister. I wished she could've had a happy life, but Shane did not need to apologize for saving our lives.

"Hayley's the one who pushed me off the bridge," I said. "Evidently, we'd gotten into an argument, and I'd followed her there."

Shane's eyes absorbed my every word, and I could see his mind racing.

"She confessed it all, right before she shot me," I said.

Shane's chest rose and fell quicker, perhaps remembering the bloody scene he'd stumbled across.

He brought his hand down and placed it on my lower stomach.

"Did the baby..." He couldn't finish his thought.

"It'll take a couple more weeks to be sure, but it seems I'm still pregnant."

The blue in Shane's eyes was back in full force, gorgeous sapphires sparkling as he smiled at me.

"When did you find out you're pregnant?" he whispered.

"A few hours before—" I paused. "I'm sorry. I *am* on the pill. I missed one, and I'm so sorry for being so negligent. I should've—"

Shane's finger pressed against my lips.

"Willow"—he grinned—"you're having my child. I'm not upset.

332 | KATHY LOCKHEART

Surprised? Yes. But upset?" His mouth curled higher. "Not even close."

Warmth rushed around my chest. I hadn't thought about it until this very moment, but if anything was going to sway Shane into changing his mind about being in a relationship, this would have been it. Seeing him so happy that I was pregnant...it obliterated any lingering fear that, someday, he might regret his decision and leave me.

"It's funny how, sometimes, you don't realize exactly what you want until you have it and then almost lose it," he said. "I want you, Willow. I want this baby. It's all I want."

But I wouldn't let hope take flight yet because there was one more obstacle in front of us, one large enough to make Shane change his mind and never want to be with me again. I was the daughter of the man who had killed his father.

"Shane, there's something I need to tell you."

How would I even begin to explain this?

"Before you came, my sister showed me a newspaper article."

Shane's palm remained on my lower abdomen, on the baby that would suffer if Shane didn't want to talk to me again once he *knew*.

"The article was about when my dad died. Evidently, he—"

"Willow!" Mom burst into the room.

Her hands were on my face, her lips kissing my cheek.

"I've been so worried," she cried. "They weren't sure with the blood loss..."

Mom had dark circles under her eyes, which were swollen, as if she had been crying.

"I'm so sorry," she said. "I had no idea what Hayley had planned."

"Mom."

"I swear, if I had known, I would've stopped her."

"Mom."

Shane looked between me and my mom, but he didn't have time to ask any questions because the door swung open and another woman entered the room. This woman was more composed, her hair slicked back into a ponytail, wearing jeans and a blue sweatshirt with white sneakers. She looked familiar, though I couldn't place her until she came around the other side of Shane's bed and took his hand.

"You're out of recovery," the woman said to Shane. "They said surgery went well."

Disapproval flashed through her eyes that I was intruding on Shane's bed. But to her credit, she put on a smile.

"This is Willow, I presume? I'm Penny, Shane's mother."

His widowed mother.

The woman who had suffered unimaginable loss at the hands of my father. My mom was a ticking time bomb, verbal diarrhea about to erupt from her volcano of guilt for having not seen this coming, and I couldn't imagine a more insensitive or heartbreaking way for Shane or his mother to find out who I really was.

I needed to get Shane alone. He deserved to hear this in privacy and have time to process it before he broke the news to his mother.

"It's nice to meet you." I smiled.

"I'm so sorry," Mom said to her. "I never would have suspected my daughter would have done anything like this."

Shane's mom forced a tight smile.

"Shane, can I talk to you in private?" I asked.

"I think she just flew off the deep end," Mom continued.

"Mom."

"She's struggled ever since she was fourteen years old. Ever since—"

"Mom! Now's not the time."

My voice wasn't terribly powerful, but it was jarring enough that everyone in the room looked at me.

"Please," I said. "I have something important I need to talk about with Shane, and it's urgent."

My mom and Shane's mom looked at each other in confusion while Shane stared at me, his brow furrowed in concern.

"Can we have a minute?" Shane asked.

Everyone lingered, seemingly unsure what to make of my outburst, but the room cleared, and Shane and I were alone once more.

"What's wrong?" he asked. "Is the baby——"

"I have something to tell you, and I don't know how to say it."

He cupped my cheek.

When a long silence passed, he said, "It's just me. You can tell me anything."

"I mean, I just don't even understand the odds of this. It's..." My lip quivered.

"Hey," he whispered and waited until I looked him directly in his eyes. "It's going to be okay, Willow."

I opened my mouth, willing the words to come out. But evidently, I was a coward. They lodged behind the lump in my throat.

I allowed myself five more seconds to absorb Shane's affectionate gaze, knowing this was the last time he would ever look at me the same way again.

And then I spoke the words that would change everything.

"Shane...my dad's the one that killed your father."

Shane shut his eyes tightly, letting several long seconds pass.

"You knew?" I whispered.

He shook his head. "No. But I..." Shane took a deep breath, one that didn't look pain-free based on his wincing. "When I was a kid, I wanted to hunt down the guy who'd killed my dad and get revenge."

Right. The superhero phase.

"I convinced myself that my mom had lied when she said my dad's killer was dead to spare me heartbreak, so I went into her room where she kept this box of important paperwork to see what she really knew. Found a report about his death, which had the name of his killer on it, but there weren't many other details—but the report did confirm my dad's killer was also dead. So, I couldn't beat him up or do anything else I'd fantasized about."

Shane swallowed.

"I'd seen his name on that report, but once I found out he was dead, my interest in him was over, and I didn't look into him further. I shifted my focus to learn more about my dad's life and started asking people to tell me stories about him."

His chest swelled slightly.

"I knew your last name was Johnson, too, but Johnson is one of the most common last names in the country. Never imagined you'd be connected to him in any way, but..." Shane pressed his lips together. "When you told me your dad was killed and your mom was being all secretive about it, there was a moment I wondered if...but then I thought it was statistically improbable. Millions of people live in this city alone. I mean, the odds of something like that..."

My mouth ran dry, drinking his every word.

"Told myself it was a crazy thought and that once we solved your case and I knew you were safe, I'd dig up the old files and prove to myself that thought was ludicrous. Because honestly"—he shook his head—"I never truly believed it could be linked. The statistics of it are..."

He sighed deeply, again wincing from the pain of it.

My heart somehow found room to beat even faster, terrified he'd push me away and never talk to me again. Because how could he ever be with someone whose family destroyed his? How could he ever look at me, the daughter of his dad's killer, with anything but disgust?

What were the odds that our families were interconnected, anyway?

Shane licked his lower lip, lost in the abyss of his own thoughts. I'm sure thinking the same thing I was. My dad was the troubled man who Shane's father had tried to help multiple times. A man evidently spiraling in financial distress until he got the eviction notice. Which must have pushed him past his breaking point.

Shane's father must've been trying to reason with him. Maybe he sensed my dad had truly snapped this time, but the honorable police officer would not leave two children in the home with an unstable man. Especially not one with a loaded gun. I could picture the entire scenario playing out, escalating to guns drawn, shots fired.

Two souls stuffed into black body bags and hauled away, leaving the remains of fractured families behind.

"I'm sorry," I whispered. "I didn't know until my sister brought me to our old house. Where it happened. She showed me a newspaper article."

It felt like tragic karma to me, learning that this newspaper article existed and then discovering it held all the answers to years of unanswered questions pertaining to my father's death.

Shane still had said nothing, hadn't looked at me in the eyes again. I don't know why I had hoped that this would have a different outcome. Selfishness, I guess.

We would have such a complicated future, co-parenting a child from two opposing families. And on top of it, if his mom blamed his dad's death on her father-in-law simply for her husband taking the same career path, how would she ever accept the daughter of her husband's killer as Shane's girlfriend? Or the mother of his baby?

But that was all wishful thinking, presumptuous to even consider that Shane would ever speak to me again.

I had no right to think about my destroyed heart in all of this. Shane and his family were the victims here, the victims of my dad's violence. My sister's violence.

I needed to give Shane his space. He deserved as much time as necessary to let this all sink in before deciding what the future held. Maybe I could even ask to be moved to another room while we both recovered.

I rolled to my side so I could hoist myself up over his bedrail again, but Shane's hand gripped my shoulder.

"Hey," he whispered. "That's a lot to process, but it doesn't change how I feel about you."

On my left side, my back was to him. I froze, too scared to grasp the hope he'd just given me.

"How could it not? My family is responsible for all of this."

"Look at me," he said.

I hesitated but rolled back over and shifted onto my right side again. So I could stare him in the eyes.

He cupped my head. "Your father is responsible for his actions, not you. You were a child when this happened. A victim to it, not a party to it."

My eyes welled with tears.

"But my sister tried to kill you."

"And you. I'm sorry that I let my hatred for Ezra blind me to the facts that might have pointed me in Hayley's direction. Maybe De Luca was right; I was too close to this case to see things clearly. And because of that, I put you in danger. I could have lost you and the baby forever."

"You have nothing to apologize for. Even Detective Rosse zeroed in on Ezra." All the evidence, both circumstantial and physical—including the flowers—pointed to him.

"*You* have nothing to apologize for," he countered.

I frowned. "You might feel this way now, but down the road, you might feel resentful toward me."

"I won't."

"How can you be so sure?"

"Because my feelings for you will never change, Willow."

How could that be? How could at least a fragment of his soul not wilt toward me?

"No matter what they did," Shane continued, "no matter what *you* might ever do, it won't change how I feel about you. My feelings for you are unconditional."

I bit my lip, trying to tame the hope swelling inside of me. I didn't want to jump onto its wave and ride it to the top, because if it vanished from beneath me, the crash would hurt too much.

"I don't understand how you could ever look at me the same again."

"Willow, when I look at you, all I see is the other half of my heart."

I studied his eyes for any hint of doubt, and when I saw none, I rested my forehead against his shoulder and wept.

All those years, the emotional rejection from my family created a hole in my chest that throbbed with a dull, constant ache. At times, that ache heightened, and it felt like someone had wrapped my chest in nails. And at other times, the pain felt dimmer, like a metronome in the background. Always there. Always hurting, varying its tempo and volume.

Shane wanted me. Shane accepted me for exactly who I was. Of all the people in the world to accept me, having it come from the one person who had every right to hate me made it all the more powerful. All the more healing. Because it meant he accepted *every* part of me, adored those parts even, so much so that he could look past the dark monster that used to chase him in his dreams.

"I'm so sorry," I cried.

He kissed the top of my head.

"This isn't yours to apologize for, Willow. I will not let the grief from my dad's death take another relationship from me. Especially not one with you."

54

Snowflakes drifted from the sky, dusting people's dark coats and the shiny black casket in what looked like powdered sugar. There was no wind in the open field of headstones, as if the gray sky was giving us a moment of silence to digest the finality of a life cut short. Around me, sniffles and whispers overshadowed the soft voice of the pastor, who stood at the front, reading from the Bible.

I thought I would appreciate the closure the ceremony gave me, but evidently, the goal of a funeral was to take whatever sadness burned inside of you and add flames to the fire.

It didn't help that Shane wasn't here to calm my nerves. While he was doing a lot better, he had at least another week in the hospital before he'd be released. Which meant my mom and I had to come here alone. Without him.

It also didn't help that Hayley had become the villain in the news articles. The girl who'd once tucked me in on the nights Mom left would only be remembered for her demons.

Finally, the pastor stopped talking and motioned for me and my mom to come to the front.

My throat battled against the swelling as I walked along the snow-covered grass. Mom placed her hand on the coffin, sobbing so hard that I couldn't make out what she was saying. I put my hand on her back, knowing nothing had the power to make her feel better, but wanting to comfort her all the same.

And then it was my turn.

I hadn't been able to pick the wildflowers myself, given it was winter, but I'd gone to four different stores until I found the exact wildflowers that used to grow in the field behind our house. The same wildflowers I had placed on dad's casket all those years ago.

I set them gently atop her casket, noting how beautiful it was— the lilac and emerald greens on top of the thin layer of snow. As if it wasn't tragically heartbreaking.

"I'm sorry," I whispered to Hayley. "I'm sorry you were in so much pain. I wish I could've helped you."

To think of all those times I'd fixated on whether she showed up for *me*. My graduations, my special events. I'd interpreted all those moments as rejections, but maybe they were cries for help.

Maybe she was isolating herself, drawing herself deeper and deeper into her abyss of suffering until there was nothing left but pain.

Until, like our father, Hayley had reached her breaking point.

I stared at the coffin, picturing my sister lying there.

And a memory stabbed my heart.

After I put wildflowers on Daddy's coffin, I hug Hayley. "I miss him."

"Me too," Hayley cries.

Mommy spent a lot of time sobbing in her bedroom these last few days. I'm scared she'll never come back out.

A fresh stream of tears falls down my cheeks. "I don't understand why he had to die."

Hayley hugs me tighter. "Me neither."

"He promised me we'd go pick flowers," I say.

"I'll take you." Hayley runs her fingers through my hair. "I'll help you pick all the wildflowers you want."

WHEN THE FUNERAL CONCLUDED, MOM AND I ACCEPTED WELL WISHES FROM those in attendance.

One of them was Tracey.

"Hey." She gently hugged me, the scent of her strawberry body wash wrapping around her hair. "I'm so sorry for your loss."

"Thanks, Tracey."

I hadn't seen her since she'd mysteriously left town.

"Emily said you left for a few days?"

Tracey pulled back and nodded. "I had a minor family emergency. Our family dog was dying, and I raced home to say goodbye before it was too late."

"Why didn't you say something?"

She shrugged. "After everything that happened with you, it was so inconsequential in comparison."

I frowned. "It's not inconsequential, Tracey. I know how much Max meant to you. I'm sorry for *your* loss, too."

The tremble of her lower lip told me she appreciated that more than I could imagine, but our moment together was cut short when a figure approached me.

"I'll talk to you later," Tracey said before walking away.

My spine stiffened.

"Hey," Amelia said. "I'm sorry for your loss."

I offered a weak smile, unsure what to say as she stood there, fidgeting.

"You haven't answered any of my calls," she mumbled.

I wished I had texted her back so she didn't resort to talking to me here.

"I think it's best if we...take a break," I said.

With a slow bob of her head, she released a sigh of resignation, as if anticipating this would be my answer.

"I have a question," I said.

Amelia rounded her eyes, as if she'd assumed this entire exchange was going to be one-sided.

"Where'd you get the scratches on your arms?"

The ones that put her on Shane's short list of suspects.

Amelia looked down. "It's embarrassing."

I waited until she blew out a breath and ran her fingers through her hair.

"I saw Ezra flirting with a girl," Amelia said. "This was the night before you fell, and I thought Ezra and I were getting closer. I got super pissed, and I confronted the other woman and went off on her."

Ezra was a nonstop flirt. Even in the beginning of our relationship and evidently even when his goal was to get me back, he was still flirting.

"The girl shoved me," Amelia said. "I shoved her back, and it just...it was stupid, and I was too humiliated to tell you about it."

Especially because telling me would mean confessing her feelings for Ezra.

"I know this isn't the appropriate time to say this," she started, "but just in case it's the last time we ever—" She looked down, unable to meet my eye for a moment. "I'm sorry for betraying you. Ezra was so charming, and I think I let my feelings get all confused, like it was a forbidden romance or something."

I said nothing.

"If it makes you feel any better, I don't think he ever cared about me like I thought he did. I think he was using me to get back at you."

Maybe. I wondered what Ezra's side of the story was. And why I wanted to hear it, along with some other things, before I could officially put this all behind me.

"Do you think we can ever be friends again?" Amelia asked.

I wasn't against forgiveness, but the reality is that we sometimes hold on to things for far too long instead of accepting that some relationships are unhealthy, toxic, or unfulfilling. And those dynamics may never change. We need to learn to identify when to keep fighting and when to lay down our sword.

"I'm sure we'll see each other at social gatherings." And I'd be cordial. "But I think it's best if our friendship took a break."

Amelia nodded in response, as if she'd expected this. "I really am sorry."

Clearly not knowing what else to say, she ambled away.

"How are you holding up?" Emily asked, the next to approach me.

I shrugged. "Numb at the moment."

She frowned. "How's Shane?"

"Improving."

To this, she gave a sad smile. "I'm glad. Sounds like you found yourself a really good guy."

I did.

"I hope to find that one day, too." She smiled. "Are you still planning to see Ezra?"

I nodded.

"Do you think he'll be honest with you?"

I sighed. "I guess I'll find out."

55

I sat on the silver barstool, one of ten lined up in a row. Each with its own portion of glass in front of it, encased with a small tan divide, as if that afforded us privacy. A rumbling of voices punched through the stuffy space that smelled of unwashed sneakers.

I could feel the nausea swelling again and popped one of my mints. A pregnancy trick I'd learned to manage my morning sickness.

Ezra walked in, wearing beige khaki pants and a short-sleeved pullover shirt, a prison guard escorting him to his seat opposite of me.

His blond hair didn't look polished anymore. It looked messy, and his eyes had hints of purple beneath them.

He glared at me, and when I picked up the black phone, he made me wait for fifteen seconds before doing the same, as if he was considering never talking to me again.

"What?" he snapped.

"How are you holding up?"

"Like you give a shit."

"I do."

Ezra glowered off to his side before leaning his elbows on the small counter in front of him. "What the hell do you want, Willow?"

Closure.

"I know it wasn't you that pushed me off that bridge."

"No shit. I told you that all along, but you wouldn't listen."

"But you sent me that threat. You broke into my apartment to leave it there. Why?"

"What does it matter now?"

"It matters to me. Those flowers are what drove their investigation over the edge, Ezra. Your threats, combined with all of the other circumstantial evidence, is what made them think that you're the one that pushed me off the bridge."

"Know what I don't get?" he snarled. "Only thing I ever did to you was kiss and text some other chicks. And you ruined my life over it. You got it in your head that I'm capable of murder when your lunatic sister has been going off the deep end for, like, two decades."

I hid my grimace.

"Word gets out fast, Willow. I know she's the one that pushed you over the bridge and then attacked you again. But you blamed me."

"I didn't suspect you until you started acting unhinged."

"Go to hell." Ezra shifted, as if he was about to leave.

"Wait," I pleaded.

He was so mad at me; it was doubtful he'd have stayed to talk for another couple of minutes if not for his immense boredom. Anything had to be better than staring at those walls all day.

I squared my shoulders. "I know that you and Amelia dated."

Ezra's jaw set tighter.

"Was it when we were together?"

I should have clarified this with Amelia, but on the day of the funeral, I'd been unprepared and preoccupied to have that conversation with her.

He tossed his angry eyes to the side, obviously debating whether or not to grace me with an answer.

"No. We flirted a little while you and I were still dating, but nothing happened until after we broke up."

It was strange that this provided me comfort. I guess I needed our love to have been real for it to have been worth the pain that came after.

"For the record," I started, "I didn't think anyone had done this to me at first. But once they realized someone *had* pushed me off the bridge, I looked at *everyone* in my life with suspicion, not just you."

Ezra's hardened gaze softened. Just a smidgen.

"And then everything escalated, and you sent those flowers. Why'd you use your own credit card to buy them? You knew they'd get traced back to you."

"It shouldn't have mattered; I didn't try to kill you, so if the cops had done their job, they would've known I wasn't your killer."

"The cops follow the evidence. And you let it all point to you. Threats can constitute a crime, Ezra. Especially when you violate a restraining order to deliver them. Not to mention, breaking and entering. So, why'd you do it?"

"Because I was pissed! You were ruining my life *again*. I'd lost my job, I got brought in for questioning, and I was sick of feeling power-less. I wanted to tell you off, but I had to settle for the card instead."

"You wanted to tell me off."

His look said, *Obviously*.

"So, you bought me flowers?"

His lips pursed. "Thought the only way you'd open the door was if you thought I was there to apologize."

"Why break in to leave them?"

"The hell does it matter now?"

"It matters to me," I said.

"I don't have time for this." Ezra stood up.

"Wait," I said.

If I didn't get all the answers, I would never have the closure I needed. Could I accept that? Yes. I'd learned acceptance through all of this, but it was worth asking him one last time.

"You tell me honestly, and I'll put in a good word with the district attorney. That's a pretty generous offer, considering everything you've done."

Ezra sat back down, his eyes filled with anger. "A generous offer? How about you drop all the goddamn charges?"

In addition to violating the restraining order, Ezra was being charged with felony breaking and entering, since he'd entered my home, intending to threaten me. If I spoke on his behalf, there was a possibility it could get bumped down to a misdemeanor.

"You intimidated me and threatened my life. Are you going to answer the question or not? Because if not? I will not put in a good word for you. The district attorney wants to make an example out of you. Trying to interfere with the investigation by showing up in the hallway and demanding I have them back down? Then threatening the victim? They're going for the maximum sentence allowed, Ezra. Your only hope of getting the charges knocked down is if the victim puts in a good word with the DA. And you know it. So, it's your choice."

Ezra licked his teeth, looked down at the ground. And eventually met my eyes.

"I came with the flowers, but you weren't home. Thought maybe you were in the shower or were feeding that stupid cat, so I went around back. Found the sliding glass door unlocked."

So, he helped himself into my apartment and left a death threat?

"You threatened to end me, Ezra."

He said nothing.

"No matter how angry you might have been, you threatened to kill me."

My heart pounded, and I asked the question I'd come here to ask. Finally.

"Would you have?"

Ezra rolled his eyes in annoyance. "I'm a lot of things, Willow. But I'm not a killer."

Some part of me relaxed. I guess the part that feared there might be more than one person in my life willing and able to hurt me.

While I felt sorry that Ezra got tangled up in all of this, it was his own poor decisions and behavior that drew the police's attention to him. And now, he had to be held accountable for the mistakes that he had made.

Sad, how I'd struggled to accept things in my life. And he'd almost lost everything because *he* couldn't accept the end of a relationship.

"Goodbye, Ezra."

I hoped he'd find peace one day.

The Garden of the Phoenix in Chicago was located just south of the Museum of Science and Industry. With the thirty-foot-tall trees surrounding the small body of water that snaked through emerald lawns, it didn't feel like we were anywhere near a large city. I could see buildings, of course, behind the oak trees, but it was as if they were peeking over them, trying to see the magic inside this park.

At its center, flanked by wide trees, condensed green bushes, and uneven boulders, was a fifteen-foot iron bridge that arched over the narrowest passage of water, which reflected the bright blue sky and overhanging branches of trees like an oil painting.

I'd never been here but had always wanted to come—especially now, in the spring, when more than a hundred cherry blossom trees transformed the grounds into a pink fairyland. I'd read that cherry blossoms symbolized both birth and death, beauty and violence. Fitting for everything Shane and I had been through in the past few months.

I was glad Mom moved to Texas, like she had planned; I think if she had stayed here, the grief would've devoured what was left of her heart. We talked more often than I had assumed we would, and so far, she had already flown back three times just to visit me.

Shane's mother, on the other hand, had a harder time adjusting to it all. Understandably, when your son finally brings someone home to meet you and that someone is pregnant with your grandchild, it's devastating to find out her father was your husband's killer. That's not something you can get past quickly or easily. But to her credit, she made the effort to get to know me. I wouldn't say that it was easy, because it wasn't. I could still see a flash of pain pass through her eyes from time to time, but I could also tell she didn't hold me personally responsible for what happened in the past. She wanted her son to be happy, and she wanted to be part of her grandchild's life.

Shane held my hand as we walked toward the bridge. A different bridge than the one that had started everything all those months ago. I put a hand on my swelling stomach, delighted that we'd decided to wait to find out the baby's gender until his or her birth. I loved having things to look forward to these days. I loved our new apartment that we recently moved into together and our new pet, Snowflake, who we'd adopted two months ago.

But most of all, I loved Shane.

I'd left my HR job to open my dream company, which currently focuses on helping unemployed people get back on their feet. I had to take out a loan for it, living off that debt for a bit, but according to my cash flow projections, I'd break even shortly after the baby was born and pull in enough money to pay the bills. These days, I used all my mad HR skills to help people write the perfect résumé, to get them proper training that would make them more attractive in the workforce, and I worked with companies in the Chicagoland area to match hardworking people with open roles. I loved every second of it.

I actually looked *forward* to working rather than dreading it.

"Is your mom having fun, planning the baby shower?" I asked.

"You kidding? She's going overboard." Shane rubbed his

eyebrow. "Yesterday, she said something about storks. I hope to God she meant cardboard cutouts, not the real thing."

I laughed.

"Fallon's eggin' her on." Shane rolled his eyes. "Keeps sending her more ideas on some shared Pinterest board. Last I heard, they were up to thirty games planned for the event."

"God help us." I smiled.

"I know. She invited a bunch of my coworkers, too, thanks to Fallon's contacts. Sounds like half the force'll be there."

I was relieved Shane had made peace with being a police officer despite being in a relationship. I would never want him to give up who he was out of fear.

Life is short. Denying yourself experiences or relationships, fearing it will end in heartbreak, will only lead to a life of loneliness and sadness. You have to go for what you want in life—fully and completely.

Just like Shane had chosen to do.

I was proud of him.

"My mom has her flight booked for it," I said. "It'll be"—interesting?—"nice having everyone together."

Shane squeezed my hand, his knowing eyes meeting mine. "The past is the past, Willow. My mom doesn't blame you guys for it."

"I know, but...you have to admit, that's a big matzo ball."

"I think it gave my mom a new perspective."

I eyed him skeptically. "How so?"

"My mom had her walls up at first, but she's thrilled because she's never seen me happier. She sees what a kind person you are. And once she let you into her heart, I think it healed her in ways it might not have otherwise. I think she realized she had misplaced her grief for a long time."

"Maybe you're seeing what you wish to see."

Shane's mouth curled up on one side. "She invited my dad's side of the family to the baby shower."

Holy cow, a two-decade-long family rift mending? My eyes exploded with tears. *Dammit.*

"I blame the hormones." I wiped them.

Shane chuckled as he swiped my cheeks.

"Enough with the heavy," he said. "We didn't come here to talk about all this. We came here to see some cherry blossoms."

Shane took my hand, and as we continued walking along the grounds, I felt like the luckiest woman in the world. To find such a remarkable guy, to have so much to look forward to.

We walked to the top of the bridge and stopped to look down at the water, pink cherry blossoms rippling through its reflection.

"Check out that one," Shane said, pointing to my right.

"It's beautiful."

I turned back around to find him on bended knee. In one hand, he held a little white box, opened with a sparkling diamond ring in its center. In the other, a couple of purple wildflowers he'd grabbed along the way—the kind I'd told him reminded me of my father.

"Willow, a long time ago, I shut the door to my heart. I told myself it was because I didn't want to risk someone losin' me. Like my dad. And that was part of it, but it wasn't the whole part."

I studied the speckles in his eyes, which shimmered.

"I'd spent so many years in a dark place, isolating myself, and I forgot what happiness felt like. What it would be like to fall in love. And the longer I spent in that cave, the harder it became to find my way out. But when I met you, that all changed. You were like my compass, showing me the way, makin' me *want* to come out for the first time in my life. I went from not wanting to get close to anyone to not being able to *exist* without you by my side. If it wasn't for you, I would have stayed in that cave forever. Alone, going through the motions of life instead of living."

His eyes shimmered more.

As did mine.

"I can't imagine spending a single moment without you by my

side. I love you, Willow. I want to spend the rest of my life with you. Will you marry me?"

I nodded, the tears rolling down my cheeks. "Yes."

Shane smiled and took the ring out of its holder, placed it on my ring finger. Then, he stood up and took my face between his hands.

"I love you," I whispered.

Shane brought his lips to mine.

Our love had healed so many old hurts and taught us to let go of the things we couldn't change and embrace the happiness within our reach.

* * *

THANK YOU FOR READING GRAVE DECEPTION! I HOPE YOU ENJOYED THE story that readers participated in writing (more on that in a minute).

IF YOU HAVEN'T READ THE REST OF THE SECRETS AND THE CITY SERIES, CATCH up with all the interconnected characters now!

DEADLY ILLUSION: SHE WAS ABLE TO HIDE THE BRUISES FROM everyone...until an MMA fighter came along. Now he'll die to protect her. Maybe even kill...

FATAL CURE: SHE HAS NO IDEA THAT THE CRIMINAL KINGPIN SHE VOWED to make pay for decimating her family, is the man she's fallen in love with...

LETHAL JUSTICE : A CRIME LEADER HAS FALLEN FOR THE WRONG woman. She's his hostage in a heist, and if he leaves any witnesses, his colleagues will kill them both.

. . .

WHAT HAPPENED WHEN SHANE GOT THAT PHONE CALL FROM HAYLEY AND he rushed to save Willow? Find out in this **exclusive FREE chapter from Shane's POV** (https://kathylockheart.com/Shane-POV/).

P.S. IF YOU LOVED GRAVE DECEPTION, I'D BE HONORED IF YOU'D CONSIDER posting a 2-word <u>REVIEW</u> on Amazon.

* * *

DID YOU KNOW READERS PARTICIPATED IN THE WRITING OF THIS STORY? **<u>As a reminder, here are some of the ways you PARTICIPATED in writing Grave Deception.</u>**

🩶 YOU VOTED FOR YOUR FAVORITE TROPES. WINNERS WERE AS FOLLOWS, and yep, all of them are in Grave Deception!
- ☑️ Friends-to-lovers
- ☑️ Touch-her-and-perish
- ☑️ Forced Proximity.

🩶 You voted for the STORY you wanted to read, and the winning story became Grave Deception.

🩶 I named a character, Tracey, after a reader (I did this in Lethal Justice, too, with Katy, and it was so fun I might have to do it in every book.)

🩶 You named Willow's favorite coffee shop Angie's Coffeeteria. :-)

ACKNOWLEDGMENTS

First, **I'd like to thank you, the reader.** You have a ton of options when it comes to books, your time is incredibly precious, and you gave *me* a chance. From the bottom of my heart, THANK YOU. Readers mean the world to me, and I'd love to connect with you! Please find my social media links at www.KathyLockheart.com.

Thank you to Susan Staudinger. Your developmental and content editing, combining with our amazing virtual sessions made Grave Deception far better than it ever would have been without you.

Thank you to my early ARC readers: Katy, Kayla, Shay, Kim, Kate, Alyson, Sam, Sara, Kim, and Sandy. It means the world that you'd take the time to read this story, and provide insight back to me!

Thank you to my husband for showing me the beauty of true love and being my biggest cheerleader. Thank you to my children for giving me a love I didn't know existed until you were born and for inspiring me to be the best *me* I can be. Always go after your dreams.

To my family for enveloping me with love, encouraging me, and embracing my idea to become a writer.

To my friends, for your never-ending support.

To Amy and Kristen, my formal beta readers. Thank you for helping make this story even better.

To my editor Jovana, your attention to details polished this story and made it the best it could be! To my cover artist, Hang Le, for bringing such beauty to this novel!

To all the authors who came before me—your success paves the road for new writers to do what they love. Thank you.

~ Kathy

LET'S CONNECT!

The easiest way to connect with me is to go to my website, www. KathyLockheart.com, and find my social media links. I interact with readers, so don't be surprised if you see me reply to your post or invite you to join a reader team!

Xoxo

Kathy

- amazon.com/Kathy-Lockheart/e/B08XY5F2XG
- bookbub.com/profile/kathy-lockheart
- facebook.com/KathyLockheartAuthor
- tiktok.com/@kathylockheart_author
- instagram.com/kathy_lockheart
- twitter.com/Kathy_Lockheart
- pinterest.com/kathylockheart